# MADDIE MIDNIGHT

A story of sex and motor racing

For my lovely wife

Alison

First published in 2016 by Morienval Press

1 3 5 7 9 8 6 4 2

Morienval Press,
4 rue des Trois Couronnes,
60127 Morienval, France.

www.morienval.com

ISBN 978-0-9554868-9-0

Typeset in Avenir Medium 9pt

Printed and bound in the United Kingdom by
Lightning Source
Chapter House
Pitfield, Kiln Farm,
Milton Keynes MK11 3LW

And in the United States of America by
Lightning Source Inc
1246 Heil Quaker Boulevard.
La Vergne, Tennessee 37086

# MADDIE MIDNIGHT

by

## KIT DEVEREUX

# One

Maddie Midnight was in a pickle, and she only had herself to blame for it. She cursed inwardly. This Winslow Davenport fellow had knocked her off balance completely, and she had somehow ended up in a discussion with a complete stranger about the colour of her pubic hair.

He was looking at her in an amused-bemused fashion.

It had been his fault, of course. He had paid her a compliment; said he liked her auburn hair.

"I'm a natural blonde," she had said, wanting to explain why she had auburn hair. But then everything had gone out of control and, to use motor racing parlance, she was spinning wildly towards the barriers and it was going to be a big shunt. How ever did that happen?

"I'm a natural blonde," she had said. "I am not auburn at all, but I have a very good hairdresser. She's so good no-one ever believes that I am a blonde, until they see me naked, at which point it becomes fairly obvious, doesn't it? Not that I am suggesting we should do that... Certainly not."

Then another thought had thrown her sideways.

"That does not mean I am keen on body hair," she said. "I'm absolutely not, but I do think it's nice to retain a little mystery, don't you? What I am trying to say is that imagination is so important, isn't it? When it comes to sex. It's so much more exciting when there is a bit of mystery."

Oh God, she thought, could the earth please open up right now and swallow me? She kept talking. It seemed like the only way out. She would talk herself to safety.

"Sex is all about power, isn't it?" she said. "We all like to feel powerful. Or dominated. Or both at different times. I mean, when you look at some of these rich men with their stunning wives, you think: 'Why?', but you know it's power and money. The men feel powerful because they have the best-looking women and the women feel powerful because they can land the big fish. They feel they are better than other women. The bigger the star - the more satisfaction they get."

She was not quite sure where the discussion was heading, but at least it had veered away from further revelations about her own 'turf management'. This was a good thing. What a girl does with her pubic hair is her own affair.

"I like to feel powerful sometimes," she said. "It's normal, isn't it? But then there are other times when all I want is to be told what to do. I know I'm not supposed to say that, but that is the truth. I think all women secretly fantasize about being dominated. Knights in shining armour. Faceless figures. It is a primal thing, but we don't want other women to know that's what we think. We're supposed to be repelled by the idea, so it's embarrassing to admit it and we don't confess. I'm not talking about kinky stuff, just enough for us to feel a little bit helpless. Enough so we don't feel we have to be in charge. It's good to have a man who knows what he wants and makes things happen. That's sexy."

Maddie paused. Her stream of consciousness had reached a natural pause.

Winslow Davenport III was still looking at her with a slightly astonished look on his face. He had not expected this. She laughed, rather attractively, and fixed him in her gaze. She felt like he was challenging her. And she loved a challenge.

Davenport was going to say something, but he paused.

The human brain is an amazing thing. In a split second it can assimilate a huge amount of information and spit out a logical answer. There's a sort of hyper-drive that kicks in when one gets into extreme situations; everything seems to slow down and yet the brain speeds up.

He had known this strange Maddie Midnight woman for about an hour. They had each drunk one Gin & Tonic, they had nibbled on some peanuts and had made fairly normal polite conversation. She was not under the influence of alcohol. He had presented her with a business proposition which he believed was pretty impressive. She had said she liked the idea and would definitely consider it. And then, out of nowhere, she had started talking about the colour of her pubic hair and had spun off into this discourse about sex.

Obviously she liked him, he had sensed that, and it was clear to both of them that squadrons of pheromones were dog-fighting in the air between them. But had he done anything to launch her into such a speech? All he had done was say he liked her auburn hair. OK, it was a flirtatious comment, but it was also honest. He did like it. It was shoulder length and gathered at the back to keep it under control. It didn't look dyed at all.

In this timeless split second, Davenport looked at her. She was bursting with life. Energy was shining out of her. She probably didn't even realize it. The word 'kooky' popped into his head. Yes, that was the right word. She was clearly bright, if a little unorthodox. Still, you do not get to be the marketing director of a Formula 1 team in your mid-thirties without being pretty good at what you do. The team owner Charlie Chiphurst and her were not an item; nor was he her father or uncle. Maddie was in her job because light shone from her eyes.

Davenport liked the electricity. He liked her mind, strange though it was; her face, yes; her body, absolutely. And she knew it. He could tell.

But all of this led to a question: what were they going to do about it? They could embrace it, or ignore it. He knew from his research she was definitely single. He too was unattached and thus there was nothing to stop them getting entangled, if that was what they wanted to do.

It was supposed to be a business meeting, but clearly he

had a choice: he could be polite and keep it professional; or he could step over the line and maybe have some fun, while hopefully not screwing up the deal.

In the same instant, Maddie's mind was also working at hyper speed. She had a pretty good idea what he was thinking. She had often wondered why men were so keen on her. She was OK to look at, but she was certainly not blessed - nor cursed - with supermodel looks. Her mother had told her men wanted only one thing and, generally speaking, she had found that to be sensible advice. They all wanted to have sex with her, all the normal ones at least. She did not really mind that. She knew where she stood. It was so much more simple than dealing with women.

She still hoped one day she would meet The Perfect Man, but he would need to be good, kind, caring and sexy. He would also have to be both naughty and faithful, which is always a hard combination to find.

When you put it all down in a list - as she had done several times over the years - it all sounded like a rather rare treasure. If there were men out there like that they had been snapped up and their women fought tooth-and-nail to keep them. Such men were never on the market for long, but she was still looking, if only vaguely.

She had met a lot of men in the motor racing world but, as a general rule, she felt it was best to avoid getting involved with them. If a girl wants to be taken seriously in a man's world, she needs to avoid too many romantic adventures.

She had tried men outside the sport, but found she soon got bored. Racing folk were different. They were weirder than normal people, unpredictable, but more fun.

The thing she had wanted to explain to Davenport about hair colour was the reason she dyed her hair. Men, she had meant to tell him, never take blondes seriously. If you are blonde it is assumed you are not very clever, so she dyed her hair auburn and a few lucky men had discovered the collar and cuffs definitely did not match.

But somewhere along the way, she had got off track.

Davenport recognised the predicament she had talked

herself into and felt the urge to help her escape. He did not really want to hear any more intimate soliloquies, if only because she was clearly uncomfortable. He leapt in to help.

"Don't blondes have more fun?" he asked. It was a lame remark, but he could not think of anything else to say.

"I get fun enough," said Maddie, unsure whether this was really true. "When I want a little bit of it, I can always get it."

That had sounded to him like a challenge.

"Do you want some fun?" he said.

It was a difficult line that he delivered as smoothly as possible. Maddie widened her eyes just a fraction. She wrinkled her nose. Her brain spooled up into hyperdrive again.

Yes, of course, she did. She wanted a night of orgasmic delights more than anything else. Maddie liked sex, or at least good sex. She knew how to lose control and let herself go, but that kind of thing was reserved for special occasions.

She had realized early on, from reading books, that women are much more complicated than men when it comes to sensuality, but she believed and always had, that it is all in the head - or 90 percent of it, anyway. Much has been written about the mechanics of the process about what, where and how to stimulate women, and men have been doing these things ever since, like working through an instruction manual. But there was no real research about the whys; about why the female body does what it does when releasing sexual tension, it was all still very vague.

She had never allowed herself to do bad sex. If she was not getting excited enough, she always backed out. She had to be absolutely ready. It was a rule she had and, as a result, nature took its course. Things happened when they should happen. She knew how she worked and never had to worry about enjoying it. She also understood that great sex is all about giving, rather than taking, and Maddie's men had to know that. If they did not, they were soon gone.

Maddie was pretty well-balanced, or at least she liked to think she was. She believed it was largely due to luck - but perhaps her practical nature had something to do with it. Her parents were decent people and she had grown up being told to like the way she looked - even during a difficult "ugly duckling" period as a teenager. Her folks had told her it was just a phase and she did not let it mess her up. Her early sexual adventures – which she did not discuss with them - did her no real harm. No-one said she was frigid, nor this was too big or that was too small. This all meant Maddie did not have any real hang-ups about her body.

She knew her body was good enough to provide satisfaction for men with their set ideas of what female sexual perfection should be. In the worst case, she thought, she could always make money whoring or appearing in porn films - there was always demand in that industry - but she was never going to be a lingerie model.

Because she was not ashamed of her body, she viewed the mirror as her friend. Every day, if she could, she would spend five minutes naked in front of a full-length mirror. It was the one time of day when she could be completely herself, without clothes and unguarded. The naked Maddie was the real Maddie. She loved to look at herself, but it was not vanity, nor delusion. She saw herself as she really was and she felt this was healthy. She knew every inch of her body and felt connected to it. She had no illusions. She was what she was: auburn, blonde or otherwise. She saw every imperfection, but somehow she had learned that each tiny flaw makes one different and unique, and they are really a source of strength and beauty.

To Maddie, perfection was over-rated and fleeting. Humans are all like ice sculptures. There may be moments when we are perfect, but beauty is ever-changing. You can capture beauty in paintings, photographs or films but it is not always there.

She liked to imagine what it was like for others to look at her. Five-feet eight inches tall, weighing one hundred and thirty pounds. Pretty normal, if a little tall. She was a UK size six, but she struggled to fill a B-cup bra. Her breasts were small, but not disastrously so. Maddie had never worried about them. She had what she had. You don't get to choose, but she liked what Mother Nature and the Good Lord had fashioned for her.

Her hips were slim and still almost girlish. Her bottom was nicely rounded and her thighs were firm and velvety. There was just a hint of softness in her waist. Her stomach was not perfectly taut, but it was flat enough for a bikini.

In a tight-fitting gown she looked elegant and she quite liked the sideways glances that resulted. The best thing was that not only did it all look nice, but it also worked perfectly, when the right kind of attention was paid to it.

The one thing she felt was odd was that she never wanted to go through all the cuddling some women need after sex. She just didn't like it. She liked to free herself from the clutches of the man and fly away, in almost manly style. She had sometimes wondered why this happened and concluded it was probably a pre-emptive strike to avoid feeling disappointed when the man left. It caused her no harm and most men seemed to like it.

By nature, when she did find a man she wanted to sleep with, she tried to be helpful and undemanding.

"I am a woman," she would say sometimes. "My body works exactly as the instructions say it should. There's no false advertising here. You get what it says on the tin."

Men liked this little speech. It made them feel safe.

Maddie was clever like that.

"Girls worry about their breasts, men about their penis," she would say, "But let's face it: average is average. Too much is as bad as too little. Girls are happy with average, as long as men know what to do with it."

All of these thoughts took place in a split-second. Then it was time for her to give Davenport an answer. Did she want to have fun?

"A girl needs a little romancing," she said. "There is no magical on/off button, you know. Sorry, but your approach is way too direct for me. I am like a racing engine. I need to be warmed up before I start to perform."

Winslow smiled and tried not to appear disappointed.

"I am sorry," he said. "I'm a different kind of racing

machine. I am into efficiency of action. I see what I like and I don't waste time."

She liked the response and the back of her mind a voice was screaming at her: you describe a powerful man and yet when one appears you turn him down. How absurd is that?

But her mouth said: "I'm not feeling the romance at all" and she frowned. She was not sure if this was directed at herself or at Davenport...

"Are you always this direct?" he asked. "It's rather attractive and, at the same time, quite off-putting."

"You ask me if I fancy having sex with you and I am the one who is being direct?" she said. "Well, if you like me being direct, then I have something that will really turn you on. Mr Davenport, or whatever your real name is. You have no chance at all of adding me as a notch on your bedpost."

She tossed back her head, shot him a slightly flirtatious look, said: "Is that direct enough for you?" and rose, turned and walked off. He watched her go, her pert rear end moving with a fluid elegance that was more perfect than anything one might see on a catwalk at a fashion show.

She's a piece of work, he thought. Sexy as hell.

As she strode away from Winslow Davenport III, Maddie Midnight felt strangely excited. She had expected a dull business meeting with a man called Mr Cornelius Rich from Texas. He had telephoned Chiphurst Competition a couple of days earlier and said he was considering sponsoring the team and would like to discuss the options available. It had all sounded wildly unlikely, but the Acquisitions Team - a professional-sounding description for Jake and Jen, who sat in the office next to Maddie reading financial newspapers and magazines, looking for leads - said it was probably worth a discussion, although they could find nothing about any Cornelius Rich.

Formula 1 teams are all structured differently, but at Chiphurst the roles are fairly well-defined: Charlie Chiphurst is the owner, the inspiration and the man who takes all the credit. He is the team's "talking head". Behind him is the indefatigable Cheryl, always bright-eyed and bushy-tailed, who has the patience of a football team of saints. She is the super-organiser who micro-manages them all with amazing skill.

Maddie is the go-getter, who makes the deals happen. She doesn't really care about taking the credit for that. She wants to be rich and respected by her peers, but is not much bothered by celebrity. She is unusual in marketing circles in that she is both a cultivator of prospects and a closer, the person who nails down the details, gets the signature on the dotted line and the money in the bank. Charlie would turn up sometimes and do a star turn, but Maddie is the one who took the deals across the finish line.

And so it was that she was sitting in the bar at the Berkeley Hotel in London at seven in the evening on Wednesday, July 23, waiting for Mr Rich to appear. It was like a blind date, she thought, though she had never been on one.

She had the image of a larger-than-life Texan type with big boots and a cowboy hat. She had decided to go for her best little black dress, paired with a suit jacket that matched, but was light enough to allow her to cuff the arms, so the ensemble was business-like without being formal. She was a black and white kind of girl when it came to clothing and hated having to get into the team uniform at the race tracks. This was always designed by men - and it never made the women look attractive.

She was one of those girls who liked to be on time and at exactly seven she looked at her watch. When she raised her eyes, there was a gin and tonic floating in front of her. The man holding it was good-looking. He had salt-and-pepper hair. He sat down, raised another glass and said "Cheers" with a neat and tidy American accent. They chinked glasses.

"Mr Rich, I presume," Maddie said.

"No, not at all," he said. "Mr Rich told me to tell you he couldn't make it and asked me to come instead and make you the proposal."

"Make me the proposal?" Maddie said. "I thought it was going to be the other way around."

The man shrugged. "I cannot answer that," he said. "I am

doing what I was asked to do."

"How did you know it was me?" she asked. "There are other women in the bar."

The man smiled.

"Madeleine Mezzanotte was described to me in great detail," he said. "Little black dress, matching jacket. Spectacular auburn hair. To be quite honest, you were not difficult to spot. I was told to get you a gin and tonic."

Maddie was surprised, but she hid it well.

No-one ever called her by her real name and not many people knew what she liked to drink.

"And my underwear?" she asked, with more than a hint of sarcasm. He smiled. She was being flirtatious.

"Probably French," he said, after a momentary pause. "Aubade or Simone Pérèle. I would guess. Something understated, but sexy."

His reply was not strictly honest. He was not guessing. Her credit card bill had given him some clues, but he was not about to tell her.

Maddie raised an eyebrow. This man knew far too much about her.

"And you are?" she asked, covering her surprise.

"Winslow Davenport," he said. "Winslow Davenport the Third."

"You have a tattoo of Mickey Mouse on your left buttock," she said. "And Snow White on the right."

"Nice try," he replied with a smile, "but you'll have to jump through a few more hoops before you find out stuff like that."

Maddie smiled back. She had managed to avoid seeming to be shocked. Something he was probably expecting. She guessed this made her seem pretty cool.

"What does Mr Rich have in mind?" she asked, fixing Davenport in a stare. She had come prepared for a sponsorship meeting and had been hijacked. She guessed there was no Mr Rich. But there seemed to be little point in leaving until she had heard what this Davenport person had to say.

Davenport did not hesitate, explaining that he had a

proposal that would be interesting to Chiphurst Competition and to Maddie Midnight herself. It was really very simple. He began to explain.

It was very clear from the first couple of minutes that he knew a great deal about the F1 industry and how it worked. The idea he proposed was, she had to admit, quite brilliant. It was surprising, completely unethical, but rather attractive nonetheless. She listened intently until he paused, took a big slug of his G&T, baring his teeth slightly as it slipped down his throat.

Maddie picked at the peanuts, twirled her G&T, and tried to remain cool and professional. In truth she was not sure what to say. The only thought that crossed her mind at this pivotal moment was the less-than-helpful notion that she hated lemon in her drink.

Davenport was not *that* well-informed.

"Tell me, Mr Davenport" she said. "What evidence do I get to show you can do what you say you can do? What qualifications do you have for this job? And where did you learn to do this kind of stuff."

Davenport smiled. A nice smile, she thought.

"Well," he said. "I used to work for a government. I guess it's pretty obvious which one. I was very good at my job, but these days they want guys who speak Arabic. I'm old school. I speak Russian. So now I have a new career in a freelance capacity. I discovered this Formula 1 thing when I was based in Berlin and I figured there is plenty of money in this world and a man with my skills should be able to get hold of some of it. I do have some useful talents, but to be fair this stuff is not rocket science. Hacking is not that hard. Anyway, no-one will know what we did. No-one will get hurt. You and I will get rich and Chiphurst Competition will be a better team and will pull in more prize money and, maybe, even a sponsor or two. What is there to argue about?"

"I think, Mr Davenport, I will have to get back to you on this one," Maddie said, rather coldly. "Perhaps we could have another meeting at a more opportune moment. I am a little busy tonight."

He smiled again. "That is not true," he said. "You are having dinner with Mr Rich. Don't you remember?"

"But you are not Mr Rich," she said, with an Arctic smile. There was a chink of ice cubes in her drink.

"Oh yes I am," he said. And then he softened a little. "Look Maddie, if I go now you will go up to your room and order room service, like you always do when you do not have an engagement. You will enjoy yourself because you like your own company, but why not let your auburn hair down just a little. Allow me to take you out to dinner.

"I promise not to talk about work any longer. Let's just have fun... I love your auburn hair, by the way."

And that was the moment at which she launched into her speech about being a natural blonde, which led to him making a pass at her. And so there she was walking away from him in the bar and he was chasing after her, not wanting her to leave.

"Look, I'm sorry," he said. "Let's be friends. I want to do business with you. OK, I find you attractive and you like me. I can tell. But we can work around that. I promise not to even try romancing you. I promise not to go looking for your on/off switch."

She could not stop herself smiling at that one. She was going to say no, but realized Winslow was right. She was a little boring. It felt safer that way. Yet he had annoyed her and her pride did not want to let him win this argument. And yet, she admitted, he was intriguing. In fact she found him rather exciting. Perhaps it was the mystery. Perhaps it was the little scar he had on his temple. She could not say. Dinner, she thought, would do no harm at all.

Just dinner.

"OK," she said, "but if I am going to have dinner with you I need to know your real name. I am afraid this Winslow Davenport thing is not very convincing."

"The name is Bond," he said. "James Bond."

She laughed again.

"Your real name?" she tried again.

"Winslow Davenport III," he said. "I'm sorry if it is not

convincing, but that really is my name. And if you continue to doubt me, I will call my father Winslow Davenport II in Virginia and get him to set you straight."

"Ring the right number at the Central Intelligence Agency and they will say anything you want them to say," Maddie said.

Winslow smiled. "That's true, but my Dad doesn't live in Langley. He lives in Colonial Beach. The zip code is 22443. It's on the Potomac River, to the south of Washington DC. They call it the Oyster Capital of the Potomac. You like oysters?"

"You should know that," Maddie said, with a little twinkle in her eye. She loved oysters, but she was not in the mood for a long and complicated dinner.

"Let's just eat Italian," she said. "I know a place just around the corner. Quite civilised."

"How very British," he said.

And so they had dinner. Just dinner. They worked their way through some pasta and then Winslow proposed sharing a tiramisu. Maddie felt it was too early in the relationship for a plate and two spoons. They had coffee instead.

He talked about Colonial Beach and growing up. He talked about his love of boats. Along the way Maddie made a few discoveries. He was close to fifty. He knew exactly how old she was, so she did not have to decline to tell him she was thirty-four.

They parted at ten thirty. Maddie half-expected Winslow to play up to the James Bond image and offer to shake and stir her, but he pecked her on the cheek, handed her a business card and said: "By the way, you do have an on/off button. I'll show you where to find it one day."

A split-second flash of laughter shot between them and then he was gone into the night. She was left standing in the hotel lobby, feeling slightly disappointed and just a little bit irritated.

"The problem with you," she grumbled as she stood by herself in the lift, "is you don't let yourself get enough sex."

# Two

Some people believe all motor racing stories involve sex and death, but in the modern age, it is rarely true. There is precious little of either in Formula 1 today. The cars are safe. Even allowing for the wildest youngsters, getting killed requires a huge amount of bad luck. And the racing drivers of the modern age are not the same type of maverick wild men they were in bygone ages. These days most of them are clean-living choirboys. They spend their days working out in the gym, politely attending sponsor functions or staring at computer screens with wild-haired engineers looking over their shoulders and pointing things out with half-chewed biros. The sad thing is this is how they need to be, to keep the teams and the sponsors happy.

Perhaps Maddie had been around them for too long, but she found most of the drivers of the modern era to be rather underdeveloped. They were usually good-looking, some were educated, but most of them were simply not very interesting. They had spent too much of their lives at kart tracks. The idea of sleeping with a modern racing driver left Maddie completely cold.

She found the other people in F1 to be much more interesting, especially the older engineers. They had lived the life in the old days, they had made their money, been through divorces and they were still there, for the love of the sport. The boys in the overalls did not impress them much.

The team principals were generally interesting, because they just happen. There is nowhere one can learn the job. The problem was they tended to become caricatures of themselves.

What was fascinating for Maddie was their manic urge to win. Everything was a competition. They fought for the best people; they fought for the sponsors; they even fought for the best seats on an aeroplane. It was a competition to be at the front of the queue for hire cars, although most never wasted any time on such menial things these days. They had become more worried about the size of the team's private jet or the motor cruiser, evidence that for some people, at least, size is important.

Maddie had often wondered what psychologists and psychoanalysts would make of such characters and what painful childhood memories would explain how they ended up as they are with this rage to be recognised. Winning in such a competitive world is anything but easy and talent is not enough. In such an environment there is no shame in winning only once, but these folk always wanted more, they wanted to be remembered in history. Teams are rarely run by people who are satisfied with life and have nothing left to prove. There is the added problem that some of the competitors are completely unethical, even amoral. Motor racing has only one commandment: Thou shalt not get caught.

The skill of the game is to find loopholes and "grey areas" that can be exploited. The officials of the international automobile federation have to find what you are doing, but more importantly they have to prove you had been cheating and often this is not as easy as it sounds. Smoking gun evidence does not convict.

But with Winslow's idea none of that was necessary...

They could never get caught. It was pure genius.

When she got to her room in the Berkeley Hotel, Maddie hung up the "Do Not Disturb" sign, locked the door and then carefully took off her clothes. The underwear, she noted, was

Aubade. She could not remember during the conversation with Davenport but now she smiled. How the hell could he have known that? And how many men really know about good underwear? For most of them lingerie exists only to be admired briefly and then removed and thrown on the floor as quickly as possible.

Maddie was happy to be naked. She stood for a while in front of the mirror, looking at herself. What would Winslow make of such a picture, she asked herself. She smiled at the thought. She wandered around the room. The hotel was a nice place to stay, if money is no object. There is an amazing rooftop swimming pool, complete with a retractable roof.

She looked at her watch. No, it was too late to go swimming. She was restless. She prowled around the room and then spotted the business card Winslow had given her. She had put it on the dressing table, without even looking at it.

"Send me an e-mail," he had said. "And don't worry. It cannot be traced."

The card was made from quality paper, but she was amused to find it did not even have his name on it. There was nothing apart from an e-mail address: burglar@watergate.com.

She laughed out loud.

Still naked, she dug out her computer, sat down on the bed and logged in to her e-mail, ignoring the busy inbox.

She clicked on the new message tab and immediately began writing an e-mail to Winslow.

*Dear Mr Davenport,*

*I have considered your suggestion and I think there is much to be applauded in the proposal. I would therefore be delighted to meet with you again to discuss the matter and perhaps draft some form of an agreement.*
*I am leaving in the morning to fly to Budapest for the Hungarian Grand Prix at the weekend, but I will be*

*back in my office at Chiphurst Competition on Monday. Perhaps we could have dinner in Oxford that evening?*

*Best wishes*

*Maddie Midnight*
*Marketing Director*

She pondered a few seconds before pressing the "Send" button. Was it too forward to ask Davenport for dinner? She looked at her name – Maddie Midnight. It looked good. It was a name that fitted her well, like a well-cut cocktail dress. No-one ever called her Madeleine Mezzanotte; not even her parents. She had often thought maybe she should go the whole way and change her name by deed poll, like Toto Wolff of Mercedes had done. He thought it odd to be Austrian and have the name of a Norse god and she thought it strange to have an exotic Italian name while being as Italian as a Yorkshire Pudding. She didn't even speak the language.

The story of how the name had come about stretched back seventy-odd years to a dashing young Roman called Matteo Mezzanotte, who had gone to war in 1940 with the *Regio Corpo Truppe Coloniali della Libia*, under the command of the glamorous General Pietro Maletti. A few weeks later, in Libya, this unit had led the Italian advance into Egypt, part of the mighty British Empire. It had probably not been a great idea, but the British were unprepared and did not put up a fight. The Italians could not press home the advantage because they ran short of supplies and so dug in and waited at a place called Nibiewa. It was the wrong thing to do.

The British, under Lieutenant General Richard O'Connor, quickly built up their forces and then counter-attacked, sneaking part of XIII Corps through a gap in the Italian line and attacking Maletti's troops from the rear. General Maletti was killed and four thousand Italian soldiers - including Mezzanotte - were captured. The prisoners were sent first to Egypt and from there to South Africa, before travelling on to England in the middle of 1941. Mezzanotte ended up at Goathurst prison camp in Somerset, where he worked for the local farmers, was paid a small amount each day, plus a packet of cigarettes a week. He learned to speak English and, as the war went on, it struck him that Mussolini was perhaps not the great leader he had previously imagined. He had done his duty and being a prisoner of war was no disgrace. There was no obvious reason to want to escape. It was better to be out of danger.

Eventually Matteo was found a place on a farm where he lived for the rest of the war. He still had to wear a POW uniform, but he was left alone most of the time, feeding and milking the cows and keeping the place clean. With all the young men away fighting the Germans and the Japanese, some of the local girls concluded the Italian prisoners were rather an attractive bunch. They, in turn, liked the rosy complexions, so different from the darker skinned girls at home. Nature did what nature does, with Glenn Miller being a little involved in the process, and although the details were rather sketchy, in 1945 Matteo Mezzanotte, known as Matty Midnight, decided *not* to go back to Italy and instead stayed in England and married Barbara Brockett, known as Babs.

Matty and Babs quickly had a son (perhaps rather too quickly), whom they called John. He grew up as an Englishman and when he was at school in the late 1950s he earned the nickname Johnny Midnight. He was clever and his proud parents watched him go off to university in the autumn of 1963. Four years later he was working "in the City" and mixing with people from far less humble beginnings. As a result Johnny Midnight ended up one weekend at a place called Brands Hatch in Kent, where some of his friends (and a secretary he fancied) had gone to watch motor races.

Johnny loved it. And so it was that, in the tumultuous summer of 1968, Midnight went to Brands Hatch to watch Chris Amon and Jacky Ickx racing their Ferraris against the British F1 teams. He was there in 1970 as well, but by 1972 he was bored of waiting for a Ferrari win and rather than going to Brands Hatch, he spent the day of the British Grand Prix trying to seduce a young lady, employing a great deal of wine and Donny Osmond's Puppy Love. This proved to be very successful, although the marriage that resulted was not.

By 1974 Johnny Midnight was back at Brands Hatch, if only to get away from his wife. Still no Ferrari had won a Grand Prix at the Kentish circuit and two years later, having split with his wife, he returned to Brands Hatch. He had given up on Ferrari and was there to cheer for James Hunt.

That evening, amid the victory celebrations, he met a Castrol promotions girl called Lizzie Morgan. It was love at first squint, for the pair had drunk rather a lot by the time they met, but when they woke up the next morning at his place, they felt rather comfortable together. She borrowed a shirt to avoid the embarrassment of catching the bus home in full Castrol colours, and that sparked the subsequent chain of events. She returned the shirt a few days later and so they had a drink and woke up in bed again. By the autumn they were married, the ceremony taking place just after Hunt's victory at Brands Hatch was taken away from him and the victory given to Niki Lauda - in a Ferrari.

For the next three years they were forever falling into bed at every possible occasion and in the summer of 1980 little Madeleine appeared. No-one could ever remember why a French name was chosen.

Given their story, there was an inevitability that young Maddie would end up going to a lot of racing in her childhood. As he made more money Johnny Midnight decided, despite his wife's complaints, to have a try racing an old MG, which he duly crashed. He bought a second and improved and so Maddie spent her childhood weekends at Brands Hatch, Lydden Hill, Thruxton and Silverstone. Lizzie was won round to the idea and they formed a little team called Midnight Motors, which Johnny always said sounded "suitably fly-by-night for this business".

After some success with his MGs, Johnny decided to run a couple of Formula Fords for spotty teenagers with rich fathers and Maddie got her first kiss from a no-hoper called Billy Wing, behind a pile of tyres in the pits at Silverstone. Usually they stayed in a motorhome at the races, and when she was sixteen Maddie snuck out one evening and lost her virginity to a mechanic called Rod (which always made her smile) in the back of the Midnight Motors transporter. Surprisingly, it was a good experience and for the next six months Maddie and Rod were often to be found grappling in the back of the team truck.

She went off to university in the autumn of 1998 and three years later her father took her on to run operations at the Midnight Motors headquarters at Silverstone.

Johnny Midnight's team was never very well-funded and the following year the boss of a richer operation, who had known Maddie since she was 12, asked her if she would help him out with his sports car team. A year after that, he absconded to Spain when the money ran out. Maddie was outraged. She swore blind she would keep the business together and make sure everyone kept their jobs. She bought the team from the administrator for a Pound and changed the name to Midnight Racing, Johnny Midnight having by then given up with his own team to concentrate on property development in the pretty villages of Northamptonshire. This was a great help as it was Johnny who put the money together to help Maddie keep the team alive. Things gradually became more stable and Maddie Midnight became part of the motor racing community around Silverstone. The team did quite well in sports cars and bought some Dallaras and entered British Formula 3 for the next three years, but the series was already waning in importance and Maddie was wondering what to do when one day there was a commotion in the workshop and she emerged from her office to find the celebrated Charlie Chiphurst nosing around the factory.

"Ah, there you are," he said. "I'd like to have a chat."

The upshot was he wanted her to work for him.

"I've got money, you've got charm," he said. "We should be able to go a long way."

And so it was that Maddie Midnight went to work for Charlie Chiphurst. Midnight Motors was sold to its chief engineer and the money was used to buy Maddie a cottage.

Charlie had been a team owner since the mid 1970s, when

he got bored of his very successful career selling household radiators. He was happy to admit he had been in the right place at the right time. They had all had Cosworth engines in those days and if one had a half-decent designer with a few good ideas, one could make quite an impression, if you could find a good driver. As he had plenty of money behind him - it just kept coming - he did not have to struggle in the same way as a Frank Williams or a Jack Oliver.

He was one of the boys and his timing was good because just when the team needed to do well, it all came together and allowed him the opportunity to get a BMW engine supply when the turbocharged engines were required in the mid-1980s.

While other teams went to the wall because they could not afford turbos, Chiphurst survived. He built up the team slowly and quietly, never achieving a great deal, but remaining in the midfield. His was a solid F1 team and in the six years they had worked together the pretty auburn-haired girl had often been seen in the background when Charlie did his TV interviews.

Charlie was now in his early seventies, but he still liked the high profile Formula 1 gave him. He did not make much money, but then he did not really need to. He had plenty of it because people were still buying radiators.

Maddie suddenly became conscious she had been staring at her computer screen, not reading the words, for quite a while. She focussed again and re-read the e-mail to Winslow. It seemed slightly flirtatious, but she could not really explain why. After a few seconds she just accepted it was what she wanted to say and clicked on the send button.

The message disappeared. She was working on something else when the reply came back five minutes later.

*Sure. Monday night is good. I know a little place out of the way. Sweet dreams. Winslow*

"Winslow," she thought. Unusual name. In her mind she turned over the sound of it: Winslow and Maddie. Maddie and Winslow. Just like a teenage girl. After that she could not sleep. At about three in the morning she decided to hit the minibar because her mind was racing along, thinking about Winslow's proposal, and she needed to slow it down.

Winslow had said that as a medium-sized Formula 1 team, the path to the top of the sport had become so difficult that it was now almost impossible. Most of the F1 team owners of today can only dream of being a Ron Dennis or a Frank Williams. They refuse to be defeated. They fight on, against the odds. Their aim is to do an outstanding job with limited resources and somehow draw attention to themselves, in the hope that an automobile manufacturer will want to partner with them. If they are lucky enough to get a factory engine deal and the money that comes with this, then they can start to hire better people and move the team up the ladder.

Maddie's job as marketing director was to find the money required each year to keep the team running. When you are looking for more than one million US dollars a year, it is not easy. There are constant presentations to be done, brainstorming sessions to try to think up new ideas, but the truth is the really big sponsors are not won by hard work. The big fish swim straight to you. Many a celebrated F1 marketing man has made his name by picking up the phone and saying: "Yes, of course, I am sure we can do that".

To get that kind of approach, however, one needs good results and to achieve those one must do a better job than everyone else. These days you are allowed to buy technical expertise from rival teams, but that has only limited value. It will move you up the ladder to a certain point, but when you get there you have to invest and buy the right equipment and the right people in order to compete and move higher.

The difference between a good car and a bad car today is down to the engine and to aerodynamics, the way in which the air flows around the car. The crazy thing is F1 aerodynamics have almost no relevance to anything other than Formula 1, which means it is money that is completely wasted. The engineers do not care. Hundreds of them spend thousands of hours every year looking for tiny aerodynamic advantages. If you start with an advantage it tends to remain if you can afford development. All the big teams work like mad to improve, but their progress is limited because their performance generally stays the same, in relative terms. The people without money to develop their cars fall behind. Some teams stop their development in order to concentrate on the following season.

It is all completely illogical.

Winslow's idea, on the other hand, made complete sense – and that annoyed her. Try as she might, Maddie was unable to find a flaw in the plan. It was completely foolproof.

In the morning she drove her Renault Mégane to the airport. She would worry about Winslow and his plan when she got back from Budapest.

The Hungarian Grand Prix is the last race before F1's annual summer break, when the race teams are all forced to take time off before the second half of the season begins. It is designed to ensure team members are able to have time with their families.

The biggest problem for the F1 community is that in July everyone becomes a traveller. Airports move slowly because they are filled with amateurs. Planes are late. Baggage-handlers go on strike, stewardesses do not have the time to be nice. Travelling is not much fun. Charlie Chiphurst had long ago forgotten what it was like to live in the real world and so arrived in Budapest in a rented Bombardier Global 600 jet. It was a lot bigger and more powerful than they really needed, but Charlie liked to spoil himself sometimes. It was all tax-deductible, he said, and he tried to convince Maddie it was cost-effective because he had brought six other people with him.

"There's a seat for you on the way home," he said, trying to stop her shouting at him.

"You're not the CFO!" he said forlornly, trying to ward off the blows. He would never understand.

Maddie left him cowering in his office in the Chiphurst motorhome and went out into the F1 paddock. It was hot and the paddock was busy with people milling about doing their jobs. On Thursday that means preparing the cars, getting everything ready, talking to the media and gossiping with other teams. The engines would not be fired up until Friday morning, but Maddie loved the energy of the paddock, even if the restrictions on passes had reached absurd levels, making it almost impossible for teams to please their sponsors. It had been like that for some time and no-one really understood why. It felt like Bernie Ecclestone  - the man who ran the F1 business - was simply doing it to prove he could. Perhaps it was because he was chasing after all the sponsorship, arguing sponsors got a better deal if they worked with him, rather than with the teams. Gradually the team sponsorship was disappearing but Ecclestone's deals with pay TV companies meant he was providing more and more of the money on which the teams relied - and this meant he should have more control over them. You had to be on good terms with Ecclestone and they all did it, albeit often through gritted teeth. One day, they all said, he would go - one way or the other - and then they would make some changes. But at eighty five, Bernie was still going strong, sharp as a tack and three steps ahead of the game, like every great chess grandmaster. Maddie was not that bothered by Mr E. He was what he was and there was no getting rid of him. The sport just had to wait. F1 was damaging itself all the while, but no-one had the power - or the balls - to take him on.

What Maddie loved more than anything was when the cars were running. The colours flashing through the corners, the engines thundering. She never ceased to be impressed by the speed with which these beautiful machines would leave a corner, nor their unthinkable ability to stop. The men who drove them might not be as charismatic as in previous generations, but they all had impressive skills. Even the pay-drivers had extraordinary abilities. If she could, she would always sneak away during a practice session to watch these men battling their mechanical beasts, fighting the machines, themselves and their adversaries. She came back in awe of what they do and she loved to pass that sense of wonder on to the team's guests and sponsors.

Chiphurst Competition had a pair of drivers who Charlie referred to as "quite useful". That was not a great compliment. He had hired better drivers in other eras, but you did the best you could. The experienced Lorenzo di Sustro was not a bad Grand Prix driver, but he had never been quite good enough. He had failed to live up to the expectations that came with him when he arrived in F1, but his results were always just good enough to allow him to hang on for another year and another year. He had made a great deal of money as an F1 driver, but his best result was still only a third place.

He was an amusing man with many stories and, predictably, was known to the team by the nickname "Disaster". He had hairy knuckles, always wore a very large heavy watch and spent his spare time in his native Sardinia, where he owned a vineyard.

"Everybody say that Sardinia wine is shit," he would complain, in English that was more smashed than broken, "but we make wine for many century. Our place is perfect place for wine. Earth come from volcano. Sun is hot. We have big hills. Our wine is beautiful in ancient times. And me, I make it better today. And European Union give me subsidy! Now very top quality. You know *cannonau* grape? She is beautiful."

His English always made Maddie smile, but it had not improved despite him having competed in 160 Grands Prix.

"You know why they call me di Sustro?" he asked Maddie one day. "There ain't no place called Sustro in Italy. So how family can come from there? My father say that it is mistake with typewriter because Italy uses QWERTY keyboard and A and S is together. So maybe the name is Austro and they type Sustro. Anyway that sounds better. My grandfather add the "di" like he is a *barone*! So maybe I am fake *barone* from Austria!"

Somewhere along the way Lorenzo had hooked up with a windswept Brazilian beauty called Rosita Silva Santos, who always wore a pink flower in her hair. She always looked as though she had spent the entire night being ravished. This was probably because that was exactly what had happened.

She spoke very little English and communicated in Italian. This meant she had a rather solitary life in F1 when Lorenzo was busy. Her only escape was to find the girlfriends of Brazilian drivers and chatter away for hours in motorhomes, discussing shades of nail polish, orgasms, celebrity magazines and all the latest fashion trends.

Rosita was not a complicated character, but she made the team a bit more colourful.

The other driver was the youngster Poppy Denso from Brazil. His father had played an important role in cutting down huge swathes of Amazon rainforest. Timber is big business and money was never much of a problem for young Poppy. He moved quickly into Formula 1, thanks to a modicum of natural talent and a great deal of money. He had done well enough to be taken seriously by all but the top teams, who did not need his cash. He had been rather wild in his first two seasons, but since joining Chiphurst he had begun to show signs he was finally calming down, at least on the race track. Away from the circuits he led a most exotic life, forever turning up with a new Russian model on his arm, and doing stupid things with cars, motorcycles, jet skis and helicopters. Charlie Chiphurst was none too impressed when he heard Poppy had flown his helicopter into a barn as a bet with some of his rich friends in Brazil.

"Actually," Poppy had explained, "it was really a very impressive thing, you know. I was flying the 'elicopter backwards."

Like many racing drivers, Poppy spoke English using strange expressions which had been learned by spending too much time with racing mechanics in the formative stages of his career. Nowadays he would not be seen dead in the company of his mechanics, but he retained their colourful expressions, such as "it's a bit bloody parky" and "Blimey, look at that boat race".

He was a good team member, but Maddie had spotted there was a serious problem that might blow up at any time. Poppy clearly thought Rosita was the most beautiful woman he had ever seen and he was quietly, but continuously, trying to convince her that he was a much better option than "the old fucking Italian". Rosita was holding out against his advances and, fortunately for the team, Lorenzo did not seem to have noticed Poppy's fixation.

"It's a powder keg," Maddie said to Charlie one day. "We need to get rid of one or the other because if Rosita ever decides to give Poppy a test drive we are going to have real trouble."

Charlie smiled and thought about saying something about not being averse to the idea of test driving Rosita himself, but decided it was not a classy thing to say. He told Maddie he would probably dump Lorenzo at the end of the season after he had heard him say "the sooner we dump this shitbox, the better" to one of the engineers.

Chiphurst was proud of his cars, which he saw as being thoroughbreds, and he did not like them being criticised by "bloody foreigners". He did, however, like the bank transfers that arrived from Lorenzo's sponsors bang on time whenever there was a payment deadline needing to be met.

Formula 1 drivers are employed to drive fast and the majority of them are super-talented, even those who come to F1 thanks to the money behind them. Motor racing has always been about money, right back to the earliest days when one French aristocrat was able to buy a faster machine than another French aristocrat. It was no different to horse racing in this respect. You were simply paying for the best you could find, a thoroughbred. In the early years of the sport many of the leading names were lords and barons, wild young sportsmen with money to burn in an exciting era of technological change. The wealthy thrill-seekers and playboys joined the game, notably Willie K Vanderbilt. But being rich does not make you fast and after a while the aristocrats and industrialists found that often their mechanics could drive faster than they could and so a new class of professional racing driver began to emerge.

Then after World War I there came a generation of young men who had survived a cataclysmic war but still wanted the excitement of being in constant danger. Many of the racers on the Twenties were former fighter pilots.

In the modern era it is still a game for the rich and the fast. All the others involved are passionate, but are basically wasting their time.

The trouble with drivers with money behind them is they struggle to throw off the reputation that they are pay-drivers and so they have to go on paying. Occasionally they are good enough to switch from paying to being paid, but it really is a rarity. The problem they have is that when a team knows a driver is there on financial merit rather than sporting merit, the attitude changes. The team members cease to be motivated to go the extra mile. They settle for things that would not be the case if they were motivated by a rising star or one of the few demanding superstars who command respect with the way they drive.

That is what was holding back Chiphurst Competition.

"What I really want," said Charlie one day, "is a gorgeous competitive African-American woman driver. If I had that I could get enormous amounts of sponsorship."

There are not many sports where men and women can compete head-to-head. Automobile racing is one of them but still there has never been a woman good enough to win a Grand Prix.

In rallying, Frenchwoman Michèle Mouton was sufficiently competitive to finish runner-up in the World Championship, but she herself says she does not see women beating men in races. Rallies are different because one is fighting against the clock, rather than competing directly against men.

Mouton believes women can drive as fast as men, and indeed some can drive faster, but that they have an inherent sense of self-preservation which is more advanced than in men. It is an instinct that has developed over the two hundred thousand years of human history, during which time men were the hunters and women the nurturers. As a result, men take risks women think about, if only for a split-second. She says she hopes she is wrong and that the right woman will come along one day. Despite this, the sport is something both sexes enjoy watching. One might argue it is a form of mating ritual. Maddie did not really care about the philosophy. She liked the lifestyle and she loved the racing.

She also loved the travelling and Budapest was one of her favourite places. She liked the splendour of the city, with its grand hotels, its parliament, castles and opera house. There was nothing better than to take an early morning walk along one of the great avenues. It was a lot like Paris, only it needed more cleaning up after forty wasted years under the rule of communism.

The Hungaroring circuit was out of town, in the sandy hills to the east of the city and she spent most of her time out there, looking after sponsors and talking about deals but she was able to slip away and have dinner with Charlie on the Thursday night. Friday and Saturday were reserved for sponsors and VIP guests.

Sunday was always a busy day with the pre-race excitement building up during the morning. At one thirty the engines fired up and the cars went out to the grid, where they lined up in qualifying order, surrounded by the mechanics and engineers, frantic camera crews, profiling VIPs and journalists snatching quick conversations with key people. And then the numbers would thin out, the national anthem would be played, the crowd would cheer, maybe there would be a flypast. Then the drivers were in their cars, cocooned from the world, connected to their teams by radio alone. Maddie often listened in to the conversations and was always amazed at how calm most drivers were. Then they would fire up the engines and the cars would head off on the final parade lap, the drivers darting and weaving to warm up the tyres and the brakes, getting everything ready. The international TV feeds would go live and the commentators would start to build up to fever pitch. The cars would line up on the grid and five lights would come on, one after another as the engine noise built up and then there would a moment of complete calm as everyone held their breath and waited for the lights to go out. This was the climax of the entire weekend and then suddenly everything exploded into action and excitement, with cars going left and right. It was impossible to take it all in, but replays would soon follow to explain what had happened as the drivers looked for the best place to be going into the first corner, daring one another to go too far. It never ceased to amaze her that they usually managed to all get through without hitting one another. That was her favourite moment of any race meeting. Afterwards, things would settle down, strategies would emerge and dices develop, but the mad dash to the first corner was the thing.

That afternoon things did not go well. Di Sustro tagged wheels with a Sauber on the first lap and had to pit to get a new nose. He dropped to the back of the field and ultimately finished a dull thirteenth. Denso was running ninth when his engine blew up.

As he stomped off towards the team hospitality unit with twenty laps to go before the chequered flag, Charlie rang Maddie and said he was leaving in five minutes if she wanted a lift back to the UK, so she needed to move quickly.

Five minutes later Maddie, pursued by her carry-on, was leaving the paddock with her team owner, his assistant Cheryl and the chief aerodynamicist Bill Poppinger. It was a squeeze to get them all in the car and Charlie was not in a good mood, although leaving before the end of the race meant no traffic. At the bottom of Bernie Avenue, named after Ecclestone, they turned right on to the motorway, going east. A couple of miles down the road there was a turn off to the south on another motorway and they arrived at the airport within 20 minutes.

As no-one else had managed to get there Charlie ordered the plane to leave as soon as possible. He didn't care. He wanted to go home.

"It's their own bloody fault for pissing me off," Charlie said as the Global 6000 thundered down the runway and left Budapest behind. "They can all get drunk at my expense and fly home tomorrow."

Maddie was not really listening. She was busy doing sums. It was four thirty Budapest time. That was three thirty in the UK. They had to cover about a thousand miles. The plane travelled at nearly six hundred miles per hour. That meant about two hours. They would be home by five. She could get home easily enough from Brize Norton, but her car was at Heathrow, which was the complication.

"I am having the day off tomorrow," she told Charlie. "Got to get my car."

The team boss made a grumbling noise, but he rarely argued with Maddie. She was too quick for him. He couldn't keep up. Cheryl, who solved problems before they even developed, was already organising transportation.

"You want a taxi home?" she asked Maddie.

"I'm OK. Charlie can give me a lift. It's on his way."

"Roger that," said Cheryl.

"I'll get someone to give me a ride to London tomorrow," Maddie said, fishing out her computer. Winslow was her man. The plane had wireless access to the Internet and she tapped out a quick e-mail. "Need a ride to London Monday morning 10:00 a.m. Will buy you lunch on the way back. You up for it?"

She did not have long to wait. The reply came back almost instantly: "Sure. Will be there."

It struck her that Winslow was not supposed to know where she lived, but it was obvious this was not a problem, so she replied with "Thanks" and did not even mention the address. That would have been playing his game.

Charlie and Poppinger were talking a lot. Bill was a Canadian and a good solid old-fashioned engineer. He had the arrogance of a technical director, but had never quite made it to that exalted status. But, to give him credit, he was not a man of half measures. It was all or nothing with Bill. Maddie liked him, but for some reason whenever she saw him she was reminded of Charlie Chaplin. He had an innate sadness that sometimes gave her a lump in the throat.

"I want a bigger jet," she heard Charlie say. "That's your job, Poppinger. If you can make this team win then I can buy a bloody great A380 with Chiphurst written on the side. Done up how I want it, like that Saudi Prince. I want a jet with a fireplace and I want to take my Aston Martins with me."

Maddie had a couple of drinks and then dozed off for a while, waking as the plane began its descent into Brize Norton. There was a Mercedes waiting for them. A bored-looking chauffeur stubbed out his cigarette as they approached and very quickly Maddie and Chiphurst were on their way through the lanes of Oxfordshire. She was home as the evening news began.

Home was a small limestone cottage in a village called Netherington. The house was nothing special. It was on the edge of the village green, which was large enough for a Maypole, but not sufficient for cricket. There was a war memorial, a small stream, and on the other side of the green was a church with a square tower, surrounded by a small cemetery. Next door was a pub called The Scalded Cat. There was a bus stop, but Maddie had never seen a bus.

The house was one of five in a row, all joined to one another. They were all set back from the green and separated from it by a swathe of lawn, fifteen feet wide with wooden posts hammered in at intervals to stop people parking there. Thankfully there was little traffic.

The layout of the village meant the residents of the five cottages never used their front doors and each house was entered through the back garden, behind which there was a private parking area where the stones still crunched when you drove in.

Entering the house through the back door meant everything was back-to-front and the central staircase was facing the wrong way. It was, in truth, little more than a two-up, two-down with a sitting room on the one side and a kitchen/dining room on the other. Upstairs was the master bedroom on one side and a smaller one on the other, with the remaining space used for a bathroom.

The house was pretty from the outside but inside it always seemed to her to be rather cold and lacking in soul. Flowers died and food grew legs and tried to walk out of the fridge, complaining of being mistreated. The freezer was Maddie's only friend in the village. That was the effect of the F1 lifestyle. And yet Netherington was a nice place. Every barn and outhouse had been converted (some by Johnny Midnight) and there was a thriving community of all ages. Horses clip-clopped through the village at all hours and kids still looked for tadpoles in the stream, while their parents relaxed outside The Scalded Cat.

Maddie considered going across the green to have a glass of wine, but she didn't really feel sociable. She was weary. She found some vanilla ice cream in the freezer and went to bed, watching bad television and eating scoop after delicious scoop. Before she drifted off to sleep she set her alarm for the morning. Winslow was coming... That would be fun.

She didn't dream. She rarely did. Sleep was never a luxury but rather a necessity and she had learned to grab it whenever she could. When the alarm went off, she was instantly wide awake. Winslow was going to be arriving at ten. She needed to get ready. When she emerged from the shower, feeling deliciously clean, she saw she had received a text: "Can come early with croissants" it read.

"Can sit outside waiting," she replied. "Enjoy croissants".

Five minutes later the phone buzzed again.

"Understood."

At nine forty-five she was putting on a bit of make-up when she looked out of the bathroom window and saw Winslow, standing in the parking area, next to a sporty-looking Mercedes. He was eating a croissant. She made herself a coffee and, sitting at the kitchen table, composed herself for the day ahead. At five seconds past ten the phone rang.

"Miss Midnight," said the voice. "Your carriage awaits."

She heard the gentle rumble of the Mercedes engine outside the door.

"I'll be there in a minute," she said and hung up without another word. She stood for a moment looking at the mirror. She looked good, she thought. She had caught a hint of sunshine over the weekend and it made her look just a little bit healthier. She wished the tan was all over and did not stop at her neckline. Not that it mattered, of course. She had no intention of taking her clothes off for anyone other than herself. Winslow was attractive enough, but there was no way. Not with him.

"Who are you kidding?" she said to herself in the mirror. "Look at you. You've spent the whole morning so far getting dressed for him. It has all been about him..."

She nodded to herself. Yep, that just about summed it up. She stuck out her chest, blew herself a kiss and headed for the door.

Winslow was waiting by the car, the door open for her.

"You've forgotten the peaked cap," she said. "I do insist that my chauffeurs wear peaked caps. Did you have a nice breakfast?"

"It was solitary," he replied reproachfully, "but really very agreeable. The croissants were rather good. I presume you have done the British thing and have already had your bacon, sausage, black pudding, eggs and beans."

"And a fried slice," she said. "Not to mention toast and marmalade and lashings of hot tea."

"It amazes me how you English girls remain so damned thin when you eat all that stuff every morning," Winslow said.

"It is all down to exercise," said Maddie.

# Three

It was time to talk business. If Maddie was being truthful she might have said she would be just as happy if they could go on talking about other things, but business was business.

"So," Winslow said, as the car accelerated away, "do you accept the theory that modern sport is similar to war?"

"In principle, yes," she said. "You do what is necessary to beat the opposition."

"You break contracts?" Winslow asked.

"We never break contracts," said Maddie. "We just don't always honour them. There is always a way in which such things can be negotiated away."

"That," smiled Winslow, "is an interesting distinction."

Maddie smiled again.

"OK," he continued. "Do you spread mistruths in order to destabilise the opposition?"

"It has been known to happen..." said Maddie.

"And you spy on the opposition?"

"We do."

"Well then," Winslow said. "Let us look a little bit more about what warfare is all about. Back in the 1830s there was a Prussian general called Carl Von Clausewitz. He wrote a book called Vom Krieg in which he advocated what we nowadays call "Total War". Before Clausewitz came along, two armies would line up facing one another and shoot. Then, if necessary, they would engage in hand-to-hand combat, which was very messy, and then one side or the other, or both, would run away. Clausewitz argued that if one wanted to win a war one must attack not just the opposing armies, but also one's rival's resources and people. If a country has no will to fight and no factories in which to make weapons, armies are useless.

"Elements of the idea derived from tactics used by Arthur Wellesley during the Peninsular War. He ordered the construction of fortifications placed on the tops of hills, so as to control the roads into Lisbon. He also did dastardly things like damming rivers to create swamps. The British then sat behind these lines while France's General André Massena blockaded Lisbon. The problem was the British were supplied from the sea, while the French had to live off the land. In the end French supplies ran short, the soldiers became ill and morale crumbled. The population also suffered. Finally, the French withdrew and Wellesley gave chase, harassing the poor old Frenchies all the way."

Maddie noted they had reached the motorway.

"Clausewitz used the same principle, but as an offensive measure," Winslow went on. "The effects of that theory were first seen when General William Sherman's army marched through the South during the American Civil War. They burned Atlanta and then went through Georgia destroying crops and buildings, tearing up railroad tracks, releasing slaves and seizing all the supplies. They wanted to destroy the will to resist and to demonstrate that the Confederates could not hope to fight the power of the Union armies.

"The same theories were used to develop all kinds of modern warfare from saturation bombing of cities to the use of saboteurs, propaganda, disinformation and even to the idea of defoliation in Vietnam."

Winslow paused.

"Motor racing teams say they are fighting a war," he continued, "but the sport has not really started to see the full potential of warfare."

"That's true," Maddie said,"but you must remember this is a sport."

"If sport is war," Winslow said, "then the theories of war should be applied."

Maddie paused for a moment. There had to be a limit to what one would do in order to win.

"I don't think one should use offensive measures against the opposition," she said. "Pushing another driver off the road is not acceptable, and I think acts of sabotage would be going rather too far, don't you?"

"Why?" said Winslow. "Can you justify that view when you look at the demands that exist nowadays in the sport?"

"It is not right..." said Maddie. "Winning is important, but it must be sporting as well. Otherwise, the achievement is undermined. That is the problem with cheating. Circumstances change, people move from job to job, and in the end all these stories come to light. If you listen to people talking about the early 1980s, you would be horrified at what they did to be successful."

"Were the results changed?" said Winslow.

Maddie shook her head.

"So cheating is deemed to be acceptable – if you get away with it at the time," he said. "It follows that in order for anything achieved to remain credible, the methods used must remain a secret. The best way to do that is to tell as few people as possible. The more who know, the easier it is for information to leak out."

"Stealing staff and nobbling sub contractors is OK, but sabotage is unacceptable," said Maddie.

"And what about espionage?" Winslow asked.

"We all do it," Maddie said. "We all have photographers taking pictures of the other cars, so we can learn about wing profiles and so on. When engineers go from team to team they quite often do so with computer data. Information passes between teams all the time. Back in the old days there used to be an engineer who had stuff from Ferrari on his cars before the Ferrari team was even able to manufacture it. He had a man at Maranello who sold him drawings.

"All I am suggesting is that you should really do this espionage stuff properly," Winslow said. "You need to use modern techniques to get what you want. Chiphurst Competition could get the technical breakthrough you require, without spending the money needed to get it. All you have to do is hack into the computers of the best team and take whatever you need. What everyone needs is aerodynamic data and if you present this data to any aerodynamicist they are going to take it and keep their mouth shut. They know they will get the glory and that will mean they will be able to earn more...

"The key thing is the aerodynamicist must not know what he is getting, nor where it is coming from. He is not going to ask. All he will get is a message telling him where to find the data. These days that can be on a disk or a flash drive. You can leave them wherever you want. Post Office boxes, cut-out library books, any of the old spook tricks.

"Aerodynamicists are as ambitious as their drivers," he went on. "Some are even more arrogant. This is actually a good sign, because a meek and mild engineer will never make it to star status. There are plenty of engineers out there who are happy to take the credit for the achievements of others. This is perfect for them. They don't have to pay, they get something for nothing and they can pretend it is their work."

"I understand all that," said Maddie.

The only person in the team who would know the full story is you," Winslow went on. "You have to find a way to pay me three million US dollars and I will hand over the data to your technical guy. I'll give you twenty percent of the money as a commission. So if you pay me three million, I'll kick you back six hundred thousand dollars. Just imagine what you could do with that kind of cash."

"I pay you for stolen items, and I get a kickback on the deal," said Maddie. "That has to be criminal on any number of levels."

"Not at all," said Winslow. "It's nothing of the sort. Chiphurst will pay an anonymous company belonging to me. This will then pay a company in Jersey called M&W Enterprises. The name doesn't matter. With the three million, the company will buy a couple of pretty nice beach front villas just outside Nassau. These will be high-revenue producers in the short-term rental market, with rates of twenty thousand dollars a week in the high season and maybe a little bit less for the rest of the year. The rents would be paid to M&W Enterprises. If the two properties are rented for six months a year that brings in rents of about a million a year. In the Bahamas there are no taxes on profits, dividends or income; there is no capital gains tax, no withholding tax and no sales tax. Most offshore or non-resident entities are exempt from other taxes as well. So the profits could, quite legally, be transferred to bank accounts in Jersey: one would get eighty percent of the money, the other twenty percent. Each account would have a debit card, allowing the account holder instant access to the cash at thousands of ATM machines around the world.

"You don't want to be getting all that money in one go because people will start to talk. This way you can live very comfortably and no-one will spot the difference. And, while the money rolls in, our properties are increasing in value as well, so one day M&W can sell them and get a nice big lump sum into the Jersey account. We are both set for life. And if you want a house, you get a Jersey-based property company to buy a nice place in the UK and you can pay rent to live there. You can set up your own consulting business and get paid huge fees from a client in Jersey. So, you pay some UK income tax on that, then you pay your rent and the money goes back to Jersey... and no-one knows the difference."

"This does not mean it is not stealing," Maddie said. "You want me to pay you three million dollars for the CAD files and aerodynamic research and development data from Mercedes AMG Petronas. My designer will then incorporate this into his car."

"And that saves you a fantastic amount of money," he said.
Maddie nodded. It was true.
"It's perfect," Maddie said. "But is it right?"
"You don't seem to be able to tell me why it is not right," said Winslow. "When you accept all the things that go on

nowadays, it is really insane that you are not doing it."

"What about billing you for it," Maddie asked. "How do I get around that? Three million dollars is going to stand out."

"Oh, I don't know," Winslow replied. "I am sure you can come up with something. Consulting fees, a commission on a sponsorship deal I had nothing to do with. All you have to do is to write something into the budget."

"What you are suggesting is theft," Maddie said, "but you believe if everyone is stealing it is not wrong to do the same thing? I see it as a moral issue. When does cheating cease to be part of a game and become a criminal offence? What is right and what is wrong in a world where morals are completely warped?"

"That's about it," Winslow said.

Maddie was thinking what a nice warm feeling it would be to have that kind of money sitting in her bank account.

What would she buy?

She had been seduced.

The only argument she had against Winslow was that it was wrong. And yet he had explained why it was not wrong and Maddie had found herself nodding in agreement. Financial security would make life a great deal easier. And with that new calmness she could change the way she lived. Perhaps her workmates might comment she was now laid back, compared to the frantic Maddie of old, but no-one else would really notice.

They were quiet for the rest of the journey. Maddie picked up her Mégane and they drove back. The sun was shining and England was at its most beautiful. It was the kind of day one wants when there is a game of cricket to be played. She was going to suggest stopping for lunch, but it was still too early and so they drove back to Netherington. Winslow climbed out of the Mercedes and went to the boot. He pulled out an armful of books and a picnic basket.

"We have a choice," said Winslow. "We can picnic in a field near here, or we can picnic in your sitting room. Your choice. Let's have fun. You don't have to believe what I say. I've brought these books. Just read them. The answers are all in this lot."

Maddie was impressed. Winslow had prepared a picnic.

"Why don't we go up the hill and you can save time and energy by telling me what is written in all those books," she said very sweetly.

Winslow put the books back into his car and they walked up Netherington Hill. At the top of the hill, they turned right off the lane and walked across the top of a field. They found a sheltered spot looking down on the village. The sun was warm and the sky was a deep blue. Maddie was hungry. Winslow laid out a picnic blanket, waterproofed on one side, and opened a bottle of wine.

"Marlborough Sauvignon Blanc," he said. "Really very good."

A real wine glass was shoved in her direction and Winslow began to pull out a series of delicious-looking things from the basket.

"Where to begin?" he said. "We have some prosciutto-wrapped prawns with orange marmalade to begin."

Maddie's mouth fell open.

"Then we will have a caramelized leek quiche, followed by something that I call Boozy Fruit, which is fresh fruit served with a little brandy."

"Wow!" said Maddie. "I'd have been happy with a couple of scotch eggs."

As they ate, Winslow began to tell her about the early days of motor racing. Everyone, he said, was stealing ideas from everyone else.

"Peugeot, for example, was racing voiturettes against Hispano-Suiza in 1909," he said. "The little cars were pretty good and both companies believed they could build cars to win Grands Prix. So they both designed Grand Prix cars in preparation for 1912. Then Robert Peugeot decided he could cut some corners and hired the top Hispano-Suiza designers. Peugeot was able to finish its car first. The engine was a huge step forward, even if most of the ideas had come from Marc Birkigt, the boss of Hispano-Suiza. He sued and won, but by the time that was all done, Peugeot had won the Grand Prix and had got all the publicity that came with the victory.

"The funny thing was the following year, Louis Coatalen, the boss of Sunbeam's racing, managed to get hold of a Peugeot when it was on a sales tour in England, in the hands of Dario Resta, who had previously been a Sunbeam driver. The car was stripped down, measured and all the important parts were sketched and in 1914, Sunbeam was very competitive. A Peugeot was also sent to the States where it was rebuilt by an engineer called Harry Miller. A year later Miller produced his own engine, which boasted a number of features inspired by the Peugeot. That is how motor racing has always worked. I could go on and on with such stories.

"You know after the last war there was a British intelligence guy called Cameron Earl. He convinced his bosses to let him go to Germany to look in the files at Mercedes and Auto Union, in order to find out the secrets of the pre-war Grand Prix cars that had dominated in the 1930s. He wrote the whole thing up in a report, published by His Majesty's Stationery Office, which included all the data about the mid-engined Auto Unions. Was it a coincidence that a few months later the Cooper Car Company produced a car that looked like a cobbled-together version of an Auto Union?"

"That was the start of the revolution that took Britain to its modern domination of the racing world."

Maddie looked a little shocked.

"It is really not a big deal," Winslow said. "The Russians did it too. They found all the Auto Union Grand Prix cars in a salt mine and shipped them off to Moscow. The idea was to build Grand Prix cars so Russia could dominate racing, but it never happened.

"It is still going on. Ferrari broke into the Williams garage in Brazil one night in the early 1980s and measured the cars from end to end. The following year's Ferrari was a much better car. I don't need to tell you about the spy photography that goes on these days. Actually Maddie I really don't understand why they bother with that stuff because nowadays there are all kinds of amazing scanners to do this stuff."

"I cannot argue with you," she said. "But it doesn't feel

right. And I think that means it must be wrong."

"No. It's not wrong," he insisted. "Show me a rule that says you cannot steal from another team? There isn't one. It would be impossible to police. You know in 1977 the only way they could stop the Arrows team using a copy of a Shadow chassis was to bring an abuse of copyright case. That was pretty obvious as the Shadow technical team joined Arrows and built a car in just a few months. They could not have done it any other way."

"Yes, but they lost the case," Maddie said.

"But they knew they were going to lose," Winslow said. "The only reason they did it was to have a car ready in time to be able to win prize money. They knew they would lose, but by the time the case ended and the High Court ruled they had broken the law, there was another new car ready to run. That was all about survival, it was not about stealing."

"Hang on," Maddie interrupted. "It was stealing. Stealing because you want to survive is still stealing."

"Is it?" said Winslow. "I am not sure I agree with that. Wouldn't anyone steal if they had to? I would. And I bet you would do it as well."

"Of course we would," Maddie said, "But this is a sport. You don't have to steal."

"So it is better to lose then?" Winslow snapped back.

"No! We are in this game to win..." she said.

"...and you will do what is necessary," he fired back. "Maddie this is not like robbing a bank. This is like peeking at a classmate's examination papers. It is not the same as knowing the answers in advance."

"Oh, I don't know," she said. "I need to think about it. Let's talk about something else."

"Like what?"

"Let's talk about you. Tell me what happened after Colonial Beach and before you met me."

"Ah-h-h," said Winslow. "Now why would you want to know about all that stuff?"

"Professional curiosity," she replied. "I want to know if I am going to get my money's worth."

Winslow took a long deep breath.

"Well," he said. "I guess the story begins with the Pilgrim Fathers..."

"I can't stand puritans," said Maddie.

Winslow shrugged.

"It's your fault, you asked," he said. "Anyway, maybe they weren't on the Mayflower itself, but they were in Plymouth, Massachusetts, not long after that. And they did well. For many generations the Davenports were a wealthy family, then a couple of imprudent generations meant my father had to actually work for a living, although to be fair we lived comfortably.

"When I was young I was scared of witches and skeletons under the beds - these things don't seem to scare kids much these days - and yet the thing that scared me most was far more horrifying. I grew up with the nuclear bomb. And yet for all the fear, I figured out that thanks to these terrifying bombs we were never going to fight another big war. And so I ended up going to the United States Naval Academy at Annapolis in 1984, doing my four years by the bay. My parents were so proud. I was commissioned as a Second Lieutenant in the US Marine Corps and went off to train at Quantico. It was 1988 and the US was not really fighting any small wars and so I was sent off to Monterey in California where I spent a year learning Russian. I missed the Gulf War because I had the wrong qualifications and then the Soviet Union collapsed so my qualifications were not much use. I was sent to Moscow to be an assistant military attaché. I never did anything really interesting.

"So you are a victim of fate," Maddie asked, mocking him slightly.

"Well, I guess you could say that."

"And after that?"

"I was moved over to join what we call The Company, but its budgets were being slashed under the first George Bush. Then Clinton came along and things got worse. More and more staff retired and were not replaced. The whole thing was geared to economic intelligence in that era and I did a bit of that, but I wasn't really interested. There was still terrorism going on, but it was at a pretty low level stuff at that time. In the end I left and went to do private security work - and that is what I've been doing ever since."

"Even after September 11?" said Maddie. "They didn't want you back?"

"Not really," said Winslow. "Maybe if they had some stuff that needed deniability, but I didn't do much of that. It pays well though. I like government work when you can get it. They pay top dollar because you know they won't have to help you if you get into trouble."

# Four

Winslow stopped talking and refilled Maddie's glass, and then his own. She found herself looking at him in a quite different way. He was tall and good-looking in a clean-cut kind of fashion. He would, she thought, look adorable in a dinner jacket. She liked the way the moved his shoulders and imagined how exciting it might be to run her fingers across the muscles she imagined she would find beneath his Brooks Brothers button-down cotton Oxford shirt.

Men always seemed to over-estimate the importance of muscles, but Maddie was very clear about what she wanted. She liked a muscular man, but not one who was muscle-bound. Wide shoulders and narrow hips always did it for her. There is an inherent masculinity in broad shoulders, suggesting confidence, dependability and strength of character. She was sure it all went back to the days when women were looking for good hunters to breed with.

Yet, Winslow had more than just that. It was all in his eyes. She didn't like men with bedroom eyes, she always felt they looked shifty, rather than romantic, but Winslow's eyes were open and relaxed. They were never darting about and yet, at the same time, she felt they were always laughing and just a little mischievous. His eye contact seemed to last just a fraction longer than perhaps it should have done, but it made her feel he was attracted to her. It made her feel special. If she was being honest with herself, she would have admitted he excited her.

When he spoke it was with a fine voice, exactly as one would expect. It was soft yet powerful and every word was well chosen. Maddie knew such thoughts were probably a bad idea, but she did not care. It was so easy to be in his company. She felt she could be herself.

She paused for a moment and realised he was looking at her in the same way she was looking at him. They each knew in that instant what the other was thinking, but she wrenched her eyes away from him and started to talk about stoats, if only to change the subject. She knew nothing about stoats, but Cheryl used to go on about them doing horrible things to her garden. Maddie knew she was floundering. He knew too.

"We could go back to your house for the coffee," he said, without much originality. She frowned and went back to talking about weasels and badgers. He smiled. When she ran out of words, they sat silently until a cool breath of air caused her to shiver.

"I think I want to go to sleep now," she said.

They packed up the basket and wandered down the hill, back to her cottage. Winslow was wondering if she would invite him in, but she smiled sweetly, said "Thank you for everything" and pecked him on the cheek. That was it.

He smiled as he watched her go, her slim hips moving with that easy elegance which got him every time. She looked over her shoulder and smiled. She looked tired.

The day will come, he thought. She's definitely thinking about it.

He turned and strode to the Mercedes. There were other things needing to be done...

Maddie went to bed and slept until the evening. That was not a great idea because it meant that when it came to bedtime she was wide awake. The heat had gone with the daylight and she sat by a fire and had some wonderful soup she had found in the freezer. There was a bottle of something red that helped the situation. She couldn't be bothered to watch the TV. War could have broken out and she would not have known. The world was going along without her. She had concluded there was no argument she could come up with to defeat Winslow, except that it seemed to be wrong. But there were advantages she could not deny. Six hundred thousand dollars in her bank account was a pretty convincing argument. She wondered whether the Citizens Advice Bureau could help. She could go to church and ask the vicar but she knew they would all tell her to leave the warped world in which she happily lived. They would tell her there was a more Christian way through life. She didn't want that. Then she thought of Fred Quirk. That was the answer. Fred would know. She rang him straight away.

Was he free for lunch?

"For you," he said, "I am always available. I would move mountains if you asked me to."

It was so very Fred.

It was a source of much amusement amongst her workmates that Maddie's qualification for being a marketing director in Formula 1 was a degree in philosophy. Engineers study engineering, but in F1 in the old days anyone could do the other jobs on offer. Office workers became journalists, caterers became marketing men and anyone could be a team manager. If you sat around and talked to those in the paddock you were constantly amazed by the stories they had to tell. Formula 1 was a world of wonderful, exotic and free-thinking characters.

Yet Fred was not a Formula 1 person, although he was sufficiently dysfunctional he might have been. He had been her tutor at university and, for a time, was widely considered to be the most brilliant young philosopher in the whole of Oxford. Sadly, Dr Quirk was also a drunk and a lecher. In the realms of academia these faults were glossed with the description "eccentric", which meant he would never move on to Nobel Prizes or any great works. He was content to amuse himself with the education of generation after generation of clever young men and women. His greatest passion in life remained the same: an ever-changing diet of dark-haired grammar school virgins, in awe of his reputation. Maddie had not been one of them, but she had liked Fred and after three years under his guidance they had stayed in touch, if only with the occasional Christmas card and a dinner once every couple of years.

The first thing that singled out Fred's brilliance was that he had the front end of an old Mini in his room and had somehow contrived to fit an engine block that acted as a drinks cabinet with a bottle in each cylinder. Maddie had often wondered during tutorials how this had been transported up two flights of stairs and through several narrow doors, but Fred never explained. Vodka was Fred's favourite tipple.

At the centre of the room was a huge oaken table upon which were heaped papers and books, learned articles and bus tickets. This was his desk, through which he loved to rummage, pausing occasionally to sharpen his pencil into what had once been a potpourri. Although the room had no chimney, he had installed a fire place for the express intention of being able to lean on the mantelpiece when he was teaching.

The strangest of all his furnishings, however, was a Second Empire chaise longue that he had for his pupils, in order that they might relax during tutorials. Dr Quirk's chaise longue was a notorious venue for the education of dark-haired grammar school virgins.

Maddie knocked on Fred's door. It flew open immediately and Fred brushed straight past her.

"Come along, child," he said. "We don't have all day. Lunch and a rowing boat await us."

"It's raining," she replied.

"Is it?" said Fred. "Oh dear. That's a bore. I was going to get you in my boat, ply you with drink and have my wicked way with you."

It was just like old times.

Maddie liked that. No matter how long it had been you could start up the relationship with Fred just as it had been left off. They returned to his rooms and Fred pointed Maddie towards the chaise longue and said: "So Maddie. What is your problem? Why am I the lucky man to spend my lunchtime with you today?"

"Philosophy," Maddie said.

"And what philosophy would that be?"

"I need to know the difference between good and bad in an amoral society," she said.

"Ah-h-a," he said. "I think this calls for a glass of wine." He lifted the bonnet of the Mini and pulled out a bottle of red wine and two glasses. He fiddled with the cork.

"I am this day fourscore years old," he said finally. "And can I discern between good and evil?"

"You are not that old," Maddie laughed.

"That, child, is the Second Book of Samuel. Chapter Nineteen. Verse Thirty-Five," he replied. "There is no answer to your problem. You are the one who has to choose. There is really nothing I can do to help you. Even if you go into the details of whatever it is that is troubling you, I cannot tell you right from wrong. The answers are inside you."

He thrust a glass of wine in her direction.

"...but it is nice to have you here. Did I ever tell you about my love for dark-haired grammar school virgins?"

Maddie smiled.

"I think you may have mentioned it," she smiled, "but I'm afraid I could never live up to your dreams. I am a blonde, although I did go to a grammar school. The rest is lost in the mists of time..."

They both laughed.

"So," he said. "How is life in the fast lane - apart from your little problem?"

They did not talk about the problem again and after a pleasant chat Maddie went back to work. There was a little time to waste. There is no testing allowed in F1 in the summer and with most of the sponsorship (thankfully) in place for the season ahead it was down to the finance people to tell the engineers what their budgets were going to be. That meant it was the time for the engineers to start screaming. Maddie knew if she was going to pull off Winslow's plan it had to be done immediately.

A Formula 1 car is not a static object. The car is forever changing, from one race to the next, there are new parts, little aerodynamic tweaks, changes in software and in the geometry of the suspension. Nothing ever stands still. But every year with the new car, there is a chance to make a big leap forward. Each year, at around halfway through the season, work begins on the car for the following season. The mistakes made on the old car are corrected and new ideas put forward. New rules are taken into account. The designers get together in about July and work out what they want in terms of suspension design, fuel tank size, gearbox size and design and the positioning of the auxiliaries. The aerodynamicists tell the designers what they want to do and the designers then work out how to package the car around the concept. There is much debate. It is a finite discussion, however, because there is a pressing need for decisions. The items with the longest lead times are the chassis and the gearbox. You also have to allow time for crash tests because they will not let you race if you have not passed them all. So you need the concept decided straight after the summer break and design work to be finished by the end of September so the manufacturing can begin. All the while, however, the aero people are coming up with new ideas, week in, week out. But they can only do what the concept design allows them to do.

Time was short.

That evening, as Maddie was fixing herself a very dull salad back at the cottage, Winslow rang the doorbell.

"I was just passing," he lied. "I thought I would drop in and say hello and see how things are."

Maddie frowned. She knew he had come for a reason.

"Did you have a nice lunch?" he asked. "Quirk is such an unusual fellow, isn't he?"

Maddie wrinkled her forehead.

"I do not like being watched," she said.

"Well, it's a bit late now," he replied with a smile. "I have been watching you for quite a while now.

"Can I do anything without you knowing about it?" she growled.

"Yes," he said, "...but only after you have agreed to this project. I need an answer. Time is running out."

"I know," said Maddie. "We have to do it now or it is gone for another year. The thing is I don't think Bill Poppinger will go for it. He's old-fashioned. He believes if you cheat you are only cheating yourself, even if the rest of the world never finds out. You know you are a fraud. Some people will accept that, they say that if they are clever enough to get away with it, that is good enough. In the end you judge yourself. That's the best you can look forward to. The worst is that someone will spill the beans and you will be discredited, revealed as a cheat and rejected from the world that you love. Maybe they won't take away your World Championships, but everyone will know and it will overshadow everything you ever achieve."

Winslow nodded.

"That is the risk you take," he said, "but think about the things that come with success: not least the money. You'll be made for life. No more struggles, no more worries about where the money is coming from. Have you ever noticed that it is only people who have money who say that money is not important? And you think they are all blameless? You think none of those rich folk ever cheated. Of course they did. That's what happens. And rich people can get away with all kinds of things. Money is power."

Maddie knew this was true. Formula 1 had its own version of the story when Bernie Ecclestone was charged with bribery by a German public prosecutor. The accusation was that Ecclestone had paid a public official in order to ensure the Formula One was sold by a German state bank to someone who would keep him in a position of power.

In the end the court accepted a financial settlement, without a verdict. That was all he required to stay on, despite being in his early eighties. It cost him one hundred million dollars. The Germans took the money because they were worried they might lose the case, which would have been a huge embarrassment. He took the deal because it got rid of the risk he might be found guilty.

Some screamed it still was a disaster for the justice system in Germany, but it happened because it was the best solution for everyone. The Germans got a hundred million in cash and created a situation in which Ecclestone emerged at liberty, but with his credibility in tatters. People said: 'does an innocent man pay a hundred million to settle a case when he might simply sit tight and prove his innocence?' Even if he was innocent, the settlement meant his name was blackened, but he took the deal.

"Justice must sometimes be pragmatic, whether we like it or not," said Winslow. "We all like to believe in the rule of law, but sometimes legal systems are no use at all.

"But in sport, the focus is always ahead. If there is a controversy, it quickly blows over and, after a while, it does not matter any more. You know that back in 1994 the Benetton F1 team had an illegal traction-control system in its software. To access it, you had to scroll down a menu of ten items on the computer screen and then continue for another three extra lines before you hit "Enter". You might argue this was a deliberate attempt to hide the system and a lot of people that year believed the car was using traction-control. But where was the proof?

"Smoking gun evidence is not enough.

"The defence was implausible at best, but the international automobile federation said that without one hundred percent proof that the system had been used, the team could not be thrown out, because in a civil court it would be hard to prove.

"The federation did not have the courage to act because it feared the Benetton parent company might take legal action, claiming damages for such a penalty and might be able to put the FIA out of business. So a pragmatic solution was found. Benetton F1 was never the same again, although the team later returned as Renault F1, and was later caught cheating in other ways.

"Those who are involved in cheating know very well what they are doing, but the human being has an impressive capacity to delude itself when it wants to. We conveniently forget what we don't want to remember. False memories become real memories. It is a neat trick. But, you know, deep down we do remember. We know we cheated. The way to escape from this is to have set ideals of morals and ethics and punish those who go beyond them, but the neat and tidy rules and regulations cannot always replace our baser instincts. Religion does not really work and elected governments are not much better. Yes, they save us from dictators, but look at the number of politicians who are unmasked every year as being crooked.

"We try to believe in good, God and the rule of law, but deep down we know the human being is corrupt by nature. What was that bit in the Bible: 'And God looked upon the earth, and, behold, it was corrupt' and so he sent a flood to drown the people he had created."

"Wickedness is voluntary," said Maddie. "We all have the ability to make the right choices."

"Yes, we do," Winslow fired back, "but we don't always do that. We act in our own self interest. It is what Darwin called natural selection. This was what was required for mankind to survive and to lift itself above the other beasts. After that we advanced still further and gained a sense of right and wrong, but inside every civilized person is a caveman who does not care if his actions hurt anonymous strangers. He will not hurt his own family, his clan, but the rest of the world, he believes, is not his problem.

"In polite society men and women will adhere to their rules but when they get a chance to cheat, with no possibility of getting caught, what do they do? They cheat - because that is what they are programmed to do."

"Experience changes people," said Maddie.

"Yes," said Winslow. "I had a fortune cookie once that said: 'Good judgment comes from experience. Experience comes from bad judgment'." That summed it up well.

"But how many people get away with it? How many people get to live better lives because they were dishonest? Half the world, I would think. Maybe more. You can believe in right and wrong, but all too often it is not in your best interest to do that. And when you cannot be caught, it makes no sense not to do it.

"In this case, the only person who can implicate you is me."

Maddie laughed.

"So I am supposed to trust a man who does not believe in right and wrong?"

Winslow smiled.

"I am arguing like a bad man would argue, but I have a moral code and I try to live by it and do the right thing most of the time," he said. "Stepping over the boundary between right and wrong from time to time does not make us bad all the time. We all want to be loved, we all want to be part of a society, in one form or another, we don't want to be outlaws."

There was a pause in the discussion. They had said all there was to be said. Maddie wondered whether Winslow was there to sell her on the project or because he wanted to have sex with her. Would a man who was trying to seduce you really admit to being immoral? Or did he believe this was part of the attraction? If he was a bad boy, why should she be a good girl? They could have meaningless sex. But was it what she wanted? Yes, at times, that was fine, but deep down she wanted more. She wanted love.

Probably he did as well.

They shared the dull salad and a bottle of something she found in the cupboard. Neither was great. The conversation was lightweight. Day-to-day stuff. And then, to avoid the possibility that they might fall into bed together, Maddie suggested a walk. Winslow immediately agreed.

"England is very agreeable at this time of year," he said.

As they wandered across Netherington Hill, Maddie decided she was going to be blunt. She believed straight-talking was always the best way to solve problems and so she just came out with what she was thinking.

"Do you want to have sex with me?" she said.

Winslow did not flinch. He was not embarrassed. He paused, stopped walking and looked at her with what seemed to be amusement in his eyes.

"A straight answer?" he asked.

She nodded.

"Yes," he said. "What red-blooded man would not want to sleep with you, Maddie. You're gorgeous. You are full of life. You're funny. Smart... Yes, I would like that very much."

Maddie liked every word she heard, but something within her told her not to let him see that. Not to succumb there and then. To hold out.

He waited for a reply and when none came he turned the question back on her.

"And do you want to sleep with me?" he asked.

Now she was in trouble, because the answer was yes and no, but she did not want to hurt his feelings. Her mind went into overdrive again. She liked him. He was attractive in a rather conventional way. He was clever. But then he was secretive, manipulative, corrupt. How could he be trusted? Yes, they could have sex easy enough, but she wanted more than that. She wanted it all and she was not about to give in to him unless she was sure he wanted more. But if she said that would it scare him away? Would he run or was he old enough not to?

"It's not an easy question to answer," she said. "You are an attractive man so in that respect, yes, I am pretty sure that if the situation arose I would rise to the occasion, but that's not what I want, first and foremost. I want more. I want a relationship. A proper one."

She paused to see the reaction.

He shrugged.

"Yeah, that is what I figured," he said. "I get it, but that's not where I am at the moment. I don't know if I'd be any good at it. Maybe that could develop if we did just do it, but maybe it wouldn't work and that would be a shame. I'm trying to do a deal here, and I don't want to mess that up with a complicated emotional situation."

"So we will have to be friends," said Maddie.

"Is that really possible?" Winslow replied.

"For God's sake, Winslow, don't be so Harry Met Sally.

That's so old hat. The world has changed. These days people work together, play together, socialise together and the sex thing is different. You can do things now you couldn't do twenty-five years ago. You can sleep with a man, I can sleep with a woman. Attitudes have changed. Sure, there are always going to be men who cannot have platonic relationships with women, but it doesn't mean every man is like that. You can be friends before you are lovers and lovers can be friends after they have broken up. Some people can be friends with members of the opposite sex – and some cannot. Which are we?"

"I don't know," said Winslow. "I guess we can try."

"Well that seems to be only choice we have..." Maddie fired back.

"That's true," said Winslow. "For now."

"Yeah, for now."

They paused for a moment. They were standing in the middle of a field. It all seemed very out of place. Maddie wanted something more than the conversation had given her. She wanted something more intimate.

"Give me a hug," said Winslow.

He was right. That was what was required. They hugged. It was nice. Did they feel stirrings of lust? Yes, of course, they did. But they were not going to give in to them. They were friends.

For now.

They wandered down the hill and Winslow headed for his Mercedes. Maddie gave him a peck on the cheek.

"See you kid," he said and drove away into the soft light of the summer evening.

# Five

When Maddie woke the next morning, she looked up through the skylight in her bedroom and saw it was a beautiful day. The sky was already a deep blue. She looked at her watch, it was still very early, but she was full of energy. She could not just lie around in bed and so she pulled on some clothes and went downstairs, made herself a cup of coffee and went out into the garden, barefoot. It was one of those beautiful crisp summer mornings one gets in England. The garden was still green, but it was a real mess. The lawn needed to be mowed properly, and the flower beds had been invaded by herbs and weeds. She thought about doing some work on it, but she was enjoying the sun on her face and the cool grass under her toes and she just stood there, taking a sip of coffee now and then. When the coffee was done, she went back into the kitchen and found some bread in the freezer. She made toast and added some tangy marmalade. It was wonderful.

Then she went upstairs and spent five minutes communing with her naked self before taking a long hot shower. Being clean was a feeling she loved. She wandered around the bedroom, wondering what to wear and picked out a black pencil skirt and a new white blouse she hadn't yet worn. She wanted to feel sexy and so chose some of her favourite

French underwear, the stuff she saved for special occasions. She never used much make-up. It was better that way. When you did use it, the effect was so much more pronounced.

When she was ready she casually looked at her watch and discovered her meanderings had taken more time than she had imagined and she was cutting it a little fine for getting to work. Charlie did not much care about that sort of thing, but Maddie had learned when running her own team it was always best to set a good example. If you were there when the mechanics were arriving and did not leave until after they had gone home, they had some respect for that. It showed you were serious.

The blue Mégane was waiting for her. She jumped in, shoved it into gear and gunned the throttle. It was ten minutes to get to work on a good day. She was going fast and it felt good. The little Renault was fun to drive. It handled well and did what you wanted it to do. She arrived at the long curling right-hander she loved. It was blind and one had to be a bit careful going through it flat because there might be something coming the other way. "Fuck it," she said and kept her foot down.

Two seconds later she knew she had made a big mistake. In front of her was a large farm truck. It would have been a squeeze if she had been going slowly but she knew immediately a crash was inevitable, unless they could take avoiding action – and there was not any space to do that. From the moment she realised this, her brain seemed to slow down, kicked into another gear. Her life proceeded frame by frame. She was not frightened at all, which she felt was odd. She watched the lorry driver swerve but even before the truck hit the earth bank she knew it was not going to help much, it would likely bounce back into her path. She saw the impact and watched the mud curl back like clay. The earth was wet. The driver looked surprised and a little worried, but Maddie's attention was drawn to his hideous choice of pullover. She winced.

The swerve had opened a small gap ahead of her, but it was going to be closed before she got there. It was her fault, she knew. She had said "Fuck it" and that had left her with no good choices. She could hit the truck head-on, to a lesser or greater extent, but it is never good to hit anything head-on. A fast-moving car and a big solid truck going in opposite directions are not a good combination, but the lane was not wide enough to do anything else. The only choice was to turn left and then see what happened. Maddie did not fancy the idea of turning herself into canned meat and so she turned the wheel and the Renault headed towards an earth bank.

She noted there was some grass at the top of it. She had no idea what was beyond that. It was not her first priority. She laughed at the thought. As the car moved towards the bank she looked intently at the earth. Was it soft enough, and the car fast enough, to convert the ground into a muddy ramp. If that did not happen and the car bounced off, she was going to be in deep trouble.

Give way, please, she prayed. Launch me into the sky. I don't mind flying. She waited for the crash.

When it came, it was not so bad. The earth compacted and the car surged upwards. She noted, with a sense of relief, that there was blue sky behind the bank. That meant no trees. That was good. If you are going to hit anything, you should always avoid hitting trees. They are the least forgiving objects. They give just a little, and absorb just enough energy to stop a car rebounding, but that is not what you want. You want the car to bounce off anything it hits, and to spin around and dissipate its energy.

If the car stops dead, without rebounding, as it does when it hits a tree, the chassis does not absorb much energy. It is the passengers who do. And that's ugly.

She felt the earth giving away and modelling itself into launch ramp, up which the Renault Mégane set off, like a ski jumper, keen to break loose from the earth. Maddie was thinking ahead. The accident was going to have to dissipate energy in the vertical plane, she said to herself. She was not sure if she had said it aloud. What this meant was that stopping the car would almost certainly mean going end over end over end. That was not great. There would likely be some severe shocks. Maddie looked at the sky and thought how beautifully blue it was. In her mind she asked the control tower for permission to take off and imagined a voice replying "Roger!" and then she concentrated on the sky. It was at that moment she began to think about Winslow. He had blue eyes. The world was suddenly a beautiful place and Maddie was happy to be alive.

The car arched gracefully through the air, clearing a busy hedgerow, frightening a number of birds, and then the arc downwards began. The dark earth was ahead. She noted that her decision had been a good one. Ahead was a ploughed field and, being England, the earth was soft from summer rain. She was happy nothing had yet been planted. She did not want to damage anyone's property. The nose of the car would dig in a little, she thought. The momentum would then flip it over. Energy would be dissipated.

At that instant Maddie had a dramatic moment of clarity. Of course Winslow was right. Life was short and brutal. If there is a chance to make it better, one must grab it. She ought to have known sooner.

It is amazing that things happen so slowly when you are having a really big accident, she thought, as she flew past a terrified scarecrow. She had all the time in the world to think. She had heard racing drivers talk about the state of mind in which the brain is working so fast that everything else slows down and one finds oneself in a world of peace and quiet, an observer of one's own fate. She wondered if perhaps this is what they mean when people say their lives flash before their eyes. There was certainly a lot of time for thinking.

Flying through the air is the best part of having a really big accident. There is not a sound. It is peaceful. She thought of Winslow again. At first she had not really liked him, but now she felt genuine fondness - and more than a little lust.

As the car arched gracefully through the air she told herself she had been a fool. She should have just called in sick and spent the morning at home, enjoying herself. That was what she really wanted to do and yet her work ethic had got in the way, once again.

Why was she always too busy for life and love?

Perhaps she had been driving a little too fast. That thought made her laugh. Of course she had been driving too fast. The fact she was laughing in the middle of an accident was so absurd she laughed even more. Thank goodness I am wearing my seat belt, she thought, as the car finally arrived at the earth, nose-first into the ploughed mud. A nice soft landing. This was the big moment. She felt the seat belt biting into her shoulder and crushing her chest, her breasts and her hips. She hoped, perhaps she even prayed, that the seat belt would not break. It would be a shame, she thought, to mess up so beautiful a body. She felt her head being wrenched forwards and she worried her neck might break and imagined for a moment lying naked on a slab in the morgue. Was she presentable? At least, she thought, if she was going to die she would be doing it wearing her best underwear. At that instant the windscreen turned opaque and then disappeared into a million pieces of glass muesli. She was happy to see it go, that meant she could not fly through it. She watched her handbag - all her things - going out through the hole where once the windscreen had been. It was a nice bag, she thought, the mud will ruin it. She reached out for it.

The noise was really quite extraordinary. The word 'obtrusive' came into her mind. Dying young and pretty, and wearing the right underwear, seemed an acceptable compromise in the circumstances. Her life was wonderful. She had it all, except a man. And in this moment of great clarity, she realised that despite every else she had, what she really wanted, perhaps even needed, was a man. The life of a 21st century superwoman left a few things to be desired and Maddie did not want to have to be good at everything. Sometimes she wanted to be weak and to have to rely on a big strong man. She laughed, knowing the thought would outrage her feminist friends. She did not care. Men and women are not the same. Some men are different from others, some women are different to other women. We can mix and match as we wish, she thought. The pressure against the seat belt eased slightly and she was aware the car was rotating onwards. She was looking at the earth. She could smell it. The Mégane was doing exactly what she had predicted and now she wondered whether the second impact would be with the rear end or whether the rotational forces would be sufficient to loop an entire loop and land nose-first for a second time. Between these thoughts of a practical and scientific nature, Maddie found the time to think about a great array of other issues in her life. She wanted to make a few notes, but remembered, with a giggle, that her handbag was out there somewhere, in the mud. The car had rotated further and she could see back towards the road and was amused to note the mess she had left behind. There was a flutter of birds, just above the hedge she had vaulted over, and a deep hole in the earth. There were lots of Renault spare parts and blue bodywork.

She liked blue. The Renault was upside-down now, probably twelve feet in the air, although she admitted to herself that she had never been much good at judging distances. Through the windscreen hole she watched the picture change and she found herself looking only at the sky. The beautiful blue sky. She thought of Winslow again. She chuckled. Maybe she should just get it done and sleep with him. The car was still rotating and she saw the earth approaching once again. She knew they were slowing down; a lot of the speed had been absorbed by the earth and by the air. A rearward impact was likely to follow and that could be nasty, although the motion of the car meant that it would probably only be a glancing blow. Perhaps it would even land on its roof. That would be good, she thought. That would give the poor car a better chance of surviving. She laughed again. That was wrong. The car, her little car, had no chance of survival at all. It was already smashed beyond repair. At work she would have used the word "fucked", but such expressions seemed out of place as she flew through the air. Girls, she thought, should not use such words - except maybe in bed. If the car landed on its roof there was a danger that this might crush down on her. She might survive, but the Renault was not coming back from this one. As she pondered this sad piece of information, she felt the rear of the car bite into the mud, and watched in amazement as little pieces of earth flew past her ears. She was crushed into the seat by the impact and wondered as she felt her vertebrae straightening whether or not the mounting points would hold, or whether the forces would tear her adrift. She wondered about her handbag again and how unpleasant it would be to have to walk through a ploughed field to pick it up. That would ruin her shoes. She laughed again.

As she had suspected the rear impact had been just a glancing blow and the Renault went into another arching flip, although she noted with some satisfaction that now she was nearer to the ground. She saw the earth beneath her again and was looking back across the field to the startled birds above her hedge. It was odd, she thought, that the accident seemed to be speeding up. The calm and the peace was about to come to an end. She sighed. It was such a shame. She had been enjoying it, sort of.

The car, she thought, was about to land on its roof. She hoped the chassis would take the blow without collapsing on her. She wondered too if the seat belt would again keep hold of her. She praised the Lord for the crash test dummies which had been sacrificed for her benefit. She wondered if it was possible to sponsor a dummy, to say thank you. She would need to look into that. If she survived. She knew that after the impact with the roof the speed would be gone. The car might slide a little further through the mud. Maddie wailed silently at the thought that her new blouse would be ruined. She wondered whether the insurance would cover that as well as the car.

The Mégane did as she had predicted and during the last flip towards the mud Maddie found herself wondering what to buy Winslow for Christmas. Then she thought about what James Dean might have become if he had lived and how it was probably better for him to go when he did.

The mud, when it came, was slightly softer than she had expected. And then suddenly there was water. Freezing water. Her blouse had become see-through, but it did not matter. The shock had taken her breath away. The dream had ended. The car, or at least what was left of it, had come to rest upside-down in a stream. The warm and secure world of the adrenaline rush was over. Suddenly everything was noise and action. Maddie was upside-down and ice cold water was pouring through the broken rear windscreen. She could not get her seat belt undone. If I was unconscious, she thought, I am sure I would die.

Maddie Midnight did not want to die young. She did not want to lie on a cold slab in the morgue with people, cutting off her sexy French underwear and looking at her beautiful young body, thinking: "Hmm, she's a natural blonde" and pondering what a waste her life had been. She wanted to live long enough to grow old, to go through the pain of childbirth and be enraged by future children in their teenage years. She wanted die in the arms of some man when they were both one hundred and eight. She did not have time to consider why one hundred and eight was a good age as she fought for more years on the earth. In her head, all she could hear was running water and the words they say at funerals: "They shall not grow old as we that are left grow old".

And then, somehow, she was out of the car, scrabbling to the safety of the muddy bank. She had no idea how she had done it. She lay there, freezing, coughing icy water from her lungs, but delighted to be alive.

When she finally lifted her head she saw a man struggling across the field towards her, through the mud. Her only thought at that moment was that her nipples were sticking out like coat pegs because she was so cold and she ought to be embarrassed. But she did not care. She was alive. The man took off his coat and put it over her shoulders. He was talking a lot. Babbling. He was wearing a horrible sweater she thought she recognised. It was only when they were halfway across the field, fighting through the mud, that she realized he was the truck driver. She insisted they stop to find her handbag, which had not flown far. Everything was still together. She scooped it up, mud and all. Her nails were a mess. The truck driver led her to a nearby house and knocked on the door. A pleasant-looking old woman opened the door and looked rather shocked. The lorry driver was still talking too much. He was in shock. The old lady ignored him. She led Maddie up some stairs to a bathroom.

"Give me your clothes," she said. "I'll get something for you to wear and a nice cup of tea." She started the bath running and Maddie began to pull off her clothes. She saw in the mirror there were nasty bruises where the seat belt had been. When the bath was ready, she slid into the water and relaxed. There was a knock at the door and the old lady came in, averting her eyes politely. She put the tea on the side of the bath and took Maddie's clothes.

"I've put some sugar in it," she said. "I've left some things for you to wear."

Maddie nodded. She was happy. She did not want to talk. She wanted to be left alone. The tea was good. She checked herself over and there seemed to be no serious damage. After a while, she had no idea how long, she washed her hair and then climbed slowly out of the tub. She wiped away the condensation from the mirror and looked at herself. Yes, she would have made a good-looking corpse.

The dry clothes felt warm, and they made her feel better, but they were not at all stylish. When she was just about presentable, she went downstairs to find the nice old lady.

"You sit down, dear," she said. "Watch TV."

The driver had disappeared and so Maddie watched the news. They were talking about a stunt pilot. Maddie wasn't really listening, but she saw the picture of a biplane hurtling towards the ground. She knew there was no way the pilot was going to pull out of the dive, but she found herself wishing he would. The plane was almost horizontal when it hit the ground - but it was no good. It bounced high into the air and somersaulted into a million little pieces. Maddie shrugged. She did not care. It had no effect at all. People will do what they will do. There is nothing that can be done to stop them.

And she knew what she was going to do. With the decision made, she fell quickly asleep, a big accident can take its toll on a girl.

Some time later, she had no idea when, she was woken up by the old lady. The police had come and wanted to ask lots of questions. And then everyone seemed to disappear. Maddie found herself all alone. She found the old lady in the kitchen and asked to borrow the phone. She wasn't sure where her mobile had gone. She called work. Cheryl sounded worried.

"Don't worry about me," Maddie said wearily, "I'm fine. I need a new car. This one is dead. And I think I need some time off. I am pretty beaten up, and not very nice to look at. We're closing the factory next week anyway, for the August break. Tell Charlie I'll be back after that."

She hung up. Now all she needed was to get home.

She called Winslow. He was a knight in shining armour, he would come to her rescue.

# Six

She admitted to herself later that if she had not been in a state of some disorientation, resulting from the accident, she would probably not have agreed to go with Winslow to his "little place" in France. All she had said when he suggested the idea was: "Does it have two bedrooms?"

He had nodded. There were three.

And so she had agreed to go.

Winslow had been a brilliant knight in shining armour, as she knew he would be. He had arrived at the old lady's house and taken charge of Maddie's life. The old lady handed over her clean clothes and Maddie thanked her far too much for her kindness.

"Oh, that's no problem, dear," she said. "This is the most exciting thing that has happened to me in years. It was nice to have some company. You go off now with your boyfriend and have a good time."

Maddie sighed. It was too complicated to explain, so she didn't try. Winslow took her home, told her to go to bed and said he would take care of everything. While she slept, he organised everything. He did not pack a bag for her because, he confessed, "that was way too difficult to even consider". In the middle of the afternoon, after she had packed her bag, he put her into the car and they headed off down the A34 to Portsmouth, where he had booked them on an overnight ferry (separate cabins, of course) to Saint-Malo. They arrived at breakfast time and Maddie continued to doze in the car as he drove south. She saw a few town names; Rennes, Nantes and La Roche something.

It was getting towards lunchtime when they came off the autoroute and on to normal roads, which grew gradually narrower. Eventually they crossed a narrow bridge and drove out into what appeared to be a large area of marshland. There were pools on either side of the road. Ahead was a small clump of trees and what Maddie could only describe as "a small castle". It had four walls and what appeared to be a gateway. Inside, on one side, there was a flat-topped tower. As they got closer she saw it was surrounded by water.

"I knew you were a knight in shining armour," she said, "but I didn't know you had your own castle! I'm impressed."

Winslow smiled.

"It's really only a ruin," he said. "When I bought the place it was completely overgrown. It had been abandoned for centuries, no-one wanted it. I got it for nothing."

There was a sort of gatepost beside the road where Winslow had stopped the car. He lifted a cover and inserted a key and, in front of them, a drawbridge began to descend.

"This is great," she said.

When the bridge had slid down into place, Winslow drove the Mercedes across and through the narrow gateway. It was a squeeze, but they emerged in what could best be described as a grassy courtyard, at the centre of which was a very large old tree. The gravel crunched deliciously beneath the tyres. Winslow stopped the car and jumped out, opening Maddie's door and declaring "M'lady, your journey is over".

Maddie was almost speechless. Winslow ambled across to the gateway and pushed another button. The drawbridge began to rise, closing them off from the outside world.

"The basics were all here," Winslow said. "I spent a summer camped here, I had to swim across in those days. I stripped away all the vegetation and seeing what stones were where. I even found the well. It's all salt water on the surface but deep underground the water is fresh. Anyway, I then started putting the obvious stones back where they ought to be. It was pretty much all there. All the big stuff anyway. The mayor came to visit one day and said so long as it looked all right from the outside, he didn't really care what I did inside. Apparently at some point when I wasn't here some officials turned up but the mayor told them to get lost because they had no interest in the place until the mad American turned up. So I finished repairing the walls. The gateway was basically OK. I used to sleep under it for a while. What was needed most of all was the drawbridge. That was the first project. Using a boat to go backwards and forwards got old, real quick. The second project was water, but by then I had found the well. That was great news because it would have cost a fortune to have it pumped here.

"The tower was the next project. It needed quite a bit of fixing, this side of it had fallen down completely. The stones were still here, so I just put back together again. I put in a couple of floors and some windows on the inside. Then I planted that climber and let it grow up the outside.

"After that was done, I started work on the house. That meant proper drainage and an electric cable. Those cost a fortune, but then I discovered the quarry where the rock had originally come from. It was abandoned centuries ago and the local farmer was happy for me to dig up as much as I wanted. He wants me to dig up the whole thing so he can get some more workable land. So, bit by bit, I rebuilt the main house. It was all pretty simple, but the local mason helped me a lot."

Opposite the house, on the other wall of the courtyard was what looked like a cloistered garden, with some arrow slits that went through the castle walls. It was green and cool and had a small fountain in the middle. Next to it, was a stone wall with a couple of large arches, each closed with a large wooden door.

"Those are the garages," Winslow explained. "I have workshops in there too. The neat thing was that the mason and I decided to put a garden on roof. It's invisible from the outside, but from up there if you stand on the parapet you can see the world. There is a view right out across the marshes. The village is away in the distance. I'd like to make a boathouse at some point, but I don't think the mayor would let me do that. Besides you cannot go that far in a boat. There are too many sluices.

"What I love about this place is if you want to be alone, you just pull up the drawbridge. You can wander around completely naked if you want to..."

"You wish..." said Maddie. "If I did that I am sure that the French Air Force would be flying over."

Winslow smiled.

"Do whatever you want," he said. "I'll not bother you. This is your holiday. I always have things to fix."

Inside the house there was one big living room on the ground floor, with a kitchen at one end and the base of the tower at the other. The windows onto the courtyard were much bigger than they could have been in medieval times, while the external walls had no openings apart from a couple of narrow vertical arrow slits that were now sealed with glass, each had its own little alcove, in which Winslow had placed bookshelves.

The room featured a big wooden table over near the kitchen and a sitting area in front of a fireplace next to the tower. There were doors on either side of the hearth, both leading into the tower: one going into what looked like an office, the other to the bottom of a staircase that climbed the tower wall to the floor above.

The floors were all made from old tiles.

"They weren't easy to find," he said, "but they are on concrete so the floor will at least stay even. It used to be just earth. The chimney goes inside the wall of the tower. That means that in the winter the roof is not a great terrace, it gets a bit smoky - but in the summer you can sunbathe up there too."

"The thing I don't get," said Maddie, "is why this is here. Why did anyone build such a place in the salt marshes."

"Just remember how valuable salt used to be in medieval

times," Winslow said. "They used to call it white gold. This whole area was once an inlet of the sea, but the river silted up the entrance and so it became a marsh. The Romans came and dug this maze of ponds to create the salt farms. They still produce some salt, but there are fish farms too and some oyster beds. They also grow this stuff called salicorne, I think the English call it marsh samphire. It's a bit like salty asparagus. I like it. They say that in the Middle Ages pirates would come here from the Bay of Biscay, the sea is just behind that forest over there. They would come and steal salt, rape the women, that sort of thing and so I guess some rich salt farmer decided to build himself a fortified farm. The good news is the lamb here is great, it comes ready-salted. The food here is great, particularly the local market. I even have a bread oven. It's great for pizza too!"

"It's perfect," said Maddie.

They climbed the stairs to a landing on the first floor. On the left was a door to a bedroom in the tower, it was clearly where Winslow slept. It had a window onto the courtyard and an arrow slit in the external wall, which looked out over the marshes.

"Your room?" she said.

He nodded.

On the right there was a corridor inside the castle wall. A door on the left opened into a bedroom, with two windows overlooking the courtyard. It seemed big and rather cold. Maddie didn't like it. Further down the corridor there was a second door on the left. There was just one window looking out onto the courtyard, but at the other end of the room was a large French window leading to a small terrace, squeezed between the bedroom and the castle wall. It was open only to the sky. There were climbing plants and a comfortable-looking chair.

"I like this one," Maddie said instantly.

Winslow nodded.

"I thought you might," he said. "Settle in, relax, make tea or whatever it is you English do and I will go and get some food from the village. Tomorrow, if you like, we can go walking on the marshes, or go through the forest to the sea."

He disappeared and Maddie settled in. She loved her room. For the first couple of days she did little but sleep. She was still aching from the crash. She slept inside or out on her private terrace.

Her bruises had become quite dramatic and so she decided not to parade herself too much. Winslow was perfect, attentive when she needed him, but happy to do other things. The warm sunshine in the afternoons that shone on to the garden above the garages was too good to miss and that was where Winslow saw at least some of Maddie's bruises. He winced.

"Ouch," he said. "They must be painful. I guess there's no chance of energetic intercourse then?"

He winked and wandered off.

She had decided that she would be happy to sleep with him, but only if it was going to lead to them becoming what she called "a proper couple". Until that happened, there would be no sex. It was a subject that lurked just below the surface, prowling through their relationship like a shark, ready to pounce at any moment.

For some reason, after the accident she had become more aware of the world. She became very sensual. Colours were somehow brighter and the sunshine seemed warmer. Everything felt more alive. Food tasted better too. Winslow cooked the most extraordinary things for her, beginning on the first night with a casserole of chicken, mint and cucumber. The second day he prepared sea-bass with salicorne and oysters. On the third he made a pizza in the bread oven. She sat reading in the sunshine in the courtyard while he worked in the kitchen. She kicked off her sandals and tilted her face to the sky and half-closed her eyes. Through her eyelashes she watched the world of yellows and greens. She could feel the wind, see the dusk and feel it deep inside herself.

As he cooked, Winslow was thinking life was pretty good. You know life is good when you actually realise it at the time. All too often you only figure out what a great time you have been having after things have turned bad.

They started going for walks in the mornings, across the *marais* and into the woodland. On a couple of occasions they went right through to the sea and paddled in the ocean. There were people there and Maddie did not want to mix with them. Winslow was all she needed.

One day, Winslow insisted they go to the local *Fête du Cheval et du Chien*, a big thing in the neighbourhood, a festival that celebrated the horse and the dog. This, Maddie read, was a complicated event, which began with a Mass at the church of St-Martin, during which all dogs and horses present were blessed by the local priest, an amiable-looking fellow from Niger.

There was a jumping competition, pony rides, a lottery with the prize of half a lamb. There were long and dull speeches by fat men who held different offices in the various clubs involved. The mayor won considerable applause by keeping his speech to just a couple of words, thus increasing his popularity. After this, as they all sat down to a lunch of *merguez* and *frites*, a bugle band, using hunting horns, entertained them. As the event wore on, the band became more and more dishevelled as extra wine was drunk. The smart green jackets over their golden waistcoats, soon had their sleeves rolled up. The waistcoat buttons came undone one after another. The music was more and more out of tune, but the band played on. The dogs panted in the shadows and the horses trampled the grass beneath them and chewed branches on the trees to which they were tied.

The wine flowed freely.

Eventually a group of clog dancers took to the stage, which produced curious tremors, some of which may have been registered on seismographs across France. After that, as the sunburn came, the performers sought shade and the loudspeakers played county and western music for the rest of the afternoon, with some of the locals singing along. Maddie and Winslow departed to the sound of drunken Frenchmen and women singing what they thought were the words of American songs.

As they wandered home they felt the cool of the evening descend upon the *marais*. With each passing day Maddie felt better. Her bruises changed from an unattractive purple to a pale yellow, which looked worse, but fortunately the sun was colouring her skin differently with each passing day and the tan hid the damage done.

"Damn," said Winslow one afternoon when he walked past Maddie sunbathing on the terrace. "You're just too attractive. I might seriously have to start thinking about giving up and committing myself to a relationship, just so I can have my wicked way with you."

"Really?" said Maddie, not taking him very seriously.

Winslow paused.

"I'll have to think about it," he said. "You are simply too sexy for me to ignore."

"Well, that's very nice to hear," she said. "Quite stimulating. Let me know as and when you want to give in to my charms."

He looked at her hungrily.

"You need a good spanking," he said.

"Yes," replied Maddie, with a smile. "Perhaps I do."

Winslow shook his head and wandered off, leaving Maddie to ponder the exchange.

Having her bottom slapped was not something that worked for her. Every time she had tried it - usually as a means of exciting her partner - she had found it was in no way pleasurable and tended to achieve the opposite reaction to that which was intended. She had fantasies about being spanked from time to time, but did not like reality. It was, she concluded, all about being helpless. There are some who will tell you it is all about Daddy and that women like it because it makes them feel they are in the strong caring hands of a father-like figure. She laughed at the thought. We are all different, she thought. Different strokes for different folks.

It amused her that when she was at work she was seen as someone serious, savvy, organised, competent and professional and yet beneath the veneer she didn't want to be like that at all. She wanted to be a woman. She didn't want to always be virtuous and homely, she wanted to be raunchy and abandoned. A little wild. And yet, she wanted a faithful and committed man.

She was tempted in that instant to call Winslow over and tell him to go ahead and give her a good spanking, but the moment passed. She had noticed since the accident that she had begun to see things much more clearly than she had beforehand. Suddenly she was able to discern what was important and what was a waste of energy. She wondered if perhaps it was some kind of shock, as she had received no bump on the head.

Clearly, her job was important. It gave her satisfaction, a great deal of fun and it paid the bills. The new deal being offered by Winslow would secure her financial future and help the team to be successful. If she agreed to it, her focus would almost certainly shift because she had come to understand that there was more to life than just work. She wanted to have a proper relationship. When she had been fighting her way out of the car in the stream her mind had brought up the subject of children. This had been something of a revelation, as she had never been in the least bit broody. She had been quite happy to see what came along and never really worried about the concept. The subject of kids had never come up.

The idea it might still happen and was something she might want was rather disconcerting. Maybe, she thought, this was part of the attraction she felt for Winslow. That was how the sub-conscious worked. He came from good genetic stock.

It was a weird thought.

Maybe he was too old, she thought. He would not want young children running about.

Whatever the details, she was aware that suddenly her priority was Winslow and making their relationship work. She wanted no half measures. It was all or nothing. It was pretty old fashioned when she stopped to think about it. In the modern age, so many relationships do not last, but she did not want that to happen to her. She wanted to live happily ever after, as they do in the movies. She wanted to grow old with her man and be so close they would finish one another's sentences. She was still getting to know Winslow, but she feared he might get bored with her after a while and drift away to other women. This was a horrible thought, but she knew she should always be prepared for the worst. Life is a gamble and unless you are lucky, it doesn't always work out well for you.

The odd thing was despite what he did for a living, Winslow always seemed to be a man who wanted to do the right thing. It was his upbringing, she supposed.

The Puritan.

He had told her, in one of their conversations, that he never wanted to cheat or to lie. He wanted complete trust in his partner.

Morality is an odd thing, she thought. On the one hand she and Winslow were talking about cheating the system, even if the system was, by its very nature, corrupt and yet, on the other hand, they were trying to create the purest possible human relationship.

Winslow's plan was quite brilliant, carefully ensuring everyone involved either did not know the full story, or had something important to lose if it all went wrong. She loved the idea that one side of the team did not know the other side was helping it to be successful. And on both sides it was only one person who knew the story. The link between the two team-mates was outside the team and unknown to everyone in the F1 game.

If it was a crime, it was almost perfect.

It was at that very moment she made her decision. She would do it. Winslow's plan could go ahead. She rushed to find him.

"Good," he said. "That is the best news I have had all day."

"No other revelations?" he asked.

"In your dreams," she said.

He gave her a broad smile and then very calmly went back to grinding up nettles.

It amazed her that Winslow got so much pleasure from cooking. He took it into his head to go through all the cookbooks he could find and try out one dish after another.

She did nothing. They went to the local markets when they could, buying the best produce they could find. His Holy Grail was to find the perfect recipe for wild herb soup. He had read of this in a book many years before, he explained, but he had never found a good recipe and wherever he went he would ask the locals. They searched the markets for salsify and sorrel, dandelions, nettles, milk thistles, yarrow and wild spinach. The resulting soups were not always very good, but such is life. You experiment and you try to do better.

They did not talk any more about Winslow's proposal, but simply enjoyed the simple pleasures of life. They cooked, they ate, they drank, they slept and they joked about sex.

One evening she was dozing in one of the old armchairs, her head resting peacefully on her shoulder and her eyelids fluttering slightly. He had been reading quietly and looked up and found himself watching her. She looked, he thought, so healthy and happy that he felt afraid to wake her, so he sank quietly into his chair and watched. How long he sat there he did not know. Then her eyes opened and she smiled.

"What time is it," she said, stretching and growling like a lioness.

Outside it was dark and cool. They went up to the terrace garden and they lay down on the grass and looked up at the sky. They could see a million stars. And there was silence, not the stark meaningless silence found within walls, but rather the silence of nature, with a distant rustling of the wind through the trees and the whispers of breeze in the marshland grasses.

The next morning Maddie did not want to get up to go to the market. She wanted to be lazy and so Winslow decided he would go on his motorcycle. It was beaten up and a little rusty, but as he began to clean it, he saw it might still work. At eleven the little engine burst into raucous life and Maddie watched him ride away, his face a picture of schoolboy glee.

She hated motorcycles.

In the village Winslow bought a few supplies and filled the bike with petrol and then set off for home. The air was crisp and clean and it pushed back his tousled hair as he gathered speed. The road was straight and clear and he eased open the throttle to see how fast she would go. The bike surged forward. He smiled, a laugh in his throat. When he came to the turning to the *marais* he braked to turn the bike but realised too late he was travelling too fast. He felt the bike go from under him. He was laughing as he hit the road and slid into a ditch. Vegetables bounced away, splashing into the ponds.

There was silence.

# Seven

Maddie saw it happen. She had been worried when he did not return as early as she expected and so she had started to walk down the road between the ponds, looking across the salt flats to the track that went away towards the village. She saw him coming and was happy. Then she saw him fall and ran frantically to where the accident had happened. Tears streamed down her face and she was panting hard when she got there. She could not see him but she heard a noise coming from the ditch. It was Winslow laughing. She looked down at him and wiped away her tears.

They picked up the vegetables that could be found and walked slowly up to the castle, Winslow pushing the dented old motorbike beside him. She made him promise not to ride the damned machine again.

"Ride that thing again and you won't ride me!" she said.

"A graphic image," he said. "And it sums up the problem. You want to control me, and maybe I don't want to be controlled. Maybe I'm not willing to give that up."

She looked forlorn.

"...but," he added, "it is nice to know you care enough about me to weep when you thought I was hurt."

He cared about her rather more than he cared to admit, and he loved being with her. But the problem was there. He wanted to be free; to be able to get up and go whenever he wanted and to wherever he wanted to go. He didn't want discussions. He'd done the whole marriage thing. It had not worked out and he didn't want to do it again. He could pretend, he thought, that would be what he would do if he followed his business ethics in his private life. That would be efficient. She'd give in and they would have sex like rabbits for a few weeks and then he would break her heart.

The problem was he didn't want to hurt her.

He was stuck.

On their penultimate day at the chateau Maddie started to think about life back in the real world. She had loved being out of the loop of F1 for nearly two weeks, but she knew it was time to get on with her job.

"Winslow," she said that morning while having coffee, "I don't want Bill booted out of his job. It does not feel right.

"In war, Maddie, there are always casualties," Winslow said. "I supposed we could try an approach to him and see if he bites, but you seem to think he is too honest. In that case it is best not to even try. Why would you feel sorry for him? What was he paid last year? Was he worth it? No. The car was nothing special. And besides I hear he has displayed some rather unusual fetish-like tendencies towards a female member of the drawing office staff and she is not happy about it."

"How do you know about that?" said Maddie, amazed that Winslow knew one of the team's biggest secrets. "Not even Charlie knows that. We convinced the girl to shut up because we needed Bill. It wasn't that bad. He just has this thing about fondling her feet."

"I know," said Winslow. "But is it right to force that poor girl, who is quite upset by all accounts, to just ignore this pervert?"

"She hasn't left," said Maddie. "She can't be that upset."

"We'll get rid of Bill when we get back," Winslow said. "Charlie will find out and Bill will get fired. All you have to do is to suggest he hires Elfin Grindvall. He's pretty new and very ambitious and I am sure he will go for the deal on offer.

It will be good to have a new chief aerodynamicist, as no-one will question a big change in philosophy.

"I know Elfin," Maddie said. "He once tried quite hard to get me to sleep with him. We were in a bar in Cassis, racing down at Paul Ricard. He's an attractive bloke for an aerodynamicist."

She remembered the evening. Elfin's idea of seduction was to tell her his life story. His mother had been an actress from Leeds. She had toured Scandinavia enthusiastically with a rather good version of "The Importance of Being Earnest" and had returned to Leeds newly pregnant, as the result of a wild night out with a Mr Grindvall of Mönsterås, who had said all the right things to her over several glasses of Aquavit. Nine months later a small boy appeared in Leeds. His mother, being a theatrical, came up with the name Elfin and the poor little bastard spent the next twenty years of his life paying for his mother's whim. Initially he lived in England, looked after by a string of nannies, as his mother had no intention of giving up her career to look after an unwanted child.

After she disappeared off to Cape Town with a production of "Cat on a Hot Tin Roof" he was sent to Mönsterås, where Mrs Grindvall was less than enthusiastic about his presence. He learned to speak Swedish and English, aided significantly by his friendship with a girl who lived next door called Gunilla Skräddar. The two of them were inseparable until they were around thirteen when her parents discovered about a number of interesting experiments that the pair had been involved in the forest behind their houses in Mönsterås. Elfin was sent away to boarding school in England, but was able to return to Mönsterås in the summer, where he used the useful term "Vill du knulla med mig?" on a number of young blonde Swedish girls with rosy cheeks who went walking with him in the woods.

When he was about seventeen his mother suddenly reappeared, having finally hit the big time by bagging a wealthy American. She retired to North Carolina, where her new husband owned a very large number of trees, and she began to show Elfin that mothers can actually be quite useful. He was particularly impressed when she bought him a Formula Ford racing car for his eighteenth birthday.

He was not a very good racing driver (even in Sweden) but quickly developed a fascination with engineering that led him to study aerodynamics at KTH in Stockholm, after which he did a postgraduate course at Imperial College, London. Unencumbered by any real sense of morality, he had done well in the sport.

"I'd say he was perfect for our project," Maddie said.

They headed back to England the next day, returning by a faster route via Cherbourg. They arrived in Netherington in the early evening. Maddie was delighted to see a new car sitting outside the house. Cheryl had delivered – as Cheryl always did.

Saying goodbye to Winslow was rather a difficult thing to do. They had grown very close in France and neither really wanted to be apart from the other. But Winslow was still not convinced he wanted to be "in a relationship". Maddie had decided she was going no further down the path of unrighteousness until he was willing to make a commitment. They were both stubborn. So Winslow kissed Maddie on the cheek, gave her a hug and walked away to his car.

"You're welcome here whenever you want," said Maddie. "But the rules remain the same."

Winslow smiled back at her.

"You never know," he said. "Maybe I will have an accident, get a bang on the head and realise what is important..."

As he drove away, Maddie felt rather sad. She was by nature positive, always filled with optimism, but this relationship was very odd, and very frustrating.

"You must follow your heart," she said sadly. "And my heart says no."

In the car Winslow was wondering whether he was a fool. Should he not just turn back and give in to Maddie? Would it work? He didn't know. He wasn't sure.

"Follow your heart," he said.

The next morning Maddie was back at Chiphurst

Competition. Everyone seemed to have more energy after the summer break. The cars were being readied to be sent to Belgium. The production department was flat out on some new parts for the races at Spa and Monza. It was a busy time. Charlie was back from his boat in Sardinia. He had heard all about Maddie's accident and, as he liked to give the impression that Chiphurst Competition really cares about its employees, he dropped in to her office to see if all her limbs were still in the right places.

"They look good to me," he said, with a wink. It was a whole three minutes before he got to the real point of his visit: Chiphurst Competition needed to save money, he said. The budget was a hundred million dollars and they had only ninety million. If she could find him the extra ten million he promised to love her forever, but he said they had to plan in case there was no money to be found.

"Cut out the R&D budget dramatically." Maddie said. "That would do it."

"Maddie," said Chiphurst with a smile. "If we do that how are we going to keep up with the others? Besides, the engineers will all scream at me and I haven't the arguments to fight them. They are right. We must concentrate on the engineering."

"Get a new aerodynamicist," said Maddie. "We know what Bill can do, but it is not enough. Is it? Bring in a new one and let him try out his ideas and that will save us a year in R&D costs. Bill always says if we give him more money and more people he will do a better job, but maybe he's just not talented enough."

Charlie looked at her oddly – this was not usual behaviour for Maddie Midnight. He shrugged and strode off to his office.

An hour or so later rumours swept through the Chiphurst Competition headquarters that Bill Poppinger had been fired. As the day wore on the stories of what had happened began to circulate. Apparently, according to Cheryl, who was not to be doubted, Charlie had received a mysterious phone call. Cheryl said that:"the guy said: 'Tell him my name is Vengeance. Charlie knows me'. So I asked Charlie if he knew a Mr Vengeance and he said he'd take the call."

Charlie had talked for about ten minutes and Cheryl could see the phone call was upsetting him. When he hung up he asked her to call Bill in for a meeting.

Bill was his usual jovial self when he arrived, but after a couple of minutes she heard shouting. Poppinger asked Chiphurst what he was accusing him of having done. Whatever the answer was it had a dramatic effect. The door flew open and a furious Poppinger burst out of the office, turned, and with a touch of melodrama, yelled: "Chiphurst! I hope you rot in Hell!"

"Get out you dirty pervert!" Chiphurst had roared back. "And don't think you are getting any more money. I am not sure you want that stuff coming out in court, do you?"

Cheryl said that if Bill Poppinger had a gun at that moment, she was sure he would have used it on Charlie. Instead he turned, ripped open her office door, kicked the water dispenser so hard he hurt his foot and stomped off, limping slightly.

Chiphurst came out of his office and very calmly asked Cheryl to call security to make sure Bill left the premises with nothing of value. She watched from the office window as Bill was frog-marched out of the factory. By lunchtime the whole factory knew Poppinger was out. It was the talk of the canteen.

Later that afternoon Maddie received a phone call from Chiphurst.

"Can you come to my office?" he said smoothly.

Charlie explained what had happened.

"He was a bloody pervert," he said. "I had a complaint. He was no good anyway. Who do we get now? There is still time to do some stuff on the new car. If we move quickly."

"Well," Maddie said quietly. "I did hear word that Elfin Grindvall is available."

"Hmmm..." said Charlie. "He has a decent reputation. Have you got a number?"

"I can find one," Maddie said.

She went back to her office, picked up the phone and rang Winslow. "The seed has been planted," she said. "It's growing fast."

"Good," replied Winslow. "Splendid! Why don't you come over when you're done at work. We should celebrate."

"Come over where?" she said. " I don't know where you live."

He laughed.

"True," he said. "How silly of me. Well, I guess we have now reached the point in our relationship when the truth can be told. Do you know The Jolly Boatman at Thrupp? Meet me there at seven."

Thrupp is a tiny place on the Oxford Canal. It seemed a strange place to be meeting Winslow, but there he was, standing at the bar, sipping a Scotch. They had dinner and then Winslow said "Let's go home". Maddie figured they were going to the car park, but outside the pub Winslow walked along the towpath beside the canal. He stopped beside a narrowboat called Daisybelle.

"Meet my other woman," he said. "This is Daisybelle. My humble abode. This is where I live, but we move around a lot. That's why I don't have a proper address."

They boarded the boat at the stern.

"Her engine is beneath us," Winslow said, in passing. They went down several steps into a cabin that seemed surprisingly large.

"This is the salon," he said. "The banquettes have storage beneath them and they can convert into single beds. There is the stove that keeps the place warm. Then there is what we call the dinette. That also serves as my office and converts into a double bed. Beyond that is the galley."

"And beyond that?" said Maddie.

"There is a bathroom. And the bedroom – with a nice big bed. And that opens on to the bow, where I have a little garden."

Maddie noted that there were no female touches at all.

"I have a motorbike," Winslow said. "Well, it's a mini motorcycle really. Made in Italy by a company called di Blasi.

They've been making these things for about fifty years. They are small, but they also fold up and I don't mean disassemble, I mean fold up. It's amazing. It does sixty miles on a tank of fuel, not that I'd want to be riding the thing for that long, but it goes at thirty miles per hour and weighs only sixty-five pounds. Daisybelle has a compartment designed specially for it. It opens on the outside and folds downwards, so that the door can act as a sort of a ramp. I can stand on it and lift the bike on and off the boat. And when I get to the Mercedes I just fold it up, stick it in a bag and it fits into the boot of the car. It's brilliant. I have a rented parking space in Thrupp for the Merc. I can go pretty much where I please. I can moor up for fourteen days at a time or just keep going. If there are longer trips, I can stop near a station and catch a train."

Maddie understood why Winslow was so protective of his independence. It cannot be easy to have a relationship when you are forever on the move and Winslow would probably have to give it all up if he and Maddie got together. Was it the kind of place she would want to go home to she asked herself? No, not really. She liked her space and her privacy. Living on a narrowboat was all a little bit too claustrophobic. No wonder Winslow also owned a small castle in France.

He had stopped talking about Daisybelle and had switched to the subject of their project. She tuned back in.

"I hacked into the Mercedes computers today and downloaded the whole thing," he said, as he handed Maddie another glass of wine, which she had not asked for, and didn't really want. "The new car looks quite promising. The basic performance is there if your guys can build it in the time available."

"Won't they know you have been there?" Maddie said. "Inside the computers? You know."

Winslow smiled.

"In the old days we had to break windows and climb drainpipes," he said, "but nowadays all we have to do is dodge a few fire walls. We can come and we can go and no-one will ever know we have been there. We're pretty good at spotting the security stuff. We can steal anything. We can read anything. We can even change things, if we are feeling nasty. There are no secrets.

"And there is no evidence?" Maddie asked again. "No trace you were ever there?"

"Only if we want to leave a calling card, which in this case we assuredly do not. One or two of the teams have got some good computer men, but these guys don't expect us. They don't think people like me exist. They know you need some security if you are in government or in the defence industries, but industrial security is pathetic. And it's primarily aimed at their own employees. We're pretty competent, but even so they are not expecting us. These guys in F1 are interested in building racing cars, they are not into boring security software. And even if they were, we would be ahead of them. If we stole a laptop computer they would be worried, but they don't think we can get into their servers, they don't think we can read their computer screens, or record their keystrokes. This is all easy stuff. You know light from laptop computer screens doesn't just disappear. It bounces off walls and can go out into the world and be read by clever satellites.

"An F1 factory really isn't that big a challenge. If we need to bug people we generally use laser bugs these days. You know the ones that measure the movement of glass caused by the sound waves from voices and then convert the waves back into voices. You should hear the result, Maddie, it is very impressive.

"We use a few wire taps if we have to, but one or two of the F1 team bosses use scrambling devices. Do you know I tried to record one the other day and he had some really weird electronic technology which meant all I recorded was a lot of electronic 'noise'. That was a professional device.

"The truth is, Maddie, that people are fools. They are just lazy. It has always been like that."

While he was talking Maddie had curled up on the banquette. She was sipping the wine, a very nice white wine, which slipped down too easily. He refilled the glass immediately. She didn't really care. He could drive her home, she thought, only to conclude it would be all too complicated in the morning, with cars and people in all the wrong places.

"I should go home," Maddie said. "It's late."

"If you think I am going to let you drive, you are dreaming," he said. "And I've had too many as well. So, unless you want to spend a lot of time trying to get a taxi and then waste more in the morning, trying to get the car sorted out, you are simply going to have to stay over."

"Have I just walked into a trap?" Maddie asked, taking another sip of wine, realising as she did so that it probably did not really support her argument.

"Do you honestly think I would take advantage of a tipsy woman?" he replied, rather sadly.

"Of course you would," she said. "If she wanted you to..."

"Does she want me to?"

"Ah-h," said Maddie. "That is the problem. The answer is still yes, she does, but not unless you commit."

"Yes, I know the rest of that speech," he said. "Don't you ever consider just letting that go? Just fucking my brains out for one wild night and then seeing what we feel like in the morning?"

"Of course I do," Maddie said. "It is quite appealing, but I know what will happen. It will be awkward and that will probably mean the end of what we have. And I like this brother-sister thing we have going. I don't want to lose that. It's very precious to me."

"Maybe it's possible to be fuck-buddies and to keep what we have," Winslow suggested.

Maddie had thought about that one too.

"Yes, there is a chance it might work out," she said. "There are examples I am sure, but how many of these relationships are really successful? On paper they are perfect. Everyone gets what they want. They get laid. There is no emotional baggage. There are no families and friends you have to put up with. You are both still free to sleep with other people and you can still play the field. So you have a higher chance of getting some nasty sexually-transmitted diseases... Then I don't see the whole sex-without-emotion thing working for long. One partner or the other is always going to fall for the other person. I crave the fulfilment of a real partner. I don't want to be a fall-back. I don't believe in recreational screwing. Every man I ever slept with was someone whom I thought might become a proper boyfriend. It was not just about the sex.

"Since the 1960s, women have wanted to believe they can remain uninvolved during sex – like men do – but, you know, I don't think many of us can do it. Sex is an emotional and bonding experience. We've done away with dominant male and submissive female roles, but it is not that easy. We are fighting against millions of years of evolution. The biological reality is most women still want the physical and emotional effects of sex to be aligned. We want to be committed. If women become fuck-buddies, most of them – most of us - are doing it because we hope that in the end the man will commit to us. We con ourselves. We know deep down what we are doing, but we try to convince ourselves otherwise. And so we get attached and start to feel things and then we look for signs our partner is feeling the same way. We begin to imagine them and then we get hurt when he walks away."

Her thoughts ran out.

She took another drink. Winslow was looking miserable.

"You're right," he said. "I know you're right, but I just don't think I can do it. I have too many scars; too much damage."

"Bollocks," said Maddie. "You're just frightened."

He nodded.

They agreed they would share the bed. They would still wear their clothes, but they were allowed to cuddle. She fell asleep with her head on his chest, his arm around her.

For a long time he could not sleep, but is was not because it felt awkward. It was because it felt right.

# Eight

Maddie woke early the next morning and remembered where she was and why she was there. It felt good. She had an urge to kiss this strange man, but restrained herself. There was no telling what might happen if she did that. So she slipped quietly from his arms, without waking him. She wrote him a nice note and having made the best of her appearance in the circumstances, she went back to The Jolly Boatman and drove home to Netherington. It was a beautiful morning, with some mist in the river valleys. At home, she stripped off straight away. Naked, she made herself a cup of strong coffee, and then showered. There was the required five minutes with herself, naked in front of the mirror, and then she dressed in new clothes and headed off to work. She would not think about the Winslow problem any more. She had things to do.

Chiphurst Competition did not even bother with a press release about Bill Poppinger being replaced by Elfin Grindvall. If anyone asked they were told Poppinger had left "to pursue a new challenge".

Grindvall had signed the contract immediately. He did not argue terms at all. He had been working for a sports car team and so there were no problems with starting straight away. The other engineers soon reported back to Charlie that Elfin had arrived, looked at the design and said: "No way". He had told them he would come back with some new ideas and, a few days later, he delivered the first CAD drawings for a new concept. There was much detailed design to be done. The aerodynamics department was buzzing with activity and the model-makers were going into action. The race team was assembling at Spa and Charlie began telling journalists "off the record" that Elfin Grindvall had made a huge difference and that the new car was going to be really special.

Maddie laughed when she heard that one.

The new car ought to be better, she thought, they are building a Mercedes. If Grindvall was clever he would take the information he had been given and make a few alterations so that no-one would ever be able to prove it was a straight copy. That way he would be protected.

Her job, she reminded herself, was to sell the sponsorship on the car and despite the optimism that now began to run riot in the corridors at Chiphurst Competition, this was not an easy task. No-one is interested in a team which did not score points in the previous season. And Charlie wanted ten million more. In the afternoon Winslow rang. Would she like to come over? No, she said, but he could come to her. She wanted to be at home for a day or two. She had to go to Spa on the Friday.

That evening he arrived with fish and chips.

"That's what you English eat," he said. "I went to this place on the Iffley Road. They say it's pretty good."

They sat at her kitchen table, and in between mouthfuls, Maddie vented her frustration about the need to find another ten million.

"It's almost impossible in this market," she said. "The pay TV thing is a disaster and we're competing against not only the teams, but also against the bloody commercial rights holder, who wants more track side signage and big partner deals.

"Is it a matter of survival?" Winslow asked.

"Well," said Maddie. "Not really survival, but certainly without that money our chances of success will be reduced."

Winslow nodded. He understood.

"I'll talk to some people," he said. "But I don't see that as being a problem. I am sure we can find you ten million. It's not a lot of money these days."

Maddie was open-mouthed for a moment.

"Ten mill is not a lot of money?" she said.

Winslow laughed.

"You should have realised by now, Maddie, that it is not what you know in life that is important. It is who you know - and who you sleep with."

"Low blow," she said.

"I wish," he replied.

"I expect you do," she sighed.

She sent him packing at ten.

"My life is too complicated for more sleep-overs," she said.

The following afternoon, as she was getting things in order, in preparation before heading off to Spa, she received a call from Winslow, telling her to get herself down to Heathrow. Pronto. A meeting had been arranged for them in Los Angeles. Charlie Chiphurst was not around and, for once, Cheryl did not seem to know what had happened to him.

"He's not answering the phone," she said, "and that usually means golf."

"OK," said Maddie, "in that case I will take an executive decision: I'm off to LA. Charlie can cover for me at Spa. There's nothing really important. No sponsor functions. I wanted to talk to a couple of drivers, but that can wait. It's only a few days before we go to Monza."

Maddie met Winslow at the airport. She winced when the girl at the ticket desk announced how much it was going to cost for a last-minute reservation, but a big sponsorship deal is a big sponsorship deal and Charlie Chiphurst would just have to understand and swallow the cost. At least she hoped he would. He rang just before they closed the doors of the plane.

"Is it a big one?" he said.

"I hope so," Maddie said. "I think it's a good chance."

"Take it," said Charlie. "Spa is not that important from

a sponsor point of view. It'll be pissing with rain, anyway. It always is. Bloody Belgium. You going to LA? Seventy-two degrees and sunny. Awful place. The weather never changes."

Maddie laughed and rang off with a cheery "See you, Charlie".

During the flight Winslow explained what was going on. He knew a guy in California called Melvin Bilski. He had done some homework to fill Maddie in. Probably of Polish Jewish stock, he said, Bilski was one of those Ellis Island names that was probably a contraction of something unpronounceable such as Przybylski.

"I guess the immigration men were allowed to play God to some extent," he said. "You know Samuel Goldwyn, the movie mogul, had a name like Gelbfisz and so when he left Ellis Island his name was Sam Goldfish.

"Anyway, Bilski's father arrived with nothing in the late 1930s, and somehow ended up in Bowling Green, Kentucky, where he started a knife-sharpening business."

"There's a big GM factory there," said Maddie, "I think that's where they make the Corvette."

Winslow ignored her.

"Bilski's father married a local girl and Melvin was born, I dunno, in 1945. That would make him what? Seventy-one? When he was still a teenager he and a school friend called Marcellus Weisenfreund decided that there had to be money in timber in the area and so they borrowed money from banks to buy a lot of forest and set up the Bilski & Weisenfreund Lumber Company. B&W quickly became one of the biggest timber merchants in Kentucky. They then invested in saw mills and stuff like that, maybe paper, and in the end they had quite an empire and sold out in the late 1980s to some guy from Oregon. So they were just about 40 by then and mega-rich. They didn't ever need to work again. That was not very interesting and so they started investing in new technology, putting money into start-up after start-up, in exchange for shares. And so they turned a large fortune into a vast fortune. In addition to buying shares in companies they bought land, wherever they could get it.

"Melvin's big thing at the moment is the media and I think that F1 might suit him. As people get more leisure time they will need more things to keep them amused. That was the logic behind his switch into media.

"And Formula 1 is media. It's content.

"The other thing is the amount. Ask him for twelve million. That way if he wants to negotiate downwards, there is room to bargain. If he says yes to twelve million, I don't see any reason why I should not be getting a commission from Charlie. He's expecting ten million, so if you get twelve I'll take the other two. And because we're partners, I'll give you ten percent of that. So you'll get two hundred thousand dollars each year, and I'll take one point eight million. Is that a fair deal?

"I had twenty percent on our other deal," said Maddie.

"True," Winslow said. "OK, so you get twenty percent. Four hundred thousand a year. One point two million over the three years."

Maddie did not believe it. This man had just given her one point two million dollars and he had not even thought about it. He did not even blink. That was odd. People negotiate, but he did not even bother. He gave her twice as much as she wanted. Winslow must be rich, she thought, but how rich do you have to be to behave like that?

He had moved on and was talking about Bilski again. He had been into motor racing since the 1980s, when he had sponsored a team in sports car racing. It had not made much sense in terms of an investment, but he had enjoyed doing it and wrote the sponsorship off as a business expense.

"About ten years ago," he said, "Bilski decided that he wanted to enjoy a sort of semi-retirement. He craved peace and privacy, but he wanted great views, hills in which to walk, but also a place to store his cars, where he could tinker with them and drive them, without the hassle of having to travel. He looked for a very long time and one day, in the hills behind Santa Barbara, he found an old ranch, in a hidden valley behind a ridge, surrounded on all sides by trees. The valley was flat and someone had cleared the land in order to create a meadow. There was a stream running through the valley, a dam had been built and a small lake created. The homestead itself was of little interest, but Bilski had spotted that up on the ridge above the valley there was an old cowshed, not in very good condition. He saw this as being the right place to build his home, with a fabulous view all along the coast. His plan was to use the footprint of the cowshed to build a house - and to use the homestead as a garage for his cars. Bilski reckoned that the planning people would be happy to see the cowshed improved, and by digging into the rock he saw that he could create an amazing palace.

"These hills are why the real estate people call the area the American Riviera," Winslow went on. "There are quiet country roads, winding along secluded canyons, with driveways disappearing up to unimaginable houses, worth tens of millions. And you cannot see any of them...

"The first thing Bilski did was to pay for a fibre optic cable to be laid up from the network down by the sea. That way he could stay in the touch with the world.

"At the beginning the only access was a dirt road that ran up the back of the ridge, passing the old cowshed and then curling down into a hidden valley. Bilski carefully upgraded the road. His architects designed a palace and soon the builders were burrowing beneath where the old cowshed had once stood, all the while making sure that all the changes blended in with the ridge.

"A year of two later the house was done and Bilski went back to the planners, asking if he might build a new section of road from what had become the main driveway, down into the hidden valley, in order to avoid everyone having to drive past the house. He showed them an elegant design for a road that would run down through the trees and then curl around the valley until it reached the old homestead.

"It seemed logical and there was no objection.

"Another year passed and Bilski told the planning office that he would like to build a boathouse on the lake and proposed running a road to it from where his new road to the homestead reached the valley floor. It would not cause any fuss. They agreed.

"The only problem, he told the planners a year later, was that visitors tended to cut across from the boathouse to the  original road to the homestead, creating a muddy mess and it would be so much better if he could be allowed to put some tarmac down. The planners agreed. Mr Bilski had always done a nice job.

"So the work was done and Bilski added a few crash barriers to make sure that the road was safe, because it ran close to the trees. And when it was all finished, Bilski had a private loop of road around the valley that looked remarkably like a racing circuit.

"That," said Winslow, "is Bilski."

When the plane arrived at Los Angeles International Airport there was a rush to clear US Immigration and to catch a commuter flight to Santa Barbara Municipal Airport, but the whole process worked well and when the small plane began its descent into Santa Barbara, Maddie finally saw what Winslow had meant. The coastline was stunningly beautiful. On the ground, it was warm. The hazy sun was sinking gradually to the west and the air was filled with the scent of bougainvillea.

They were met by Bilski's chauffeur, who went by the name of Buck. He had a huge shiny black Chevrolet Suburban. As the shadows were growing longer, they drove about twenty miles. The roads grew narrower and then the Suburban pulled up at the gate. There was little exceptional about it. Maddie was expecting a grand entrance, but there were two gate posts and two solid but well-aged wooden gates. There was nothing manicured.

The gates swung open, but this revealed only a hillside covered with oaks and scrub. The driveway curved around to the left, passing a sun-bathed cottage on the left. It was neat and tidy. The road curved back to the right, into the trees, and arrived at the bottom of what an architect might have called an *allée*. This ran gently uphill between two rows of ancient oak trees, identical, but all different. The branches overlapped above their heads, creating the feeling of a tunnel, draped with occasional wisps of Spanish moss.

It all drew the eye up the hill, but there was no great mansion, as one would have expected.

As they drove on upwards, Maddie could see a simple stone archway ahead with walls on either side, all covered in creeper. On the left a road peeled away and disappeared down into the woods.

"That goes to the homestead," Winslow said.

They went through the stone archway. There was another avenue of two-hundred-year-old oaks and then a brightly-lit gravel circle, at the centre of which was a simple stone fountain, surrounded by well-cut grass.

The Chevrolet came to a stop. To the right was an old wall, covered in flowering vines with an archway through it. There were ornate wrought iron gates, but they looked as though they were permanently open. Behind the archway was an ivy-covered wall, a simple marble statue and some low box hedge. They went through the arch and followed the white gravel path around to the left to three wide stone stairs that took them down to a  doorway, with two huge wooden doors, which were open. Beyond this, on the right was a dark hallway, which felt like a tunnel. Ahead of them was sunlight.

They emerged into a courtyard with arches in either side, each with its own French window. There were a variety of bushes to soften the stone. On the right, under a trellis, hung with ancient vine, was a perfect outdoor table and matching chairs; unpretentious, but just right.

Ahead of them was a wall fountain and two archways through which Maddie could see only blue sky.

A sprightly grey-haired gentleman appeared from one of the doors on the right, smiling broadly and holding out his hand.

"You must be the famous Maddie Midnight," he said. "Hi, I'm Bilski. Just call me Bilski."

Americans tend to gush a little too much for the English, who are more reserved and feel uncomfortable when things are overdone. Bilski's greeting was correct; his handshake was firm. Maddie decided that she liked him. He had kind eyes and a cheeky grin. He would have been very successful with the ladies in his day.

Being rich is not something that everyone can do, and there are even fewer people who do it well. Those who have made vast fortunes tend to be overly keen to show the world how much money they have. The result, all too often, is flashy cars and watches, overblown mansions and gaudy women. In the modern age, there is a shocking amount of plastic surgery.

Charlie Chiphurst always said that being rich was a state of mind and it did not matter what you wore, nor the car you drove. The best waiters and doormen recognised wealth when they saw it, even if the people did not make it obvious. It was a question of well-cut clothes, good quality fabrics, but most of all an innate, yet understated, confidence. Charlie had it right: if you have nothing to prove, why do people spend so much time trying to prove it?

Bilski had class. Most castles and palaces rise up to impress the visitor, to underline the power of the owner. Architecture had always been about building to impress, to show power, but Bilski's place was the opposite. He had built what he wanted, not what some designer told him he should have. It did not rise, but rather descended into the ridge, merging into the rock.

"This is a place where one lives out of doors," he said. "I always wanted a courtyard like this. This is the top floor. The rest of the house is below us."

He led them through the archway where there was only sky and both Maddie and Winslow stopped in their tracks. The terrace had a view of the entire coastline, spread out below like a giant train set. Framed on either side were trees that hung down to a perfect length. A stone staircase descended from the terrace and beneath the courtyard was a large reception room. At one end was a view of the Pacific shoreline, at the other a transparent wall with stone pillars and a swimming pool with glass at the far end, looking out into the woods behind the house. The trees were bathed in mottled sunlight.

"It's a wonderful place to swim," Bilski said.

The reception room had various doors. Bilski showed them through one on the right side. They passed a cloister with a lawn and a stone fountain. There was a corridor with nooks and crannies and old wooden doors on both sides. Finally they reached a big oak door.

"This is my guest house," Bilski said. "It has a lovely indoor pool at the base. Please settle in, your baggage is probably there already. My people are very efficient. Freshen up and let's meet in the courtyard in perhaps twenty minutes?"

"That would be fine," said Winslow.

They were shown into a pair of magnificent guest suites, one above the other, each with a private balcony. There was every luxury one could imagine. Maddie had a quick change of clothes and a wash and brush up and then found her way back to the courtyard to find Winslow and Bilski already chatting.

"Come in, come in," Bilski said. "Or I suppose I should say 'Come out, come out'. I always think of the courtyard as a room. I suppose you could call me a troglodyte, when you look at the house, but the truth is that I live with the light. I cannot live without it."

They returned to the terrace as he talked. Below the house, at the bottom of a high cliff was forest, falling steeply away.

"You must need a drink by now," he said.

Bilski's butler Benedict appeared as if by magic when the word "drink" was uttered and Bilski suggested that it was a good moment for some gin and tonics. They talked for a while. Bilski liked to talk, but she noticed that he was a careful listener as well. He did not miss a thing. He had sharp, bright eyes, but perhaps there was a hint of loneliness in them.

"I suppose," Bilski said finally, "we should get down to business before dinner."

Maddie did not beat around the bush.

"We are looking for twelve million dollars a year for the next three years," she said. "It's a good deal because we will be making a big step forward next year and the rate card will rise when we are successful."

Bilski smiled.

"So, how can you be so sure that you will move forward? The team's record in recent years has not been exactly stellar."

"That's true," Maddie said, "but we have a new chief designer, an aero specialist. That is the most important thing in F1. We are confident that this will help us move up the grid and score better results. That is why this is such a great opportunity. I think we will make enough of an impression to give any sponsor huge value in their investment. You will get real value for money in Years Two and Three."

She launched into her usual presentation about the value of F1 sponsorship: the global market penetration, the B2B possibilities; the hospitality.

Bilski smiled again.

"So you know how to sell," he said, as though expecting an answer. But he did not give her time to say anything. "OK, let's do it. I'll give you guys twelve million a year for three years. You can relax now. Get me a contract to sign. Give me bank details and we're done. Maybe I will give you the whole lot up front. Then you can earn some interest off it. Would that be fine?"

Maddie was so startled by the speed of the decision that all she could do was nod. This was a big deal, but she clearly understood that for Bilski the money was not important.

Bilski winked at her.

"In my world," he said. "This is small potatoes... You cannot imagine how much money I spent on that avenue of old oaks coming up to the house. It's actually rather shocking, but it is so very nice."

Maddie wanted to be ecstatic, but all she really felt was relief. It was a huge anti-climax. It had been almost too easy. What she needed was to sit down. Maybe a short nap.

"I think dinner would be a good idea now," said Bilski. They walked along the terrace, through another archway, to another open area, with an outdoor pool, lit with flaming torches. Winslow slid up behind her.

"You just have to know the right people," he whispered in

her ear.

Bilski talked, as old men do, about the good old days when the world was a better place and about the excitement he had felt when the Bilski & Weisenfreund Lumber Company was first set up. He talked about Bowling Green with its famous Lost River and the cave in which they had started a nightclub, just as a side line, when he was younger. And he talked of Beech Bend Raceway where he had first acquired a taste for speed.

"Nowadays," he said. "It's an automotive centre. They have a Corvette factory and a Corvette Museum. But it's still kind of a nice place."

Perhaps, he said, one day he would retire back to Bowling Green.

His friend Weisenfreund was still his partner in a variety of businesses, fifty years later, although Marcellus had long ago retired to live in the Virgin Islands, with a woman half his age.

Bilski said, with wonder in his eyes. "I'm not sure I could manage a woman in her late thirties. Perhaps I should try it some time."

Maddie took the reference with a smile.

"Perhaps you should," she said, "but I'd make sure there was a good prenup. She might just be planning to try to screw you to death."

Bilski laughed.

"Not a bad way to go," he smiled.

"Depends how good she is," Maddie said.

Although the wine flowed Bilski remained in complete control throughout the evening and eventually when he saw that his guests were tiring after a long day, he suggested that they make themselves comfortable and, without further comment, wished them a good night.

"Tomorrow," he said. "You must come and drive on my circuit. Shall we have breakfast at eight?"

Maddie and Winslow nodded and then they meandered back to the guest suites. On the way Winslow put his arm around her waist and she did the same. There was just a peck on the forehead when they got to the suites and then

Winslow was gone.

She was still buzzing and so decided to try the magnificent bath tub for a good long soak. When she emerged, warm and pink, she spent a few minutes naked in front of the large mirror and then slipped quietly into the huge bed and fell instantly asleep.

She woke early, found a large dressing gown into which she snuggled and went out on to the balcony and sat down looking out across the Pacific. Winslow had been right about the view. It was startling. Maddie just stood and stared. This was the top of the world.

Breakfast was perfect and Bilski then insisted on taking them to the hidden valley behind the house in a golf cart. Maddie was not good at pricing old cars, but it was clear that there was a lot of very expensive machinery.

"What would you like to drive, my dear?" he said.

"Why don't you drive me?" she said.

He was delighted with the idea and took her around the track in an open-topped BMW from the 1930s.

"Maybe I can have one of your Formula 1 cars," he said, with a broad smile. "I could probably kill myself it around up here"

"Maybe you could," Maddie said, "but if you like I will talk to Charlie about it. It might be a bit noisy."

In the mid-morning Buck the chauffeur appeared. It was a sign that Bilski had to go back to work.

"Thank you so very much for coming," he said. "It's been an absolute delight. I will certainly have to think about your advice on 30-year-olds."

She smiled demurely. "Just beware of the gold diggers."

They had not really planned their return and when they reached the airport they discovered that there was no flight to LAX for several hours and then the flight out to London did not leave until late in the evening.

"We're not in any rush, are we?" said Winslow. "It's Thursday. The team is away in Spa. Why don't we just stay for the weekend?

"If we fly tonight, I will get to Spa on Saturday evening,

at the earliest," Maddie said, thinking aloud. "It's bound to be raining there. I love Spa, but Santa Barbara is a very agreeable option. Let's bunk off."

"And do what?" said Winslow.

"I don't know," said Maddie. "It was your idea."

Winslow shrugged.

"You know, Maddie, sometimes I think I am just about ready to give in and say that I will give it a try. You cannot believe how much I'd like that. Then I get cold feet again. I don't want it, but that is what happens…"

Maddie smiled at him. It was a pale smile. Should she tell him how she felt? How she sometimes ached because they were not together? No, she thought, probably not. Don't want to scare him away. She would keep that to herself.

"In any case, we have a lot to do," he said, changing the subject. "We need to set up a Panama firm so that Bilski can pay a company with the Chiphurst name, if only for his accounting. So the thirty-six million dollars can go to Chiphurst Realisations SA in Panama. We can get two nominee directors. A bank account for that company would then be opened. There are more than a hundred banks in Panama. The legal tender down there is US dollars so it is not a complicated transfer because there are no foreign exchange controls and no restrictions on capital flow in and out of the country. Taxation in Panama is strictly territorial so money earned outside the country is not taxed, nor is there any requirement to file any financial returns.

"The best thing would be to buy some ninety-day certificates of deposit from another bank. These can be used as collateral for loans issued by a third bank. The money loaned can then be deposited to a company called Blue Windmill in the Cayman Islands. As soon as that has happened, Blue Windmill will transfer thirty million to a bank account in the Bahamas, owned by a company called Chiphurst Enterprises and the entire sum will then sit there, earning interest. The remaining six million will be transferred to M&W Enterprises in Nassau. The Blue Windmill account then closes down. In Panama the deposit certificates are sold and the loans repaid. Chiphurst

Realisations SA disappears. The money is where we want it to be and there are no questions to be asked."

It was true, Maddie thought, there was a lot to do. That would take the best part of a day to set all that in motion. And there was the contract too.

They decided to check into a hotel near the airport, leave their luggage there and have a big Mexican lunch. They could do the paperwork later. She rang Charlie before he went to bed, to tell him that they were getting close to a deal, but needed to stay a little longer to work out the details. The practice at Spa was not going well. One of the cars had been crashed badly.

"Hopefully, I will have good news on Monday," she said, to cheer him up.

"You deceitful hussy," Winslow said.

"True," said Maddie. "Showing your man that you are capable of telling lies is probably not a great idea. Still, you're not my man so I guess that is OK."

"We all tell lies," said Winslow. "Some are just bigger than others."

# Nine

"When God was creating the earth," Winslow said, "on the seventh day he had a rest, played a round of golf at Pebble Beach and had a couple of drinks with the angels. He woke on the eighth day feeling relaxed and filled with energy and new ideas. He decided to build the most beautiful road in the world and so he constructed Highway 1. And even he was impressed by what he had done. Highway 1 was exquisite."

It was Friday afternoon and Maddie and Winslow were in a convertible Ford Mustang, as black and cool as Maddie's wardrobe. They had negotiated a deal that would allow them to return the car to LAX on Sunday , and they were booked on a night flight from Los Angeles to London, arriving late on Monday. She would thus be able to go to work on Tuesday. They had spent the rest of Thursday evening and Friday morning setting up companies and bank accounts to ensure that everyone had money where it was supposed to be. Maddie would then inform Charlie Chiphurst about the deal and they reckoned that the old curmudgeon would probably either take her out to lunch, or drop dead from the shock of a job well done.

So their plan was to drive up Highway 1, as far as they could make it on Friday night and then stop in a hotel. Winslow talked about the joyous nature of the Monterey Peninsula, of Cannery Row, Carmel, Pebble Beach and Seventeen Mile Drive. He knew the area well, having spent a year there learning to speak Russian. The plan was to potter around on Saturday and then find a place to stay that evening before a leisurely run back down to LA on Interstate 5, a trip of about five and a half hours on a Sunday.

"Shall we book some hotels?" said Maddie, ever the one with the practical nature.

"No," said Winslow. "That would tie us down, wouldn't it? We'll just find places as we go. It doesn't have to be fancy, does it?"

Setting off from Santa Barbara after lunch on Friday seemed to be a sensible time to depart. Google suggested that the journey would take about five hours. It sounded reasonable enough and so at about two thirty they climbed away from the sea, up the freeway that leads to the Gaviota Pass. The coastal forests gave way to golden grasslands, dotted with raggedy old oak trees. The sky was blue, but with subtle wispy cirrus clouds that seemed like great waves, frozen in the air.

Where there was water, there were luscious green paddocks, lined with white fences and filled with elegant horses. They stopped to visit the mission at San Luis Obispo and then joined Highway 1 and headed north. Very quickly they were back into the golden hills. They passed a signpost that said: "Monterey 135 San Francisco 249".

It was just a few miles to Morro Bay, with its great rounded rock and three tall factory chimneys, but they skirted around and were soon beside the ocean again, right on the beach in some places. From the road they could see big rollers crashing on to the golden sand.

They passed through Harmony and Cambria and arrived in San Simeon. Up on the hill they could just see the twin towers of Hearst Castle, the insane one hundred and fifteen-room mansion built by newspaper magnate William Randolph Hearst, one of the richest men in the world in his day. It was on top of a hill that he called *La Cuesta Encantada*, the enchanted hill. There was no time for them to take a tour of the castle. Somehow it had become five o'clock. There was still no real sense of urgency because it was only ninety miles to Carmel and they still had three and a half hours of daylight.

Maddie was reading from a tourist guide.

"The road from San Simeon to Carmel was started in 1919, about the same time as Hearst began building his castle, but the highway was not finished for eighteen years. Convicts from San Quentin were used for the construction of a sinuous but spectacular two-lane road.

"Along the way there are nearly forty bridges to be built, including a number of elegant structures that reflected the Art Deco style that was popular in the 1930s, notably the impressive Bixby Bridge."

"It is not the fastest road," Winslow said.

The other thing they noticed was that the place names ceased to be Spanish. They went through Ragged Point, Soda Spring, Redwood Gulch and Mud Creek, which all seemed to derive from the nature of the coastline.

"I guess this is because the coast was so rugged that the Spanish gave up and built their missions inland," Winslow said.

The problem is that once you are on this wonderful stretch of road there is nowhere to turn off, because there are no roads through the Santa Lucia coastal range. There are numerous lookout points, all of them spectacular, but the road was not built for speed, nor for comfort. They stopped several times to admire the beauty, but there is only so much magnificence that one can absorb in a single day and gradually the journey became a slog, as the road ducked and weaved, often in a hair-raising fashion, as it clung to the hills where they met the sea.

There was not much traffic, but when you are behind a slow-moving car, truck or trailer you are always slowed down. At six they were still seventy miles from Carmel and were beginning to wonder whether Highway 1 had been such a great idea. They were not going to make Carmel before nightfall.

"We don't want to be driving this road at night," said Winslow.

The other thing that they noticed was that there were not many hotels along the road. It was beautiful, but people tended to pass through. Eventually, they saw signs to a place with the name of Treebones and Maddie decided it would be wise to stop and get some advice about the places that lay ahead.

Treebones was a strange place, with a series of what looked like Mongolian yurts perched on the hillside. The man at reception said that they could rent one, but there was a two-night minimum.

"We had a late cancellation," he said. "You are very lucky. Take my advice: grab it. North of here, you won't find anything. It's all booked. It's the summer holidays and this weekend is the Concours d'Elegance at Pebble Beach. Hotel rooms up there are like gold dust. I can guarantee you won't get anything in Big Sur, Carmel or Monterey. Even the jails will be full!"

Winslow shook his head in disbelief.

"I completely forgot Pebble Beach," he said. "That's like having a Grand Prix in the area. Everything is booked and people pay crazy money not just for hotels, but also for tickets to attend. They stand about and drool over these expensive cars. Coming up this way this weekend was probably not the smartest thing we could have done."

"I disagree," said Maddie. "Rich people who like cars. That is sponsor-hunting heaven. We can go tomorrow."

"It costs like six hundred dollars a ticket," Winslow said.

"Wow!" said Maddie. "That makes a Grand Prix sound pretty cheap."

When the man in reception told them how much it cost to stay in a Mongolian yurt, they were taken aback.

"Good lord," said Maddie. "It's a damned tent!"

"We prefer to call it glamping," said the receptionist. "It's a luxury form of camping, blending the natural experiences of outdoor camping with more glamorous and luxurious amenities."

"And," said Winslow, with an ironic smile, "it's the only damned tent in town. We don't have a lot of choices here. And look at the view. It's amazing. I don't care about the money. I'll pay. I'm tired. We can stay here for two nights. We can go up to Pebble Beach if you really want to, but I guess that by the time we arrive, there won't be much sponsor-hunting time before we have to turn around and come back here again.

Maddie was unimpressed. The receptionist began explaining that yurts don't have bathrooms, but that the communal showers were very nice. She rolled her eyes.

"I don't do camping" she mouthed to Winslow. He smiled, shrugged his shoulders. "The restaurant looks nice," he said. "You do have wine?"

The receptionist nodded energetically.

"We have a fabulous selection of very great Californian wines," he said. He was about to launch into a speech but saw Maddie's face and stopped. She knew that she had little choice but to give in, but her mood darkened again as they were carrying their bags from the car park to Yurt 13.

"I cannot believe I am doing this," she said. "They say that you should get a flash-light, so that you can go to pee at night. And cellphones don't work either."

"They haven't been working since we left San Simeon," Winslow said. "Anyway, this is supposed to be a bonus. We're getting away from the world. Going back to the earth."

"California," said Maddie. "The land of fruits and nuts."

"Nicely put," said Winslow.

Maddie noticed that the one good thing about Yurt 13 was that it was close to the facilities at the main lodge - and it was big. There were two double beds and a heavy curtain that could be drawn between them, to create the impression of privacy. Maddie could survive with that. She could sleep in the same room as Winslow.

A yurt is made from wooden poles and has a canvas roof and walls. It is not the kind of hotel room one books for a honeymoon, unless you want the whole world to know about your sexual adventures. Some people do not care about that sort of thing, but Maddie was not one of them. If she was going to cry out in the night, she did not want the next door neighbour smiling knowingly at her in the morning.

"I hate that," she said.

Winslow smiled. "OK," he smiled. "We'll just have to do it quietly."

"In your dreams," she shot back at him.

"It has been..." he said.

The guy at reception had told them there would be some noise at night, but it would come mainly from the seals down on the beach below and, of course, from the ocean and the wind. He also cheerfully informed them that guests were asked to adhere to a "quiet time" between nine at night and eight in the morning.

"Perhaps he should have used the word 'inmates'," said Maddie.

Despite the drawbacks, she had to admit that the yurt was really rather pleasant. It had electric lights, a stove for heating and a sink with hot and cold running water. The floor was made from polished pine and there were a number of windows. Outside a redwood deck offered extraordinary view of the coastline.

"They even have a pool with an ocean view and a hot tub," said Winslow, trying to cheer her up.

"I didn't bring a bathing costume," she said.

She did not begin to perk up until they got to the restaurant. The menu included things such as sriracha and gremolata, neither of which Maddie had ever heard of, and thus she considered it pretentious.

She had to admit, however, that it all tasted very good.

"I am very happy to be here," Winslow said. "It's a lot better than the two of us sharing the backseat of a Mustang."

"That sounds interesting," said Maddie.

With a little help from the wine, she began to mellow as the evening progressed. The seared tuna with wasabi mashed potatoes helped the process and, as they walked back to the yurt, she slipped her arm into Winslow's. They sat for a long time on the deck. The light had gone, but it was a clear night and there was a dazzling array of stars above them.

"It makes you feel so small and insignificant, doesn't it?" she said. "Earthly problems cease to matter when you look at a sky like that."

They had acquired a second bottle of wine from the restaurant, in expectation of needing postprandial refreshment and, as they chatted into the night, the level of the bottle gradually dropped. Finally the air became a little chilly and they moved into the yurt, closing the door and the curtains. They lit the fire and quickly the yurt became warm and cosy. Maddie was completely relaxed. She did not even worry that soon she would be sleeping in the same room as Winslow. Perhaps, she thought idly, they might end up in the same bed, if the mood took her when the right moment came. That would be nice.

Winslow too was relaxed. As they sat in front of the fire he began asking Maddie questions, something he had never done before. She was a little surprised. She had just assumed that he already knew all her secrets, as he seemed to have been spying on her rather a lot.

"Tell me," he said, "why is a girl like you doing in a world full of men, some of whom are really not very nice. You are asking for trouble, aren't you?"

"I guess so," she said. "Well, it's certainly not boring. The people are a bit weird, that's true. No racing driver is normal. If they weren't racers some of them would probably have turned into serial killers, slicing up their victims and leaving severed breasts going round and round on record players and other gruesome things like that. Or they would be grease-covered mechanics, hitting the booze every evening because life never quite delivered what they intended. In the end, you know, I learned not to ask questions. I am not here to judge them. I just watch them doing it. I think the healthiest way to look at the sport is to imagine that you are a Martian, flying by in your space craft, discovering the universe, and as you are whizzing past Earth you look down and you see a race track. When you try to analyse what you are looking at, it does not make a whole lot of sense. You see people climbing into little boxes on wheels and going round and round in circles - wiggly or straight, it is all pretty much the same - and they do this as fast as they possibly can. You see them crash and they get hurt. And then if you look closely you see them paying the man who owns the box on wheels to do this. The average Martian would be confused.

"Fundamentally racing is an absurd occupation. They always say that the fastest way to make a million dollars in racing is to start with two million, but there is a lot of money involved. And a lot of people have got very rich. The drivers would probably be dead were it not for racing. They would have stuck their cars into trees when they were kids if they had not learned to control their speed by going karting. They are selfish because they would not be where they are if they were not. You never hear a driver say anything much more than "I want". But you know what, Winslow? They are fascinating. Most of the team bosses are failed racing drivers. It is like being in the circus and I don't think I could ever do anything else in life. It would all be so terribly dull."

Winslow smiled at the description. It was a classic Maddie stream of consciousness.

"That reminded me of your speech when we first met," he said. "You remember the one about blonde pubic hair and how sex is power and how you like doing what a man tells you to do. Well, you haven't ever done anything that I have ever told you to do, at least not when it comes to sex."

Maddie smiled.

"So what is it that you want me to do?" she said.

He looked at her as if to say: 'Are you serious?'

"I don't know," he said. "I know that I want to see your body. Naked. I want to see Maddie Midnight's truth. I've tried to imagine it so many times and I'd like to explore it. I'd also like to give you pleasure, Maddie. I want you to be happy in life. I really do. There's a whole lot of stuff I want to do, and get you to do. But I'm still not sure about getting into a relationship."

He looked so sad at that instant that Maddie wanted to take him into her arms and console him. One of Winslow's many attractive features, she thought, was that sometimes he was still a little boy on the inside.

"It's nice and warm in here," she said, very quietly. "It's not too cold to get naked. Why don't you just tell me what you want me to do and we'll see if I am willing to do it."

Winslow sat bolt upright. Was she kidding? Was she drunk? Would she really do whatever he told her to do? His mind went into one of those hyper drive moments. How far should he go? If she was really into being told what to do, he could have a lot of fun. What had she said? All women fantasize about sexual submission, but it didn't need to be kinky. As his mind raced he noted that Maddie was looking stunning.

He hadn't even noticed that day. She was wearing a powder blue shirt over a simple striped sailor's top and a black knee-length pencil skirt and some simple pumps. It was all so simple, so elegant and so very beautiful. He noticed too she was breathing deeply. She was excited by the idea of pushing their relationship a little bit further.

"Stand up," he ordered, trying to sound manly without being domineering. Maddie looked him in the eye, stood up and waited.

"Take your shirt off," he said. She raised an eyebrow, but began to obey his instruction. Her fingers moved slowly and deliberately, undoing one button after another until none were left to do and then she slipped the shirt off her shoulders and placed it carefully on the back of the chair. The sailor top was carefully tucked into her skirt, to accentuate her waist.

"Untuck the shirt," he said. "Let it hang free."

Maddie did as she was told.

"Take off your skirt," she heard him say. "I want to see your legs."

Now they were getting serious. Carefully, she found the side fastener and zip and opened the top of the skirt. She slid it down her legs to the floor and stepped out of it. She picked it up and folded it neatly next to the discarded shirt.

"You have lovely legs," he said.

She was wearing cream-coloured hipsters, with a low waist

and panels of lace. But the shirt covered most of them. Winslow wanted to see more than that.

"Do those panties have a little bow at the front?" he asked.

Slowly she pulled the shirt up to show him. It was, he noted, exquisite underwear. Simple, not flashy, revealing her elegant body without showing too much.

"And I presume that you having a matching bra," he said, breathlessly. She smiled at him and he watched as she slowly pulled the striped top over her head, folding it and putting it on the back of the chair.

The bra and hipsters matched.

"What do you want now?" Maddie asked, her voice quiet.

"I want to blindfold you," he said.

She opened her mouth, slightly in surprise.

"And why would you want me to do that," she said.

"So you cannot see my face," he replied. "I want it so that you can only hear my voice, and maybe feel my fingers and my tongue. Sensations are much more intense if you cannot see, nor know what I am going to do next. And I want you to have intense sensations."

"That sounds good," Maddie said. "We'll see about the touching. This is not capitulation on my part, you have to understand that. This is just a little experimentation, some reconnaissance, if you like. To see what you are missing. It is a bit like when we were children, playing doctors and nurses."

"I never did," said Winslow. "I had a very protected upbringing. No naked girls at all. I didn't have a sister I shared baths with. I didn't discover any of that sort of thing until I was in my teens."

"How handsome you must have been," Maddie said.

Winslow shrugged. He'd never really thought about it like that before. He'd felt awkward at the time, but being a sportsman, he found girls seemed to like him all right, some girls anyway, but not always the ones he wanted.

"Do you understand the rules," Maddie said. "We're just exploring, pushing back the boundaries a little. We're not going all the way."

He laughed. He had not heard that expression for many

years.

"I understand the rules," he said.

With that assurance, Maddie turned and walked across the yurt to her suitcase. She looked inside. He admired her bottom. It was perfect. Rounded but not too much. Pert.

She pulled a light scarf from her suitcase, folded it twice and walked back towards him. He watched her body move.

"You'll have to tie it behind my head," she said.

"Happily," he replied. He moved behind her. She held the scarf up to her eyes. He took it from her on either side and tied the two ends together with a basic knot. Once that was done he remained behind her and ran a finger down her backbone, until it reached the top of her hipsters. Her skin was soft all the way down to the lace.

She shuddered at his touch.

"Turn around," he ordered in a whisper. She turned to face him. He put a finger on her lips and then slowly drew it over her chin and down her neck until it reached the top of her sternum. The skin was silky. His finger slid down the valley between the two hillocks of her breasts, skipped over the lace of her bra and then continued down to her belly button, pausing for a moment as he listened to her breathing. Then it continued downwards until the finger arrived at the little ribbon bow. He wanted at that moment to tear whatever clothing was left from her body.

"I bet you want to undo my bra, don't you?" Maddie said, reading his thoughts.

"Of course I do," he said hoarsely. He wanted to unclip the lace, slip the bra off, cradle her breasts in his hands, feel their gentle weight and watch the nipples harden to his touch.

She heard him breathe, but he didn't touch her. He decided to surprise her and kissed her gently on the lips. She responded, but it was just a fleeting kiss.

"Don't do that again," she said. "Unless I tell you to. If you do, then the games will stop."

"I thought I was the one giving orders," Winslow said.

"You were," Maddie said. "But now it's my turn. Maybe if this works out all right, you can be in charge again, but right now, I'm taking over. Take my bra off."

"Turn around," he said, putting a hand on each of Maddie's shoulders and gently turning her away from him. He then ran his hands in towards her neck. Then he let one of his fingers run down her backbone again. When it reached the bra strap, he stopped and gently eased the two sides together until the clasp was undone and the tension released as the weight of her breasts pulled the fixings apart. She sighed. It was always a good feeling to have her breasts freed from their bondage. She let the bra straps fall forward down her arms and then she caught one side, slipped her arm out of it and in one flowing movement released herself and threw the bra in the direction of where she thought the chair must now be. Amazingly, it landed on top of the other discarded clothes.

"Now come round in front of me," she said. "Feast your eyes, but don't touch. You have no right to touch.

"They are perfect," he said. "So perfect I feel that I want to kiss them."

"That's not an option," said Maddie. "Do you like them? I always have. I think they hang nicely. I love the way that my nipples darken when they go hard. I can feel them doing that right now. It must be good to watch."

Winslow was beginning to feel rather uncomfortable now, not because of the gorgeous almost naked woman in front of him, but rather because of his reaction to her. He wanted to be free of his clothes. He felt constricted.

"Winslow?" said Maddie softly, reading his thoughts, despite the blindfold. "I want you to be naked now. I want to know that you are as naked as I am."

"You're not naked," he said.

"I will be," she said. "Take your clothes off."

Winslow stripped, trying not to be too hurried. Maddie could not see him and stood waiting. He looked at her body. This was an exciting game. When he was ready he stood naked before her.

"I'm ready," he said.

"We are going to explore a little more and then maybe we

will sleep together, and I mean sleep. Winslow? I want you to kneel down in front of me."

"Ditto," he said.

This time she laughed naughtily. "Who knows," she said. "Maybe I will. Our deal is that you won't have sex with me, but as President Clinton proved way back, it does not mean that I cannot have sex with you."

"I love the law," said Winslow. "It is so strange."

Winslow knelt down.

"Now," said Maddie. 'I want you to take off my panties."

"The pleasure will be all mine," he said.

"I doubt it," she said. "I think I'll probably enjoy it too."

Winslow ran his fingers up the outside of Maddie's legs, past the knees and right up the thighs until he reached the top of the broad band of lacy material. The tiny knots excited his fingers. He wondered as he did this what he might now be touching if he had traced the same upward path on the inside of her thighs. That was a pleasure that was yet to come, but now he was sure that even if she would not allow it, she was ready for him.

Gently he slipped a finger under the lace on each side and began to slowly pull the hipsters down Maddie's silken legs. She enjoyed the feeling of freedom that this gave her. When the downward journey was completed, she stepped elegantly out of the underwear and stood in front of him.

"You see," she said. "I wasn't lying."

"I can see," he said. "Maddie Midnight, natural blonde. Who would have thought it? Do I get to give the orders now?"

"Take control if you want to," she said. "I'm all yours."

# Ten

Winslow knew what he could and could not do. He had accepted the rules of their little game, but just as she has come up with a Clintonian way to get around the restrictions, he too had formulated a plan.

"In a little bit I will take you to bed," he said, very firmly. She recognised that it was an order, not a request. "We will be naked. Under the rules we have, I can touch you, but not in a sexual way. I accept those rules, Maddie. I respect your wishes. It is what I want as well. It must be all or nothing. But that does not mean I cannot show my feelings for you and give you pleasure. There are many ways to make love if we use our imagination. We can hear. We can see. We can smell. We can taste. So what if we cannot touch?"

He stood up, took her gently by the shoulders and turned her around. He paused for a moment, smiled to himself and then turned the blindfolded figure twice more.

She swayed a little, feeling disoriented. "I don't know where I am. I've lost my bearings. That's not fair."

"It was entirely deliberate," he whispered into her ear. "I want you to be detached from all earthly realities; to be a little helpless. That way you can concentrate on my voice. I want to use my voice to excite you.

"You can do that," she breathed back at him.

"Maddie, I want to see the inner slut in you. I know it's there. I've known that since the very first speech you made to me in the hotel in London."

She moved slightly

"Just stand still," he ordered. "I'm looking at you. My eyes are devouring you, every inch of you. Just as you do yourself, Maddie. But I am looking at you differently. I am not analysing, I'm not looking for faults. I am admiring you, I am trying to create a reaction. I'm exploring you with my eyes. If I cannot touch you, I will look."

Quietly he circled her, leaning in close so that she could smell him and hear his breathing. She did not know where he was, but she was excited.

"Let me tell you a little story," he went on. "What would you like? Straight sex, a rape fantasy, a lesbian adventure, a good spanking? Nope, none of them will do. Not tonight. I am going to talk to you about scientists. About a reality. I read somewhere that researchers at some university have discovered quite recently that around eighty percent of women - eight out of ten - are capable of having an orgasm without any physical stimulation. They get off using only their brains."

"I wish," she said quietly.

"They say it is just a matter of throwing away inhibitions and opening the mind," he said. "It is about relaxing and exciting the brain with erotic stimulation and after that it is all just chemistry. The chemicals in your brain will do the rest. I bet you're one of those of eight out of ten, Maddie, I reckon somewhere in your past something like that has happened to you."

She shook her head.

"You just have to let go of all fear and anxiety, just concentrate on pleasing yourself, excite your mind with erotic thoughts, imagine your wildest dreams, get into that mental zone and the chemicals will do the rest. Just think what that could mean if you find that trick. Don't think it is impossible."

Maddie groaned.

"I'd love to," she said. "But I don't think I'd ever get out of bed if I could do that to myself."

"You're turned on, aren't you?" he said.

She nodded.

"Well, just relax. Believe in the amazing abilities of the human brain. Eighty percent, Maddie, eighty percent. Let your thoughts run free, let me talk you to a spontaneous orgasm. Or, if you don't know how to get there, let me get you so worked up that you touch yourself. Just imagine what it would feel like if you touched yourself, knowing I was watching you, knowing you were turning me on. You can imagine that feeling, can't you? You know what it feels like. You play with yourself a lot, I bet. You know just how to do it. The only difference is that this time I am watching you. You are not hiding away. You are doing it openly. Shamelessly. Brazenly. You want to be a slut for me, don't you? You want me to dominate your mind. You want to submit yourself to my voice, to my eyes. Can you feel me watching you? Just imagine what I might be doing as I am watching you. I can do what I want, you cannot see me."

He could hear her breathing a little faster.

"Think about the pleasure that you know you can get with your fingers," he said. "Let me watch you do it."

He sensed her resistance.

"I don't think I can do it," she said. "I'd be embarrassed."

"That's fine," he said gently. "We must go one step at a time, but I want you never to forget what is possible if you can let yourself go."

"I want that," she said. "I really want it, but I think it takes practice."

"We can do that," said Winslow. "Now relax, let me guide you to bed. And when we get there I will just hold you."

He touched her shoulders, she shuddered slightly, and he turned her gently towards the bed. He pulled back the covers.

"Get in," he said, "but keep the blindfold."

When she was settled, he turned out the remaining lights. There was only the glow of the stove. He climbed into bed next to her. "Roll over," he said. She turned on her side, with her back to him and he undid the blindfold and threw it aside.

"Lie on you back," she said. "I want to put my head on your chest." She curled herself around him. Her head and arm were on his chest. He could feel the gentle weight of her breasts on his side. She had thrown her leg over his, so they were intertwined. Her thighs were on either side of his leg. He thought that he could feel her soft pubic hair, but he wasn't sure. They lay twisted together for a long while, both lost in their own thoughts. He was just beginning to fall asleep when he felt her hand gently sliding down from his chest. It moved almost imperceptibly across his stomach and then went lower. She wanted to discover him.

"That's against the rules," he said.

"No it's not," she whispered. "I'm making the rules. You have seen all of me, in almost every detail. I cannot see you. That's not fair. So I am feeling you. You replaced one sense with another, so can I."

Her hand had found what it was looking for and she held him gently. She could feel him reacting to her touch. He could not stop that. Even if he could, he didn't want to stop it. She giggled sleepily.

"Down boy."

"Right now, I could so easily lose it," he breathed.

"Hmm," she sighed. "That sounds nice. I'd like you to do that one day. But not tonight. The inner slut in me is tired. Too much excitement in one evening. She wants to sleep."

Maddie paused for a moment. "You feel very nice," she said faintly. "It feels perfect for me."

In a minute or two he felt her breathing change and her hand stopped its gentle movements. She was asleep.

He lay still, listening to her breathing, feeling her hand still there. He had done a few unusual things in bed in his life, he thought, but this was quite strange. At the same time it was something different, something new. She was a great woman. In the soft glow of the light from the stove he could just make out her face. She was at peace.

Outside the wind was rustling through the trees. He could

hear the sound of the surf down below and the occasional bark of a seal on the beach. There was no human sound at all. Gradually he faded into sleep.

She woke to find herself still on his chest, her hand still holding him. She smiled and thought back a few hours. It had been an interesting experience. She had enjoyed herself. She dozed, wondering if what he had said about spontaneous orgasms was right. She would have to look into it when she got home. She moved slightly to free her other hand and she felt him stir. She moved the hand down between her legs. Without any real purpose she let her fingers explore just a little. It felt good. She had the whole world in her hands. She was tempted to play with him and let him take her, there and then, in the quiet of the morning. It would be so easy. Just a few movements with her hands and the process would be set in motion. She knew that it would end well, but she restrained herself. Luscious it might be, but she had a higher purpose, a bigger picture. She stopped her fingers, admittedly with some reluctance, and very gently extracted herself from his arms and tiptoed across the yurt. Sticking her head between the curtains, she stood naked, looking out at the Pacific Ocean. She giggled silently at the picture that Winslow would see if he woke up: a naked headless woman. After a while she tiptoed to her suitcase and found a simple white sun dress, so light that it was almost see-through. She slipped it on and quietly left the yurt and headed for the showers.

When she returned Winslow was awake.

"That was a fun night," he said.

"It was," she said. "We're sailing pretty close to the edge."

"We are," he said, "but if we weren't comfortable with that, I guess we wouldn't be doing it."

They had a quick breakfast and then headed off towards Pebble Beach. Maddie was back to being her usual self. The soft woman he had seen during the night was gone. She was the maid in shining armour again.

"I want to meet at least two billionaires," she said.

She would be disappointed. It took them nearly two hours

to get to Pebble Beach and it was clear that the big event was not until the following day, when fifteen thousand people would pack on to the eighteenth fairway of the Pebble Beach golf course and feast themselves on what Maddie called "automotive porn". There were a lot of smaller events going on around the town, but it seemed like most of them were private affairs, car launches and such things. They found themselves wandering around Monterey and then Carmel before going along Seventeen Mile Drive and then heading back the sixty-odd miles to Treebones.

On the return journey, they discussed what to do on the Sunday. They needed to be at LAX by about six in the evening, which meant going to Pebble Beach made no sense at all. If they left Treebones very early in the morning they could be up there by about nine, but the big guns would probably not arrive until just before lunch and they would need to leave by one to get back to Los Angeles.

"It's pointless," Winslow said.

In the end Maddie agreed and they planned to leave in the late morning, return south on Highway 1 to Cambria and then cut through the coastal range on the Green Valley Road to Paso Robles. From there it was an easy run along the 46 to Interstate 5. They would be at the airport in five hours. They could even stop for lunch on the way.

When they got back to Treebones, Winslow sensed that Maddie was a lot more relaxed than she had been the previous evening. It was only natural she would feel this way, given their experiments. She changed for dinner in front of him, quite casually, not concerned that he might see her.

They had another agreeable dinner and, as they had the previous evening, they took an extra bottle of wine with them back to the yurt and sat on the terrace, drinking, chatting and looking at the stars.

"What games shall we play tonight?" Winslow asked finally, when there was a pause in the conversation.

"You tell me," said Maddie.

"I don't know," he said. "Last night just happened. I don't want tonight to feel artificial. I just want to do what we want to do..."

"...which is?" said Maddie.

Winslow shrugged.

"I guess we'll just have to see what develops."

They fell into silence. After a while Maddie said she felt like a shower and went inside. Winslow followed and watched her change into the light white dress and then disappear into the darkness. He waited for a while, nosing about in the yurt and then decided he was bored and stripped off his clothes, brushed his teeth and climbed into the bed. She would be back soon.

When Maddie returned she laughed at him. He looked so funny, with just his head poking out from beneath the covers. She wandered around the room doing things. Her dress clung to her curves as she moved. Then she began to turn off the lights. When the last light was gone, he was aware of her moving towards the bed. He heard the sound of the dress being pulled over her head and sensed her naked body close to him. She slipped into bed beside him and felt her way to him in the darkness. She smelled clean, her hair was still a little bit damp. He was lying on his side facing her and so she turned, fitted her body in front of his. He put his arm over her and cupped a breast. It was against the rules he knew, but she did not object. He felt the nipple harden against his palm. He gently nuzzled her neck. She knew that if she moved her body just a little he could be inside her.

Once again, as she had in the morning, she felt herself close to a precipice of lust. It would be so easy to just give in and let their passion take its course. But she knew once more it was not what she wanted. Yes, she wanted Winslow to take her, but only when he was ready for their relationship.

So she turned around and lay on his chest, just as she had the previous night. He listened to her breathing softly. She was turned on, he could tell, and he wondered if she might give in to the passion and break the agreement they had. Once again he felt her hand stray down his body and she began to play with him. At first it was gentle and playful and slowly she increased the intensity.

"Oh Maddie," he groaned. "What are you doing?"

"I'm torturing you," she whispered in the darkness. "I'm allowed to touch you because I want to be in a relationship with you, but you're not allowed to touch me because you will not commit. That's fair. The way I look at it, this is a bonus, a chance to see what I can do, with no requirement to purchase. It's like taking a new car out for a test drive. So I wouldn't complain too much if I were you. You're getting something for nothing."

He laughed at that.

She moved slightly and he felt her lips on his nipple, sucking it and biting it lightly. He was getting more and more turned on, and she knew it. He was breathing more deeply.

"Maddie if you keep doing this, you know what is going to happen," he whispered.

"Oh, yes," she said. "I'm not some high school virgin, I know exactly what will happen. I am just deciding what to do about that. Maybe I'll stop... leave you frustrated. What do you think?"

Winslow groaned.

She laughed. "This, my dear Winslow, is a perfect example of female power. Right now, you would do just about anything if I asked you to, wouldn't you?"

"I would..."

"That makes me feel powerful. Yesterday, you were feeling the power when you had me stripping in front of you. Today, it's my turn."

Winslow knew exactly what he wanted to happen and the prospect of that happening was getting closer by the minute. She knew this, of course, and the intensity of her manipulations was designed to achieve exactly that.

"I'm still not sure," Maddie said. "Maybe I'll slow things down. That will give me more time to think. That might be a good idea. I don't want to make the wrong choices at this stage."

She slowed her movements.

Winslow groaned again.

"You like that?" she said, "a change of pace." She slowed

down still more. He could feel him pulsating in the darkness.

She stopped moving her hand. Winslow was breathless.

He felt her hand move further down.

"Oh God, Maddie," he said. "That feels good."

"I have an idea," she said. "I can just stop... or I can do this..."

He felt her slide her body further down, moving under the covers. She burrowed her way to where her hand had been and he felt her mouth on him. He gave in to the pleasure. She was playing all kind of tricks with him with hand, mouth and tongue. She was making quiet whimpering noises and Winslow wondered whether perhaps she was using her other hand for some other purpose. The thought that she might make them both orgasm excited him. Gradually the tempo increased. Her head moved faster and faster and she was using her hand as well. The inevitable conclusion was close. He could not hold back any longer. His body surged uncontrollably and he let out a silent cry of ultimate pleasure. He was panting hard and his body twitched with aftershocks. Her mouth was still there.

As his pleasure subsided and he began to get his breath back, she felt her slide back up the bed and she then took her place on his chest again.

"There," she whispered. "No mess. Everyone happy. It's time to sleep."

"It's not the right time to say it," Winslow whispered, "but Maddie Midnight, I love you."

"No you don't," she said. "If you did you would have committed yourself to me and we would be making love properly, like a couple of horny teenagers."

He laughed quietly.

"You'll have to give me a bit of time to recover before we start doing that," he said. "I'm not eighteen any longer. It takes me a little longer to go back into action."

"I don't want you to do that," Maddie admitted. "As I told you that was just a test drive. I enjoyed it, but let's not make it into something it was not."

They fell silent and after a couple of minutes she was aware that his breathing had changed. He was asleep. A typical man, she thought. The minute they get their rocks off all they want to do is to go to sleep...

She listened to his heart beating beneath her and felt his chest moving up and down. She had loved the feeling of making him lose control. The inner slut loved the abandon required to keep her mouth there. She did not have a problem with that. Men liked it. She wondered for a moment what the word was for women who were frightened by sperm. She knew it was not the obvious, because spermophobia is the fear of germs, not of sperm. It did not really matter, but it would be a fun word to learn. She was happy too because while he had been reaching his peak, she had been using her fingers on herself. It had been close, but he was done before she came. It was not his fault. She had given him a good working over. She should have started on herself a little earlier. Was it frustrating playing this game with Winslow? No, not really. She wanted satisfaction, of course, but her goal was to win Winslow. When she had done that, she would let rip...

In the morning Maddie did not want to laze around in bed. She was hungry. She woke first and slipped away to the showers once again. Winslow was gone when she returned but soon afterwards he reappeared, smelling clean and rather wholesome. She kissed him on the cheek, to highlight their new-found intimacy. Oddly, she felt that while they were not yet lovers in the traditional sense, they had crossed a line of intimacy and the sexual act itself was not so important. It would be when it happened, but the need to hurry the process along was really urgent. It would be best, she felt, to let Winslow assess what had happened, decide what he wanted to do. She was hoping that she had done enough to change his mind. But she wasn't sure.

They had a good breakfast and after checking out, they set off to enjoy the magnificence of Highway I once again. For Maddie, Yurt 13 had seemed a bad idea at the start, but it had turned out to be a lot more successful than she could ever have imagined. Perhaps in years to come they would remember this as the place where it all started with Winslow.

He was having similar thoughts as they checked out, but pretended to busy himself getting everything to the car.

They did not rush it. The journey to LAX was nice and easy. Traffic in the city was not too bad and it was not long before their plane thundered down the runway, rose into the dark sky and curled away towards London. Eleven hours later they landed at Heathrow. They shared a kiss, a proper one, before going their separate ways to their different parking spaces. As she drove home, Maddie considered the situation. Was he really coming around to the idea of being her partner? It certainly felt that way. She was excited at the thought.

In another car, on another road, Winslow was wondering about the future as well. Maddie was great. She was everything that he wanted in a woman. She was a lot younger than him, of course, but they were a good match.

And he was going to tell her all that on Tuesday evening.

# Eleven

On the Tuesday morning, Maddie was keen to give Charlie a pleasant start to his day and so she made sure that she was in the factory at 8am. Racing teams are temperamental beasts and the team had not done well at Spa. The boys seemed to be a little down in the mouth.

One or two said a cheery "Good morning", but most just nodded or grunted. She hoped that a cheerful presence in the canteen would raise their spirits.

When Cheryl arrived Maddie asked her to make an appointment with Charlie, as soon as he appeared. She then spent the next hour catching up with paperwork, dotting the i's and crossing the t's.

Eventually, at around nine thirty, the phone rang.

"Charlie just turned up," Cheryl said. "Funnily enough, he wants to see you. It must be love..."

Maddie laughed, put the phone down and strode down the corridor. She gave her boss a huge smile as she walked into his office.

"Charlie," she said. "Will you give me a pay raise if I land a deal worth ten million dollars this year, plus another twenty million sitting in the Bahamas, earning interest in a bank account called Chiphurst Enterprises. This means that we can have about eleven million next year and even more the year after that?

Chiphurst looked at her, thought for a second, and then replied. "Absolutely not. That's your damned job."

Maddie laughed.

"OK, I'll tell the guy that I have just got to agree to that deal that we are not interested," she said.

"What guy?" said Chiphurst, shoving a letter from the Inland Revenue into the shredder.

"The guy who I went to meet in California."

Chiphurst looked up.

"Really? You found some nutter willing to give us thirty million dollars up front."

"I did," she said. "Actually it should have been a better deal. I could have got thirty-six million, but I had to pay a big commission to the guy who put me together with this Californian character."

Charlie thought about it for a second. "Fair enough," he said. "He got the other six?"

Maddie nodded.

"Decent deal for him..." said Charlie.

And then his face lit up.

"Midnight," he said, "you're a bloody miracle-worker."

He paused for a second, as another thought entered his head. "Is this man a criminal?" he asked. "No, don't tell me. I actually don't care where the money comes from..."

"I believe he's private equity," said Maddie. "He's a class act and I think he owns a whole bunch of different unrelated businesses. He is going to use the sponsorship to promote various brands that he controls. He said he will let us know what he wants on the car. I have told him the space he can have and we will figure it out from there."

"Private equity?" said Charlie. "Well, I guess that he can afford it. I should probably try flogging half the team to him. Fifty percent, but I stay on as chairman.

"I doubt he'd fall for that one," said Maddie.

"With an option to buy the other fifty?" said Charlie.

He thrust his finger on to a button on his phone on the desk. "Cheryl love," he said. "Can you book us a table for two at the Manoir. Twelve thirty. I have to spoil Ms Midnight. She's been a very good girl."

If only he knew the truth, Maddie thought. She was not a good girl at all. In fact she'd been a naughty girl in lots of different ways. A very bad girl.

She spent the rest of the morning making sure that all was well with the Bilski transfers. The money had been sent to Panama. It would be in the Bahamas by the Wednesday morning.

The lunch was, of course, magnificent although Maddie felt rather bad about eating so grandly. She had planned to give Winslow an evening to remember to say thank you for everything he had done, but here she was pigging out on Raymond Blanc's best creations. The gazpacho was, she felt, from a parallel universe, the Chassagne-Montrachet slipped easily down and the Welsh lamb tasted like lamb used to taste. By the time they returned to the office it was the middle of the afternoon. She felt perfectly fed, but could tell that a big dinner was not going to happen.

She reached for the phone to ring Winslow. As she did so, the phone rang. It was him. He sounded happy to hear from her and they agreed to meet that evening at The Perch & Pike in South Stoke, on the River Thames, close to where the Daisybelle was now moored.

"I'm next to a beautiful water meadow," he said, "and the weather is gorgeous."

It was nearly eight before she finally reached South Stoke and parked the car at the pub. She still wasn't in the least bit hungry. Winslow was sitting patiently in a small garden. He looked very relaxed. They had a glass of wine and Winslow had some fish and chips. She watched him eat. After a second glass of wine, with the light just starting to fade, and a soothing mellowness coming over her, Maddie led him to the car and he told her where to drive. It was not far. Up the main street, known oddly as "The Street", and then down a narrow side road called Ferry Lane. At the bottom was the river and an old dock where once there had been a ferry that went backwards and forwards to the village on the opposite bank. Winslow said someone had told him there was still a ferry that went across, but he had never seen it himself. They got out of the car and wandered along the towpath, hand-in-hand, and there, moored beside a solitary tree, was the Daisybelle. Maddie suspected, and seriously hoped, that Winslow had finally decided to commit himself and she was ready for that to happen. It would be nicer for them to get together on the Daisybelle, moored in a lovely place, rather than in some anonymous hotel room, or even in her own rather miserable house. It would make the Daisybelle somewhere special for both of them.

There was no awkwardness at all between them because both sensed what was going to happen and so there was no pressure. It was a glorious summer evening. The river was silent, the water meadow golden and there was a sense of happy expectation.

"Stay there," Winslow said when they reached the boat. He clambered aboard and returned moments later with a small lantern, a blanket, a bottle of rum and two glasses. Dutch Courage, she thought. The rum tasted good and the pair of them chattered away about nothing in particular. They sat and then lay back on the blanket, as the darkness closed in around them. Soon they were gazing up at the night sky.

Winslow then seemed to decide that the time had come for action. He sat upright and said: "Maddie. I'm decided. I'm ready to do this. I think you're fabulous, and sexy and smart, and I want to be with you, as much as we can be. When you're not around I get lonely. It was never like that before you came along. I've changed and it took me a while to understand and to accept. I apologise for being such an ass and making you wait. I should have stopped all this messing about when we were in France."

Maddie was smiling broadly.

"I don't care," she said. "It is better this way. Besides it was fun trying to convince you."

"Yes," he said. "It was."

She felt great. She had got him. She had planned for this moment and wondered many times what it would be best to say, but she had never found the right answer.

"The good news," she said finally, "is that the inner slut is now officially unchained. She's running free and wild. Take me to bed immediately and fuck me until I weep."

Winslow laughed out loud. "And there was I, thinking that you were such a nice young lady."

"Oh, I am," Maddie replied, "but it does rather depend on the room. I cannot remember who said it, but there is a famous remark about the perfect wife being a lady in the drawing room, a chef in the kitchen and a whore in the bedroom. I'm afraid that I can only lay claim to two of those talents. You can do the cooking..."

Winslow stood up, held out his hand to help her up and together they climbed aboard the Daisybelle, with the blanket, the bottle and the glasses rather getting in the way. There was no ceremony, no wild tearing at clothes. He led her to the cabin and, in a fairly leisurely fashion, he started to undress her, taking his time, button by button, clip by clip and clasp by clasp. She watched him enjoying the task and it excited her.

"What a beauty," he said.

When she was naked, Winslow told her to lie on the bed and, almost immediately, he was there beside her. For a while they nuzzled and exchanged kisses and then gradually things began to escalate and for an indeterminate amount of time they pleased one another. It was as perfect as love-making can be when two new people are together for the first time. There was still a lot for each to learn about the other, but by the time they drifted to sleep, each was completely satisfied. Her last thought was that it had been a wonderful experience, and just what she needed.

When she woke up in the morning she had to admit that she felt rather tender. How on earth, she wondered, did girls in porn movies go on and on as much as they did?

Winslow stirred beside her, breathing gently. She ran her fingers through his hair. There was no mystery in him now. She snuggled up to him in a gentle echo of the night before. When he opened his eyes he looked at her in a way that she could hardly describe. It was a look she had waited years to see. And then he laughed.

"You see," he said, with a twinkle in his eye, "you have become a notch on my bedpost. And to think you said it would never happen..."

She growled at him, playfully.

It was only seven, but Winslow was feeling energetic. He said that they should get up immediately.

"Do you know what the best thing to do in the morning is?" he asked. "Throw on your clothes. We are going for an adventure."

Maddie was not very interested. She was more into the idea of having a lazy morning, and getting to work a little late. But Winslow would have none of it.

"What you need, girl, is exhilaration," he said.

"I've had plenty of that already, thank you" she groaned. "What I need now is gentle laziness."

He refused to give up. In the end, she rolled out of the bed, her joints clicking in protest. She immediately stubbed her toe on a built-in cupboard and sat down on the floor and pouted into the mirror. She did not want to go out into the world looking like this. Winslow pulled her to her feet, shoved her into the little bathroom and gave her a playful slap on the bottom.

"Don't shower!" he said. "If you do, you'll just have to do it all again later, so there really is no point."

"I am not having sex any more" she said.

"I wasn't thinking about that," he said. "But It is not a bad idea. Come on. Hurry up. Let's go out while the world is still quiet. It is better this way."

She squeezed a toothpaste tube, ran a comb through her nest of ruffled hair and rounded up her breasts and barricaded them into their flimsy hammocks. She borrowed one of Winslow's jumpers to hide the whole sorry mess. She wanted coffee, but he refused to make her one. He just wanted to get going. Finally, he dragged her off the boat and along the towpath to Ferry Lane.

"Do you think I would be doing this if it wasn't going to be the best fun?" he asked.

She grunted.

They arrived next to an old shed and Winslow pulled open the door. There was a dirty old Land Rover inside. He told her to jump in and at the first turn of the key, the machine burst into life. She was tugging at strands of hair which were not falling where they should be falling. He looked at her and laughed again.

"You look great," he said. "Do you know people pay a lot of money to get that tousled look you have right now."

"I think that they call this the 'just-fucked' look," she said. "I cannot believe I am doing this..."

He drove up Ferry Lane and then turned left up the valley towards Newnham Murren, where there was a lane, heading up the hill. The old Land Rover roared as it climbed up the scarp of the Chilterns. At the top of the hill there was an old pub called The Crown. Winslow pulled off into the car park and stopped. He climbed out and Maddie followed, curious to see what he was up to. In the back of the Land Rover was a tarpaulin. He pulled it back to reveal two bicycles.

"His and hers," he said. "So all we do now is get on them and head down the hill. It's miles, downhill all the way, no effort at all. It's a brilliant way to wake up. In a perfect world there would be someone to drive the Land Rover back down the hill, but I will run up here this afternoon and pick it up - if I have the energy."

It did not sound such a bad idea after she heard what it was. She had not ridden a bike for probably ten years and suddenly she couldn't remember why she had ever stopped. It had been great exercise, a good way to burn calories and to tone up one's thighs and bottom. She climbed on to the bicycle and pushed off, circling the car park a couple of times, remembering what it was like ride a bike and then, following Winslow, headed towards the hill.

The morning was beautiful and the views ahead were spectacular as they began to build up speed. The faster they went, the better she felt. She suddenly didn't even care that she looked a mess. If Winslow liked it, what did it matter what the rest of the world thought? Freewheeling on a bike is fun. And this run went on and on. They tucked down to go faster and by the time Winslow finally put on the brakes and they began to slow, she felt great.

"Wow, Winslow," she said. "You really do know how to make a girl feel good."

The run from Newnham Murren back to the boat was easy, with just one small rise to worry about, but Maddie found the whole experience exhilarating and started talking about taking up cycling to tighten up "all the saggy bits". They cycled right down to the bottom of Ferry Lane and left the bikes leaning up against the fence where the towpath began.

"I'll put them all back later," Winslow said. "Now, we need the second best thing of any great morning: the great British fry-up. Totally unhealthy and utterly magnificent. He began to go to work with bacon, sausages, black pudding, eggs and goodness knows what else, while Maddie stripped off and went to the tiny bathroom, where she enjoyed a warm shower. It wasn't quite as good as great sex, but it was better than free-wheeling. She emerged feeling great.

Winslow delivered the food and they ate, glowing with happiness. Even the coffee tasted great. By the time it was all done and the last traces had been wiped from the plates, it was time to get going.

"I need to swing home and get some new clothes..." she said. "We'll have to figure something out about that. You don't have a lot of space on this here barge."

They kissed goodbye and she shouted back "see you tonight" as she departed. There was not even a question about whether they would be meeting, just where and when. The problem was that it was Wednesday morning and on the Thursday she would need to be at Brize Norton early to get Charlie's plane to Monza. It would be best, they concluded on the phone later in the day, for him to come to stay with her at Netherington.

"If I must," he said.

"I'll make it worth your while," she said. This was as convincing an answer as he could imagine.

That evening they made up for time which was going to be lost and it was a weary Maddie who arrived to meet Charlie at Brize Norton on the Thursday morning. A cup of coffee helped and soon the two of them were in lively conversation about the future of the team. The arrival of major new money at Chiphurst Competition was something of a game-changer and Maddie was keen to talk to Charlie about the driver line-up. The money from Bilski meant that finally they could pick their drivers based on talent alone.

"This team does not pay for stars," Charlie would often say. "We manufacture them. We give good young guys great cars. We have rock solid long-term contracts, so if these hot shoes want to move on, they have to pay us to let them go. Otherwise they stay with us and we enjoy success together. We should always remember that the key to success is engineering. The day we forget that is the day that we fail."

The hike in the F1 budgets and the economic crisis had meant that Chiphurst had slipped back in the F1 pecking order and so had to rely on pay-drivers. Bilski's money meant that Charlie could once again afford to choose.

Chiphurst was tough and he knew how the sport worked. The big sponsors always want the fastest men. There are plenty of folk with hard luck stories about how they would have made it if they had money, but the truth was that no genius racing driver ever missed out on a top drive. Being a great racer is not just about driving fast. It is also about getting the right team around you, the right machinery and being in the right place at the right time. And it is about not being afraid to make a change if you feel the change is necessary, whether there is a contract in or not.

"What we need is the next superstar," said Charlie, as he watched the coastline of England slip below the plane. "The trouble is I haven't seen anyone who fits the bill."

Maddie knew the answer. Charlie did not really get out there and look very much. He might sometimes watch the races that supported a Grand Prix, but he would not know a Formula 3 car if it was about to run him over. Charlie was not unusual in this respect. The F1 teams all tended to rely on a group of talent-spotters who see the kids racing karts and sign them to management contracts. There was a time when a good manager would be able to fund a youngster's route to the top, but that was no longer viable. The driver development schemes of the modern age are funded by teams and sponsors and it is a dangerous career path, because if they lose interest in a driver, his career can be destroyed. Red Bull has destroyed many more F1 careers than it has made.

Maddie liked to keep an eye on young talent and believed that one should always look beyond the results and meet the individuals. She would sometimes go to national race meetings on weekends off, to see what talent was out there. If she liked what she saw she would go and meet the driver.

She had done that the previous year, visiting an old friend who was running a Formula Renault team. Was there anyone special? she had asked him. Her pal had pointed out a kid from New Jersey, with the unfortunate name of Jimmy Buckett. She had watched the race and decided that it would be worth meeting Buckett, to see what he was like; to see if he had the fire and the brains required to be a star.

Things did not begin well. The team had been preparing for dinner when Maddie wandered into the awning, set up next to the transporter. She walked to the back and emerged in the sunlight just as Buckett was sitting on the barbecue, wearing his fireproof overalls, and shouting "Great balls of fire".

Oh God, Maddie thought. A real dork.

But, as the evening wore on, she began to change her mind.

"Hey, Hot Dog," she asked, "why did you sit on the barbecue?"

"Hot Dog?" he said, quizzically.

"Better than Fried Chicken," she said.

He smiled.

"Yeah, that's true. OK, I'll be Hot Dog, but you need a nickname too. It's only fair. I think we'll call you Cougar."

That did not bother her at all. And so they became Hot Dog and Cougar.

"I sat on the barbecue because I thought the guys would

like it," he explained. "Every great racing driver is close to his mechanics, he cares about them, knows the names of their wives or girlfriends. He has fun with them. Treats them right. And he does it not because he thinks he needs to do it, but because he cares. He needs those guys. OK, I'm a kid, but I've been around the racetracks since I was eight and I've learned a lot of stuff."

The speech got Maddie's attention and she asked about his background. He seemed surprised.

He had grown up, he said, in Green Brook, New Jersey.

"It's basically a suburb of New York. My mother and father were both lecturers at Rutgers University. It is a nice place to grow up, a little bit of old town America, but within easy reach of The Big Apple. You could go straight into Penn Station in about half an hour. We didn't have a lot of money, but my parents believed in good education so I got sent to a place called the Pingry School, which was pretty nice. We used to go on holidays in the Pocono Mountains, just over the state line in Pennsylvania, about seventy miles from home. It was another world. And I first saw racing cars up there at the Pocono Raceway. The whole region was mad about the Andretti Family and I guess that was where I got the crazy idea about becoming a Formula 1 driver."

So he had started karting at eight. It was the usual story. Except that Jimmy Buckett knew about the history of the sport.

"I discovered that Mark Donohue had been at the same school, even if the school had moved since his days," he said. "That was cool."

Every weekend, he explained, the family would go to kart races and every Monday he would be back at school, telling the other kids how he had won this and that. He made up interesting stories about racing girls to keep his schoolboy friends amused.

"It wasn't true, but it made me a bit of a hero," he said, "and, of course, the girls like to hang out with a racing driver. That was cool."

He had wanted to go to Princeton, but he had to choose

between school and racing.

"I had a few sponsors by then and one of them said he would help me make it in Europe. So, a year ago I had a huge fight with my parents and told them that if I failed as a race car driver by the time I was twenty-one, I'd go back to Princeton and they could pay for me! If I was successful then they did not have to worry. I would get rich."

Buckett explained that he was always reading and that The Great Gatsby was "a cool book".

"Come on," Maddie said. "I've never heard a racing driver talking about Gatsby before."

"I read a lot of different stuff," he said. "Sometimes history, sometimes literature. I even do philosophy occasionally - and trashy detective novels."

Maddie was surprised.

"Can you talk about Steinbeck and the politics of China as well?" she said. "Racing drivers don't do that sort of thing. They talk about cars, girls and fitness training."

Buckett laughed.

"A lot of these guys gave up going to school when they were twelve," he said. "They were earning money as professional kart racers - and school really didn't seem to be much use to them. I understand that. If you're earning tens of thousands as a teenager, and getting all the girls, you end up thinking that there is not much that you can learn from other people. It never enters your heads that you might not be successful. So they all decide to rely one hundred percent on their God-given talent. I'm doing it my way. I'm not the Gatsby type. I don't have to re-invent the past and be something I am not."

"And you're how old?" Maddie asked.

"An ageing nineteen," he said.

"Wow," said Maddie.

"No, you're not old enough to be my mother," said Buckett. "Not unless you were a very bad girl in High School."

Maddie smiled.

"Yeah," said Jimmy. "I bet you were bad."

"Naughty," said Maddie. "Not bad."

"Naughty is good," said Buckett.

"Forget it kid," said Maddie. "I don't do schoolboys, but for your information I am still naughty."

They spent the evening in enjoyable banter, but beneath the chat, Maddie recognised that Jimmy was not your average teenage racer. He seemed so grown-up and down-to-earth.

"I know most people think my name is stupid," he said, "but it's really not. It's really useful. People don't forget you, when you have a name like that. It is like Jenson Button. Your name is your brand. I think it's a fun name and it is great when I screw up because I can say things like 'different shit, same Buckett' or 'you need to kick the Buckett'. It is a great way to diffuse tension."

She watched him race again a few weeks later and was impressed that a man - well, a boy really - who drove with such fire and passion could emerge from his car after the race with such icy coolness.

They had a couple of dinners together after that and Maddie's respect for Hot Dog had grown. He wasn't in the best team, but he was driving the cars well and achieving results that he should not have been able to do.

"You know what I want?" he said one evening.

"I can imagine," Maddie said.

"No, I mean seriously," he said. "Yes, sure I want to win races and be a star. I want to get the girls and the jets and all of that, but what I really want is to be able to say, if one day I find myself heading towards a concrete wall with no way out, that I have lived my life to the full. Done the best that I could have done with the cards I have been dealt. Beyond that we cannot really control anything."

As Charlie Chiphurst's jet crossed the French coast, Maddie decided it was time to tell Charlie about Hot Dog. She knew that soon Chiphurst would be talking about "my new discovery", but she did not really care.

"This kid had got that little bit of magic," she explained. "You see it sometimes when two-tenths of a second suddenly vanishes from a lap time and you don't know how it happened."

"Get me a meeting," said Charlie.

As the plane circled in to land at Orio Al Serio Airport in Bergamo, Maddie and Charlie agreed that she would get Buckett under option. It would not be hard, she said, no-one else was paying him any attention.

"Let's get this done," said Charlie. "Ring this kid and set up a meeting today. Then fly back to Brize, get him to sign something and be back here for dinner with me."

"Really?" said Maddie.

"Chop chop," said Charlie. "Strike while the iron is hot."

# Twelve

Standing on the tarmac in Bergamo, she phoned Hot Dog's mobile and told him that she wanted to meet him for lunch.

"So you have finally decided to give in to my boyish charms?" he said.

"No, saddo," she said. "I'm afraid you're just going to have to continue giving yourself hand-jobs until you find someone dumb enough to do it for you."

"Ouch," said Buckett.

They arranged to meet in a hotel in Oxford at midday.

"I'll check if they do rooms in the afternoons," he said.

"Are you old enough to have a credit card?" she asked.

He hung up, laughing at her response.

In truth, Jimmy didn't really want a girlfriend. He was too busy with his career. In any case, he was a little suspicious of girls who liked racing drivers. They were easy to exploit - which could be fun - but it was not really very fulfilling. Sometimes he wondered if an older woman might not be a bad idea, but he worried they might want to have babies, which was the last thing he needed. So he would hang out with his trainer and if he felt the need for a little action there was a very amenable girl who worked with one of the other team and had proved, on occasion, to be very accommodating, without being in the least bit demanding.

Jimmy and Maddie met as planned.

"What's up?" he said.

"Charlie wants to offer you a contract," she said.

Buckett nearly fell off his chair. He looked at her, trying to judge whether or not she was serious.

"I am not so sure," he said. "I thought I might try to get some better results and then maybe the top teams will be battering down the door."

She laughed. He was cocky, but then he was also right. Chiphurst's record in recent years was not much good and results were all that mattered. Buckett had struggled through poor teams throughout his career and he knew that it could do you more harm than good.

"I think the best way is to come to us, score some decent results, learn the ropes and then move on," she said. "Or you can stay with us if we get better. We are going to have a much better car next year. We've just taken on a new chief aerodynamicist and we are all pretty excited. Our sponsors like the US market so that might be good for both of us. We have faith in you and there are not many folk out there who see what we see. We want your name on a contract. You don't need to bring any money, but you do have to commit to us. If you do that we could run you in the Friday practice on Austin."

Buckett smiled.

"That would be uber-cool," he said.

"What a horrible expression," Maddie said. "Where did you pick that up?"

Jimmy shrugged.

"What are you paying?" he asked.

"We'll pay your expenses, flights in Economy, cars, hotel rooms in hotels which we would book for you. You pay the extras: telephones, minibar, port channel, gym and so on.

"Fair enough," he said. "How much salary?"

She mentioned a suitable figure.

"What about bonuses?"

"Yes," said Maddie. "We will give you money per point and a lump sum if you win the championship."

Buckett laughed out loud.

"Personal sponsors?" he asked.

"Yes, we can make provision for a few small extras."

"Endorsements?" he said.

"Yes, you can do some of that, with our permission."

"I own my own marketing rights?" he asked.

She nodded.

"And sponsor days?" he said.

"We'll be unreasonable," she replied.

He paused for a second.

"Oh, and you will pay fines imposed based on personal misconduct," she added. "We pay if it is our fault."

He nodded.

"I don't see any problem with any of that," he said. "I will sign the deal if it is one hundred percent sure that I race for you next year."

"It will be an option in our favour for a couple of months," Maddie said. "If we take it up, the deal will be solid."

"Yeah, that's fine," said Buckett. "You can take it up any time in that period. Can I have a top team get-out clause?"

"No," said Maddie. "But we don't mind talking about it, if they come and ask you. We don't want to hold you back but we don't want to get dumped at a moment's notice. The deal is a one year plus four with our option each year. You happy with that? We'd tell the media it is a multi-year."

"Fair enough," said Buckett. "That is good for me."

"Works for me too," said Maddie.

They shook hands.

Maddie paused for a moment.

"I'm impressed," she said. "I don't remember seeing a young driver doing his own negotiating. It has been years. Everyone has a manager these days."

"I don't see the point," said Jimmy. "They cost a big percentage and what do they really do? They just talk to people and in the end they do what I want them to do. Why do I need a manager? Once you get hold of a contract, it needs a lawyer anyway. I have a sensible accountant. What else do I need?"

"Someone to hold your hand?" said Maddie.

Buckett laughed.

"You want that job, Cougar?" he said.

They were quiet for a moment and then Jimmy said: "Wow! I just became a Grand Prix driver."

Maddie laughed.

"Not bad for a nineteen-year-old," she said. "I'll buy you a drink. I don't think they will sell you one otherwise."

They had a quick lunch while the team's legal counsel prepared a contract. This was signed at Brize Norton about ninety minutes later and a few minutes after that Maddie was back in the air, bound for Bergamo.

She slept all the way.

By the time she arrived back at Bergamo, it was getting towards the evening. Charlie was already back at the hotel and had ordered his helicopter to go to Bergamo to pick Maddie up.

A few years earlier, Charlie had decided that he hated getting in and out of the Monza circuit and so had told Cheryl to find him a helicopter and a hotel where one could fly to. He probably knew what the result would be. Helicopters took off from a large field between the modern back straight and the original back straight from the 1920s. It was about two hundred metres from the paddock but, as the crowds were always very insistent, walking was not an option, and so they would go by minibus. Once there, they would fly to the Villa d'Este, about twenty-five miles away, on the banks of Lake Como. Fans did not get past the gate there. It cost a fortune, but Charlie did not care and it was always a nice experience.

As she flew there from Bergamo, above Montevecchia, with its strange pyramid-shaped hills, she wondered whether it would be worth once again trying to explain to Charlie that mixing with the fans - even for only five minutes a day - would be a good thing to do. He was not interested and would probably never understand that the race fan is the customer.

The Autodromo Nazionale at Monza is probably the

most evocative racing circuit in the world. It is a place that has everything that a race fan might want: speed, history, ghosts, atmosphere, but above all else, as far as Maddie was concerned, it had passion.

No matter how cynical or jaded one becomes with Formula 1, if you are a fan at heart, Monza is the place to cure any malaise, for there is nowhere on this earth where the joys of going motor racing are as strong. The hopes and dreams of the Ferrari fans always give Maddie a boost of extra energy, although she never ceased to be amazed by the chaos of Italian life. They wander across the street, wearing the latest chic sunglasses and chatting on their mobile phone without ever looking to see if they are about to be mown down by someone wobbling along on a bicycle with a basket filled with vegetables, or a Fiat being driven erratically by a man who looks like an extra from The Godfather.

At every entrance to the Autodromo someone was always arguing that they should be allowed in because their cousin was someone important. It was annoying, but it had all the exuberance and creativity of the Italian nation. There were laws, of course, but no-one ever seemed to pay any attention to them. As a result every Italian Grand Prix weekend was an adventure, if only for the daily trips into and out of the circuit.

"Them fans is all fucking mothers," said Lorenzo di Sustro, when they arrived in the paddock the following morning. "Today one tries to jump on me motorbike. He falls off! I know they are my same nationality, but they is crazy."

It was a relatively dull day, but that evening she was able to chat with some of the engineers, before being whisked off to the Villa d'Este again. What did they think of Grindvall? she asked. How was he doing? The response seemed to be positive. The new car was beginning to look really good. The aero boys were excited at the ideas that he had brought with him. They reckoned the concept was a good one. They talked about drivers and who they would like to see in the cars.

"Not these wankers," said one.

The rest of the weekend was a bit of a blur. Di Sustro and Denso did not do anything wrong, but on such a fast track there was no chance of scoring points. The cars were all so reliable that scoring from the midfield was tough. If the top five teams all finished both cars without drama, no-one else had much of a chance.

The race on Sunday was over quickly and within minutes Charlie was dragging her out of the paddock to get to the chopper. They were at Orio Al Serio for just a few minutes and then they were in the air. By six they were on final approach into Brize Norton. Maddie rang Winslow from the plane. He was on the Kennet and Avon Canal, at the Dundas Arms, near a place called Kintbury.

"I've booked their Secret Garden," he said. "It sounds wildly exotic."

She stopped off at home for five minutes, dumped her bag, picked up some new clothes and departed to find her man. He was waiting with a picnic basket, under a graceful willow tree, where the river and the canal met.

"My car is becoming a mobile wardrobe," she said. "It's not quite knickers in the glove box, but it's heading in that direction."

She was happy to see him, and keen to talk.

"Things are really coming together for next year," she explained. "I've paid you the scam money from my marketing budget. We have a budget meeting coming this week. Charlie has no real interest in it, unless the team is short of cash. So we basically put the numbers in front of him and he signs them off. I'm going to argue with the engineers about research and development and tell them that most of the R&D is coming from inside Grindvall's head (or his computer) and that this is a huge saving. We have a new concept design for free and we need to understand that and get the most from it, before trying to develop it. There's some logic in that and I will tell them that with the new sponsorship deals we need more activation. They don't know what activation is and they don't really care, but I think they will go for my idea. That way everyone will be happy and it will all get signed off.

We're using the marketing budget to pay for engineering and that annoys me, even if they don't know that - and can't know that. It's stolen engineering, but that's not the point. Grindvall is the only one who knows that it is not all his idea, but he does understand that if it works it will make him look very good, so he's happy about that.

"How did you get the data to him, by the way, I completely forgot to ask."

"Do you need to know?" said Winslow.

"Not really," said Maddie, "but you never know. It won't do any harm."

"I used the old library trick," Winslow said. "You get an old cookbook and you use a sharp knife to cut out a hole in the middle of the book. You don't even need to glue the pages. You put a disk or a drive in the hole you have made. I went to Oxford Central Library and put the book in a place here no-one ever looks. They all use the Dewey Decimal system and I use Section 417, historical linguistics. There is not massive demand. Then I sent your man Elfin instructions to look for a cookery book in Section 417, take what is inside and leave the book behind. So he opens the book, finds the memory stick, puts in his pocket and departs. I go back later. It can be days. I make sure there are no odd people hanging about and then I remove the book. He has his data and has no idea from where it came, nor why he has received it. But he doesn't care. If it makes him look good then he's fine with it, he'll go home, look at the stuff, recognize its value and then load it into his computer. He then makes some cosmetic changes in the design, he makes sure that transfers all the data to new files, with a new UUID. That means 'universally unique identifier', which means that every file is different. If he just changes the file names, the UUID stays the same and is traceable. Then he goes to the office, loads his files into your computers. Then all he has to do is throw away the memory stick and his own laptop. If it was me, I'd wipe the thing, put it into a block of concrete and throw it in a river. After that he cannot be caught.

"The Chiphurst boys see his stuff. They all think Grindvall

is a genius."

"I find it amazing that no one will spot the similarities," said Maddie. "I guess these cars all look a bit the same."

"One or two of the engineers may have suspicions," said Winslow, "but they would not be able to explain how it was done. Having high-performance scanners will only give you the external shape and they don't know that the internal design is the same as well. You don't see one team letting another look at the details, do you? So, how would they know?"

Winslow smiled.

"There's always espionage," he said, with ample irony. "Anyway, it is not in anyone's interest to make accusations against their own team, particularly if the car is producing good results. So as long as you keep your mouth shut, it's completely untraceable. In any case, I've got you where I want you. You've taken a kickback, so if you start getting troublesome I can always shop you to Charlie. You cannot prove a word of our story, even if they could find the money. They could not trace it back anyway. There was some obscure offshore bank account that no longer exists. All records are gone. If the police raid my office, all they will find is paperwork backing up my story, all of which has been signed by you."

"Every detail is covered," she said.

"Of course, you build plausible deniability into everything. If they cannot prove it, they cannot convict you, so they won't even charge you."

"Unless I've been recording this conversation," she said, with a smile.

"A good point," he said. "However, for your own protection, I will need to give you an all over body search, just to make sure you don't have any hidden microphones about your person. A girl can easily get killed wearing that sort of stuff."

Maddie pulled herself to her feet, walked across to the nearest tree and put both hands on the trunk. She stuck out her bottom in his direction, spread her legs a little and looked back over her shoulder and said: "I assume this is the position?"

"There are lots of different positions," said Winslow. "We can explore some of them when we get back to Daisybelle later on..."

Back at work the following day, Maddie had plenty of work to do. The Singapore Grand Prix was coming up. F1's first night race had quickly become one of the most important of the season, with the high rollers of Asia all flying in to do business, but it was always a very tiring race for Maddie.

It is an odd affair. The F1 teams never change their time zone and so continue to work on European time, Maddie's internal time clock, which was extremely adaptable thanks to many years on the road, reacts to daylight and so once the sun is up, unless the hotel room had shutters and no light at all can get in, Maddie is awake. All means that even if she goes to bed at six in the morning, as most of the teams do, she would still wake up at eight. You can do that for a few days, but it wears you out.

Early on Saturday morning - it was about two in the morning - the paddock was quiet. She and Charlie sat down in the team hospitality and agreed that it was time to make some decisions about drivers. They had decided that Lorenzo had been given sufficient chances to be an F1 driver. He hadn't made it and his presence did not motivate the team at all.

It was time to put a stop to that.

They pondered about Poppy Denso. He was talented, but seemed to be too a much of a playboy to be focused as an F1 driver needs to be if he wants to fight for the World Championship.

"Do you think you can learn this stuff?" Maddie asked.

"No," said Charlie. "I think you've either got it or you haven't."

"And we don't think he's got it?" she said.

"He hasn't got it," said Charlie. "But, to be fair, there are worse options. We could keep him for another year and see how he does. His money is certainly useful, and he's not an embarrassment. We could keep him, see how he matures and then dump him if he makes no progress."

"And we agree we will take Buckett."

"That seems entirely reasonable," Charlie said.

"OK," said Maddie. "I'll take up Jimmy's option tonight. Are you going to tell Lorenzo?"

Charlie nodded.

"I get all the good jobs," he said.

"Yep," said Maddie. "That's why you get paid the big bucks..."

The following evening, as the teams were coming in for breakfast, before the qualifying began, the team put out a press statement saying that Chiphurst Competition would be having a new driver line-up.

Lorenzo di Sustro was not happy.

"You are bastards," he said. "You don't care shit about nothing. And you replace me with this American school children! It's 'orrible."

In the end, Charlie's patience ran out.

"Sod off now if you don't like it," he shouted. "I don't give a toss. Alternatively, you can try and get a good result and maybe you can get a drive somewhere else next year."

Lorenzo went quiet after that. He did not qualify well, lining up on the grid directly behind Poppy. He left early, not bothering with the usual strategy meetings.

Things were even worse on the Sunday. He was in a thunderous mood and it was clear that something had happened. Rosita was nowhere to be seen. Maddie twice had to tell Lorenzo to moderate his language in front of sponsors. Denso seemed to be finding the whole thing very amusing. What they did not know, until a few weeks later, was that on the Saturday evening Rosita arrived in Poppy's hotel room in a distraught state, having argued with Lorenzo.

Poppy - ever the gentleman - comforted her in the only way he knew how. She felt better after that and sent Lorenzo a text message that said: "Você é um babaca. Vai tomar no cu." This was not polite. She made it worse by adding a couple of kisses to the message, that simply served to enrage him still further.

If he had known that the SMS was being sent from Poppy's bed, Lorenzo would probably have committed murder.

When Maddie asked him what was wrong, Lorenzo explained that Rosita was a "vaca" and that he sincerely hoped, from the very bottom of his heart, that she would go to Hell and burn there for eternity.

There was little Maddie could say.

"The world is full of wild women," she said. "I am sure that you can find one tonight, after the race."

Lorenzo considered the idea for a second, nodded and half-smiled.

A few hours later, the cars lined up on the grid. Poppy had not had sufficient sleep and confused himself with software settings, and so when the lights went out and the field surged away towards the first corner, his Chiphurst went backwards. It was not supposed to be possible to do that, but racing drivers and software engineers are not always a good combination.

Lorenzo, on the other hand, intent on showing his manhood by overtaking his young rival, made a stunning start and accelerated straight into the rear of his reversing team-mate, having no chance at all to swerve left or right. The nose of one car hit the gearbox of the other squarely and Poppy was too busy pressing buttons to notice the impact because at the very moment that the two cars hit, a forward gear in his car engaged and the car jumped forward. The impact was such that Poppy's rear view mirrors fell out, prompting Charlie to remark after the race that perhaps the mechanics might use something other than chewing gum to secure them. Denso thus had no way of looking behind him to see what had happened. In any case, Lorenzo was not there. The impact was such that his suspension broke and he climbed from his car and stalked into the pit lane.

The car had been pushed away by the time the field came back. Lorenzo saw Charlie on the pit wall and reported that his team-mate was "a stupid fuck pig" and left immediately for the airport, hoping to get out of Singapore before the race ended.

Denso was blissfully unaware of all of this. He had a faster car than some of those around him and so he began to make up positions, although it was by no means easy. It never crossed his mind that his team-mate might have had trouble because he had started in reverse.

"I think we need to do some work on the starting thing," Charlie muttered after the race.

Maddie, who had been entertaining guests, had very nearly dropped her drink when the two Chiphurst cars collided, but she soon had the VIPs cheering Poppy's rise through the field and everyone went home happy, although eleventh place was really nothing for Chiphurst to get excited about.

Poppy did not stick around for long after the race. He had something important to do, he said.

He wanted to find Rosita.

Some stayed to party the night away, but Maddie joined the exodus of F1 folk, heading straight to the airport and took a very early morning Emirates flight to Dubai. It got her home to England by midday on Monday. Winslow was waiting for her at the airport, with a bunch of flowers.

"What have you been up to?" she asked, suspicious of a romantic gesture.

She texted Charlie and Cheryl and told them to expect her on Wednesday and spent the whole of Monday afternoon and Tuesday on Daisybelle, making very slow progress. It was a delight to slow down a little and they even found the time for energetic afternoon naps. They were still very much in the honeymoon phase of the relationship and all was very rosy in the garden.

By the Wednesday, news about Rosita had leaked out inside the team and Lorenzo had telephoned to say that either Poppy had to be fired, or he would leave Chiphurst. Charlie yawned into the phone and said, "Fax me your resignation".

He reached for the phone and called Maddie.

"We need Buckett now," he said.

She put down the phone and called Jimmy.

"Hey, Hot Dog, where are you?" she said.

"I'm cruising around," he said, not being very specific.

"Well, cruise that pert little American arse of your's into the factory right now," she said. "We need to do a seat fitting and get some overalls made for you. And we want you in the simulator for the next two days."

"Cougar," he said, "are you kidding me? Is this for real?"

"What is it they say?" she said. "This is not an exercise."

"Well, fuck me," said Jimmy.

"No thanks," she replied. "You're too young. It would feel illegal. I prefer more mature individuals."

If she was being entirely honest, Maddie was glad to see the back of Lorenzo, although she was not at all impressed by what Poppy and Rosita had done to him.

"What could I do?" Poppy protested when called in to face the music. "It was Lady Nature. Fate. Whatever your English thing is. She is a hot girl. I am a hot guy. She likes me. I like her. We both hate him."

Charlie shrugged.

"Men!" he said. "Bastards, the lot of them. Apart from me, obviously."

Maddie and Cheryl had a laugh at that one.

Maddie had never been a girl's girl. She had always preferred the company of men and generally found women to be less appealing. She liked Cheryl. Everyone liked Cheryl. But they were buddies rather than friends. Her only close girlfriend was Katie Looper, her official best friend. Nowadays she was known as Baroness Haig, and used the name Caitlin, but to Maddie she was still Katie Looper.

They had been friends since the day they first met, on their first day at Junior School, at the tender age of eight. The class was arranged in alphabetical order and they were put together. Each morning the roll call was read out: "Lacey, Lacey, Looper, Mezzanotte, Morgan, Murray..." During their teenage years they had shared all their secrets but then, imperceptibly, their lives had begun to drift apart. After school they saw one another less. They stayed in contact with birthday and Christmas cards and occasional phone calls. They met now and then. They were there when the other needed a shoulder to cry on.

Katie had moved to London quite quickly and had married very young - Maddie was the bridesmaid - but the marriage had been short. It was a terrible story. They had gone on holiday to Spain when Katie's husband went for a swim one afternoon, leaving a note that said "Gone for a swim" with a single x beneath the message.

He never came back and his body was never found.

After the initial shock, Katie slowly began to realize that the law was going to ruin her life. She had accepted deep down that her husband would never return, but the law left her in an unhappy limbo. She was stuck in a house that she could not sell, but could not afford to keep. She borrowed money to pay the mortgage, but it would be seven years before her husband could legally be declared "presumed dead", at which point the insurance company would settle the mortgage and she would become the beneficiary of a substantial life insurance policy. Katie had descended into a state of depression, unwilling to get into another relationship.

Ever practical, Maddie had bought her a vibrator for Christmas.

"It's great," Katie had confessed some time later, when they had drunk a little too much rosé. "To begin with, the buzzing was a bit off-putting, but when you get used to the sound, it becomes quite a turn-on. Your subconscious tells you that the noise signals an approaching orgasm and that makes it exciting. The only problem is that you cannot cuddle a vibrator."

Maddie offered to cuddle Katie if that was what she wanted and Katie confessed that a month or two previously, she had been so desperate for human contact that she had joined a gym, hoping to find an available man, but had ended up experimenting with a girl instead. She said that sleeping with a woman didn't feel like she was being unfaithful to her husband. It had been gratifying, but after a couple of passionate sessions, she had concluded that lesbianism was not really her thing.

Maddie giggled.

"You should have called me," she said. "I've always been

curious and we could have both given it a try. Now, you know what it's like and I'm still stuck being vaguely curious."

Katie looked at her, as if considering the idea, but then she turned away, poured another glass of rosé, and said: "I had no idea you were curious."

It went no further. Katie went on living in her strange sexless limbo and waited for the law to tell her that her husband was dead, so that her life could begin again. By the time that happened she was thirty years old. The one bit of good news was that, during her wait, house prices in London had gone completely crazy and so when finally she sold the house she had so much money that she was able to buy a considerable mansion in the Chilterns, with no mortgage at all. She had become a wealthy woman, although most of her generation were by then married and having families. There were no good men left on the market.

One day, Katie was sitting at home, reading a bad book, when there was a knock at the door and a good-looking man with a blue scarf asked her if she might be willing to vote for him in the next General Election. She invited him in for a cup of tea and, after some small talk, they discovered not only that they shared the same political opinions, but that he was single, his last girlfriend having recently run away with a wealthy Russian.

"A very wealthy one," he said.

He confessed that his life felt incomplete without a partner and so she told him her story. Two hours later they were in bed together. She voted Conservative, but was more of a liberal in bed.

Tarquin Haig was elected a Member of Parliament three weeks later, with a landslide victory, which the TV pundits said was largely due to the fact that he always looked so happy. A couple of months later they were married in the Chapel of St Mary Undercroft, in the Houses of Parliament. Maddie was the bridesmaid again.

Katie sold her house and moved into the Haig Family's stately home, a considerable pile known as Tattling Hall, hidden away at the end of a very private driveway, not far from the village of Nettlebed, in Oxfordshire, close to where Maddie and Winslow had enjoyed their bike ride.

Maddie continued to see the happy couple when she could and as soon as she confessed that she might have met a new man, Katie interrogated her about Winslow. She felt that Maddie was so relaxed and happy that this one must be serious.

Thus it was that Maddie and Winslow received an invitation to dine with the Haigs at Tattling Hall on the weekend after the Singapore Grand Prix.

That Saturday evening they made their way through the darkening lanes, as great combine harvesters worked the wheat fields, their headlights ablaze. Finally they reached the lodge house of Tattling Hall, with its gates permanently open. They drove up a long avenue of plane trees, which almost certainly dated from the days of the first Duke of Wellington. Finally, the driveway curled to the left, around a spinney of trees, then dropped down slightly and crossed a low stone bridge, over a stream. The road rose up again and as they crested the rise, they went over a grille. They had entered the deer park. Ahead of them was the hall, pretty with welcoming lights.

The driveway curved elegantly to the right, passing through a small clump of trees, and then swept the left to emerge from the copse at the front of the house.

"Will you look at this place," said Winslow, obviously impressed.

"A bit draughty, I should think," Maddie said.

# Thirteen

There was a time, and a glorious time it was, when the English countryside was a patchwork of large country estates, where Darcys, Bingleys and Wickhams wooed and won their ladies with their gentlemanly manners and their impressive annual incomes. Today, this world is to be found only in novels. Great house after great house has been pulled down and the land, assembled so carefully through the generations, has been sold off, piece by piece. The elegant mansions, their intricate gardens, flooded valleys and deer parks with follies, observatories, mazes and icehouses, have all but disappeared.

Stables and dairies have been converted into offices, trout farms have gone back to nature and boathouses have crumbled to dust. The age of ballrooms, libraries, orangeries and private chapels has passed into history and the gentle pace of village life, with its landed gentry, country clergy and busybodies, is no more.

For this, equality is to blame. The upkeep, requiring dozens of servants, from kitchen maids to butlers, and gamekeepers to gardeners, was only possible when the staff was paid in pennies, in housing and were being fed off the land. As wages rose, so hundreds of these estates became untenable and were broken up, the houses sold, gambled away or burned down for the insurance money. Others fell slowly into ruin.

The thirteenth Baron Haig of Tattling, Tarquin's grandfather, had faced just such a crisis in the 1930s, when his revenues began to fall dramatically behind the expenses. He solved the problem not with a frugal approach, but rather by being ambitious and, mindful of the American love of "class", he travelled to the United States and spent some time mixing with the industrial barons on the golf courses of Pennsylvania.

As a result he married an attractive heiress from one of the steel towns. Her fortune allowed the Haigs to purchase an impressive portfolio of property in Central London, while her family benefited socially from its new-found aristocratic connections.

The rents from the London estates meant that the Haigs were able to go on living at their splendid and much-loved Tattling Hall, the Georgian manor house, hidden away in its own valley in the Chilterns. The mansion was just a small part of a thousand-acre estate with extensive beech groves on either side of the valley and highly productive farmland beyond that. The farms continue to operate, but have switched from mass production techniques to the more lucrative organic methods, which allows the farm shops to do a roaring trade in fruit, vegetables, jams and marmalades, hams and sausages and even some baked goods, postcards and, ironically, wistful books about old English country estates that have long since disappeared.

The many estate cottages and the converted stables and dairy add to the revenues and the Haigs live well, without needing to burden themselves with going to work in the mornings. Thus Tarquin was able to busy himself with politics, while his father, the fourteenth Baron, inspired by Daphne du Maurier's novel Rebecca, set off to Cornwall, in search of his own Manderley and duly settled there, where the weather was kinder and the daffodils bloomed early.

Tarquin was left to run Tattling Hall.

"To be quite honest," Winslow admitted, one night while lying in bed, "I haven't got a clue about the English

168 - Maddie Midnight

aristocracy. I can tell lords from ladies, but beyond that I have no idea."

"Well, if you forget the royals," Maddie said, playing with a solitary grey hair on Winslow's chest, "it's really not that complicated. You have dukes, marquesses, earls, viscounts and barons, in that order. We don't have counts and countesses. They're foreign. So these five ranks are what we call the peers. They are different to baronets and knights. In the case of baronets, the title passes from one generation to the next, but knighthoods do not, but you call them all "Sir", so that is pretty easy.

"Peers are a bit more complicated. The person with the title is the peer; his family are members of the aristocracy. The titles are almost always connected to places, so Tarquin's father is Baron Haig of Tattling. He could also be known as Lord Haig, but if he were a Viscount he'd be Lord Tattling. Got it? Tarquin has no title until his father dies.

"It only gets complicated when it comes to the children. The eldest sons of dukes, marquesses and earls have what we call courtesy titles, also belonging to their fathers. This is why the Marquess of Celery can become the Duke of Halibut overnight, if his father dies. This means that you can have a pair of earls, one called "the Earl of Toothpaste" and the other "Earl Toothpaste". The latter would be the first son of a marquess, the 'the' tells you the difference in their rank. The younger children are lords and ladies, but they can only use their actual names, like Lord Peter Wimsey, so as not to be confused with peers. Got it?"

Winslow sighed.

"That is as clear to me as the rules of cricket," he said mournfully. Maddie laughed.

"You call Tarquin Tarquin until I tell you to call him 'My Lord.' Got it?"

"Got it."

Winslow had this in mind as they were ushered into the Hall by the butler. They passed a splendid stone staircase that was lit by a cupola, before joining the rest of the party in the drawing room.

"The twelfth baron gave instructions that anyone who did not reply when accosted on the property at night should be shot," Tarquin was saying. "Alas, one dark night he was out walking, failed to respond to a call and was gunned down by his own gamekeeper."

The audience tittered at this misfortune.

Tarquin and the handsome Katie came over to greet them and after handshakes, pecks and hugs, began to introduce them to the other guests.

Tarquin was the sort of "chap" that one can only find in England. At Eton he had been the hero of the fifth form, a charging force on a rugby field and a stylish cricketer. He thought the best of everyone.

Katie certainly impressed Winslow. She was quite beautiful, he thought, her blonde hair was cut short, and framed her face perfectly. She was vivacious without being loud, stylish without being pretentious and she fitted with Tarquin. Her long black dress and diamond earrings were perfect. He sensed her sizing him up, with just a quick flash of her eyes.

When dinner was announced they went through a magnificent oval room to the panelled dining room, which Tarquin said opened on to a sunken walled garden. It was too dark to see. At the dinner table Winslow had been carefully seated next to the hostess and across the table from a man called John de Vane, who was even more of an Adonis than Tarquin. He had slicked-down hair and greedy eyes and said he was "in television".

He was thoroughly enjoying the attention being paid to him by Katie, although he had come to the party with a blonde called Estelle. She would have been a bright young thing had she been bright, but she had little to say for herself beyond an obvious love for horses. She was better suited to Wellingtons than to ball gowns.

She was sitting on Winslow's right, across the table from a girl called Temperance, who had none of the style nor class of Estelle. Temperance had very big teeth and a rather weak chin and, as she drank more and more, she began to exhibit an alarming tendency to shriek a little too loudly when laughing. She was the partner of a man called Bellows, who was the heir to a biscuit fortune and was sitting to Estelle's right. The name made Winslow chuckle as it summed up its owner in two different ways. He was full of air AND talked too loudly. He was a broker of Eton stock who had been a couple of years senior to Tarquin. He took great pleasure, and far too much time, recounting how he had once caught Tarquin smoking and had him rusticated.

"Of course," he barked at one point, "I don't ra-a-rely have to work, but one needs a challenge in life, doesn't one?"

As the evening moved on Bellows's volume gradually reduced and by the time coffee was served he was smiling benignly, almost wistfully, across the table at a man called Max Wysocki who, Tarquin had said, was a Polish prince and who did "stuff in finance".

"It's quite difficult being Polish," Max said with a flawless Berkshire accent. "I have to be M-A-X because no one can spell Maksymilian - with a 'k' and a 'y'."

"Well, at least you don't have any silent 'z's like most Polish people," said Maddie.

It did not take Maddie long to grab the bull by the horns and ask the obvious question: "Are you really a Prince? Should we be calling you 'Your Highness' or something?"

Max smiled, as though he enjoyed answering the question.

"In Poland," he said, "there are many Princes and Princesses. I read somewhere that in the Eighteenth Century there was a census and this revealed that in a population of seven million, there were seven hundred and twenty-five thousand aristocrats."

Temperance shrieked with glee. It was a ghastly noise, a little like a horse being put down.

Maddie concluded very early in the dinner that Bellows and Temperance were not her kind of people and she understood from looks flashing around the table that she was not alone in this assessment.

Maddie was not much interested by de Vane and Estelle, while Max seemed amusing enough. The only guest who really sparked her interest was the girl called Izzie, sitting across the table from her, between Max and Tarquin. Initially she thought that Izzie must be Max's girlfriend, as she was very much the kind of woman that a financier would love to have on his arm. What intrigued Maddie were the looks that flew between Izzie and Katie. They clearly knew each other well. Izzie's body language told her that she had little real interest in Max. Maddie was aware that as much as she was studying Izzie, Izzie was studying her.

They were of the same basic build and wore the same style of black dress. Maddie's wavy auburn locks were very different to Izzie's short dark hair. This drew the attention to her extraordinary grey-green eyes, that sparkled more than they should, and always seemed to be laughing mischievously.

She wore almost no make-up, just a hint of dark eye-liner.

Maddie searched for the right word to describe the haircut and concluded that the only description that came close was "pixie". It was boyish, yet somehow incredibly feminine at the same time. Maddie recognised it was a haircut which required a lot of self-confidence.

There was something about her that seemed familiar to Maddie, but she could not quite pin it down. It emerged in the course of the meal that Izzie worked as Tarquin's assistant at Westminster and was, to use his expression, "a bit of a laser beam when it comes to the old intellect".

Izzie did not say a great deal early in the evening, allowing others to have their moment in the spotlight, but gradually she emerged from her shell. Maddie felt an immediate affinity, although she was not quite sure why.

The dinner was a great success, the venison in particular being flawless and tender. In the course of the meal Maddie had time to study the other end of the table and was delighted to see that Winslow and Katie were getting along well. To keep him amused Katie had given him a very quiet and completely uncensored run down on the other guests, memorably pointing out that Temperance was rumoured to be "an absolute tiger in the sack", which was good news for Bellows because he was such an ass that without money he might struggle to find a woman willing to be his partner.

As the evening progressed Temperance quietened down. Her orchid, once gloriously vulgar, became limp and her designer dress was splashed with tiny wine spots, most of which by some miracle of physics seemed to have come from Bellows's mouth. She did not seem to mind. He would buy her another.

It was unfortunate for Maddie that she had Bellows on her left, but having Tarquin next to her at the end of the table enabled her to gradually escape from the biscuit baron and, by the end of the evening, she was in lively discussion with Tarquin and Izzie. This began with a discussion about urban foxes and the need to restore fox-hunting, despite the protests of those described by Tarquin as the "daft do-gooders".

"Where are the defenders of our poor chickens?" he said. "Have you ever seen what foxes do in a hen house? It's shocking. It makes Colonel Sanders look like an angel."

They then fell to discussing the slipping standards of behaviour in British society, particularly when it came to politeness, table manners and etiquette. These days, it seemed, everything was allowed, if you had money.

"Standards are so important," Izzie said, "but people seem to have lost track of that. I do think we need to try and build a better society, based on stronger social structures and the family unit. Equality and social mobility are fine as long as we have morals and manners, but money, nor class come to that, should excuse bad manners and poor morals. I am not sure if it is down to poor schooling or bad parenting, but I think that one key element is that families have stopped having meals around the table, as they used to do. I was reading somewhere that these days almost half the families in England do not eat dinner together in the evenings. Today people eat watching the TV or playing on computers. I think that's terrible. Eating dinner together is really important for family cohesion."

By the time coffee was served Bellows was entirely silent, his eyes glazed over in an alcoholic haze, and the focus had switched to Izzie and Maddie, who were vigorously debating the value of the BBC World Service.

"I love Maddie," Katie whispered to Winslow. "She's so feisty. So clever. And Izzie is very passionate and intelligent too. They have a lot in common."

Aside from jousting with Tarquin and Izzie, Maddie was happy to watch Winslow dealing with de Vane, Estelle, Temperance and the Polish Prince. He seemed at ease with the girls, but she got the very clear impression he was not very keen on either de Vane or Max. It was almost imperceptible, but Maddie knew Winslow quite well and she could see from the way that he narrowed his eyes that he did not like Max. She wondered why. She also got the feeling that the two men already knew one another.

"No," Winslow said on the way home, "I don't know him at all, but I recognise the type. He was too slick for me, you can bet that he is some kind of a crook."

"Well you two should have a lot in common then," Maddie laughed.

Winslow was not on any position to argue that one...

"Who was that lovely creature across the table from you?" he asked. "You two seemed to be getting on very well."

"Her name is Izzie," Maddie said. "She's so clever, so fresh and so beautiful. Did you see her eyes? I was jealous."

"I've always found clever women to be very exciting," Winslow said.

"Even if they're ugly?" said Maddie.

"Well, within reason," he said. "Obviously they need to have the right body parts in the right places, without anything missing or being so huge as to be off-putting. No moustaches nor mono-brows. I also draw the line at girls with humpbacks. They cannot lie down properly..."

"Winslow, that's terrible," said Maddie, pretending to be shocked.

"We should have Izzie over for dinner some time," he said. "I'd like to get to know her. You know, look deeply into those deep green pools..."

It was very late when they got back to Daisybelle, which was by then moored down near Bath. They had a very lazy

Sunday morning.

"When you are away I'm going to take the old girl down to Avonmouth and we are going to go out into the Severn Estuary and up to where the river begins. You have to get a pilot to do that, but it will be fun and it means that I can then go up the River Avon to Stratford and join up with the Grand Union there."

On the Monday morning Maddie drove to Birmingham and flew off to Dubai, changing planes to fly on to Tokyo. It's a long flight and the time difference is against you, so if you leave on a Monday, you don't arrive in Tokyo until the Tuesday evening. She had a meeting planned on the Wednesday and would then head down to Suzuka by train on the Thursday morning.

A chauffeur with white gloves and a sign that read: "Maderaine Mezzanotte" met her at Narita Airport. He bowed, handed her a mobile phone that made some very strange noises, and they set off to Tokyo in a Nissan Cedric of dubious vintage. They were soon stuck in a huge traffic jam. It was morning back in England and so Maddie spent the trip on the phone, checking to see that all was running smoothly back at base. She had a quiet dinner all alone.

The next morning she presented herself at the offices of the Yutaka-Genkin machine tool company and spent the morning making a presentation. It was quickly clear to her that Yutaka-Genkin was not going to come up with the six million dollars that Chiphurst was pitching them for. They might supply a few free CNC machines, but that was it. Maddie returned to the hotel. She considered going shopping, but did not have the energy and so walked to the Imperial Palace and wandered around the gardens for a while.

Having a chauffeur is all well and good, but the long trek out from Tokyo to Nagoya, followed by a run down the coast to Shiroko, is not a journey that one takes in a car, if you can avoid it. It may seem odd, but a lot of F1 people travel by train in Japan. It's just easier. The trains are far less confusing than the roads. They are almost always on time and so you know where to get off. The precise time is printed on the ticket. All you need to be able to do is to navigate your way through Japanese stations - which is no mean achievement.

In Japan they are experts at fitting a lot into the smallest possible space and that means that their stations are often wildly complicated, because unlike Europe, where the stations are generally spread out in two dimensions, with tracks parallel to one another, in Japan stations are three-dimensional, with tracks on different levels. It is not even that simple in Tokyo, where the main station has numerous levels and two distinct sides, which only connect to one another on certain floors. One can be lost there for hours.

Maddie knew her way around. She was booked on a Nozumi Super Express bullet train at seven thirty in the morning, from Tokyo to Nagoya. If all went to plan, she would arrive at the Suzuka circuit in the late morning.

She was just drifting off to sleep when her phone rang. It was Cheryl. She apologized for the timing, but it was an emergency. She needed to ask Maddie for a favour. Could she look after Buckett and get him to Suzuka. He was new to Japan.

"Get him to my hotel at six thirty and I'll get him to Suzuka," she said. "If he's late, I will be gone."

Thankfully, Jimmy was there when Maddie emerged from the lift the next morning. He was excited, but admitted that he was completely out of his depth.

"This place is tough, Cougar," he said. "I mean, it's really an alien environment. I saw that movie *Lost in Translation* and this feels just like that.

"It's a lot easier than it used to be," Maddie said. "Being a European in Japan is frustrating, but there is always lots of laughter to offset the pain. It is not a country geared to outsiders. They used to call us all "aliens", but now we have been downgraded to foreigners. I used to like being an alien."

The trip itself proved to be uneventful. Jimmy was asking questions all the way. He still said "cool" far too often, but he was good company. Once they reached Nagoya, they found their way through the many tunnels in the station to the Kintetsu Line and took a Limited Express to Shiroko. A limited express is the fastest way of getting from A to B because the "limited" does not apply to the speed, but rather to the number of stops. Thus, according to Japanese logic, a limited express is faster than an express.

From Shiroko Station, it was just a short taxi ride to the Suzuka Circuit Hotel. Maddie was happy to be there. She told Buckett how to get to the paddock and told him she would meet him there. She went to her room, stripped naked and spent fifteen minutes wandering around. She then had a shower, dressed again, putting on her Chiphurst team uniform and headed out, walking through the racing-themed amusement park that they called Motopia, and then through the tunnel to get to the paddock. The Japanese fans are amongst the most enthusiastic and informed in the world and although being in Japan can sometimes be a little strange, one is always able to pick up a little of their energy.

In the paddock all was quiet. Charlie had not yet arrived. The team was ready to go and Maddie spent the afternoon drinking coffee and chatting with whoever came by. With a new driver, the team had a lot of visits from the media, particularly as some of them were trying to stir up controversy about Jimmy's age. The appearance of Poppy with Rosita at his side also caused some comment, but no-one in the media made the connection between this and Lorenzo's departure. It was better that way. The coverage for Chiphurst was generally positive. A new driver usually gives a team hope that things will improve.

The practice sessions on Friday were a baptism of fire for Buckett and he ended his first day in F1 a fair way behind Denso. It would be a good test to see if he could keep cool.

It was only a short walk back to the hotel and Maddie was considering the idea of going to the Japanese style spa, but by the time she had dealt with all her e-mails there was no time and she and Charlie went straight to dinner. It may seem crazy to go to Japan and eat Italian food, but that was what Charlie wanted to do.

On the Saturday, Buckett did a great job and qualified

twelfth, two places ahead of Poppy. The Brazilian was shaken and told his engineers that it was all Rosita's fault, because she had kept him up all night. New girlfriends, he shrugged, it is always like that...

Maddie knew how he felt. Being with Winslow was a great pleasure, but she did not sleep nearly as much as she had been doing when she was a single woman.

It was raining on Sunday morning, which promised to make things interesting as Jimmy had never driven an F1 car in the wet. The rules allowed for an extra session because practice has been dry and he soon began to find his feet. Poppy was well aware of the need to do better than the newcomer and was so determined to do a better job that he spun off on the second lap. When the race ended Jimmy was twelfth. It had been a polished and confident performance, but as things were getting exciting in the battle for the World Championship, his achievement was largely overlooked.

There was no time to worry about it. The teams had to get everything packed up as quickly as possible as they had to race in Russia the following weekend. There was not a minute to waste. While the team would go straight to Sochi on a charter flight from Nagoya, on the Monday night, there were other choices for the drivers and the management. They could rush off on Sunday night and fly back to Britain for a couple of days at home, before going out to Moscow and changing planes to get to Sochi. Or they could go to Tokyo for a couple of days, before flying to Istanbul, from where there was a plane each day to Sochi.

Charlie was not keen on going to Russia at all. He did not like the look of Vladimir Putin and felt that it was unwise for F1 to be going there, but he knew that his absence would be noted and concluded that the best thing to do was to arrive late and leave early.

Thus he and Maddie went home and planned to fly to Russia on the Thursday. In order to make it worthwhile they needed to be out of Japan on the Sunday night and so they arranged for a chauffeur to take them directly from Suzuka to Osaka Kansai Airport, as soon after the race as possible.

There was a late night flight to Dubai and from there they could get flights and be home by lunchtime on Monday.

It is only a hundred or so miles from Suzuka to Osaka, but the idea of driving themselves at night in Japan was more than Maddie or Charlie could stomach. The alternative was not without stress, however, as the driver, complete with spotless white gloves, steadfastly refused to drive above the speed limit, which was indicated by an irritating electronic chime. By the time they got to the bridge that links Kansai International Airport to the mainland, Maddie was having to stop Charlie from strangling the poor man. Fortunately, they arrived at the terminal before that happened and it was not long before they were fast asleep aboard the plane, winging across the world to Dubai.

When Maddie touched down in Birmingham she called Winslow.

"I am at your house," he said, with a giggle. "I broke in, but you would never know it. I didn't leave a mark. Get down here and I'll have dinner ready when you get in."

"It is not dinner time," she said, puzzled by the remark.

"It is in Japan, and I am sure your body is still functioning on Japanese time."

Maddie could not argue with that logic. She would be very happy to have a home-cooked meal and to have a little attention as well.

When she arrived Winslow poured her a very large glass of red wine, and she pulled herself up on to the top of a kitchen cabinet, crossed her legs and watched Winslow cooking. She liked a man who knew his way around a kitchen. When the meal was over and the washing up done, Winslow suggested a walk and Maddie was reminded that it was not actually bedtime as her body was telling her.

The air was cool outside. Autumn had arrived. Maddie did not mind. It was the season that she liked the most. There was something wonderful after the way the world turned golden and knuckled down to prepare for winter. She loved the old traditions and the evenings when one wanted to come home to a hot soup or a solid shepherd's pie. The harvest festivals of years gone by have largely been kidnapped by the church although some big farms still host suppers to celebrate the end of the harvest. In the village of Netherington someone had hit on the idea of a harvest supper as a way of getting residents to know one another better. It was a great idea and Maddie wanted to be involved. She loved Halloween, Guy Fawkes and even celebrated Thanksgiving if given half a chance.

This year, she thought, I'll have Thanksgiving with Winslow and Jimmy...

Maddie was content. Life was better than good. With Winslow, with money and with an exciting future, it all looked very positive. She was happy - and she knew it. What else could she possibly want? She had no biological urges to be a mother. It just did not seem to be for her.

She had sent Izzie an e-mail from Japan, inviting her to dinner, and a reply had come back saying that it would be "delightful". Tarquin and Katie were not available that evening and, after a discussion with Winslow about inviting Max the Polish Prince to make up a foursome, they decided that it would be more relaxing to have just the three of them, if Izzie was happy with that. Maddie sent a second e-mail, explaining the situation and asking whether she minded it being "a very informal affair". Izzie replied that she had enjoyed her conversations with Maddie very much and would be more than happy not to have others interrupting.

Maddie thought it might be best to invite Izzie not only to dinner, but also to stay over, so that they could all drink as much as they wanted to and the evening would be even more relaxed as a result.

"I am afraid that my place does not have a deer park," she wrote, "but the village does boast a stream, with tadpoles, and we do have a bus stop. There is even a pub!"

Izzie wrote back declaring the plan to be "a thoughtful and sensible idea" and it was all set for the weekend after the Russian Grand Prix, before Maddie and the Chiphurst team went off to the race in Austin, Texas.

Before that, however, they had to get through the Russian GP weekend. On paper, Sochi seemed like an interesting place. The town was situated where the Caucasus Mountains meet the Black Sea. It has a little of the same feeling as the Côte d'Azur, except the beaches are black and the water cold, but very blue. Inland from the coast are mountains, where one can ski and between the beaches and the ski slopes there is a land of vineyards and orchards.

Sochi was chic back in the Communist days, with Stalin having built a dacha in the area, carefully disguised in case of bombing raids. He had encouraged the construction of health spas, known as sanatoriums, where well-behaved Soviet citizens were sent for their holidays.

Putin had wanted to develop Sochi as a world class year-round resort and so had, at vast expense, encouraged a bid for the Winter Olympic Games. The F1 race came along in an effort to use the same facilities, the track running around the buildings in the Olympic Park, and the F1 visitors staying in the former Olympic Village.

As a result they had no sense of being in the real Russia. The circuit was fine and the teams were able to feed themselves in the F1 paddock, but for most of the F1 fraternity it was a question of getting through the weekend and getting in and out as quickly and painlessly as possible.

Buckett and Denso qualified thirteenth and fourteenth - a fairly unexciting result - and in the race they made little progress and finished eleventh and thirteenth.

Getting out of Sochi on the Sunday night was not easy, the best option being an Aeroflot flight at five in the morning on Monday. This arrived in Moscow at around eight, and a connecting flight would get them to London by eleven. No-one likes a flight at five o'clock, because it means minimal or no sleep.

"Hey Cougar," Jimmy said after the race. "What are you doing tonight?"

"No idea," Maddie replied. "What do you have in mind?"

"A load of vodka and some raunchy sex?" Buckett said, with a smile.

"They won't serve you," she fired back, "but thanks for the inspiring offer. I'll give it a miss."

"How about dinner then?" he shrugged.

"That's a far nicer idea," Maddie said. "I think I might enjoy that. You can count me in."

They spent an agreeable evening together, discussing a range of subjects which Maddie never thought she would talk about with any racing driver. There was no point in going to bed and so they pushed on into the night. They were joined at two in the morning by a monosyllabic Charlie and they then headed to the airport. They were back in London in time for lunch - and happy to be there.

Maddie went straight home and Winslow came to see her that evening. They spent a pleasant week seeing one another each night, either at the house or on the boat.

"If this goes on," he said, "we're going to have to move in together somewhere."

She raised an eyebrow. Winslow Davenport was suggesting such a thing. Whatever next?

At work, the factory was humming with activity. The team had given up developing the current car and was concentrating all of its time and money on Elfin Grindvall's new CC15.

# Fourteen

Winslow had decided that for their dinner party with Izzie he would make his "exceptional and very evil" mulled wine. This, he reasoned, would warm them up and make them merry, even if it was a sombre October evening, something which is quite likely in England at this time of year.

Maddie spent several hours on Saturday afternoon, tidying up the spare bedroom upstairs, so Izzie would not have to sleep with Maddie's rarely-used bicycle and a bunch of filing boxes, filled with fifteen-year-old bank statements, which she somehow could not convince herself to throw away.

In the end the room looked fairly welcoming and she hoped Izzie would feel at home. She wondered what kind of home Izzie had grown up in, and what she would think of the cottage. Maddie was like that, always worried that things were not quite good enough.

As the darkness descended on the village, they lit a fire and by the time the doorbell bell rang, the house was toasty and warm and filled with delicious cooking smells. It felt like a home, which it rarely had before. Maddie showed Izzie up to the room so she could leave her travelling bag and "freshen up" and then waited downstairs in front of the fire until their guest appeared.

Izzie looked neat and tidy, fit and healthy. Maddie had

forgotten how attractive she was, with her bright green eyes blazing out at the world.

Maddie handed her a glass of the mulled wine.

"This stuff's lethal," she said.

"Good," said Izzie.

While Winslow worked his magic in the kitchen, the two girls did a quick tour of the house, as one does on such occasions, and then they settled down in front of the fire.

"It's not very grand," Maddie said.

"No, it's lovely," said Izzie. "I wish I had a place like this. I live in a pretty small flat in London. I'd much prefer the open air feeling in the country. I love fresh air. It feels good to be here."

"Where are you from?" Maddie asked. "I realised this morning that we really don't know very much about you. We didn't really get around to that, did we?"

Izzie told her story. It was exceptional and yet at the same time rather undramatic. Born in the village of Iver, which was then becoming a suburb of London, she was the daughter of the local bank manager, at a time when banks still had such people, before the invention of the call centre. Her mother had been a housewife, like so many of her generation, but she had started working as a secretary when Izzie went away to school. They needed additional money to help pay the school fees.

The family would not normally have sent Izzie to private school, but she was deemed to be an exceptional child and her parents had been encouraged to apply for a scholarship at Wycombe Abbey, one of the top girls schools in the country. The scholarship was worth about half the fees, and once she had won a place, her parents scrimped and saved, sold off family heirlooms and borrowed money in order to ensure that Izzie would be able to complete her education.

It was a school where the emphasis was on academic excellence and there were exceptional facilities, which allowed the girls to try new things and find out where their talents lay.

"It was great," said Izzie. "I realised it was stupid to be a rebel and waste the opportunity, so I did everything I could that did not cost extra money. I learned to dance, I read book after book after book. I did all the sports that I liked doing. I even know how to sword fight. I worked as hard as I could. I knew the sacrifices that my parents were making for me and I really wanted to do well. The one down side was that it was very protected from the real world, so I was really a rather innocent young girl, if you know what I mean."

Maddie nodded.

Izzie had gone on to win a place at Oxford to study Philosophy, Politics and Economics (PPE) and spent the next three years still working hard, but managing to develop a few more social skills as well. The PPE course is a classic route for aspiring politicians, but she was never interested in going down that path.

"I really didn't know what I wanted to do," she said, "so I applied for a thing called a Kennedy Scholarship and went off to study politics at Harvard. That was brilliant, they paid for all the tuition, gave me money to live on and even helped me with airfares and travel within the US. When I came back to the UK, I started working as a political researcher. It is not a boring job. You do everything from making coffee and writing speeches, to telling whopping great lies to the media. You need to be able to turn your hand to pretty much everything."

Maddie listened intently. She had not really thought about it, but she realised that Izzie was still very young.

"Maybe one day I'll decide that I want to become a Member of Parliament, but I don't know," Izzie said. "Maybe I will marry a lord and produce lots of baby lords and ladies. Who knows?

"I spent too much time studying and not enough time learning how to have relationships," she concluded. "But don't worry, I like small bedrooms in unpretentious houses. I grew up in a bedroom just like that, so I will be very happy."

At that moment, Winslow arrived and, with a flourish, declared that the ladies must go immediately to the kitchen table. They laughed and followed his orders. The meal was brilliant: a great chunk of roasted lamb, laced with garlic, with steaming hot vegetables and gravy to die for. This was followed by a delicate chocolate tart that Izzie had brought with her from London. Even the French would have liked it. Having gorged themselves, they returned to the sitting room and settled down, with the fire crackling quietly.

"This is so nice," Izzie said, stretching out in the armchair. Winslow noted, guiltily, that she had long and rather well-shaped legs.

"I work too much," she said. "I sometimes forget about the real world and how to relax. Tarquin and Katie are always inviting me to things and I am pretty sure they both want me to meet someone, but it feels like they are pushing men in my direction, like that Max bloke. The Polish prince. I'm not really bothered. I just want to have some fun and some exotic - and erotic - experiences. I don't really even define what those should be. I just let things happen and go with the flow. It can be interesting - and a bit weird sometimes."

"What do you mean?" Maddie said.

"The world of politics has some pretty extreme people," Izzie said. "I guess we are all a bit weird, but some of them are really out there. There are always love affairs going on, and not always involving women. Sex is a weird thing, isn't it? It is much more complicated than just missing your wife, or whatever. I guess it is about power most of all. That's what I think, anyway. These powerful men want to feel powerful - or in some cases powerless - in their private lives. They want to dominate or be dominated.

"We interns and office assistants are the primary targets for lecherous MPs who have flats in Dolphin Square. You know, they tell the wife that they are busy doing committee work, but they want sex that they can't get at home. They want to be spanked, or to spank you. They want to tie you up, dress you up as a nanny or a nurse, or a policewoman. You name it."

"Really?" said Maddie.

"I try to avoid that scene," Izzie said. "I don't really want to end up in the newspapers as some twisted politician's mistress. I'm better than that.

"But I live in Dolphin Square. It is all around me, although you don't ever really see your neighbours. It is quite anonymous. You can keep yourself to yourself. It is a huge place. And it's a nice easy walk to Parliament."

"So what is your social life like?" asked Maddie.

Izzie laughed.

"My social life?" she said. "I'll go to a pub sometimes on my own on the way home. That's about it. You meet all kinds of people in that neighbourhood: randy politicians, spooks from MI5, people up from the country, tourists. Sometimes I go home to bed with one of them. That's my social life. I suppose you'd call that promiscuous, but I feel that I am catching up for all those years when I studying. I don't want responsibility and commitment, I just want to have fun and get laid."

"That's a rather manly attitude," said Winslow.

"True," said Izzie, "but I guess I am not really the norm. I'm certainly not your average homemaker. I am definitely more of the hunter type. At least at the moment."

"It's ironic given our conversation the other night about how society needs morality, families and relationships" said Maddie.

"I did mean it," Izzie said. "I do think we need to create a more cohesive society, but in the end, we have to do what works for us as individuals, don't we? Society is changing all the time, you tend to have times when people are more promiscuous and then the pendulum swings back and they all become prudish again."

"You mean it is changing right now?" said Maddie.

"I get that impression," Izzie said. "But you might not notice if you don't really embrace the social scene. It seems to me that people these days are more willing to experiment than they ever used to be. If you think about it, we've seen a lot of changes in the last hundred years.

"After the First World War, in the 1920s, there was definitely a new kind of woman. She smoked, she drank, she danced, and she voted. She cut her hair short, wore make-up and I suspect that some of them did quite a lot more than that. If you think about it, it's not really surprising. If you were an aristocrat or in the middle classes about half the men - the officers - had been killed. There were not enough good ones to go around. It was terrible and I guess that women became more promiscuous, if only to try to get themselves a man. Those who didn't either went the other way and slept with the working classes, in the finest tradition of Lady Chatterley, or they became lesbians and moved to France."

Maddie laughed.

"Things them seemed to quieten down in the 1930s and 1940s," Izzie went on. "There was the Great Depression and the war, although I think there was a fair bit of sex going on in the war years, because people were worried about dying young and were away from their families, but it wasn't like the First World War. The scale of human destruction, at least for the British, was much less. After the war the country was up to its neck in debt and the economy was a mess and so it was not until the mid-Fifties that things really got going. And I think it came from the States with Little Richard and then Elvis, but it was still three or four years before Britain started down that path and the whole sexual revolution did not kick off until the mid-1960s, when the kids who did not remember the war began to really express themselves. It was pretty much anything goes after that, but there were still a lot of taboos.

"But I sense change now. I was reading a survey recently - a scientific one, rather than in Cosmo - which said that sixty percent of women had admitted that they were sexually attracted to other women and fifty percent of them said that they had same-sex sexual fantasies. It also said that forty-five percent of women admitted to kissing another woman.

"Really?" said Winslow. "That's a lot."

"Did they try to explain why?" said Maddie.

"Yeah, they think that they understand," Izzie said. "Like most academics, they have theories, but I'm not sure they are backed up with much in the way of fact. They think that more and more women are encouraged to have support networks of girlfriends, you know the whole 'Sex and the City' girl group thing. Women have always been more affectionate than men. Society says it is fine for girls to be friends with girls and it is all very touchy-feely. I think they believe that this has been spilling over into physical relationships. Maybe it was always like that, but in the old days there was a lot more stigma and being 'queer' required a lot more courage, so there was less of it happening and what there was tended to be hidden."

"That all makes sense," said Maddie.

"And let's face it," Izzie added, "There is the aesthetic side to it as well. Naked men always make me laugh with all their dangling bits and bobs. Women are nicer to look at, nicer to touch. They are softer and they are definitely more sensual."

"I'd agree with that," said Winslow.

"So these days, the whole thing has become not only more visible, but also less scandalous," she continued. "And as a result of that more girls think they'll try it, to see what it's like, without fear of the repercussions. I wouldn't say it was exactly normal, but a lot of women have tried it. And of course men love that idea. It's the classic male fantasy, isn't it?"

Winslow nodded.

"Well, I haven't done it," said Maddie.

"Maybe," said Izzie, "but I bet you've fantasized about it a few times."

"I have!" said Winslow.

Izzie smiled. "I have too."

"Yeah," Maddie admitted, "me too. I have to admit that I am sort of curious about what it would be like. But I'm really not sure I want to try. I think it's a bit dangerous. Did you ever do it?"

Izzie nodded. She was not shy about it.

"I was like you," she said. "I was curious and I figured that I should give it a try before it was too late. I was a member of a gym near where I was living at that time. I was going there some evenings, working out, getting sweaty. Then one evening I saw this really lovely woman. She was beautiful and sexy. We started talking and it seemed that she was pretty curious as well. Anyway, I definitely had a girl-crush on her. So one evening we went out for some drinks, let our inhibitions go and ended up at my place, experimenting. We were learning as we went along, but it seemed to work all right. It was good. Very good. We did it a few times after that, but then she confessed that the whole girl love thing wasn't enough for her. She wanted - needed - what men had to offer and she wasn't really satisfied with what we could do together. So we stopped doing it.

"A year or two after that I started working for Tarquin and moved up to London, so I didn't see her again, which I thought was probably a good idea. I went back to being a bit more normal. I still liked female company sometimes, but men were just as good. And then one day Tarquin comes into the office and says: 'Hey, I'm getting married next week. I'd really like you to come to the wedding'. I worked with him, but didn't really know him socially and I thought he was just being polite, but I got myself a silly hat and I was there in the chapel under Westminster, all dressed up."

"I was the bridesmaid" said Maddie.

"Yes I remember," said Izzie. "You looked very pretty. It was a nice wedding, wasn't it? Anyway, there we all were and the bride came in on her father's arm and I nearly fell off my chair. It was her! Katie, my friend from the gym. And she was marrying my boss..."

"It was you!" said Maddie. "Katie told me the story, but she didn't say who it was."

"Wow!" said Winslow. "Now that's a pretty wild story. What did you do?"

"She didn't see me until after the ceremony, at the reception. It was probably better that way. Tarquin introduced us and it really was a delicious moment. She was completely surprised. She just stared at me with her eyes wide and then they filled with laughter. We shared our secret without saying anything. We didn't tell Tarquin. It didn't seem right to do that, particularly not on his wedding day!"

"Did you ever tell him?" asked Maddie.

Izzie shook her head.

"I suppose we should have done..."

"Do you two...?" Maddie asked.

"No," said Izzie. "We've not done it again. I've wondered some times if Tarquin would like it, if we all got together, but I think he's probably a bit strait-laced for that. Not to mention the rather important fact that he is my boss."

Maddie smiled.

"Fair point," she said. "Probably not the best career move, although you never know with the English. They don't give much away on the surface, but they can be pretty perverse."

They laughed.

"You know," Maddie added. "I was really jealous of Katie when she told me that story about the girl in the gym. I wanted to have the same experience."

"You didn't even know me!" said Izzie, with a flash of her green eyes and a wicked grin. "How did you know I was any good?"

Maddie blushed and made noises to suggest that she had not meant the comment to come out the way it had sounded, but Izzie touched her arm and she stopped talking. The three of them gazed at the flames dancing in the fire.

"So you are still playing about with both sexes?" asked Maddie, her courage returning. She was fascinated.

"I've had a couple of adventures," Izzie said. "Just one night things. There is a little bar hidden away down an alleyway off The Strand, where you can find the kind of girls you are looking for. I'm just having fun really. I like a bit of this, a bit of that, but it is not just about sensory things, is it? Don't you have times when you just want to be wild?

"Maybe it's just me," she went on. "Maybe it was all those years being chaste and sensible. There are times when I want to break free, go commando and bra-less into the world, and just let my body go: dance wildly, shake my hair free, feel my hips moving, all the time knowing that the people watching me are getting turned on. It's great. It's sweaty, it's lustful, it's earthy. I'm getting off by showing off. I have a little fantasy about the guys on the dance floor just grabbing me and banging me there on the ground. I don't think I'd ever be brave enough to actually do it, but it's a good fantasy. A powerful one. You know what it's like. Anyway, to answer the question: yes, I like the difference between the two experiences and I am still doing it now and then."

"And combining them?" Winslow said.

"Sure," said Izzie, "but that's not as easy as you think. It's complicated, but it has happened."

They fell silent, the air filled with impure thoughts.

"And you guys?" Izzie said.

"Very happy," said Maddie.

Winslow nodded; "Very much so."

"Not experimental?"

"A little bit," said Maddie. "Hey, we're still a new couple so we are enthusiastic, inventive and very definitely still exploring."

Winslow smiled.

"I guess we'll get round to more kinky stuff eventually," he said. "But right now what we have is so good that we're satisfied with it."

"That's good," Izzie smiled. "I sort of guessed Maddie would be a tiger in the sack. It's all the energy she has. When I first saw her at the wedding I thought that."

"Really?" said Maddie.

"That was my very first thought," Izzie smiled. "I thought: 'Wow, she's hot'."

Maddie recognised that Izzie was coming on to her, to them. She liked it, but it terrified her. Was it a good idea? Izzie had said it herself. It was complicated and she didn't want any complications with Winslow. What if he liked Izzie better than he liked her? What if she liked Izzie more than she liked Winslow? There were too many questions, but she knew that the opportunity was there, right in front of them. She was tempted to grab the chance. She could see that Winslow was really into the idea, which was no great surprise. Men are men. She could also see that Izzie was turned on by the discussions. Her cheeks were a little flushed. Maddie admitted to herself that she too was turned on. It was the image of Izzie dancing wildly that had done that. She wanted to see Izzie lose control.

Maddie sensed that all three of them were looking for a way to broach the subject and get through the last barrier of inhibition. Yet no-one was making the decisive move.

Why could Izzie not just walk over and kiss her?

Why could she not go to Izzie and kiss her?

Winslow wandered across to the CD player and fiddled with a new disc. He had bottled out. Maddie reached for her glass, found it empty and proposed a refill for all of them. She was just as much of a coward...

In the kitchen, she splashed some water on her face, to try to cool herself down. She stood there for a minute or two, looking out of the window into the darkness, wondering what to do, breathing heavily.

Suddenly she was aware of a presence behind her. She knew it was Winslow and half-turned to kiss him.

"I know you want to," he whispered. "So do I."

"Do you think she really does?" Maddie asked.

An amused look came into Winslow's eyes.

"Of course she does," Izzie whispered into Maddie's other ear. Maddie jumped. Izzie had snuck in with Winslow, and had silently slipped behind her. Izzie and Winslow had got together to ambush her. She felt Izzie kiss her neck, so lightly that she groaned out loud.

"Now," Izzie said very quietly, "we decided that we would come in here and we would take you upstairs to your bed, strip you quite naked and then the two of us are going to get you very worked up. You are going to get so hot that you won't know what to do. And then Winslow is going to fuck you. I hope he will then fuck me too, and when we have worn him out and done unspeakable things to him, we can send him to sleep with a little private sex show and I'll show you a few tricks that I have learned in my life as a lesbian."

"No," Maddie sighed. "That's not what I want. What I want is to see you dance for us. Wildly, like you described. I want to see you shake your hair free, and watch your body move. And then Winslow and I will make your dance floor fantasy come true."

She could see that Izzie's eyes were sparkling at the thought. Izzie was hoarse when she said "Go next door, I'll be there in a minute".

Winslow took Maddie by the hand and led her back to the sitting room. She was thinking that the house was about to change forever, at least for he. She would always know what had happened there.

The fire had died down and Winslow threw a couple more logs on to the glowing embers. The wood began to smoulder and then, almost instantly, tiny flames began to lick along the edges of the log and the fire took hold again.

Maddie was nervous. She lowered the lights and lit a candle to keep herself busy. Winslow pulled out his iPhone and his dancing fingers turned on the Bluetooth and found a dance mix he hoped would give Izzie what she needed. The music began, the rhythm simple and throbbing.

And then suddenly Izzie was there. She was barefoot and looked very different. She had ruffled her hair and they could see that beneath her blouse she was naked. She had pulled the blouse out from the skirt and it was half-open, as though it had been buttoned in a hurry. The skirt clung to her curves. She was pretty skinny but Maddie noted that she had a very sporty body. The flames in the hearth were reflected in Izzie's amazing green eyes.

The three of them began dancing as most people dance, but then she and Winslow stopped and watched as Izzie built up the tempo, her eyes closed, swaying to the music and getting wilder and wilder, twirling around, her breasts and hips thrusting, her hands moving over herself lewdly. As she cavorted in front of them they caught glimpses of the naked body beneath. The veneer of the civilized world was gone and it was like they had been transported back thousands of years, to a dark cave where a mating ritual was taking place.

Maddie had no idea how long this went on for. Time had ceased to be part of their universe. Izzie's exertions had made her skin glisten in the firelight and the blouse was now sticking to her breasts. She was ready for them. Maddie and Winslow closed in. She had no idea what he was doing, she didn't care. She grabbed Izzie's short hair and, slightly roughly, pulled her head back and kissed her on the mouth and felt for her firm little breast. The three of them sank to the floor in a blur.

What happened after that Maddie could never properly describe. It was all mixed up in her mind, she remembered only images of certain moments and moving from one pleasure to the next. It was the most intense sensory experience of her life and several times she was driven to orgasm. Her body spasmed, she could stop neither her cries of joy, nor her moans. Her legs trembled uncontrollably as her body flushed with warmth and then she was invaded by a surreal calm, which faded slowly as she lay twitching and panting, her skin aglow, but her mind at peace.

Her body was not her own. It functioned on its own, driven by tongues and fingers and Winslow. Her muscles ached with the exertions, she mumbled incomprehensible words, asking for it to stop and for more - all at the same time.

# Fifteen

At some point Maddie fell asleep, or passed out. She had heard that some women can lose consciousness as a result of too many orgasms (apparently caused by not having enough blood left in the brain) and she wondered if perhaps that was what had happened. She didn't know. When she came to, the fire had ceased to glow, the reassuring orange embers had turned to a silvery white and were crumbling to dust. The fire had consumed all the energy in them. And yet heat still radiated from the hearth.

Winslow was asleep on the couch. Izzie was dozing, her face on his thigh. Maddie touched her leg.

"Shall we wake him?" Izzie whispered.

Maddie shook her head. "I want you to myself for a bit."

They tiptoed upstairs naked and together got into Maddie's bed and lay there, gently caressing one another.

"That was amazing," Maddie whispered. "I cannot really believe it. It is so powerful."

"The first time is always a bit special," Izzie said, "but Maddie please don't fall in love with me. You must be harsh and drive away all thoughts of affection. Think only of your lust, not of me. I want you to see me as an object of pleasure. A sex toy. You two love each other, and I don't mess that up. We don't want to complicate matters, so just love him and fuck me."

It was quite a speech and Maddie did not like it.

"But we want you to feel fulfilled," she said.

"Don't," said Izzie. "I am happy. What we did was great. I like you two individually and together... but I don't want to love you. That would mess it all up. I just want to be an object of your lust, someone to fuck. Please, please, please, don't love me. That would spoil it. One day I will find what you and Winslow have. I am sure of it."

Maddie felt an overwhelming urge to protect Izzie and they held one another close until they both fell asleep.

When Maddie woke, she was aware that she was lying on her side and that Winslow had joined them. He was behind her, his right arm draped over her body. He was breathing gently in his sleep. She smiled. Poor thing. He had worked hard. She opened her eyes, expecting to see Izzie lying next to her, but there was no one. For a split second her sub-conscious asked whether it had all been imagined. A fantasy. But her body told her it had been real.

She wanted to find Izzie and so, very carefully, she extracted herself from Winslow's arms, threw on a shirt and crept out of the room. The guest bedroom door was open, but there was no one there. The bed had not been used. She went downstairs, trying to avoid making the staircase creak. Izzie was sitting in the kitchen, wearing only her blouse, with just two buttons done up. She was looking out of the window, across the misty valley.

"You OK?" said Maddie.

Izzie nodded.

"Just a little post-coital melancholy," she said. "It's quite normal."

"A coffee will help," said Maddie.

She began making coffee, but it felt awkward. They had shared a memorable and very intimate experience, but were not supposed to show any affection. It just did not work for her. She had to say something.

"I want to be affectionate," she said. "It's natural. We've just done something weird and amazing and I want you to know that I liked it."

Izzie nodded. "I know you liked it, and I feel the same, but I also know from experience where it will lead. It's a chemical reaction, emotional bonding is a part of the whole sex thing. It cannot be avoided. But we must avoid it."

"Why?" said Maddie. "I care about you, even if you don't want me to care. I like that feeling and I don't want to not feel it. I know what you are saying is probably true, but it doesn't feel right. I cannot just use someone, even if they want to be used. It's not fair. Not right. Morally."

Izzie laughed quietly: "What's morality got to do with it? That's just a social structure, a means of control which we buy into if we want to. But if it doesn't work for us personally, we do what we want to do. Don't we? We've just done that. Freedom is fun, but with it comes danger. That's where we are now. We're in the danger zone. That's what happens. When we get what we think we want, sometimes we realise that it's not what we really want at all. Last night we chose instant gratification and we didn't think much about the consequences. Now we have to deal with them. All I am trying to do is minimise the pain that could come."

"No, you're not," said Maddie. "You're running away from love. Maybe because it frightens you. I know that feeling. Of course it can go wrong, but it doesn't have to. It doesn't always. I like to be positive and hope it will work.

"Yes, but three into two doesn't go," Izzie said. "Come on, it is an unbalanced number. Are we going to live together happily ever after in some *ménage à trois*, with no jealousy."

"We could give it a try," said Maddie. "Relationships are relationships."

"Statistically the chances of success are much smaller," said Izzie. "There would be six links in the chain, compared to two, that means it is three times as likely to fail. And that's without even thinking about practical matters, like how society would react or living too far apart. Believe me, it's better my way."

"Isn't life about taking risks?" said Maddie. "We all grab happiness whenever we can and in whatever form we can get it. That's fine, but happiness isn't real if we are not behaving as our hearts, brains, bodies, whatever, tell us to behave. Using people is not a win-win situation. It's sad. It's that look on your face when you were staring of out the window just now. We all need affection. Sex is sex and it's great, but what we miss when we don't get it is not the act itself, but rather the intimacy and the affection that come with it."

Izzie sighed. Maddie was right. But so was she: affection would only lead to trouble.

"Just don't fall for me," she said. "If that happens you will mess things up with Winslow. He's a great guy. I'd hate to be the one to ruin it. And I don't have control over that, because I cannot stop you or Winslow or both of you falling for me. All I can do is not fall for you."

Maddie poured two coffees and they sat together staring out at the misty valley. They could hear distant church bells, coming from far off down the valley. The sky was still pale but it was going to be a good day.

"You know what? said Izzie. "It's good to be alive..."

Maddie turned towards her new lover and kissed her on the shoulder.

"It is..." she said. "The one thing missing is toast. Good toast is almost as good as sex."

So they had thick slabs of toast, cut from a proper loaf and smothered with too much butter and glutinous orange marmalade that made Maddie think of sunny days in Spain.

The rest of the day was spent recovering from their adventures. They went to the pub in the village in the early afternoon, just hanging out. Winslow enjoyed the fact that other drinkers were envious that he had not one but two great-looking women. Little did they know...

As the shadows were lengthening, they walked back across the village green and Izzie announced that she had to get back to London. She had to work in the morning. Maddie proposed that she drive Izzie to Oxford to catch a train. They looked up trains and saw that the five thirty-eight would get her to Paddington by six forty-five and she could then catch the Underground home to Pimlico. Izzie gave Winslow a kiss and a hug - nothing too affectionate - and the girls were off to cover the nine-mile journey to the station. They didn't say much, just enjoying the company of the other. They didn't really know what to say, but for a while they held hands, and Maddie drove one-handed. It was probably a little too intimate for Izzie, but she let it slide. She liked Maddie.

At the station there were lots of people, but Maddie wanted to say goodbye properly. She parked in the multi-storey car park and they kissed.

"We shouldn't do this," said Izzie.

"I know," said Maddie. She felt guilty that Winslow was not there with them, but she wasn't sure if kissing Izzie was cheating or not. She would need to ask him.

"I'm away for two weeks," she said.

Izzie knew already. "We can meet up when I get back."

Maddie walked Izzie to the platform and they hugged, nothing too demonstrative in public, and then she watched Izzie head off down the platform. Maddie knew that she would turn for one last look and a smile.

When Maddie got back to Netherington, Winslow had created some creamy lasagne. They drank rough Italian red with it, using water glasses. There was no ceremony. They soon retired to bed and, lying together, they began to talk about what had happened.

"When you went out to the kitchen," he said. "Izzie didn't hesitate for a second. She got out of her chair and she came straight to me. She leaned in close, so I could smell her scent, and she said something that I'll probably never forget. 'You're such a lucky man,' she said. 'Maddie is so hot. When I look at her, I just want to play with myself. Let's go get her and fuck her. We can share.' Honestly, Maddie I didn't know what to say. I was so turned on by the whole thing that I just followed her."

Maddie stroked his face.

"It's a bit confusing," Maddie said. "I love being with you, but that was an amazing experience. I cannot really describe it. It was erotic overload. It was so powerful. But now I don't know what to feel. I am not a lesbian, but I loved the way she touched me. It was so womanly. There was no roughness and while I like a man to be manly, I really loved the difference. I want both. But I am confused. I mean if I sleep with her without you, just the two of us and you know we are doing it and give me permission, is that cheating? It would feel like it. I kissed her at the station, you know, really kissed her, and it felt like I was cheating on you.

"I hadn't really thought about that," Winslow said. "Infidelity is no different if it is a man or a woman. No, that's not true. I would accept you sleeping with a woman much more easily than with a man. That's illogical, but that's how I feel. It's an ego thing. I guess that if you are with Izzie I am not in competition with a man, and so I don't feel so bad. That's weird. Anyway, the question is not so much about cheating, is it? If I know you are doing it, then it's not cheating. There's nothing underhand about it, no betrayal. It becomes a question of acceptance. Am I willing to share my lover with my other lover?

"How would you feel if the roles were reversed and I was sleeping with Izzie when you were away at races?"

"I wouldn't like it very much," said Maddie. "I'd worry that you would like her more and that you would dump me. Yes, I know that sounds insecure, but we're all insecure. Isn't that why the human race is so successful? Because we worry and so we always prepare for the worst."

"You'd better not tell too many people that theory," Winslow laughed. "There's a huge industry built on insecurity - all those shrinks - we don't want them all being unemployed.

"It's ironic," he added. "I don't mind the idea of you and her without me, but you hate the idea of me and her without you. Anyway, I don't think we are looking at this in the right way. We should be asking: 'Is Izzie going to be faithful to us?' Of course she isn't. She's into experiences and sensuality, not relationships."

"That's not true," said Maddie. "She wants love more than anything, but she settles for pleasure until love comes along."

"She's still going to sleep with someone else if she feels

the urge, isn't she?" he said.

Maddie nodded. It was true. Izzie was a free spirit, a child of nature.

"My view is that we get on with life," he said. "It was an great experience, an adventure, but life goes on. And life is Winslow and Maddie. If Izzie flits in and out from time to time, like a bright little butterfly, they we can go chase her, like we used to chase butterflies when we were kids, but we don't really want to catch her."

Maddie liked the image more than the argument. It was Izzie's theory dressed up differently: use me, but don't love me. And she didn't like that. She liked to respect people.

"But maybe Maddie the way to respect people is to let them do what they want to do?" Winslow said.

"If I did that then surely you would be seeking my permission to fuck any woman you found attractive?" she said, "and in the end you would exploit that..."

"So, Maddie Midnight, we must respect our relationship or else all is lost."

"So we can sleep with Izzie as a couple, but not individually?" Maddie said.

"I don't know," Winslow sighed.

Maddie was still feeling odd when she got to work on the Monday. It had been such a strange experience that it simply did not feel real. She did not think that anyone would believe her if she told them that she had spent the weekend experimenting with bisexuality and threesomes. She laughed at the thought of Charlie's face if she did try to explain it.

She was off to Austin, Texas, on the Wednesday and the next two days were spent preparing for the final races of the year and pondering what they would do in terms of marketing at the winter tests. Bilski had e-mailed with details of the sponsorship he wanted to see on the car: a hire car company which he was expanding in the Middle East and a private bank in the Bahamas. She handed over the information to the graphic designers. She and Charlie spent three hours arguing over the colour of next year's car. He wanted to stay with Chiphurst orange, but Maddie said that it was "horrid" and was arguing for a green with blue sidepods.

"That's too much like the 1991 Jordan," Charlie said.

"Charlie," Maddie said. "That was twenty-five years ago. "A whole generation has been born and graduated from university since then. If we are stepping up into the big league we want to make sure we have our branding sorted out. Ferrari is red, Mercedes silver, Red Bull has claimed purple of late and Williams is still blue and white. We have a good chance to grab blue and green and make it our own. Yes, Jordan did use it a long time ago, but so what? It looks a lot better than orange on TV, the trucks and the uniforms will be better. If you have white signage on blue, you get the best chance of being able to read the names of the sponsors. It's science!"

In the end Charlie gave in and the graphic designers were sent off to come up with new liveries.

Before they departed there was a management meeting to review where the team was. The current year, they admitted, was basically written off. They would keep Poppy Denso and Jimmy Buckett next year. They had enough money, but could always use more. The new car was going to be new and exciting and they debated whether they ought to have a big car launch in order to mark what they hoped would be a change of era.

"Be that as it may," said Elfin, "we want the car for every available minute when we are allowed to test, and I am not compromising on that. Charlie, this is an engineering company. Everything that comes to us, comes as a result of the results we achieve, so that must always be the priority. How many times have we seen teams that are all marketing and no substance? We have to do it."

Charlie knew he was right.

"I'll tell you what," he said. "Maddie, if you can find the money to pay for a fancy car launch and guarantee that it won't influence the performance next year, then we will have a big launch. I want something different, though, not bloody Cirque de Soleil, dry ice and thumping music. I want something original, that people will remember."

That was a challenge. F1 car launches had taken many different forms over the years, but few had been memorable. There was always the dry ice and the thumping music that Charlie hated.

"Oh, by the way," he said. "I'm having a meeting in London tomorrow evening. I'd like you to come along."

"Charlie!" Maddie said. "It's my last day at home for a fortnight."

"What's the problem," he said. "Got some man we don't know about?"

That was mean, she thought, but she did not want the others to know, and so she said nothing. That evening she told Winslow. He did not seem to mind. There were things to be done with the boat, in preparation for his trip to sea.

"I'm sure we can manage one night without sex," he yawned. "Lovely though they all are..."

He headed off in the morning, whistling as he went. Maddie suspected that he was looking forward to a few days without having her around.

She booked a room at the Hilton at Heathrow's Terminal Five. It was simple and easy. She wondered if, after Charlie's annoying meeting, she might have the chance to catch up with Izzie, for a dinner or a drink. She called and Izzie said that she might be able to do something at Dolphin Square, but it would not be before nine. Tarquin had a lot on. They arranged to meet at a pub near her flat.

"What am I doing?" Maddie asked herself on the way to London.

The meeting that Charlie had organised was about some sort of charity arrangement and Maddie found it interesting enough. For Charlie it was some kind of a tax write-off, but it made sense.

She rang Winslow after the meeting and a couple of drinks. He was moored for the night down near Bath and was happy to hear from her. She said that she was going to head off soon to the hotel at the airport.

"Not tempted to go and see Izzie?" he asked, without a hint of any innocence. He was too smart for her.

"Yes, we're meeting up," she admitted, rather quietly. Winslow laughed.

"It is just to drink," she said, but she was not sure whether she really believed it.

"It's funny," said Winslow, "I knew that this was all a bit overpowering for you after Saturday night. I don't know if I am happy for you or jealous for me. But as I said before I am glad it's not another man. I wouldn't put up with that."

"I know," said Maddie. "And I wouldn't do that."

"So why do you feel the need to do it with a woman?" he said. "It is strange, but I don't feel that I have any objection. Really. I am happy for the two of you. As long as you come back to me. But, to be honest, I am a little irritated that you can do it and I can't."

"I don't think I would like that," said Maddie.

"I know," he said, "but don't you think you should know how it feels to be in a love triangle? I'm finding out, so I think it is only fair that you should know as well."

"It's selfish of me to behave like this," she admitted, "but I just want to see her. And I've told you about it, so I am not hiding anything. If you call me in the morning, I'll tell you what happened."

"Well, that sounds entertaining," he said. "Graphic detail, I hope. Send me pictures! And Maddie, don't beat yourself up about it. She is a stunning girl."

"She is," Maddie said.

She rang off and began to walk. It was not far from Hyde Park Corner to Pimlico. She didn't fancy going by Tube and she didn't want to be there too early. She would pick up the car later. She walked along Grosvenor Place, beside the garden wall of Buckingham Palace. The map on her phone told her to walk past Victoria Station and then down Vauxhall Bridge Road. It was not as grotty a neighbourhood as she remembered. It was still too early and, not wanting to sit on her own in the pub for too long, she walked on until she got to the bridge itself and stood for a while looking across the river at the imposing MI6 Building. She wondered what was going on inside. She then walked slowly back to Pimlico Tube

Station. The pub was opposite. Izzie was there.

They had a couple of drinks and shared a portion of scampi and chips, eating with their fingers, as they chatted. It came to a point, at about nine thirty, when decisions had to be made. Maddie was getting a little nervous. She didn't know how to say these things and confessed this to Izzie.

"It's not any different to men and women," Izzie laughed. "You simply say: 'Want to come to my place for a coffee?'"

Maddie laughed.

"I'd like that," she said.

They walked down to St George's Square, with its elegant townhouses, each with its own portico and lush trees in the gardens. They were shedding leaves now and it reminded Maddie that she would be missing Guy Fawkes.

Izzie looked at her oddly.

"Never mind," she said. "We can do the fireworks tonight, if you like."

Maddie laughed.

"You have no shame," she said.

"What is there to be ashamed of?" asked Izzie.

"I don't know," said Maddie, "but I am not ready to come out yet!"

"You're not a lesbian," said Izzie. "Nor am I. We're just a pair of horny girls, getting some extra thrills."

Maddie smiled.

"You have a way of making everything sound so simple," she said, "and so naughty."

They turned into Chichester Street and after a short distance Izzie pointed to an entrance. "Here we are," she said. It was all rather anonymous but, after a series of corridors and a lift, Izzie showed her into the apartment.

"It's a one bedroom with a decent kitchen and a nice view of the gardens," she said. "About five hundred Pounds a week."

And then she stopped talking.

"I can go on with all this blah-blah-blah," she said. "But I don't want to. Come here and kiss me, right now!"

They did not get any coffee.

# Sixteen

It was probably close to midnight when Maddie began to think about practical considerations, as she always tended to do at inopportune moments.

"I've got to pick up my car and then go out to Heathrow," she said. "I am booked into a hotel near there. I fly in the morning."

They were both completely naked, lying side by side.

"That's complicated," Izzie said.

"That reminds me," Maddie said, "we need to take a selfie of the two of us doing something that will get Winslow excited.

"He knows about this?" Izzie said, with a curious look.

"Sure, he does," Maddie said. "We share everything."

"Yes, that's true," said Izzie. "You have certainly been sharing me>"

They laughed a lot while trying to come up with a suitably risqué photograph, enough to be titillating without being blackmail material, and once this had been despatched by email to Winslow, Maddie began to make noises about having to leave.

"You cannot leave," said Izzie, nibbling on one of Maddie's earlobes. "I have not done with you yet. This is your first attempt at pure lesbianism and although it has been a valiant effort, I am sorry to say that enthusiasm does not necessarily equal skill. You need a few more lessons before you graduate from the Sapphic Academy."

"God," said Maddie, "that sounds like some grubby porno paperback about a private school for girls".

Izzie giggled. "Besides," she said, "it's a well-known fact that women always feel emotionally vulnerable after orgasm. The bigger the event, the more vulnerable they feel. I have just witnessed what appeared to be a series of fairly powerful explosions along these lines, and I believe that it is unsafe for you to go out alone, as you must be feeling extremely exposed. I don't want you to feel abandoned - you know that is one of the primal, primeval or primordial fears of womankind. I never know the difference between those three words."

"But I have to go," said Maddie.

"I know," said Izzie, "I'm just going to come too... if you see what I mean."

They put on their clothes, not bothering to do anything to smarten themselves up, and hailed a cab outside the main gate of Dolphin Square. That took them to the overpriced car park at Hyde Park Corner, from where Maddie drove them down past Harrods and out of London on the Cromwell Road. Without traffic they were at the Hilton by shortly before one. They checked in and by one fifteen they had resumed their lessons. At some point in the smallest hours of the night, Maddie lay back, gasping with joy, and thought: "Thank God, I can sleep on the plane".

By the time she left at eight, Izzie was joking that Maddie was probably just about ready for some post-graduate research. She did not go with Maddie to the airport, but took the Heathrow Express to Paddington and went straight to work, having had the foresight to put some clothes in her bag before they left Dolphin Square..

Maddie settled happily into her seat and was asleep before the plane left the tarmac. She did not wake up for the next eleven hours.

"You're an impressive sleeper," said the stewardess when

she awoke as the plane began its descent into Austin–Bergstrom International Airport.

The problem was that the flight arrived in Texas late in the afternoon and by the time Maddie had reached downtown and checked into her hotel, the evening was closing in, but her body was telling her that it was still the morning.

"This isn't jet-lag," she told Winslow on the phone. "This is sex-lag."

She went out for dinner with some of the Chiphurst engineers, but it was not long before they began to drift off to bed and Maddie ended up out in a bar, listening to music with a bunch of photographers. She went to bed at four in the morning, but she was still not tired, so she got up and set off for a walk instead.

Austin is a strange town and not at all what one would expect in Texas. It is not a big place and the only major street seemed to be Congress Avenue, that runs up to the State Capitol building, which looks like a copy of the Capitol in Washington. The locals pride themselves on not being like other Texans and have a campaign that proclaims that their goal is to "Keep Austin Weird". The city has a great deal of charm and its enthusiasm for Formula 1 was clear from the start, which meant that the city really went to town to create a party atmosphere for the many visitors.

Friday was Halloween and the houses and gardens had orange pumpkins in them, some with candles. It made Maddie feel a little homesick, but she cheered herself up that evening by having dinner with Charlie Chiphurst, who seemed to want to eat half a cow at one sitting. He tottered off to bed at midnight and Maddie joined some F1 folk in a bar for a few drinks, before heading back to her room at about two.

Outside the town was one big party. It was too early to call London and so she sat in bed and watched terrible TV shows. The lack of sleep was beginning to get to her by Saturday, but it was a good day for the team as Buckett, keen to impress in his homeland, became the first Chiphurst driver to qualify a Chiphurst car in the top ten for two years, and with Poppy Denso fifteenth, a good result looked possible. Charlie wanted to go out partying, but Maddie was ready for bed when she got back from the circuit at about seven. She texted Winslow to tell him she was back and a few moment later the hotel room phone rang.

"Hello gorgeous," he said. "We've just been talking about you."

"We?" said Maddie.

"Yeah," said Winslow, trying to sound matter-of-fact. "I'm at Dolphin Square with Izzie."

"That's not fair," said Maddie.

"It is fair," said Winslow. "You did it to me the other day. I'm just returning the favour. Anyway, it was her idea. She has a great plan and I thought it would be fun."

"What plan?" said Maddie.

"Well, you know Izzie," he said. "She has a very brilliant mind, but a lot of impure thoughts and she says that she thinks that the sex industry is not keeping up with technology and that we should try doing some three-way phone sex, with bluetooth headsets."

Maddie laughed out loud.

"Well, that's certainly creative!" she said.

As she was speaking, she turned on her Skype and rang Izzie. A moment later she could see the bedroom in Dolphin Square. The image was not very clear, but she could see Izzie standing in front of the camera, wearing only her underwear.

Maddie's mobile phone rang, making her jump.

"Hi," said Izzie. "If you look very closely at me you can see I have this thing in my ear that looks like a big earring." As she spoke she moved in closer to the computer and showed Maddie her new bluetooth headset. "It fixes in your ear without sticking out very far, so it looks like jewellery. Anyway, it means that you can tell me what to do and I can do it. And you can see the result. And I can hear you..."

Winslow appeared in the picture as well. "My headset is not as chic as Izzie's," he said, "but it works fine". So you can talk to me and, if you mute her, she won't hear you. Same for me."

"Try it," said Izzie.

Maddie muted the hotel phone. She spoke first to Izzie: "You are a dirty girl, aren't you?" she said. "I can't see that you're excited. I can see your nipples sticking through your bra."

"They are," Izzie said, feeling her breasts so that Maddie could see her. Maddie smiled. This was odd, but it made her feel powerful, and made her want to tell them what to do.

"Take your bra off and get down on your knees in front of him," she told Izzie.

She watched on Skype. Izzie removed her bra and knelt down in front of Winslow. Maddie muted the mobile and used the hotel phone to talk to Winslow.

"Pull her hair," she said.

She watched Winslow obey her order and listened to Izzie groan. "Pull out your cock and give it to her," she said. She then muted both phones and watched. That way she had a hand free. She watched Izzie toying with Winslow and listened to the noise of them getting excited. For a trial run, she thought, it's not bad. Phone sex requires two things, a good imagination and a free hand, so perhaps the pictures were not necessary. She turned Skype off and listened. It was better that way. The imagination is much more powerful than moving pictures. She was aware that things were building up in London. She listened intently.

"Take him all the way," she said to Izzie. She listened some more until she heard Winslow groan.

Maddie took Izzie off mute again: "Well, that should stop you fucking my man tonight," she said.

She heard Izzie laugh.

"Is that a challenge?" she said. "You tuck yourself up in bed over there and sleep. I'll get him going again and get him to fuck me properly."

"You bunch of perverts," Maddie said to both of them. "I'm going to bed. We need to have a think about how to perfect this system. We could make millions marketing it at Christmas. The Virtual Threesome Kit. Good night, happy fucking."

"Happy fiddling," said Izzie.

"Good night sweetheart," said Winslow.

"Wow!" she thought, "that was a weird experience."

She wondered for a time what was going on in London, but she was so tired that she soon fell asleep. She had vivid and rather troubling dreams and woke early, deciding to go out for a run to clear her head. Yes, it was fun to experiment, but she was beginning to worry about the whole Izzie thing. Where was it going to end? She wondered too whether Izzie's skills had impressed Winslow. It was rather funny, she thought, all her efforts to get Winslow into a relationship and now, all of a sudden, the poor fellow had two women. Did she actually love him? Yes, she did, but the whole Izzie thing was confusing her. Time and again her thoughts came back to Izzie. She really was a fantasy come true and while that was exciting, it was also difficult. She knew Izzie was right about using and being used, but she could not think of it that way: it was not in her nature. She wished it was. She concluded that it would be wise to end it all when she got back, but she knew that would not happen. The fire was still burning.

She had a shower and went for breakfast and then drove out to the circuit. It was still early, but she was kept busy until the race began. She watched the orange cars, and cheered with the VIP guests. She did all she was supposed to do, but her mind was not really on the race. It was focused on a bed in Pimlico. As luck would have it, Buckett scored a World Championship point. In F1 a point can sometimes be worth tens of millions of dollars and Maddie knew that Jimmy's result cemented the team's future for a couple of years. Charlie Chiphurst danced a jig on the pit wall with Elfin. He wanted to go out and celebrate, but Maddie was tired. She let them go off without her, saying that she would catch them up. All she wanted to do was talk to London.

As the teams were stripping out the garages, Maddie sat alone in a little office in the hospitality area, created with modular partitions.

She rang Winslow.

"Still at it?" she asked.

"No," he replied, with a laugh. "Actually, I was sleeping it off. It's midnight here. It was fun and I like Izzie very much, but sex is just sex. We both felt that it was not the same without you being here. That was what made it great. We both missed you. I don't think we'll do it again."

"Oh Winslow," she said. "I really do love you."

"I know," he said. "And a week from now you'll be on your way home to me and we can have a few days living the fast life on the canals..."

She laughed. "I guess that your trip up the estuary got cancelled."

"It got Izzied," he said. "When she called, I gave up and called the whole thing off. I wasn't sure how to say no to her - and I didn't really want to."

"I like that," Maddie said. "The verb 'to Izzie'. How would you define it?"

"To be led astray by a bisexual?" he suggested.

"Perfect," said Maddie. "Go to sleep, sweetheart."

She ended the call, paused for a few seconds and then rang Izzie.

"Hello girlfriend," Izzie said, in a very small voice, sounding as though she had just woken up. "It's good to hear your voice. Are you missing me?"

"As I recall I'm not supposed to miss you," Maddie said. "You are only there to be used. Isn't that right?"

"Yes, that's right," said Izzie. "Come back soon and use me some more. I would like that very much."

In truth, Maddie was missing Izzie almost as much as she was missing Winslow and she sensed that Izzie had similar feelings, but was pretending not to. They chatted for a while but Maddie was aware that there was a lot of banging and crashing going on around her. Suddenly a section of the partition wall disappeared and the cheery face of one of the team's riggers appeared in its place.

"Oops, sorry," he said. "I thought everyone was gone."

Maddie smiled.

The walls were literally coming down around her.

She went off to join the party for an hour or so. She had

two days to kill in Austin, but she was not really seeking company. Charlie flew off to meet some "buddy" in Miami, while the other team members disappeared quickly as they were needed down in Brazil. Maddie took the hire car for a tour down to San Antonio on the first day, and visited the Alamo. On the second day, she just wanted to be lazy and sleep as much as possible. On the Wednesday morning, she set off for the airport and bumped into Buckett. They were on the same flight to Brazil. He had spent his time fighting off Texas belles, playing a little golf, with the inevitable training sessions thrown in.

On the ride from the airport into São Paulo, the fast motorway is bordered by verdant greenery, the air warm and fresh. A few minutes later there comes the first whiff of the piquant air of the city, a sickly sweet-smelling mixture of sugar-cane alcohol exhaust fumes and the brown polluted river. As you near the city, the roads become bumpy and the first shanty towns spill to the edges of the highway. Then you hit the traffic jams and stare disconsolately at buildings covered with incredible amounts of graffiti.

When people think of Brazil, they think of golden beaches, beautiful women, sunshine and samba. Perhaps it is like that in some regions, but not in São Paulo. On paper, Brazil is well on its way to being Utopia. The perfect world. It is a huge, rich, beautiful, multiracial country, where all creeds and colours live side by side, but somewhere along the way, the dream has gone wrong. The rich are very rich and the poor, very poor. In São Paulo they live side-by-side. Bits of the city are pleasant enough, but you need armed guards to live in these neighbourhoods.

For most of the F1 people, their ticket home is their most treasured possession during the Brazilian Grand Prix weekend, which is a shame because Interlagos is a truly great racing circuit. Built on a grand scale, it offers a real challenge to the Grand Prix drivers.

There is an incredible passion for the sport in Brazil. You don't get polite applause from a Brazilian crowd. They either love you or they hate you. It is a place that frightened

Maddie, but at the same time fascinated her.

Most of the Formula 1 people stay in a hotel compound, on the way out of town towards the Interlagos circuit, and so they never really get in amongst the people. They go in and out of the track in minibuses with darkened windows. They keep the doors and windows locked.

They hoped that the Brazilian Grand Prix might provide Chiphurst with the chance to score more points because odd things have often happened at Interlagos, where there is a history of difficult weather conditions. The team was tenth in the Constructors' Championship and that meant that the Formula One group would be paying them about sixty million dollars the following year. Moving up the order would increase that money, but it was going to be difficult and there was a danger one of the smaller teams might fluke a point or two and Chiphurst would lose its money.

On many occasions, Maddie had tried to argue that F1 had a stupid business model, because the teams were never able to agree on anything, least of all restricting spending in order to stop everyone trying to build faster cars. This is how F1 works and one can argue that it is pure competition.

The truth, however, is that whoever invested the most money should win, as long as they use the money wisely. Many big corporations had come in, expecting it be easy. They all said: "It's just like any other business", and they all failed as a result. Formula 1 is not like any other business.

The smaller teams have no real chance to beat the big players, unless they can find loopholes in the rules to exploit. Without that, progress is dictated by money. It is like an arms race, the big teams spend money on every silly little development, but only because the other teams have them.

The really stupid thing is the technology on which all the money is being spent is completely worthless to anyone other than an F1 team, so it is basically money being thrown away. The rules make it impossible to design radical new things and yet each year the teams spend a large sum of money to design their own chassis, although no-one can really tell one from another, because they are all pretty similar. The performance differential comes from the aerodynamics, but these are so specialised that they have no value at all for the automobile industry.

This drove Maddie crazy, because it makes no sense at all. It would have been so much more logical to have cost caps and then use the additional revenue as profit, opening the way for the teams to make profits and to become more valuable businesses.

The teams have never really understood the concept of working together, while at the same time competing on the race tracks. This left them open to being divided and conquered by Bernie Ecclestone. He was so successful at doing this that he was able to create an empire trading all the commercial rights and then began to sell parts of his empire, raising billions, while at the same time retaining control. This was great for him, but the sport ended up being bled dry by financiers, although it was not wise to say such things, because speaking out of turn was frowned upon.

The governing body has the responsibility to protect the sport, but the federation allowed itself to be neutered by accepting a substantial pile of cash, which allowed the president to keep the member clubs happy, while pursuing his own personal dreams to become some kind of United Nations road safety ambassador.

The sport had become a cash cow for the financial types, who cared nothing for the thrills and traditions. No-one liked the situation, but no-one did anything about it. The problem was that the teams were still peopled by racers, rather than by businessmen.

The race at Interlagos would become a special memory for Charlie Chiphurst and for young Jimmy Buckett. For once, the luck fell in Chiphurst's favour and somehow Buckett managed to finish the weekend in an astonishing fourth place, aided by the fact that a lot of his rivals crashed. It moved the team to ninth place in the Constructors' Championship and added a little money to the pot. But, most of all, it took the pressure off.

Maddie was swept along in the excitement of it all and it

was not until they were on the plane home on Sunday night that she began to think about things. Buckett and Charlie Chiphurst were up at the front of the plane and had rather a lot to drink. So much, in fact, that Buckett had made what sounded like a serious improper suggestion to her, which she decided to ignore. Buckett was not going to struggle for long to find women willing to play with him, but she was not going to be one of them. Perhaps I should do it, she laughed to herself a few minutes later, I would probably end up making a pile more money if I hooked up with him.

Her mind had then turned to a problem she could see developing which had yet to enter Charlie Chiphurst's head.

Poppy Denso was starting to come apart at the seams. He was supposed to be the team's number one driver and he was getting beaten. The F1 press were writing about Buckett more and more and it was only a matter of time before they started asking about Denso's future and for a young and insecure Brazilian hot shot this was going to be very hard to take. What was needed was force of character and Poppy just did not have it. It was going to end in tears.

There was a ninety-minute layover in Madrid, but all went to plan and by mid-afternoon, Maddie was back in Heathrow, had collected her luggage and was off to pick up her car. She drove home at a gentle pace. She talked to Winslow on the phone for a while. He had finally completed his adventure at sea with the Daisybelle and was now on the River Avon.

"This canal doesn't half meander about," he said. "And it has some really strange places. I'm at a village called Wyre Piddle."

Maddie laughed.

Winslow said that he had not seen Izzie, but they had discussed a get-together at Maddie's at the weekend.

"See you later," Winslow said. "I'll be there by nine."

She rang Izzie at work. She sounded happy, but said that she couldn't talk because she was busy.

Maddie was all on her own for a few hours and, to be quite honest, she was happy to have some time to herself. The motorway was dull driving and Maddie was thinking ahead:

it was cold and the house would be freezing. She would need her big thick socks, a fire and a shot of rum.

Grog, as Winslow called it.

She thought suddenly of her brilliant vegetable soup. She had made a huge pot of it a few weeks earlier and had frozen it in containers, so that she could grab a quick easy meal when she needed one. She had a sudden urge to eat a steaming bowl of it. She needed comfort food. It happens sometimes when you travel a lot. You just need to feel that you belong somewhere.

Another thought then crossed her mind: fresh, crusty bread, like they used to make before supermarkets took over from bakeries. She stopped off on the way home to buy a loaf. It smelled delicious. It was early evening when she reached home. It was already dark. She parked the car, grabbed her bag and the bread, and juggled them until she got to the door and put the key in the lock.

She was home.

# Seventeen

Her first thought when the door opened was that the house was surprisingly warm, and she was in the process of registering this strange fact when the lights flashed on and Winslow and Izzie jumped out to surprise her.

Maddie was floored.

"You pair of con artists!" she said. "I nearly jumped out of my skin."

"No need to get too carried away," said Izzie. "We'd be quite happy if you just jumped out of your clothes."

"I will," said Maddie, "but the first thing I need is a bath. If you two clowns think I have the energy for a threesome right now, you're dreaming. I'm tired."

"That's OK," Izzie said. "You can watch..."

Winslow laughed out loud.

"I want a bath, a fire and some vegetable soup," said Maddie. "Good wholesome vegetable soup with big slices of bread with lots of butter. And a very large glass or two of red wine. When I have had that, we'll see."

"Off you go then," said Izzie. "Winslow and I will conjure up the necessary. You go and wash away your sins."

Lying in the bath, Maddie could hear the noise of the house living around her, and it made her smile. Houses are meant to live and she had always found her cottage a sad place until Winslow and Izzie arrived on the scene.

When she went downstairs, dressed in some old jeans and a huge warm sweater, the fire was crackling in the hearth and a steaming pot of soup was sitting on the table, with glasses of wine waiting for them to sit down.

It was perfect. After the soup was done, Izzie said: "I'd really like fruit cake now. With currants, sultanas, raisins, dried cherries and orange peel. And brandy of course."

"Hmmm," said Maddie, "that does sound good."

They considered rushing around the countryside in search of fruitcake, but in the end the desire was not quite as strong as the temptation to stay in the warmth of the cottage. Maddie curled up on the couch, put her head on Izzie's lap and her feet on Winslow.

"It's nice to be home," she said. "Let's talk about fruitcake. It is almost as good as the real thing."

"You mean like phone sex?" said Izzie.

It was clear that Izzie was feeling rather amorous and wanted to incite the others to acts of wildness. Maddie was tempted, but before things really got going she began to doze off. Her heart was not in it and she was soon in a deep sleep, oblivious to whatever it was that Izzie and Winslow got up to. In the morning she vaguely remembered being woken at some point by ecstatic cries, but she was not really sure whether it had been a dream or not.

When she woke up, Maddie found herself spooning the naked Izzie, with Winslow curled up behind her. It was around 6am and Izzie was wriggling. She was awake. A few moments later she slipped quietly out of bed and Maddie listened to the noise of the shower. She pondered getting up to soap Izzie's body, but she was cocooned in warmth and was too lazy to extract herself, until it was clear from the quiet rustling that Izzie was about to leave. She pulled on her old jumper, which covered very little, and went downstairs to say goodbye.

"You're crazy," said Izzie. "You didn't need to come down. Crazy, but adorable."

"I feel like I deserted you last night," Maddie said.

"You did check out," Izzie whispered, "but that's the glory

of a *ménage à trois*. If one partner's not in the mood, you always have another option. I have to say that Winslow did what was required of him in an admirable fashion!"

They smiled and hugged and, after a lingering kiss, Izzie slipped out into the morning mist. Maddie went back to bed with Winslow and they woke a couple of hours later. They had some lovely toast with what was left of the loaf and then went their separate ways, Maddie promising to meet him that evening in Evesham. She got to work at ten, but there was no sign of Charlie. He turned up an hour later, saying that the dreaded jet lag had got him.

The discussion that morning was a proposed visit to a UAE corporation that the acquisitions team at Chiphurst Competition (better known as Jake and Jen) had suggested might be worth approaching. Initial contact had been made and a Mr Mohamed Al-Rehab had replied, saying that the board of the Penkoz Corporation would listen to what Maddie had to say. Penkoz sold insurance and wanted to expand beyond the Middle East and it was felt that having their name on the side of a racing car was a good idea.

One of the joys of marketing Formula 1 is that one becomes an expert in many different industries and Maddie spent the day learning all about sharia law in insurance and how this might be applied to do business with guests and government officials in the F1 environment. It all sounded decidedly difficult and unlikely, but Maddie was always willing to try. A meeting was arranged for the Wednesday before the Abu Dhabi Grand Prix. So Maddie had a week to come up with some convincing arguments. Together with Jake and Jen, she worked up a number of different packages to pitch to Penkoz, and looked at the risk factors, not least the fact that the firm would be represented by an American driver.

"If they come up with the right kind of money," Charlie said, "I don't mind dumping Poppy, but is there a Muslim out there who is as quick? I don't want the team being seen as having pay drivers. It is a shame Mexico isn't Muslim... We could get whatshisname, the Mexican kid."

Maddie rolled her eyes.

There was no sneaking off early and so Maddie didn't get to Evesham before eight. Winslow had made her a dinner of bangers and mash, which she loved, but rarely ate because of the need to stay slim and presentable. Later in bed they discussed plans for the weekend. They laughed at the idea of the three of them on the narrow boat. It was a squeeze for two.

The problem was solved the next day when Izzie rang saying that she was going to have to call off the weekend because Tarquin needed her in Washington with him.

"It's OK," she said. "A bit of cooling off is probably not a bad idea. I always get the feeling with you two that I'm a little in the way."

"Not at all," said Maddie, "but we do like a bit of time together as well..."

They spent the weekend with Daisybelle in Stratford upon Avon, and on the Monday Maddie went to London for a meeting with one of the team suppliers. That evening she caught up with Izzie, hot off a plane from Washington.

"Hot being the operative word," Izzie said as they went up in the lift at Dolphin Square, after another shared scampi dinner. This time Maddie didn't bother with a hotel room.

As they lay in bed later, Izzie was thinking out loud: "How do you F1 folk ever keep a relationship going?" she asked.

"Well, we're just very efficient when we get home," said Maddie, with a rather naughty grin.

It was an early start the next morning to catch the Emirates flight to Dubai. She was booked into the Kempinski, a strange hotel which gives one the opportunity to stay in a ski chalet, overlooking a man-made ski slope, in a desert climate. From her room she could look down at the locals trying out their skiing skills, while at the same time enjoying Alpine style décor and a fake roaring fire. If you turned down the air-conditioning, you might even start to believe that you were in the Alps.

Maddie loved staying there, particularly in the autumn and winter, because it reminded her of the seasons she was missing back home, and at the same time served as a good reminder that the world in which she was operating was largely fake.

As she was checking in, she spotted Omar Rymer-Jones, the marketing director of the Super Dubai F1 team. The team was based in Buckinghamshire, but flew the UAE flag despite being largely British by nature - like most of the F1 teams.

Rymer-Jones was not a bad type and so she suggested they have a drink together. After a couple of drinks, they had dinner, gossiped a little and then went their separate ways to their Alpine lairs.

Neither asked what the other was doing there.

In the morning a chauffeur was waiting for her in the lobby. He was wearing a suit and had a peaked cap. It was very professional. In some countries the drivers let their enthusiasm for their country get the better of them and they chatter on about the latest developments. Not this one. Not a word was spoken as the sleek black air-conditioned Mercedes slid effortlessly through the streets to arrive 10 minutes later at Penkoz House. The building looked impressive enough, if you like modern architecture. Maddie was not keen on the large neon sign on top of the building, but otherwise if was fine. Mr Al-Rehab was there to greet her. He was efficient, if rather urbane and she did not trust him. She made her presentation, trying to pick up signals as to whether the company was keen on F1 and she wondered if their reticence was because she was a woman. In the overall scheme of things, she did not really care. She only wanted their money. If forced to admit it, Maddie would say that she was not overly keen on this part of the world because she did not like the way women were treated. Someone had tried to explain to her on a previous trip that the idea of women being covered from head to foot was an expression of their freedom. Women, it was argued, dressed as they did because they believed in their God and wanted to follow his rules. Dressing modestly was one of these rules. The argument was that this freed the women from the need to conform to the unrealistic stereotypes that valued them only as sexual objects, for their looks and their body shape, rather than their intellect.

Maddie was not about to convert to Islam, given that consensual extra-marital sex could result in flogging or even being stoned to death. She wondered, in an amused fashion, what they would make of her current relationship status. Would that warrant crucifixion? She did not have any real desire to find out.

Mr Al-Rehab thanked her for her presentation and showed her to the door.

"We will let you know," he said.

The silent chauffeur took her back to the Kempinski. She was all alone in a very foreign land once again. Omar had checked out and so in the afternoon she went for a wander around the mall, noting the large number of lingerie stores which suggested that beneath the veils there is still plenty going on. She decided to spend some time at the hotel's elegant swimming pool, which had the bonus of a swim-up bar and no-one complaining about bikinis. When the sun began to fade, she returned to her chalet and took a long hot bath, deciding that she would stay in and spoil herself with a burger and some fries. After watching the TV for a while she rang Winslow. He was at a place called Lapworth on the Grand Union Canal and was busying himself with something called a head-to-toe beef pie, made from beef cheeks, steak and oxtail.

"Sounds horrible," said Maddie.

They chatted while he ate, but life on a canal boat is rarely filled with excitement. It was a similar story when Maddie rang Izzie. Parliament from the inside is never as exciting as the TV news suggests. Izzie had managed to escape early and was at home in Dolphin Square, drinking wine and eating fruitcake, which she had bought in response to their cravings over the weekend.

"I bought this massive great cake," she said, "and I'm working my way through it, but if I have a big bum when you get back, you'll know what happened."

It had been a nice relaxing day and Maddie drifted off to sleep easily. There was no great rush in the morning to cover the seventy-five miles from Dubai to the Yas Island circuit in Abu Dhabi. It is an evening race and so the timetable is a little odd. Teams run on European time and so breakfast is served at midday, and lunch at four. Maddie decided not to have a second breakfast and got down to the usual race weekend work with sponsors and prospective sponsors.

Abu Dhabi is always a busy event and the day rushed quickly by. At about six her mobile rang. It was Mr Al-Rehab and she prepared herself for the brush-off that she felt was inevitable.

"Hello, Miss Mezzanotte," he said. "I trust you are enjoying the hospitality of the Emirates. I thought you would like to know that after much consideration with regard to your most interesting proposal, the board of Penkoz decided that it was not quite what we were looking for..."

Maddie sighed.

"...however, we would very much like to become the title sponsor of Chiphurst Competition, or rather Penkoz Chiphurst Racing as I believe it will be called. We would like you to draw up contracts for a three-year deal at twenty-five million dollars a year. We feel that forty million a year is rather excessive given the state of the F1 market at the moment, but if you are willing to settle for twenty-five then we will be happy to pay it. If we could meet again on Monday it would be most helpful. I will send a chauffeur to get you. I presume that you are flying out of Dubai."

Maddie was momentarily speechless. She said inane things such as "thank you" and "right-ho" and "I'll be there", but they were all rather mixed up in the delivery process and she feared that she had not done as well at being professionally cool as she perhaps ought to have done. When Mr Al-Rehab hung up, she kept the phone by her ear for about 10 seconds and then spent about half a minute, trying to stop herself from hyper-ventilating. Then she went to find Charlie. She found in his office upstairs in the team's private hospitality building.

"Would you marry me if I found you a twenty-five million dollar a year title sponsor for the next three years, with options?" she asked.

"No," said Chiphurst, "but I'd give you a damned good shagging and promise you the earth!"

"I'll pass on the shagging," she said. "Nothing personal, but I might pass that reward on to my Mum. I suspect that she could probably use a bit of that sort of thing."

Charlie frowned at her, but in an affectionate way.

"Go to work," he said. "Your mother's virtue is clearly at stake."

"No," said Maddie, "I fear not. My work is done. I am going to sign contracts with Penkoz on Monday in Dubai.

"You didn't!" he said. "You beauty! You did a deal? Go and buy yourself a frock, we're going dancing!

Charlie grabbed her and led her in a little dance around the office.

"How shall we spend it?" he asked. "We don't want to give away too much to the taxman, do we?"

"Bloody racing people," said Maddie, "what's wrong with keeping some of it and giving it to me?"

"A bonus?" said Charlie. "No problem. I'm not going to pay you a commission, but a bonus is a very fine idea. Let me think now. How about a hundred grand?

"Done," said Maddie. "Tax-free and offshore I hope."

"*Bien sûr*," Charlie said. "Wherever you want it."

"I am sure that there is a corporation somewhere that will happily receive the money," she said. "Personally-speaking, I don't really want it. The tax man takes far too much. I will let you know the details."

Maddie could not remember the last time she had seen Charlie as happy as he was. He had the budget to go racing properly, with more than enough to give the team a good profit. All that was now required was a competitive car.

They agreed not to tell anyone the news until the deal was done and Maddie spent Friday firing draft contracts backwards and forwards with the legal department (otherwise known as Norman). The race weekend was not too bad. Buckett messed up in qualifying - as young drivers do from time to time - and was seventeenth on the grid. Poppy Denso was twelfth, his relationship with Rosita having lost some of the heat of its passion.

The race was dull. Denso crashed at the first corner, after a collision with a Ferrari, while Buckett had mechanical trouble and came home a dismal fifteenth. It was a disappointing finish to the F1 season, but Maddie agreed to have a few drinks with some of the team and then went off to bed, leaving the others to party through the night. She needed to be on good form on the Monday, others would not be, although most were staying on for a test, so there was a little time to recover.

In a few days it would be December. The F1 calendar is long and brutal and it annoyed Maddie that those who created the dates did not go to all the races, so they had no idea of the physical damage it did. If they did go to races, they travelled on private jets and so the human damage was less than for those who travel the world in the back of a plane. It summed up the attitude: the teams and media were seen as simple cannon fodder. Maddie did not care if those in charge were old folks, they should take the pain with the people who earn them the money. Maddie was ready to go home. She was tired and run down, everyone was at the end of the year. She would go to Dubai, do the deal and fly home.

The silent chauffeur was there for her at seven the next morning and she was at Penkoz by nine. The negotiations dragged on. She was hoping to be on a flight in the middle of the afternoon, but there were delays and that meant another twelve hours in Dubai. The meeting finally ended at five in the afternoon and the papers were signed. Maddie headed for the airport, where she knew she could get a meal, a drink, a shower and a change of clothes in the lounge.

The flight left in the early hours of the morning and arrived in London at breakfast time. Driving home, she had an overwhelming urge to stop for a good old-fashioned British breakfast - the full works, preferably with black pudding and fried bread. It was an odd craving, but life on the road had taught Maddie to do what her body told her to do.

The human body is an amazing piece of engineering. When you need a certain nutrient, the body demands a specific type of food. If Maddie was lacking iron, she would crave a steak or some spinach; if it was calcium, she would obsess about cheese and if she felt she needed chocolate it was either magnesium or sex that was required. She had no idea why her body might require bacon, eggs and fried bread, but she knew it was best to deliver what was being demanded. She stopped on the way home and amazed some workmen by ploughing through a huge fry-up.

"Pretty impressive for a wee lass," said one, "and a skinny one come to that."

Perhaps it was meant as a compliment. After finishing a cup of great coffee, she was on her way again. She knew that she had about an hour before the digestive process would make her sleepy. She parked up at home, went into the house, put on her thick jumper and went happily to sleep on the couch.

The season was over.

# Eighteen

At the end of each Formula 1 season a large percentage of those who travel to all the race take a break. If they have kids at school there is not much that they can do, but for the single or divorced member of the F1 world, there is plenty of potential for a relaxing holiday before Christmas, perhaps even in the sunshine. The problem for the team bosses, drivers and media is that it is also the time of year when everyone has an awards ceremony or a party. There are also a number of trade shows.

A week or so after the season ended, the following year's calendar finally came out.

"Those jackals would have us racing on Christmas Day, if they could," Charlie grumbled when he saw the calendar. There were twenty-one races, from the middle of March right through to the end of November. There were three consecutive weekends without a race in August, so that those with families could spend the school holidays with their children, even if the family has fallen apart.

"They keep trying to tell us that they are putting value into the sport," Charlie went on, "but I am afraid I don't see it that way. They take half the money and then they borrow against future profits and load the business with debt. And they never invest a penny. It is take, take, take. And they really don't care if we all drop dead from exhaustion, as long as they are pulling in the dollars to keep their investors happy and earn them big bonuses. It is terribly depressing because the chances are that we will never be able to find a financier who actually likes the sport and is willing to forego some of the profits to ensure that F1 is as healthy as it could be.

"And we are so stupid that we cannot all get together and force them to change, because we cannot even agree on a day for a meeting, let alone a strategy. We get together when Ferrari needs a lever in its negotiations to win itself an even bigger share of the money and once they have done that, they cease having any interest in anyone else. Next time, believe me, we are not going to help them out."

By December the teams are already well into the build process of the cars for the next season. The first chassis is prepared so that it can be used for a series of different crash-tests that must be gone through, in order for the cars to be declared legal to race, and even to test. As the track tests begin in February, there is time pressure to get all the crash-testing done as early as possible. The teams employ entire departments of engineers who are there simply to make sure that the cars can be twisted, squeezed and smashed into solid objects. It is why F1 cars are so safe these days.

For the marketing people, the run-up to Christmas is party time and when they return to work in January, it is all about planning for the season ahead. It is not a busy time for acquisitions, because the key people one wants to talk to will rarely be around in December. Thus it is a good time to go on holiday.

For Maddie, it was the time of year which she considered to be *her* time. Charlie Chiphurst and F1 owned her from March to November, but December, January and February were for her. She had to work, perhaps, but she would not do more than was necessary and she took a lot of time off, as she was allowed to do. This was particularly important because it is hard enough balancing two lives, but Maddie had made things difficult for herself by having two lovers. The good thing was that she did not need to hide one from the other, and indeed could combine the two very successfully. But life was more complicated, both emotionally and practically, even if it had been a fascinating and rewarding experience.

She liked both Winslow and Izzie and it was clear they liked each other as well, and everyone seemed to be content to go on with the arrangements they had. That made things difficult with dinner parties, because one did not take two partners to dinner. It played havoc with seating plans...

In the past, Maddie had often gone away during the Christmas break, her aim being to disappear from the F1 scene completely and, if possible, not to even hear it being mentioned. To achieve this she tended to go the Americas, but she had concluded some years earlier that the best option in December was probably to go to the Bahamas. So she would fly to Nassau and then transfer to a small plane to go elsewhere in the archipelago.

This year she had decided to try out Abaco Island, or to be more specific, a tiny cay off the coast of the island. It had looked amazing and had cost a fortune, but her intention was to spoil herself. She had spent Christmas several times over the years with Katie, although since her marriage to Tarquin she had been decking the Hall with boughs of holly. Maddie was not sure what she was going to do. The house has been booked before her relationship with Winslow had begun and things got even more complicated when Izzie arrived on the scene.

Out in the islands, people did not worry themselves about who was sleeping with whom. If there was a man and two women travelling together, so be it. They did not care. Similarly, the islanders did not care about the antics of Nico Rosberg and Lewis Hamilton. They were focussed on more relaxed worries, such as what to have for dinner. Out where the trade winds rustle the palms, the only thing that raised more than a lazy smile was the fear that one day there would be another Hurricane Floyd, a monster of a storm had ripped through the cays in the autumn of 1999, its one hundred and fifth mile per hour winds destroying anything in its path that was not properly secured.

Maddie had been back from Abu Dhabi for just a few days when Winslow informed her, as gently as possible, that he was probably going to have to be away for part of the Christmas period. He said that he did not know the exact dates. When she asked what he would be doing, he shrugged and said that he could not answer, but said that he could guarantee that he would not be sitting down to eat turkey, stuffing and Brussels sprouts. He added that he would not be in the arms of some secret lover. It was more likely that he would be somewhere hot, sandy and, probably, rather dangerous.

The world where intelligence and special operations meet is not one about which Winslow was going to go into any detail. Maddie wondered exactly what it was that specialist electronic surveillance operatives get up to when they are not hacking F1 computers, offering expertise in eavesdropping counter measures or "frying" electronic bugs. She wondered if perhaps he had other skills that he had not mentioned.

The upside of this situation was that Winslow's disappearance would be very lucrative, allowing him a "leisure-intensive" life for months to come. The downside was that it might be dangerous, as those who get caught when doing freelance government work in the wilder parts of the globe, generally end up in places where one does not wish to be. As independent contractors, they all know that they are entirely deniable and that it is highly unlikely that the airborne cavalry will be sent in to rescue them if they fall foul of the bad guys. Some simply disappear and while Winslow liked to think that they quit because they had enough, and were gone to lead different lives, he knew very well that some of the stories had not ended well. Two bullets in the back of the head was quick and efficient, and preferable to other techniques employed by some of the barbarians out there. The less dramatic disadvantage of doing whatever it was that Winslow did in the world was that "the light footprint" tended to be used at weekends and over holiday periods.

At heart, Maddie was a bit of a busybody and she liked to know more than she needed to know, and so in the course of their relationship she had devised a scheme to identify some of Winslow's skills, by seeing how he did if they went boating, diving, climbing cliffs, parachuting and camping, but they had not had time to do any of it. She already knew that he was extremely fit and very disciplined in his training regime. The only clue he gave her came one day when they were discussing what he really did for a living and he had waffled on about computers and electronics surveillance.

He had asked her later whether she had ever heard of "the Gamma men" or something he called the "Onzième Choc". When she replied in the negative, he said it was because he was reading a book that referred to them, but she thought it was a rather odd explanation, particularly as she had seen that he was reading a cookery book.

Later, when she was alone, she googled both expressions and discovered some fascinating stories about Italian navy divers who had done brilliant work during World War II, blowing up Allied ships. The Gamma men had worked from the Trojan Horse of the Gibraltar, a ship with an underwater trapdoor through which they would depart, riding converted torpedoes to attach explosives to the hulls of enemy ships and then returning to their ship undetected.

The details of the Onzième Choc were very fuzzy, but it was some kind of special French unit that did similar things in the post-war world.

On another occasion Winslow had used a very strange expression about "a PhD who can win a bar fight". It was so out of place that she googled it and found it was a reference to the ideal candidate for the OSS, America's version of the SAS, which later became the Central Intelligence Agency. It did not really tell her anything other than he knew how to talk the talk of the covert world.

Maddie decided the best thing to do would be to go on holiday, Winslow or no Winslow. She wanted her moment in the sun, to recharge her batteries and top up her tan.

So she decided she would ask Izzie.

It amused her to try to put Izzie on the spot on the telephone, when Maddie knew she was working in the office in the Houses of Parliament and was not free to speak openly. Tarquin did not even know that they were lovers, which added to the spice of the conversations.

Maddie was often outrageous.

On one occasion she had been feeling rather frisky and had called Izzie and whispered into the phone: "I was thinking about you and touching myself."

Izzie did not miss a beat.

"Ah, yes, she replied. "I wish I could spend more of my time doing stuff related to the digital revolution. It is one of the most exciting things for our generation. It is bewildering what comes, isn't it? They don't really have good instruction manuals, so I always end up using the 'suck it and see what happens' principle."

"I know what happens," said Maddie. "It's about to happen right now..."

"Sometimes you just have to let yourself go," said Izzie and then she listened to Maddie until she was done.

"Thank you," she said. "Your input is very much appreciated here."

Maddie loved Izzie's ability to think on her feet and say absolutely the right thing. She was fascinated by what Izzie would say to the suggestion of going away together.

"I don't suppose you want to spend Christmas and the New Year frolicking half-naked with me on a desert island?" she had asked.

Izzie paused, for a split second: "I don't believe in half measures. I think it should be all or nothing."

"Nothing it is then," Maddie said.

"Great," said Izzie, quick as a flash, "I shall look forward to seeing all of you. Tell the little ones that I will give them lots of kisses when I see them."

Maddie laughed.

"The little ones like the sound of that..."

And so it was that Maddie and Izzie took a plane from London one morning in the run-up to Christmas. Nine and a half hours later they were in Nassau, where they switched to a small plane for an hour-long flight to Treasure Cay Airport in the Out Islands. The evening was coming on when they arrived. An agent from the rental agency was there to meet them and drove hurriedly the few miles to a small but quaint port, with a few shops. He explained that there were already some supplies at the house for them to use on their first night. He suggested they return to the port the next day.

"They have a very good list of places to go to buy things," he explained. "You can come here or go down to Treasure Cay, if you want a longer trip. But right now we need to hurry, because I have to get back by nightfall. I don't recommend navigating at night. Don't forget to buy conch. It's fantastic."

Halfway along the waterfront there was a strange little pier, with an old-fashioned shelter at the end, like one might see at an English seaside resort. A small boat was tied to the pier and they climbed quickly aboard. Very soon they were heading out to sea.

The trip was about twenty minutes.

The cays are generally low and flat, rising no more than 10 feet above the water. They have dense, thorny vegetation. Some have trees, native coconut palms, the gnarled and twisted Lignum vitae, the wispy grey-green casuarinas, and occasional citrus trees.

As they approached the island where they would be staying, they could see that it was a little different. It rose higher from the water on one side. The agent explained that there was a ridge of rock and that the water had flowed around it and deposited sand on the leeward side over many centuries, gradually forming two curving sand bars that finally met and the gap closed, leaving water trapped between them. Over time, vegetation had sprung up and complex root systems had bound the sand together and then more vegetation had taken root and eventually the sand bars were covered with trees and the lagoon inside had become completely hidden. At some point, perhaps in the age of the great pirates, someone had landed on the island, discovered this strange phenomenon and decided to use it. The height of the trees was not sufficient to hide a big sailing ship, but the pirates reckoned that if they dug a channel into the lagoon, with rocks on either side to stop erosion, they could create a wonderful hiding place for smaller vessels, with masts that could be taken down. The channel was dug at an oblique angle, to disguise its entrance and later someone had added an L-shaped jetty that added to the camouflage.

From the sea, one could see the jetty, but the channel was completely invisible, hidden by trees and bushes. It was only when you went behind the jetty that you saw the channel, cutting through the trees, perhaps thirty yards in length, but deep enough for a skiff. The trees had grown above the gap, creating a tunnel of greenery.

"You'll see when you explore that there were cannons placed on either side of the jetty," the agent said. "To deter unwanted visitors..."

At the end of the channel, he steered the boat round to the left and they emerged in a wide open lagoon. They could see a small wooden dock and, to the right of it, a white house, some lush lawn and a beach of white sand. Another skiff was tied to the dock. They drew up alongside and climbed out.

At either end of the lagoon was a curving sandy beach. They were perhaps half a mile apart. The side of the lagoon opposite the channel was rock, but sand had found its way into the nooks and crannies and vegetation had taken root. Green bushes ran along the top of the rock, all the way to the far beach, giving the impression from the sea that there was nothing in the middle of the island.

"This is amazing," said Izzie. "It's like we have our own secret world. You would never know what is here."

The agent smiled and helped them get their suitcases on to the dock. He gave then a hurried tour of the single-storey white colonial-style house, with a veranda all around. The path from the dock continued past the house, through occasional palms to the beach.

He explained that the best way to get to the other beach was by boat, as there was only a path that ended about halfway along the rock, at a lookout point. There might once have been a cannon there, he said, covering the secret channel.

Behind the house they saw another path that crossed the

lawn and curled away into the trees. This, he explained, went through to the jetty and the fortifications and he pointed to another track that forked off behind the house and climbed up what appeared to be a dune, covered with trees and bushes.

"There's a lookout point up there," he said. "It's nice. There's a sort of hollow at the top. It's like a private garden. If you climb up the side, you can see for miles."

He told them about the electricity and the water supply and showed them a large notebook, filled with explanations. He explained that they were only a couple of miles from the main island, but at the nearest point this was completely uninhabited, as the coastline was protected.

"There's a small town on the other side of the big island over there," he said, pointing. "But you have to trek through the forest and you cannot buy much there apart from fuel, so honestly I wouldn't bother."

He looked at the sky and then at his watch.

"Look," he said, "I have to go. I have to be back before it gets dark. If you need anything, my office is near the dock we left from."

They walked him back to the skiff and waved him goodbye as he steered the skiff into the secret channel and disappeared from view. They looked at each other and, without a thought, embraced. Izzie was so excited that Maddie was not even allowed to unpack, nor change her clothes. They had to explore. They climbed the dune behind the house and found the hollow, just as the agent had described. They stood on the edge and could see his skiff chugging through the waters back towards the mainland. They ran down to the white beach, close to the house. Izzie looked around and then stripped down to her underwear. She unhooked her bra, slipped out of her hipsters and, throwing Maddie a seductive glance, walked into the water.

"Come on, " she said. "Get them off. You want an even tan, don't you?"

It felt a little odd to be stripping off in the open air and, for some reason, Maddie felt the need to be alert, lest someone appear. She knew that there was no-one and no reason for any inhibitions. They swam side by side for a while and then returned to the shore and, quite naked, went to explore the house. It was perfect, with a big comfortable wrought iron bed. They jumped about on it, to see if it made any noises.

"You'll squeak more than this bed does," Izzie said.

"I hope so," said Maddie.

A look passed between them and they might have made love there and then, but they knew there were things to do. Maddie went to the kitchen to see what there was to eat and Izzie unpacked. When that was done, she found Maddie cooking rice and vegetables and grilling some fish. She had already opened a bottle of wine.

They were both still naked.

"This is absolute heaven," Izzie said.

Maddie looked up and smiled.

Izzie lit some torches in the garden and, as the darkness enveloped them, they settled down on the veranda to eat. They drank wine and, after everything was cleared away, they went down into the garden, hand-in-hand, and lay together in a hammock, hanging between two coconut palms. Gently they began touching one another until they were sufficiently excited to need the bed to further their adventures.

That night, they both squeaked and groaned more than the bed frame, and fell asleep, intertwined and flushed, but very satisfied.

The house was not designed with privacy in mind. There were no curtains and so Maddie woke with the light and lay there, watching Izzie sleeping. She was on her back, with her legs together and one foot over the other. Her right arm lay beside her body, her left reached out slightly across the bed. Her young breasts were taut and topped by brown nipples that never seemed to be anything other than alert. Her stomach was perfectly flat leading to the downy mound that was the very core of her being. This nest fascinated Maddie and, even then, in the morning light, she wanted to go down there, gently ease Izzie's legs apart and use her lips and her tongue to awaken her friend. Maddie was turned on.

Izzie opened her eyes, saw Maddie, smiled and stretched luxuriously, first pointing her toes and then curling them back towards her body. She recognised the look in Maddie's eye and understood instantly what it meant. She put her legs on the bed and slowly pulled her right one up towards her body, keeping it flat on the sheets. She watched Maddie's face. She lay like that for just a second and then did the same with her right leg. It was a clear invitation and Maddie did not hesitate. She did not care whether Izzie touched her or not, all she wanted was to give pleasure and it was not long in coming.

Soon Izzie lay panting, spread-eagled on the bed, with tiny spasms still rippling across her stomach and a look of pure serenity on her face. Maddie slid up beside her, kissed her on the lips and then departed to the kitchen to make some coffee.

A few minutes later Izzie, still naked, joined her and they sat watching the sun rise. Then they went down to their beach and swam across the lagoon, to the sands at the northern end. The vegetation behind the beach was impenetrable. They knew that the island extended another half a mile beyond where they were, but there was no way to explore, except by boat.

"We should be careful with the sun," Izzie said. So they swam back across the lagoon, ate some fruit that had been left for them. Maddie said that they should get dressed and head for town, as early as possible and made a list while Izzie showered. She followed and then they threw on some clothes, although neither wore much, and they were ready to go. Maddie gathered up her hair as best she could, while all Izzie had to do was to run her fingers through her short hair and she looked perfect.

They went to jetty, fired up the engine of their skiff and, after a little practice in the lagoon, headed into the tunnel of trees and out through the L-shaped dock to the ocean. The turquoise sea was completely flat and they covered the distance to town with relative ease, looking out for dolphins or turtles on the way. They tied the skiff up at the dock and went in search of supplies. They bought fish, meats of various kinds, conch, rice, vegetables, eggs, milk and fruit. Maddie found it unthinkable to live without bread and so added flour, salt, yeast and some oil to the basket. They agreed they needed wine - and plenty of it. They added all manner of other things which took their fancy and, by the time they were finished, they struggled to get it all back to the boat. They had enough food for a week. Before they cast off, Izzie ran back to the shop and returned a few minutes later with two large sun hats. The two Amazons then set sail, back to their island. There were still no other boats out and by the time they reached the island they had both taken off their shirts. They wanted to be naked again.

They had almost forgotten it was Christmas Eve, but after unpacking and putting everything away, Maddie looked on the computer and found an email from Winslow. It had been received at four in the afternoon in London, but referred to watching a sunset and Maddie concluded that their lover must be somewhere in the Middle East.

After a lazy lunch they walked down the path to the L-shaped jetty that guarded the entrance to the lagoon and explored the old fortifications. There was even a rusting old cannon. They then tried the path across the rocks to see how far it went and found themselves in the lookout post, where they were sure there had once been another gun, opposite the entrance to the lagoon. Then they went back to the cool of the palms around the house.

As evening drew in, they started to drink wine and a bottle had gone by the time they began thinking about dinner. They wanted to try the conch and followed a recipe they found in the house. The first step was to pound the conch until it was tender, then marinate it in lime.

"Look at this," said Izzie, reading from a cook book. "Conch has more protein than steak and almost no fat. Brilliant. My kind of food."

They sautéed the conch meat for a short time and it was ready to eat. It was delicious. They followed up with some cheese which had cost them a fortune.

There were no more messages from Winslow that evening and so, as Christmas Day began, they went to bed. They were too tired to make love.

It was a strange kind of Christmas. They had bought one another small presents and then at lunch time, they made some more conch and ate it with some bread that Maddie had baked. They were still at that stage in their relationship where they were constantly touching one another and they lived without any inhibition, making love whenever and wherever they felt the urge. Perhaps it was the sense of availability that came from nakedness or the knowledge that no one could hear their joyous cries. They became more adventurous and more expressive, as they experimented in every way they could imagine, to see what pleasures they might discover.

"It must be all the fresh air," Maddie said. "I'm not usually quite this much of a nymphomaniac."

By the end of the week they could count not only the kitchen table, the hammock and the hollow on top of the dunes as places they had made love, but also in the boat, drifting in the lagoon. They ceased to worry that someone might visit and were so relaxed that they often walked around the island without a stitch of clothing.

In the days that followed they developed a routine of sorts, although each day was a little different. They would wake up with the light and slip into bikini bottoms. As neither had to worry about being overly endowed, the bra ceased to be an item of any value. They wore loose shirts and nothing more. They would throw a few items into a wicker basket. They didn't even need towels as the sun dried everything almost instantly. Maddie worried about the state of her hair, but it looked great and Izzie's pixie cut was exactly what was needed in such a climate. They would take the boat out to the cays, where there were miles of empty beaches and hidden bays. They would pick a place, explore a bit - just to be sure they were alone. Once they were sure, the shirts came off and after a few minutes one or the other would decide that wearing clothing felt wrong. Each knew the other's body as well as they knew their own. Maddie reckoned that they has left civilisation behind and had become savages. They ate with their fingers and followed every whim that entered their heads. After a couple of days neither needed to worry about the sun as their bodies had turned honey-coloured and more sunshine only darkened the skin further.

They did not eat much and exercised a great deal, mainly swimming. In the afternoons they would return to the lagoon and spend their time naked on their own beaches. There was so much sunshine that Maddie could see her hair lightening by the day and even the dark-haired Izzie began to go slightly blonde.

In the evenings they would sit on their veranda and enjoy the cool breezes. They saw no one and had no real desire to go to town for more supplies. The sleepy village seemed somehow frenetic in comparison to life in the lagoon. Some nights they would sleep in the hammock, a pair of naked nymphs wrapped together. They fell asleep one night on a blanket in the hollow at the top of the dune, after they had enjoyed a picnic dinner.

Every couple of days they would look on the Internet to see if there was any word from Winslow, as both missed his manly presence, but they were as happy as it is possible to be in this world. Although neither wanted to admit it, there was a quiet sense of dread that this unreal existence would have to come to an end at some point and they would then be required to return to reality.

They visited the village twice more for supplies, but the minute they got home they were naked again - even before the groceries were put away.

"Why would we be ashamed of our bodies," said Izzie. "We are gorgeous and sexy..."

There were times when Maddie had to bite her lip to stop herself from telling Izzie that she was hopelessly in love, and she sensed that Izzie was finding it hard to live by her own rules.

On New Year's Eve, with no word from Winslow, they drank a lot, danced and at midnight they kissed and Maddie almost

242 - Maddie Midnight

broke down and declared her feelings. There were moments when she wondered if she might give up Winslow - and all other men - and just stay there forever with Izzie in this world where civilization was discarded with their clothing. They had become feral human beings.

Izzie continued to whisper every earthy desire that entered her head, and to state her willingness to be used for Maddie's pleasure alone. Yet at the same time she was trying to avoid the fact that their relationship had gone way beyond her own rules. She understood that this was developing into a problem because when Maddie walked out of the room, she felt as though the lights had gone out. At times she thought that she and Maddie were fused together and she wondered where her body ended and where Maddie's began. She also pondered whether she had crossed some invisible line and become a total lesbian, because she no longer felt the need for any form of masculine games, touches, smells or tastes. Maddie was all she needed.

# Nineteen

In the hundred or so centuries that cover the history of civilisation, man has come up with an impressive array of brilliant inventions. He has harnessed fire and, to some extent at least, the power of the sun, wind and water. He has invented the wheel and developed farming, to provide himself with a regular supply of food. He has created democracy, religions, arts and philosophy. He has learned to fly, has begun to explore the vastness of space and has developed astonishing machines that provide instant access to knowledge and expertise, no matter where you are. He has overcome a multitude of diseases and doubled or trebled his own span of life and continues inexorably to understand and improve the human condition.

But, despite all of this, man still cannot hold back the march of time. Things change. Everybody still dies, even if their lives are longer than those of their ancestors.

Maddie and Izzie were aware, after just a couple of days in this paradise, that all too soon it would end and that they would have to go back to normal. This drove them to enjoy every minute they had, savouring each and every experience with joy and enthusiasm. Everything tasted better, every sensation was stronger, and they wanted every minute to last just a little longer, in this secret and delicious world.

But time marched onwards, never dawdling, never stopping to enjoy the view, and as they came to the end of their adventure, a sense of sadness settled on the pair of them. Soon this amazing time would be just a memory.

"I feel like I used to feel at the end of the school holidays," Izzie said, one afternoon as they lay on the north beach. "I want time to stand still. I didn't want to go back to growing up. I wanted to run free for the rest of my life."

Soon, too soon, it was their last night. They tried to make if feel like a celebration, rather than a funeral, but it was a battle. They grilled the last conch, and ate rice with crab meat and green peas. They drank all the wine that was left. They danced on the beach in the darkness and swam naked in the lagoon in the moonlight. And they made love with a ferocious passion, as though it could be the last time.

In the morning they were weary and slow. They cleaned the house, packed their things and grumbled at one another. Then they climbed up to the hollow and watched out for the agent's skiff to appear. When finally it was sighted, they went back to the house, took their cases to the jetty and walked one final time on their beach, beneath the palms. And then the sound of the chugging motor in the channel brought the holiday to a close. The magic was gone. It was just business as usual after that.

The journey home to London was one of quiet reflection. They could not face the thought of the cold, nor the knowledge that at some point they would have to separate and go their different ways.

They had heard nothing at all from Winslow and were beginning to worry. They did not know where he was. As they waited for the luggage to arrive at Heathrow, Maddie must have looked miserable because Izzie said: "Come with me today. I don't want to be alone. We'll crank up the heating, dance naked and pretend we're still on the island."

It was a Sunday and as they drove into London it was clear and cold. People were swathed in coats, hats and scarves. It was England. They stopped to buy some food and arrived at Dolphin Square in time to start cooking lunch. They had decided that they needed roast beef. It was clichéd, but it was what they wanted. Comfort food. They had Yorkshire Pudding as well, and potatoes roasted crisp, and parsnips too. And some wine. They had even bought an apple pie, but neither was capable of eating any more, so it was consigned to the fridge for tea or dinner or breakfast, come to that.

They watched The Scarlet Pimpernel with Anthony Andrews and Jane Seymour and by about four they were ready for chocolate. Both had lost weight on the island and Izzie declared that it was beyond her control to fight a primal urge to store some fat for the cold winter ahead.

"I have searched you at length, Maddie said, "and I see very little fat. I think you're right!"

Dolphin Square is not the Bahamas, but while the venue was different, the sentiments were the same and later, after some delicious apple pie, they ended up with Izzie asleep, her head in Maddie's lap.

Maddie did not feel like sleeping. She was thinking about her life. It had been an amazing year. She had found love in abundance. Too much of it, in fact. She had earned a decent salary and saved much of the money, because she did little else but work or stay at home with one lover or the other, or both. She totted up the numbers in her head and concluded that she had collected one point nine million dollars in "commissions" which the taxmen in the UK had no right to grab. Her assets were earning money. She wasn't quite set for life, but she was well on the way. She might even stop working if she so desired and could spend a lot of years simply enjoying herself if that was what she really wanted to do. And yet, what she wanted to do was to go on doing what she was doing. She liked racing and was really looking forward to the season ahead.

She recognised that was like a drug she needed each year in March. And this year was going to be special. It was Chiphurst's big chance. Winslow had offered her the opportunity, and she had grabbed it and made it happen. This would be her triumph, even if Elfin and Charlie would get all the glory. She didn't care much about taking the credit. She was winning every way.

Saying goodbye the following morning was tough. They shared a piece of toast, fresh from the freezer, and then with a squeeze of the hand and an affectionate look, they went their separate ways: Izzie to the Houses of Parliament and Maddie to the M40, bound for Chiphurst Competition headquarters. She was happy to be driving against the flow of commuters. She went straight to work and spent the morning being complimented about her tan.

"Is it an all over tan?" some of the boys asked, each believing than they were the first to think of the question. "You'll never know," she said with a smile, "but if you insist, yes. ALL over. Every inch of me is that colour."

It was true...

"I am glad you're back," said Charlie. "Maybe you can make sense of what is happening in this sport."

He explained that late the previous Friday evening, too late for the newspapers to pick up, a press release had appeared from CVC Capital Partners, explaining that the company that controlled the commercial rights to F1 had been sold.

The buyer was a Panama-based company called STD Inc. The big surprise was that the last line of the press release said that the CEO of the Formula One group, Bernie Ecclestone, had decided that it was a good moment to retire and was moving to a coffee plantation in Brazil.

Ecclestone was not answering his phone and it emerged that he had departed for Brazil just before Christmas and had not been back. None of his staff knew what was going on. It had all been done above their heads. There were rumours he had been told his services were no longer required and he had immediately sold his shares in the company. The Ecclestone Family Privatstiftung, a trust fund in Liechtenstein, had sold its shares as well.

STD had bought them all. The Ecclestones were out.

"Wow!" Maddie said when she heard the news. "Now that is what one calls an earthquake. I go away for a few days and the whole sport changes. Unbelievable."

"I did try to call you," Charlie said, "but your phone was

turned off."

For Maddie, STD was a noble name, stretching back to the 1920s when the Sunbeam Talbot and Darracq firms were merged and led the British vanguard into racing on the continent. The team was successful enough to win a Grand Prix with Sir Henry Segrave driving, even if they did recruit Fiat engineers to make it happen.

"As far as I am concerned STD stands for sexually transmitted disease," said Charlie. "Or it could be an abbreviation for standard, or standard deviation, or save the date, or stabbed to death, seize the day, short term debt, standard trunk dialling, it really offers no clues. We need to find out who these people are."

The apparent desire for anonymity had led some to conclude that it must be a criminal organization, as it was argued that secrecy would not be required if it was all legal.

That morning, as Maddie had been driving up the M40, another press release had appeared, stating that STD Inc had named Harvey Powers as the new CEO of the Formula One group.

No-one in F1 had ever heard of a Harvey Powers, which to the industry meant that he was not the right man for the job. The announcement came with a brief synopsis of his career. He was fifty-five and an American. He came from the strangely-named town of Truth Or Consequences, New Mexico, and had been previously been the head of corporate strategy and business development at Disney, his job being to make the company bigger and better. He had worked there for ten years, joining the empire soon after he sold his own e-mail marketing company for one hundred million dollars. That business had been a start-up, which was built and sold in just six short years. Before that he had spent ten years working with the consulting firm McKinsey which had recruited him from a commercial law firm. He had studied for a combined law degree and MBA at Harvard.

"That's impressive," said Maddie, after reading the résumé.

By the end of the day, she was feeling weary. She really wanted to talk to Winslow and rang his mobile again, only for it to go straight to answer phone. She missed him. It was January 5 and it had been nearly two weeks since she had heard anything from him.

There was nothing that she could do.

She knew Winslow had no official connection with the US government and if he was involved in something deniable they would know nothing about him. The British would probably not even have a record of his departure as he had almost certainly been travelling on a false passport. She had never seen any documents on the Daisybelle and she presumed he had a safe deposit box somewhere, although she had read that a lot of banks were getting rid of the devices in order to save money and because a number of police raids had shown there was no protection from the law in a safe deposit box.

The only solution was to wait for him to come home.

If he ever did.

She rang Izzie and, despite having just spent two weeks together, they still managed to talk for two entire hours. Izzie suggested they look at the news to see if there might be some event that Winslow could be involved in. The problem was that unless there was a loud bang or a body, there was often no trace of effective undercover action. If there were clandestine people involved, journalists rarely knew who they were. They also had no idea about what he had been doing, so reports of an extreme Islamic warlord being killed, for example, might have been something involving him, but it could be reported as one faction killing another, even if there was no evidence to support such a claim. If the other leader was killed it would be billed as a revenge attack.

Tracking down those who behead journalists on video, for example, might take a while. And the chances were that when such a person was found and dispatched into the waiting arms of Allah, the victory would not be trumpeted because the sudden and unexplained disappearance of a leading figure would send fear through any movement and make the members aware that they too risked disappearing, with no information for their families and friends. This also sowed seeds of doubt that perhaps the person who had disappeared might have decided to switch sides, to save his or her own miserable neck. If one simply disappeared there would also be questions about one's status as a martyr: Was the missing person a martyr or a coward? Who knew? With a drone, a car bomb or a mobile phone that blew off someone's head off, there was no doubt, but if someone just disappeared they were missing believed killed. It was all in contravention of international treaties and conventions, but with no perpetrators and no victims, it was hard to accuse anyone of anything.

Maddie could only, but she tried to remain positive. Winslow would be back when he had finished doing whatever it was he was doing. He was a solid reliable man.

She concentrated on the launch of the new Chiphurst car, but activities were disrupted on the Thursday when Powers made a visit to meet Charlie Chiphurst.

He seemed to Maddie rather an odd-looking fellow, rather plump with elaborately-styled hair and expensive clothing, although his taste for tweed jackets and corduroy trousers was oddly English for an American.

He explained that his strategy was to restructure the Formula One empire, creating new departments and recruiting new people to head them, but he said in the short term he would leave Ecclestone's empire as it had been.

Talking to other teams, Maddie discovered the F1 fraternity did not really know what to make of Powers, except he seemed open to new ideas and was willing to listen. He had not had time to do very much, but his presence had done one important thing: it had changed the atmosphere in the sport and everyone seemed to be happy about that.

But even if no-one knew who was really behind Powers, he was insistent that there was no plan for the business to be floated on the stock exchange and said that the plan was for investment, in order to build up the sport, rather than grabbing every penny, as the previous owners had done. The teams were happy for there to be change, as long as they went on receiving their prize money payments, as before, They did not really care whether the new owner was the

Catholic Church or the Hells Angels as long as money kept coming on a regular basis. Such is the way of racers.

Maddie wanted to know more and decided that the most efficient way to track down the new owner would be to look at the lawyers involved. Every dodgy fortune requires a dodgy lawyer, who will act as the nominee for the real owners. By looking at other companies in which such a lawyer is involved one can often piece together evidence and that may lead to the identity of the real owner.

For most F1 teams the winter months pass very quickly. There may not be races to go to, but there are crash tests to be done and new cars to be built. In January it is all about preparation. Getting ready for launches, tests and the races, still two months away.

Maddie's priority was the relaunch the team, with its new livery and its new car. She would not be going testing. She had no desire to get on any planes she didn't need to get on, unless Charlie rented a jet, in which case she might go with him for a day trip.

She still had time to feel the rhythms of the factory, with the production teams churning out parts and the new cars building up week by week. The R&D boys and girls were already working on upgrades for the third or fourth race, making the car faster. The factory was humming.

Thinking up a new idea for an F1 car launch that has not been done before is a pretty difficult task, but Maddie had long had an idea that she wanted to turn into a reality.

It was simple and powerful.

All the teams have show cars that look like the racing cars themselves, but they are built with cheaper materials because there is no logic in spending the kind of money required for a car that does a completely different job. Thus show cars can be destroyed much more easily than the actual racing cars. Maddie had always wanted to do exactly that and introduce a new car by dropping a heavy weight on to an old show car and crushing it, but having the new car on mounted on the top of the weight.

When she first mentioned it, the health and safety people

at Chiphurst screamed and said it was impossible, but Maddie had some engineers design an hydraulic system to allow a concrete block to drop in a controlled manner. Concerns about flying wreckage were overcome with a low see-through wall around the base of the presentation area.

The car to be destroyed was a mock-up of the last Chiphurst, in all of its orange splendour. As it was an old car no-one would look very closely. No-one expects an old car at a new car launch and Maddie decided to have Charlie unveil the old car and then say something like "someone's screwed up here" and then return to the dais, press a button and the new car would descend on top of the old one and crush it.

"Smashing," Charlie would say.

Maddie had the foresight to commission two fibreglass mock-ups of the old car: one to test the idea, to make sure it all worked, and the other for the event itself. The stress analysis department assured her that when the block of concrete dropped on the fake car, it would be crushed completely flat. They were right.

The launch was set for Thursday, January 15, which meant that the team would be the first to unveil its new challenger. It was rather early, but the engineers were keen to get as much mileage as possible in testing, in order to understand the car completely. Being the first launch is always good because it attracts more publicity.

The fact that the Chiphurst would not need to actually run until the start of February meant that it was a inevitably bit of a con. The new car would have the same shape but that was about all. Maddie's view was that it would do for the required images.

There were ten days to go. Each evening she returned from work and rang Winslow's mobile, but it continued to ring out, with no-one answering. She rang Izzie and said she was worried. Izzie soothed her. On the Friday before the launch she went to London and she and Izzie spent the night at Dolphin Square.

On the Saturday they spent the day being tourists in London, walking along the Thames, having lunch in China

Town and going to see a movie in the evening. When they returned to Dolphin Square, Maddie saw that there was a missed call on her mobile, which she had turned off in the cinema. She was excited to see that it came from "Winslow Mobile".

She rang him immediately.

"How are you?" she said. "Where are you? Where have you been?"

Winslow did not answer the questions, but he was very keen to apologise.

"I really am terribly sorry," he said. "I had to leave my mobile phone and a load of other things in a bag in the Left Luggage at the airport. They wanted me to be completely untraceable, so I left the country on a different passport. I am not going to tell you anything else, but I did not get hurt and, if I am honest, I was really rather bored most of the time. Not much happened. Except for about 10 minutes at the end when we did what we set out to do. Anyway, you can believe me when I say I thought only of you two. Why would a man do anything else?"

"Men are strange," said Maddie. "Where are you now?"

"I was at Heathrow," he said, "but as you did not answer I decided that the best thing to do would be to go back to Daisybelle. I'm on my way back there now. Where are you?"

"I'm with Izzie at Dolphin Square," she said. "Why don't you come back and join us?"

"No, I am nearly there now," he said. "It would take a couple of hours to get back and I am tired. Give Izzie a kiss from me. Maybe I'll come tomorrow. There are still some things I have to do."

"What could possibly be more interesting than being with the two of us?" Maddie said.

Winslow laughed. It was true. He really was incredibly lucky to have met Maddie and Izzie. It was something he had thought about a lot when he was away. He was well aware of his good fortune. And yet, a soldier is a soldier and completing the mission was important.

"I'll come down tomorrow," he said again. "I promise."

"You had better," Maddie said, "Izzie and I have almost forgotten what it is like having you around. We need to be reminded why it is that we require men. When we were on the island, we discussed that and the only thing we cannot do without you is to conceive children - but as neither of us has any urge to be a mother right now, we concluded that men are entirely useless."

"I'd be happy to remind you both our uses," he said. "Or perhaps I should say, the pleasures that men can bring you."

"I'm sure we'd be happy with a refresher course," Maddie said. Izzie nodded.

"I will wing my way to you tomorrow," said Winslow, "like Cupid with his bow."

"I never understood that idea," said Maddie. "Cupid would not have been very efficient aerodynamically, would he?"

"He was a bit of hunk in his day," said Winslow. "He's only become a chubby chap in recent times. He was originally a man so gorgeous that even the delicious Psyche, who I imagine looked a little like Sophie Marceau, got excited and fell head over heels in love with him."

"I can't say I know the story," Maddie said. "I was never really excited by mythology. I'm too practical by nature to have gods and mortals all mixed up. If god was one of us, we'd be bumping into Zeus and Venus down at the supermarket."

"Ah, Maddie," said Winslow. "It's great to know that you haven't changed..."

As promised, Winslow appeared on Sunday and the three of them had lunch together at a pub called The Marquis of something or other. They then wandered back to the apartment and hung out until it was time for some hot chocolate. After that things warmed up somewhat, after Winslow asked to see their all-over tans. He was impressed.

They went their separate ways in the early morning: Winslow returning to Daisybelle, somewhere up near Warwick; Maddie heading off to prepare for the car launch; and Izzie going back to Tarquin's office at the House.

The return of Winslow was a relief and a pleasure and it fitted neatly in with the general mood of Maddie's life.

At Chiphurst there is always a sense of optimism in January. It is the time when a F1 team is at its happiest, unless it wins a great deal, in which case each victory brings a burst of joy. If not, January is as good as it gets, because belief in possible success tends to lift everyone on a cloud of hope. They all think that maybe this year will be different and that the struggles will all be worth it. The team charges along, powered by enthusiasm.

Later, when the races begin, the hopes are modified or abandoned, as the reality of the situation in revealed. Those who have been through the cycle many times know that it is best to rein back the dreams and keep one's feet firmly on the ground. It is a tricky balance between being realistic and avoiding deflating the hopes and dampening the energy that is inherent in a company of ambitious dreamers.

The worst thing one can do with the media is to make overly optimistic statements and raise expectations too much. The sponsors and the media will be sucked along in the excited flow, but they are easily disappointed and then tend to be harsh in their reaction when a team fails to achieve what it hoped to achieve. They feel they have been sold a nag when they have invested - emotionally at least - in a Derby winner.

Charlie was smart enough to know this trick and so the Chiphurst Competition launch, while designed to show the team in a new light, was planned to be a fairly low-key affair without jugglers, acrobats and fireworks, but with sufficient *canapés* and *gourmandises* to avoid the suggestion that the team might be short of budget.

In F1, the results always do the talking and so the simple approach is usually the correct one. F1 is a competition between engineers, with a bunch of marketing people going along for the ride. If the marketing people run the show, a team is rarely successful and loses its way. The Williams team was for many years famous for its tea-and-biscuit launches at windy race tracks, but results showed that how one launches the car does not affect the lap times.

Once the new car presentations are out of the way, the realists take over. The cars are trucked off to sunnier climes in Spain and run against one another in tests, and everyone tries to figure out who has done the best job. It is a time of subterfuge and holding the cards close to one's chest and not giving away the brightest new ideas, lest others "borrow" them. Everyone in F1 knows that in theory copying is not going to win races, but they do it anyway... trying out new concepts in wind tunnels and in the mind-blowing world of computational fluid dynamics, in which the whole process is assessed with virtual air, running over a virtual car. This is cheaper, quicker and much more flexible an approach than the traditional testing methods. It is a time of year when the cars run round and round gathering data which feeds the driver simulators, used when real testing is not allowed. The complexity of these machines is simply astonishing, as they replicate every possible detail of a real racing car, building in variables such as tyre wear rates and fuel loads, and even weather. This all means that the development of a car can be much more efficient, as long as the simulator correlates exactly to the car running on the track. If one copies a basic competitive package and advances from it, then one can not only catch up with the top teams but can also challenge them.

There is frenetic activity throughout February as the cars are moved from one track to another and run as much as they can be. New parts are flown out by the day, problems are solved.

It is a time to have your drivers lifting off in the final sector, or recording a lap time from a different point on the circuit to everyone else.

Expectations are modified, but you still don't know the true story until you get to final qualifying in Melbourne on the second weekend in March. That is where the gloves truly come off.

# Twenty

Everything was in order on the big day, with the venue in London decked out nicely. Maddie even invited Izzie to attend, but she called off, saying she was too busy at the House of Commons. It was probably better that way. Maddie was running around a lot. The launch itself went well. Charlie did a decent job saying that Chiphurst was not big on car launches and so he had decided to do it himself and pulled the covers off the old car with little ceremony.

"Oh bugger," he said. "They've sent the wrong car."

The assembled media was perplexed.

"Well, gents - and ladies," he said. "As you can see I've unveiled the wrong car."

There was a laugh.

"But the thing I don't really understand is that I have a button here, which has a big sign that says: 'Press here'. I guess I'll have to give it a try and see if we can do a little magic."

He pressed the button. There was a swishing noise and the slab of concrete crashed down on the old car, completely smashing it. On top of the slab was the new car.

There was a sharp intake of breath around the room.

"Smashing!" he said, as planned. "Well, that seemed to work. I bet none of you got the shot!"

A cameraman at the back of the room said "Wrong!" loudly and Charlie smiled. "I expect you'll be able to sell that one a fair bit then," he said.

"Ladies and gentlemen, I have a speech here somewhere," he went on, "but I cannot be bothered with it. The gist of it is very simple. The old Chiphurst Competition has gone. We've got a new car, new partners and a very competitive driver line-up, or at least we think we do. Time will tell, I'm sure, but I'm delighted. Now if you chaps want some photos I will call up the drivers and we can pose with the new car. Sadly, the old one is rather two-dimensional."

That raised a laugh and then it was into the photographs, the TV interviews and the written press sessions.

The assembled media were each given a folder with all the details of the new car, with a large blue explosion on the cover with the word "Smash!" in a suitable font. They were happy. There was a finger-food kind of lunch and by about three the team was able to sweep the last of the hacks out of the door. Maddie relaxed.

Charlie gave her a big kiss on the forehead and said: "Take the rest of the day off!"

And that was that.

Maddie was left in an empty hall. Sometimes life is like that. One moment you are at the centre of everything and then suddenly you are completely alone. It was not quiet for very long. The truckies from Chiphurst appeared a few minutes later to take away the new car, the equipment and the wreckage of the old one. By five the venue was beautifully clean and Maddie was ready to leave. She didn't want to go home alone, and so drove her car down to Pimlico and stuck it in the car park under Dolphin Square. It was too early to disturb Izzie, so she walked through to Victoria Street and on to St James's Park.

It was dark and quite cold, but London had an energy that Maddie loved and she was happy to walk and soak up the power of the city. She found herself at Horse Guards Parade and walked through to Whitehall. The Guards had long since turned in for the night and there was no one about as she passed through the gates. She crossed over to the Banqueting House, remembering from her school days that it was through one of the windows above her that in 1649 King Charles I walked on to a scaffold, to be beheaded. It is a sobering thought to remember where blood has been spilled.

She wandered on, past the Royal United Services Institute, and an area of green that they call Raleigh Gardens, in front of the Ministry of Defence. There were a series of statues of celebrated Generals: Slim, Alanbrooke and Montgomery. She was opposite Downing Street, but her attention was drawn to the left with the blue neon arc of the London Eye, just across the river. She hurried on, the streets were busy with tardy government types heading home. She ducked into The Red Lion pub and rang Izzie. It was seven.

Izzie answered instantly.

"Hi," Maddie said. "I'm here, at The Red Lion. How's it looking?"

"It's not so bad tonight," she said. "Tarquin is off at some conference somewhere. Give me ten minutes and I'll be there. How was the launch?"

"It was good," said Maddie.

"You can tell me all about it," said Izzie.

Maddie ordered a couple of drinks and waited. Izzie was as good as her word. She was excited about Maddie's day. The launch was on the TV news, with the footage of the old car being crushed. It was a huge success.

They stayed about an hour, although Maddie found it hard not to show any affection in public.

"It is strange to have to hide emotions when we are together," she said.

"I know," said Izzie, "but this is not a desert island and in Westminster there is still a lot of stigma, even in the Twenty-First Century. I don't want to come out, because I'm still not sure what I am. Maybe I should have figured it all out years ago, but I like men and women and I don't really have a decision."

"Why should you?" said Maddie.

"That's the point," said Izzie, "until I decide if I want to try to get elected, I don't want to label myself one thing or another."

"Fair enough," said Maddie. "If it's a career decision, then it makes sense. I'm the same. I really don't know what Charlie would make of it. He'd probably ask to join in!"

Izzie pulled a face and laughed.

"Anyway," she said. "I'm not the only one who is hiding. They reckon that about six to nine percent of women are gay or bisexual. That's a government figure, I think. Anyway, there are six hundred and fifty MPs, one hundred and forty-seven of them are women. Twenty-two percent. That's pretty poor when you consider that fifty-one percent of the population are women. It's nearly a hundred years since women were allowed to vote for the first time, but progress has been slow. And statistically there should be four or five lesbians in the House of Commons, but only two have come out. So lesbians are either not selected, not elected or they are frightened to be open about their sexuality."

"Maybe we should both stand for election and become the first lesbian couple to both become MPs," said Maddie.

"I think Winslow might be a bit of a problem..." said Izzie. "The House is just about ready to accept women who sleep with women, but I fear defibrillators would be required if we tried to explain that we all sleep with each other. I guess they would need a select committee to discuss trisexuals."

"What's a trisexual?" said Maddie.

"I believe they use the expression to describe people who will try anything."

"Not me then," said Maddie. "I have very set limits. Men and women are enough for me!"

"No toys?" said Izzie.

"No toys," said Maddie. "I don't need them."

"I could search your house and I wouldn't find a single sex toy?" said Izzie.

"Not one," said Maddie. "Don't you remember? You're my sex toy."

Izzie smiled.

They wandered slowly back through the streets of Westminster and stopped off on the way at the place they liked to eat scampi and chips and, as was now the tradition, they shared a plate, eating with their fingers. It had become almost a trigger in their sex life. Once the plate was cleared they were always keen to rush back to the apartment and did not waste time with coffee or chit-chat. And yet it was not all explosive sex. That evening they retired to bed quite casually. Izzie was still in her bra and underwear, Maddie was wearing a shirt, but had discarded her bra and knickers. They enjoyed snuggling.

"Nothing beats pre-sex snuggling," Maddie said, as she kissed the top of Izzie's head.

"Not even a nice orgasm?" said Izzie, looking up at Maddie, with very large suggestive eyes.

"OK," said Maddie, "I will revise my previous assertion. Nothing beats snuggling before a nice gasping orgasm."

"Right," said Izzie, "we have done the snuggling, so we need to do the nice gasping orgasm thing."

She disappeared beneath the duvet and Maddie sank back, relaxed and enjoying Izzie's expert explorations. She still had a little voice in the back of her head saying "But you're not a lesbian," and yet, whenever Izzie started on her, the voice was drowned out by the passion. Maddie was amazed that someone could have this power over another person. It had never happened to her with a man, not even with Winslow.

What was it that made the difference? Maddie had believed from the very start that women are simply better at making love to women because they know what their lover wants and how they function. Everyone is a little different when it comes to what turns them on, but the mechanics of the human body are pretty much the same from one body to another. The secret is that it is not the places that one touches that are important, it is how you touch them. Men tend to have a 'to do' list and they work their way through the different stages: breasts, a little oral sex, penetration and then climax. They tend to stay at the same pace, believing that this will turn on their partner. But with Izzie it was completely different. She would graze on Maddie, first here, and then there. She would touch her all over, her hands, her feet, her stomach, the small of her back, her buttocks and breasts, of course, but also her scalp, knees and thighs. She would tug gently on Maddie's hair. The touch was different in different places, with finesse and sensitivity depending on the spot. She always seemed to know the pace to match Maddie's arousal.

The other thing that Maddie loved was that when the orgasms were subsiding, Izzie would go to sleep. She always made sure that her lover enjoyed a stress-free afterglow. She knew that Maddie didn't like being held and so she would simply whisper about how amazing it was to make love to her and then she would get on with life.

That is not to say that their lovemaking was in any way one-sided, although Izzie did always tend to take the lead. She was, if you like, the "man" in the relationship. She liked that. She showed Maddie what she wanted and Maddie did what she was told to do. And it worked. Izzie's climaxes were just as shattering as Maddie's. The two were well-suited in this respect.

Afterwards, Maddie would lie there, thinking "I'm not gay", but she loved every moment. Of course, she loved it when Winslow was there with them. She loved to be possessed as only a man can possess a woman. She loved to be penetrated. She loved the roughness that contrasted to Izzie's gentle ways. And Izzie liked it too. Maddie had concluded almost from the start that, like her, Izzie was not really a lesbian, but simply enjoyed the sensuality. She had watched Izzie squirming and twitching on top of Winslow and knew exactly the pleasure that she was feeling at that moment.

That night they made love for what seemed like hours and then Maddie sensed that Izzie had drifted into sleep. The alarm was set for six in the morning and Maddie sighed. She would not be getting much sleep.

At that time of the morning, getting to Oxford would take

at least ninety minutes, even as an anti-commuter and then she would need half an hour to change and clean up and then another twenty minutes to get to the factory.

To get there at nine she needed to leave London at six thirty. Maddie would slip out of bed, into the shower and then they would share a quick cup of coffee and a lingering kiss. She would then disappear, leaving Izzie to run a bath. She loved to soak herself, rather than be showered in a few short minutes.

With the car launch out of the way, the team at Chiphurst Competition were able to finish building the car. Once that was done there was the exciting day when the engine was fired up for the first time. There was no reason why anything would not work, because it had all been tested on rigs and simulators so it was really just a question of whether the assembly had been done correctly.

The next big excitement was to see how the car went in comparison to its rivals in testing and the first finished car was sent off to Barcelona for the initial test of the year. Maddie flew down with Charlie for the first day of running. The team had decided to allow Poppy Denso to have the first run. All seemed to go well. Systems checks were done, data was gathered, and most importantly nothing fell off the car or caught fire. Towards the end of the day, Poppy was told that he could do a little performance work and began to push the car to its limits. They didn't want him to do any complete laps but were keen to know how fast the car would go in different sectors. By adding up the best of these they could come up with a lap time that would give them an idea. On his third fast run Poppy let out a whoop of joy on the radio.

"Repeat," said an engineer sternly.

Poppy came slowly into the pits and drove the car straight into the garage. The team pulled down the door. Poppy climbed out and walked out to the truck to chat to his engineers, while the mechanics went over the car like fingerprint men at a crime scene.

"It's a brilliant car," was all that he said. We don't tell

nobody about it..."

Elfin considered for a brief moment trying to explain to the Brazilian that double negatives make a positive, but concluded that it was probably not the right moment.

Poppy was fast, but he was not awfully intelligent. He would never be a World Champion.

Everyone was happy. For the rest of the day, Poppy lifted off the throttle at different points on each fast lap. The engineers knew what was going on, but the opposition could only guess. They would find out at the first race. F1 people like psychological warfare, it adds to the pressure on the others to have to perform all the time, but Chiphurst was not just playing mental games. Teams can use testing as a publicity stunt. By setting good lap times, they can get lots of column inches, which they can then show to potential sponsors and, now and then, they might find a foolish entrepreneur who falls for such things and pays out millions, only to be disappointed later on.

The problem with showing your real speed too early is that the other teams will then direct their spies to try to out where the advantage is, and one can lose it as quickly as one found it.

"This car might not win races," said Charlie Chiphurst on the flight home, "but it will certainly make a good impression. So what we need to do now is to carefully manage the PR side. We want maximum impact at the first race. Testing never gets much real coverage, so we want to avoid setting good lap times. We want to give everyone a really big surprise in Australia. The bigger the story, the more coverage you get."

"Word always leaks out," said Maddie.

Charlie ignored her.

As part of the restructuring of the engineering team under Elfin Grindvall, there was going to be a new race engineer for Jimmy Buckett. His name was Dave Blenkinsop and he was six feet four inches tall and broad as a barrel.

Elfin reckoned that Blenkinsop's direct ways would be just the thing for Buckett.

Jimmy was dozing in a deck chair in the paddock when his

new engineer arrived.

"Are you a wanker?" The giant from Barnsley said, looking down on the callow American youth from a very considerable height.

Buckett opened one eye, looked the engineer up and down and then closed his eye again and said: "I guess that you are either a market researcher, who used to play basketball, or that clipboard means that you are my new race engineer."

"Aye," said Blenkinsop, "I am and I know you think you're dead cool, but to me you're not. You're a wanker until you prove otherwise. I like quick. I don't like excuses. You get to be called Driver if you're quick. Until I decide that you are quick, you're called Wanker."

"Fine," said Buckett without opening his eyes. "If you can make my car go quicker, I will call you Sir."

"Cocky little fucker, aren't you?" said Blenkinsop. "I have just a little bit of advice, by the way. I've been around F1 since you were in what you Americans called diapers. If you want to do well, overcome your innate meanness of soul and take your mechanics out for some pizza and cheap wine from time to time. If you feed them they will be your slaves. They will love you. Motor racing isn't hard. You give English mechanics pizza, you give Germans anything edible - because there is nothing edible in their country - and they will all be happy."

"What about the French?" said Buckett.

"Who cares?" said Blenkinsop, "no-one likes the French, but they don't care because they like themselves plenty!"

And with that gem of wisdom he strode off in the direction of the engineering truck, to spin some more home truths to anyone who was willing to listen.

Later, he explained to Buckett and Denso that he came from Barnsley.

"That's Yorkshire," he told the drivers. "Confuse that with Lancashire and I'll punch your nose. Wars have been fought over such matters."

He was also keen that they knew how to spell his name correctly.

"It's with one p at the end," he said. "Only one."

Blenkinsop was a man who knew what he liked and was happy to tell anyone who wanted to listen. He had learned to play the F1 game at the feet of Patrick Head at Williams.

"I don't like bullshit," he said. "I don't like liars. And I think most drivers are wankers, but if I get a good one, I'll be happy and as sweet as a goldfish."

Poppy Denso looked puzzled when he heard this. So, in England, he thought, little fishes can be sweet. It was very confusing.

On the second day of Buckett's test, Blenkinsop called him "Driver" and Buckett said: "Thank you, Sir."

The lap times remained deliberately unimpressive and the journalists were suitably downbeat in their reporting, but Buckett knew. And Blenkinsop too.

Back at the Chiphurst factory things were buzzing with excitement. One never really knows how competitive a car is going to be until you go up against the others in serious competition, but the testing seemed to suggest that a lot of the teams had made a big improvements in aerodynamics over the winter. The lap times were very close. It was going to be an exciting season.

One day, in the canteen, Maddie found herself sitting with Blenkinsop, discussing whether or not he thought that they had a winning car. Elfin had told Charlie that it was a winner, but Blenkinsop was not so sure.

"If you look at the other cars," he said. "You can see a lot of copying of last year's Merc. It's not just our car. A lot of people have had the same idea. We cannot know for sure until we go racing, but I think that with a lot of teams having copied the Mercedes, I expect to see a lot of cars being very close to us. The good news is that the drivers will come into a play a lot more, and we have one good one. It will also be grand for the sport too, because we should have some cracking races, but I do think that it is all a bit odd. When I was a lad, learning at the feet of the great engineers of the day, I were always told that if you copy, you're a follower. You're not a winner. We learned to be the ones who jumped ahead, not that followed behind. Now the design types, like Elfin, get very touchy when someone says that they have been copying. I understand that, but I'm just saying that a lot of the cars this year look a bit the same - and I think it is very odd."

As the start of the season drew closer, Maddie began to feel both excited and a little melancholy. The racing would mean she would have less time to spend with Winslow and Izzie. After Winslow came back, they saw each other most evenings, either at the cottage or on the Daisybelle. Maddie's car quickly became a wardrobe on wheels.

"I've been wondering if I should put the chest of drawers in the boot," she said one evening. That would be the most efficient thing."

Izzie was their weekend treat, although Maddie saw her sometimes if she went up to London. They shared a few plates of scampi and chips and there were a few early morning runs up the M40 to Oxford. Maddie enjoyed having a relatively stable life for a while, and she knew that she would miss it when the travelling started again.

The last week of February rolled into the first week of March and Maddie packed her bags for the opening race, which was held as usual in Melbourne. It felt odd and she worried whether she had forgotten things, which never happened when the season was up and running. There was a fond farewell with her two partners on the Sunday night and she flew out on the Monday.

In the F1 world, people meet on planes all the time. It's only the really big names who can afford their own private jets and one regularly bumps into drivers, technical directors, team principals and journalists on commercial flights. Inevitably this means that a lot of business is done on planes, or as the result of meetings on planes and in airports. Flying in business class, there are some flights where every single passenger in the cabin is involved in the sport.

Maddie boarded the plane in London and noted some other team people were there. There were a few knowing nods, but there was no-one to whom Maddie really wanted to talk. Upstairs in an Emirates A380, one can hide away from the world in one's own little space, without having to deal with anyone else. There is wireless internet, food, drink, electricity and endless videos and music. You can sleep easily, particularly if you're an F1 person, who knows how to sleep anywhere. If you want to chat there is a bar at the back, where the lotharios practice their seduction skills on stewardesses from a wide array of nations.

Maddie watched movies until they reached Dubai and then, after a couple of hours in the Business Class lounge, she boarded a second flight, non-stop to Melbourne. She intended to sleep all the way.

Thirteen hours later, the A380 lumbered into Tullamarine International Airport. It was early on Wednesday morning (Melbourne time) and Maddie was feeling energetic. She was quickly through immigration and baggage collection and was soon in a taxi, heading into the city. She liked Melbourne and started the day with a good solid Australian breakfast at the hotel, before heading out to Albert Park with a chauffeur that the team employed each year in Australia.

# Twenty-one

For a large percentage of the racing fraternity, the Australian Grand Prix is the most popular race on the calendar. The locals are friendly and they talk vaguely the same language as most F1 people. They have some exquisite wines. Maddie was not too keen on the pretentious menus that they always seemed to have in the chic Melbourne eateries. Olive oil could never be just olive oil, it has to be virgin, or even extra-virgin. Cheese has to be matured on some exotic kind of native hardwood.

Everything comes glazed with a bizarre form of marmalade or foam, and all meat and fish come from a named region, and even from a specific farm.

Beef cannot just be beef.

That evening she went out with a couple of Chiphurst engineers and ordered "Tasmanian wok-fried goat with a raspberry glaze and green tomato marmalade". Just for fun, she completely flummoxed the waiter by asking him to explain the difference between a Tasmanian wok and one that would normally be found in mainland China. The manager was called to try to explain that it was the goat rather than the wok that came from Tasmania, but Maddie just smiled and said something about menu-writing and grammar.

In March the weather in Melbourne is usually good,

providing the palefaces from Europe with the chance to pick up some southern hemisphere sunshine, after the wintry months back home. Melbourne is a city that has entirely embraced Formula 1 racing. Trams are painted to advertise the event, every shop adopts a Grand Prix theme and the papers are filled with F1-related stories, usually negative unless they involve a local driver.

Albert Park, where the racing takes place, was once a swamp where the citizens used to dump their rubbish but, as the city expanded, it was turned into a public park and in the 1950s hosted the Australian Grand Prix, on the roads that ran through it. The race faded away because of protests from home owners, who did not like to find the remains of Maserati 250Fs on their neat front lawns. It was not until the 1990s that the local government decided to revive the idea and took on a small number of tree-hugging opponents, who claimed to be ecologists. Corporate Australia won that battle and the resulting race track was brilliant, setting new standards for temporary facilities, while also providing Melbourne with a public park which was no longer a place where only derelicts, drunks and drug addicts hung out.

Because the race track is on streets, some of which are not used much, the Albert Park circuit is always very dusty on the first day of the new season, and teams often confuse themselves about the performance of their cars and their tyres. As more and more rubber sticks to the road, the surface becomes grippier and the lap times come down. There is a tendency on the Friday for some of the wilder and less experienced drivers to overestimate the levels of grip. Poppy Denso did exactly that and piled his brand new car into one of the tyre barriers at very high speed.

"I bet that scared your shit out of you," he told the track marshals after the crash.

Poppy was not really sure what to say to Elfin Grindvall and Charlie Chiphurst and so he stayed at the scene of the crime until after the session was over. To Denso's surprise Charlie just nodded when the Brazilian did finally return to the pits, although later, in the privacy of the team hospitality,

Chiphurst was heard to call his number one driver "a bumbling, blank-headed berk". Denso asked his engineers to translate exactly what Charlie meant and spent the rest of the day pouting, with his eyebrows lowered.

Then Buckett spun and damaged his car as well.

"The good news is that we can probably build one car using parts from the two wrecks," said Elfin, with a large wink.

There were not a lot of spare parts available and the drivers were instructed not to crash the cars again. Saturday was the day when the gloves finally came off and Charlie was delighted to see his cars scramble through the Q sessions to take seventh and ninth on the grid.

"I could have been fifth," Buckett told the engineers.

"I could have been third," Denso responded, keen not to be outdone by his young team-mate.

Buckett laughed. He was not really bothered about playing games with Denso. He knew he was a better driver and no amount of psychological warfare would change that view.

And Poppy knew it too.

When the Q3 session ended, Charlie was caught on TV dancing a brief tango on the pit wall with one of his engineers. The smarter observers noted how small the gaps were between the top teams and the fact that there were seven teams represented in the top ten, but Chiphurst had done a better job than most. The team was bubbling with enthusiasm and, at one point, Maddie found herself chatting with the mechanic known only as Oily Rag, when he was on a break and having a cup of tea. She reminded herself that she really must try to find out his real name.

"I've been around this sport for a few years," Oily said, "but I've never seen anything like this. The cars are so close together. Everyone is pretty much of a muchness. It looks like it will all be down to set-ups and the drivers. I know the rules are a bit restrictive, but all the cars look very alike to me. I've never seen that before. I guess that everyone copied the Mercedes. They were bloody quick last year. I don't know if we can win or not, but I think Jimmy is bloody good and I bet you we see some really great races from him this year."

Maddie thought back to a similar conversation with Blenkinsop. It was strange how everyone seemed to have done the same thing and copied the Mercedes. She knew how Chiphurst has done it, but wondered about the others. Was it possible, she thought, that they had done similar deals with Winslow? Commercially, that made sense and she had never thought to ask Winslow if their deal was exclusive. She had just assumed it was. The thought did not last for long. She had a fancy dinner to prepare for, with some of the big regional customers of Penkoz, and even Mr Al-Rehab was in town. They did not get to sleep until late, but with a late afternoon race they had some time to relax on the Sunday morning.

That day, Albert Park was packed as the F1 cars headed out to line up on the grid. There was huge excitement up and down the pit lane. It is always like that at the start of the F1 season, but there is also the fear that the drivers will get too excited and crash into one another on the first lap, after a winter of controlling their innate aggression. Sometimes it just happens and, more often than not, the first lap is the moment when these crashes occur.

Up in the VIP hospitality, overlooking the start-finish line, Maddie had her guests tuned into the action and ready to start cheering for Buckett and Denso. As the cars came round on their final parade lap, with the engines idling, everyone was standing up and watching out of the windows. As luck would have it, they were right opposite where Buckett and Denso were lined up, one in front of the other

The start lights began to go on, one after another, and the engine grumbles turned into a roar. Then the lights went out and suddenly there were cars going everywhere. Maddie loved that moment more than anything else in F1. There was something slightly orgasmic about expectation suddenly turning into wild release.

In the circumstances, it is always easy to confuse one driver with another, if you are trying to follow the overall activity, but Maddie was watching only Jimmy Buckett. He made a decent start and went into the first corner using an inside line, thus reducing the chances he would be knocked out in someone else's accident. He emerged from the corner in sixth and scrambled up to fifth during the rush towards Turn Two, as one of the cars ahead lost momentum at the exit of the first corner. Maddie rushed across the room to watch the TV screens, but there was no shot of Buckett.

All the cameras were on a tangle of cars left behind at the first corner. There in the middle of the mess was Poppy Denso. He had tried to go around the outside of everyone but had slid into the car in front of him and ridden up over it. The two cars then slid off into the sand trap, taking a couple of others with them. Yellow flags were being waved everywhere and there were boards with the letters SC being shown. Maddie explained there was a Safety Car period and the race was running under caution while the damaged cars were removed.

"A crash is good for the sponsors," she said, stretching the truth somewhat. "This way you get more air-time."

At that moment the TVs in the hospitality conveniently began to show replays of the crash from a number of different angles, and in slow motion, and the Penkoz customers were happy to see the name on the cars.

For the next few laps the field circulated behind the Safety Car, growling with displeasure at not being allowed to run free. Then the Safety Car turned off its lights and a message saying "Safety Car in this lap" came up on the timing screens.

"OK," Maddie said. "When they come past us, they are racing again."

Buckett had done a great job making sure his car was at the right speed and the right distance behind the car in front and as he crossed the start-finish line he was already alongside the fourth-placed driver. Maddie could hear the track announcer screaming Buckett's name as the two cars went side-by-side into the first corner. Please don't let them collide, she thought. Buckett braked later and was ahead, but at the exit of the corner the car drifted wide and his rival ducked to the inside and the two disappeared from view, side-by-side once more. They turned to the TV screens to see

Buckett and the McLaren go through the next turn together. It was a right-hander and Buckett refused to give way on the outside. He was out there on the edge, but it meant he had the advantage into the next corner, a left-hander.

He was fourth.

The race switched a little more to strategy and, by pitting before the third-placed driver, Buckett was able to lap faster and was ahead when the pit stops were finished. He was third and Charlie Chiphurst was jumping about like a schoolboy in need of a pee. The second-placed car was ten seconds ahead on the road and Jimmy was closing the gap, but both drivers had well worn tyres and so the fight gradually stabilized. It was just a case of getting the cars home. Maddie prayed quietly the leader would be hit by a thunderbolt and the engine of the man in second place would turn itself into metal muesli, but lap after lap the gap stayed about the same. She told the VIPs that if Jimmy could use his rubber more efficiently he could make up time and added that they might call him into the pits and give him new tyres, which would allow him to not only make up the time he would lose in the pits, but also to catch and pass the man ahead.

"I don't know if they'll do it," Maddie said. "But usually we take a risk if there's a risk to take."

Down in the pits Blenkinsop was calling the shots.

"OK," he bellowed into the radio. "We're doing this. Don't mess it up."

Jimmy peeled off into the pit lane, jumped on the brakes at the last second and wrecked what was left of the old tyres. The Chiphurst was at rest for just two seconds, during which time all four wheels were changed.

"Fuck me," said Al-Rehab, rather impressed by what he had seen.

When Jimmy rejoined, he was twenty-eight seconds behind the car in second place, and he had fourteen laps to go. The track was clear and his tyres were soft and new. He could use them to do qualifying-style laps, at least for a while before they began to lose their edge. At the end of that first lap the gap was down to twenty-five point one. Next time around it was twenty-three point four then twenty-one point eight, then twenty point six. Jimmy was on schedule.

Next time around he had made a big effort, or the guy ahead had made a mistake, because the gap suddenly dropped to seventeen point six and then fifteen point one, twelve point three and ten point two. There were six laps to go and ten seconds to find - and an overtaking move to do.

It was not going to be easy.

The good news was Jimmy's rivals were suffering more and more as their older tyres gave out and so next time around the gap was down to seven point three and then four point eight. Everyone in the Chiphurst VIP area was cheering him on. Was there ever a better way to build a sense of team spirit? Maddie thought. Next time around the gap was three point two.

The TV cameras were now following Buckett as he closed in on the Red Bull ahead. Both drivers were getting more ragged, but in every sector Buckett was closing. On that lap Jimmy clawed back another one point two, the gap was two seconds and he had two laps to go.

Down on the pit wall Charlie Chiphurst had a very pink face. He looked like he was holding his breath. That lap the Red Bull locked up twice under braking and Jimmy was right on his gearbox as they set off on the last lap.

The team heard Buckett on the radio, talking to himself. "I am doing this" he said. "I'm doing this."

If it was going to happen, it was going to be in Turn Three. They all knew it. Here the driver jumps on the brakes and the car goes from one hundred and eighty-five miles per hour down to sixty-five. It's a place for the brave. The Red Bull did not have the grip and so the driver was trying to put his car on the piece of road that Jimmy needed, but he did not know where that was going to be. Buckett jinked to the left, then instantly went right. The Red Bull lurched left, but Buckett was alongside him on the inside. The two cars skittered towards the apex of the corner. Buckett got there first, eased the power down a fraction faster and the car pulled ahead. The place was won. Everyone around Maddie was cheering and she could see Charlie, down on the pit wall, waving two fingers in the air. It wasn't that she wasn't happy, but deep down she knew it wasn't quite fair. They had copied the car. She saw Elfin down on the pit wall. He was smiling broadly: no sign of a conscience there, she thought. He was the only other person in the team who knew. Everyone else was ecstatic. This was the fairy tale they had dreamed about for so long.

Buckett pulled away from the Red Bull in the final part of the last lap and duly crossed the finishing line, waggling his car from side to side in celebration and whooping into the radio. Everyone was hugging and cheering. Maddie was worn out and sat down. She knew that she couldn't get down to the pit lane in time to watch the podium ceremony and so she picked up a glass of champagne and downed it in one.

Her VIPs were all excited, but gradually they calmed down had a drink, exchanged business cards and then headed off home. She did not wait for the last one to leave. She made her excuses and went down into the paddock, to celebrate with the team. She felt rather drunk.

Buckett was tied up with the media, doing interviews for the written press and then the TV crews. It would be a while before he returned. Charlie was busy talking to other journalists and so Maddie sat with Elfin and they asked the hospitality girls for some wine. They chinked glasses and sat, smiling at one another, not really needing to talk. Racing people can be like that sometimes. Success does not need words. She could not help but feel the irony of the moment. They were the only two team members who knew the secret of how their success had been achieved. And one of them didn't know that the other one knew the secret. It was a brilliant scam, she thought.

Later she, Charlie, Elfin and Jimmy agreed to have dinner. Blenkinsop went along too. They invited Poppy, but he and Rosita had other plans. After eating, the party planned to go dancing. The rest of the crew had turned up by then, as tarted up as they could manage after a busy day at the races. The motorhome girls, the mechanics and engineers were all going on a bender. There would be some damaged heads by the morning.

Charlie was smiling from ear to ear all evening and, as usual, his political-correctness failed him spectacularly.

"You know, Maddie," he said. "I reckon that I would have less fun than I am having now if I was with two honey-covered lesbians."

Maddie smiled. "Yes, you probably are," she said. "Lesbians wouldn't be in the least bit interested in some old pervert watching them."

Charlie laughed out loud.

"That's harsh," he said.

"That's truth," she replied, with a sweet smile.

He shrugged. She was probably right. She usually was.

Maddie was feeling weary and was not really in the mood to party. She was happy for everyone. It was good to see them so elated and it was satisfying that she knew it was she who had made this all possible. But there was something not quite right. She stayed long enough to be polite and then slipped quietly away into the night.

She had agreed with Charlie that she would take a week off between the races and Winslow had said he would fly out to meet her in Sydney. He was due to arrive on the Monday evening.

Maddie was having a quiet breakfast on her own when Charlie appeared, looking remarkably fresh for a man who had been up drinking until "at least three". He said that he had left Buckett dancing on a table with three Australian girls, all called Jessica, but added that he would put money on an Emily, who had been lurking in the wings all evening. The remaining mechanics would no doubt have divided the Jessicas between them.

"Emily clearly knew how not to be obvious," Charlie explained. "And I think young Jimmy has done sufficient Jessicas to know that you get a better bang for your buck - if you'll pardon the expression - from an Emily."

"Or a combination," said Maddie, with a wink.

Charlie made some remark about that particular thought

being rather bad for "his ticker" and ordered himself a disgraceful breakfast involving sausages, bacon, beans, eggs and "a very large Bloody Mary".

"And crispy toast," he added. "Don't let them put it flat on a plate. Toast must stand up on end so that it does not go soggy."

There was still no sign of Buckett by the time Maddie and Charlie finished their breakfast. Chiphurst was off to Kuala Lumpur, to buy or sell some real estate, and it was agreed that they would meet again a week on Tuesday at Sepang.

"I'll call if I need you," he added.

"My phone may be switched off," said Maddie.

Shortly afterwards, Maddie took a cab out to Tullamarine airport and caught a flight up to Sydney. She checked into the wildly-over-priced downtown hotel they had booked. It had a huge king-sized bed, a marble bathroom and a spectacular view of Sydney Harbour Bridge and the Opera House.

She had a lazy afternoon, sleeping for a while and then going for a walk around The Rocks. She had planned to take a cab back out to the airport, but had read somewhere that there was now a train that went almost door-to-door and so she decided to give it a try. It was amazingly efficient.

She convinced Winslow that it was much better than a taxi, but it was still eleven at night before they got back to the hotel room, hung up the Do Not Disturb sign and tumbled wildly into bed. They did not venture out of the room until the following evening when, in need of sustenance, they went looking for a restaurant, down on the waterfront. They spent the next few days exploring Sydney. It felt a bit like what Maddie imagined a honeymoon might be like. They were just having fun.

They did not talk about motor racing, but one evening Maddie remembered that she had a question to ask him.

"No-one suspected anything in Melbourne," she said. "Elfin behaved as though the success of the car was entirely down to his genius alone..."

"... as he would," said Winslow.

"And no-one but me knew the secret," she added. "I felt

rather lonely."

"I know," said Winslow, with a reassuring smile.

"Yes," said Maddie, "we're crooks together and I cannot sell you out to the cops because you have a trail of paperwork that proves that I am the guilty party."

"I do," said Winslow. "You are at my mercy really."

"I do have a question, though," she said. "It was something that Blenkinsop, the new race engineer, said. He was sure that there was something strange going on. He told me. He said that too many of the cars look like last year's Mercedes. He'd never seen anything like it. He told me that he reckons a lot of copying has been going on."

"And?" said Winslow.

"Well, the mechanic they call Oily Rag said the same thing."

"It is always possible that other designers have been looking at the Mercedes," Winslow said. "Maybe they have mates in the team. That sort of thing happens all the time."

"Yes, I know," said Maddie, "but I wanted to understand the technology that we have today that could make that happen."

Winslow yawned.

"Well," he said, "I very much doubt that anyone has physically broken into any F1 factories. Most of the security efforts in F1 in the last ten years has gone into software, designed to stop one's own staff downloading data and selling it to someone else. That used to be the way they did it. Someone would copy files on to a disk and then either give or sell the information to a rival team. You cannot do that these days without leaving traces, but very few of the teams seem to have considered the possibility that external organizations can find what we call backdoors into their systems, bypassing the usual authentication procedures."

"You mean hacking?" said Maddie.

"Yes," said Winslow. "Getting into their systems. Nowadays everyone is switching across to cloud storage and that means there are going to be more opportunities because cloud service providers often store the data in more than one place and in the same server as data belonging to many others.

"Not long ago a computer security company in the US set up a number of servers and loaded them with different operating systems and widely-used programmes and invited hackers to try to break in. They offered a prize of five thousand dollars. It took just four hours for that prize to be won and it was done by someone without much hacking experience.

"So one needs to look not just at password access, but also at whether things need to be encrypted. These days hackers can use what we call dictionary attacks to work out passwords or decryption keys by trying thousands of likely possibilities. So one needs to have complex passwords. Passwords also need to be changed regularly, but people hate doing that.

"The other thing is that one can capture data en route to the cloud storage, even if it is encrypted. Nothing is really safe. Hackers can attack the cloud itself rather than the individual users and some governments can in any case get access if they want it. In the US, for example, all that you need is a subpoena requiring the cloud company to open their clients' data for government examination.

"I remember reading about the Renault F1 computers in France being hacked. It must have been fifteen years ago. They said that the hacking was traced to former members of the Stasi - the old East German Secret Police. It seems that whoever went into the computers deleted a load of data about the Renault V10 engine. Renault said that it had been a big blow at the time, but no-one knew much more than that. And they could not say whether the data had been stolen as well as being deleted, but it probably was."

He paused for a moment.

"Nowadays there are also these amazing laser devices that they use for process control, to make sure that everything fits exactly," he said. "These cut down inspection time and are much more consistent that traditional measuring methods. They are great for things like making racing seats. You just scan the driver's back and the seat will fit exactly. This means that all the parts are exact matches. You can also scan a rival car and reverse engineer it. It is virtually instantaneous.

"With the laser, you cannot do all the internals, you would need an x-ray machine to do that, but if you have the exact measurements of the bodywork, then you can design a chassis that would fit beneath it. If a team put one of these laser things in the pit lane, they could get an exact 3D scan of any rival team's car. It might help if they could scan the car without its bodywork, but that would be difficult. You can still build something pretty much identical.

"I heard about a great scam with these laser machines the other day," he went on. "If you takes one of these devices into a bank vault, disguised as a security camera, you can do all kinds of things. Everyone expects to see cameras in banks these days, so no-one thinks such a device is out of place in a safety deposit vault. The staff never go in there and customers don't really think about it. So you go back a few weeks later, take the scanner away and depart. You then go through the data that it has scanned and you can make copies of the keys that people used to open their boxes. Once the device is gone there is no crime, because the people being robbed are almost certainly not going to report the loss, because it is probably illegal anyway. And if there is no sign of the boxes being forced open, then it is a perfect crime, isn't it? No-one knows how it is done and no-one reports it."

Maddie was impressed.

"Any other ideas about the F1 thing?" she asked.

Winslow shook his head.

"I cannot think of any," he said.

"Oh, I can," said Maddie...

# Twenty-two

Winslow waited to hear what she had to say, his face a picture of curiosity.

"Well, how about this," Maddie said. "Someone else has got the same data that you gave Chiphurst, and perhaps they have sold the same information to four other teams and made a great deal more money?"

Winslow shook his head.

"No, I promise you. I did a deal with you guys alone," he said, rather hurt that Maddie would have even considered the possibility that he would do such a thing.

She believed him, but it did not really answer the question. Did Winslow really know the whole story? The scam, as it was, made sense. He had managed to extract three million dollars from Chiphurst Competition in exchange for the design data he had provided. That was a good profit margin. There was no need for anyone else to be involved.

Having said that, Maddie's suggestion was slightly worrying because he had to admit, if only to himself, that there was one key fact that she did not know: he had not been working for himself. He had been hired to do a job and he had done it. The money that Maddie had given him for the data had not gone into his bank account, but rather had been transferred to an account controlled by the person who had employed him. Houses had been bought in the Bahamas, but they did not belong to him. He had been given a generous lump sum for his role. That was it.

The other thing that Maddie did not know was he had not been the one who hacked into the Mercedes computers. He did not have the skills required to do that. He was an operational type, not a computer nerd. The data had come to him in the mail.

And so, he concluded, it was entirely possible the same data might have been sent to other teams and there were identical scams in parallel to the one with Chiphurst.

He was happy with his role in the whole process. He had been paid a good fee for his services and it was none of his business if there was more to the story than immediately met the eye. They had all made money or were going to enjoy more success than previously. There were no losers, or at least the losers did not know they were losing and so they had no reason to complain.

But Maddie was right. There might be four or five Winslows out there and the profits from the scam might have ramped up to between ten and fifteen million dollars. When he stopped to think about it later, when Maddie was in the shower, it was pretty obvious that it would be possible to do a lot with no-one knowing about it.

If you want to keep secrets in any covert organization, you have to create independent cells of people who do not know about one another. If there is no interaction between them, you have perfect security. If you want to keep things really secret, you then need to have cut-outs; intermediaries who are in contact with the cell leaders. They don't need to know the people in the cells, nor what a cell is actually doing.

Winslow realised that it was possible that he was just a cut-out and he had no real idea who he was working for. He could be a pawn in a far bigger game. There had been many occasions in the espionage world when people found out (in horror) that they had been working for the opposite side than they thought they were, without even knowing it.

If there were four other Winslows, doing exactly what he

had done, who would know? There would be four more car designers who had taken the data, but were ignorant of its source. They did not care and they were not about to admit anything. They had been given something that made them look good and they were not going to be stupid enough to have kept files that did not belong to them.

There would be four commercial people other than Maddie, but they were not going to tell anyone what they were up to because each had been compromised by having been paid very dubious commissions, which their team bosses did not know about. Thus, if they felt the need to reveal the story, they would be in the firing line for being dishonest and disloyal.

The more he thought about it, the more Winslow suspected that he might just be a part of a much bigger scam and the man who had commissioned him was probably not the person who had thought up the idea. In the course of this thought process he concluded that Maddie did not need to know more than she already knew. He did not want to divulge information that might compromise the operation. As a soldier, he knew his duty was to his commander or, in this case, to the person who had paid him. He did not need to know more.

In the shower, Maddie was also thinking.

If someone could raise fifteen million dollars by simply copying some files, there was no real need to look for other motives, she thought. In any case, the idea was not at all bad for F1. The fact the teams had similar cars meant the racing was better. It was a win-win situation. There really was no need to ask any further questions.

On the Monday night, after a terrific week together, Maddie flew off to Malaysia and Winslow disappeared back to London.

The Malaysian Grand Prix is held at the Sepang circuit, located right next door to Kuala Lumpur International Airport. These two facilities are a long way from Kuala Lumpur itself and very few F1 people stay in the capital. There are hotels in the new cities of Putrajaya and Cyberjaya and the usual airport hotels as well, although most of these are somewhat lacking in character. They are, however, quite convenient. Some people prefer a longer drive down to the beach, where there are plenty of resort hotels as well.

Formula 1 arrived in the country back in the 1990s, as part of a long-term national economic plan, with the goal being to switch Malaysia away from its reliance of hydrocarbons and palm oil. The intention was to create a high-technology-based, diversified economy, allied to more tourism. The country has moved slowly in that direction, but nothing moves quickly in Malaysia. The planned motorsport industry never really took off and the arrival of the Singapore Grand Prix cast a big shadow over the race at Sepang.

The race always seems to be rather tiring, not because of the travel required to get there, but rather because of the heat and humidity, which mean that by the end of the day, no-one is in the mood to do anything energetic.

After the excitement in Melbourne, the race was always likely to be a bit of a let-down for Chiphurst Competition. It is hard to avoid that. Buckett qualified well, in sixth on the grid, but Poppy Denso and his engineers struggled to find a set-up he liked and so he was a poor sixteenth, even if the gap from pole to sixteenth was less than a second. The race was worse. Buckett's car had an electronic glitch of some sort and failed to fire up. He had to start from the pits and although he was quick, making up for all the time was difficult, although  to finish eleventh in the circumstances was a very good effort. In part he was helped by the fact that Denso had another collision at the first corner, taking out three other cars. He blamed the crash on another driver and that did little to win him any sympathy from the team. With Poppy it could never be his fault. Charlie began to mutter about the need to find a replacement and asked Maddie to look at the available options.

When she stopped to have a think about it, there was only one sensible choice. He was young, cheap and fast. He was also British and, as Charlie always liked to be seen promoting young British racers, he seemed like a good bet. His name was Kyle Mason and he came from Hoddesdon, a rather drab place in Hertfordshire.

"Get him in for a meeting next week," Charlie told her, "And make sure Autosport finds out. Let's see if we rattle some performances out of Poppy."

The following day there were stories on the Internet linking Mason with a Chiphurst deal. Poppy was going to be rattled.

That week the F1 circus moved from Kuala Lumpur to Bahrain, and Maddie spent a couple of days en route doing business in Dubai, talking with Penkoz about their sponsorship activation plans.

She had wanted to go home, but it made little sense. On the Thursday she spoke to Izzie and Winslow and discovered that they were going to be getting together that weekend and she felt rather left out. Perhaps it was selfish and irrational, but that did not change the way she felt, nor her insecurities. She was feeling rather disaffected all weekend and just wanted to go home. She spoke to the two of them on the Friday night, when they were enjoying a meal aboard Daisybelle and she was forced to admit that she was having some serious pangs of fear. It was not jealousy. It was strange because she was happy that her two lovers were pleasing one another, she was happy to share, but what got to her was the fear that they would forget her and that she would lose both. She felt threatened. Being in a *ménage à trois* is anything but easy.

She tried to concentrate on the racing and not think about England, but the fear remained, lurking in the shadows in the quieter moments.

Buckett was again competitive, qualifying sixth on the grid, but Denso seemed confused and disheartened and was back in twelfth place. He looked haggard. Maddie felt a little the same, but in the morning she still looked young and fresh in the mirror.

She was struggling to cope with the relationship, but did not think she could end it. She just wanted to go home to be with them, to know how they felt. After a month away from home, as a result of the illogical calendar that had been created, Charlie was also keen to get back as quickly as possible and so he had rented a private jet for the Sunday evening. With the race starting at six in the evening and finishing by eight, there was going to be a rush to get up to the airport, on the other side of Manama, for a nine thirty take-off. It would then be a six and a half hour flight to Brize Norton, but they would get three hours back, thanks to the time changes, and so they would touch down at around one in the morning. She would go straight home, but she knew it was too late to meet Izzie and Winslow.

The race proved to be a relatively unexciting affair, although Buckett again drove well and finished fifth. Denso finally scored his first point of the season, with a solid but uninspiring tenth.

"My season has begun," he told the TV crews, at the end of the race, but when he got back to the team itself, there were only the mechanics left. Everyone else, including Buckett, was gone to the airport. The message was clear: there was nothing to celebrate with a tenth place. No one cared. The team that he had once led had become Team Buckett.

The only thing that one must do in motor racing is to beat your team-mate. He is the mark by which you are measured. He is your ally and yet, at the same time, your worst enemy. Another rival may beat you on the track, but you are driving different cars and you cannot fairly be compared, but with your team-mate it is him or you. It's a gunfight and there is no margin for error. If you don't kill him, he will kill you.

There is a purity about that contest that is refreshing. Racing is a complex sport, but beneath it all is a basic, very simple, truth.

For Charlie Chiphurst, Maddie Midnight and Elfin Grindvall that evening, the only truth that mattered was completely unrelated to Poppy Denso. The take-off time was the take-off time. It was not to be missed.

Before the race began, their luggage was loaded into the boot of a Mercedes. The driver was told to be ready to move at a moment's notice. He was aware that his value would rise or fall based on his ability to get his passengers to the airport. They did not care if there was traffic. There were always alternative routes. He had to get it right.

As soon as the chequered flag fell, Charlie, Elfin and Maddie were on the move. There was no time to wait to congratulate Buckett. There was no thought of congratulating Denso. A podium finish might warrant the decision to delay the plane, but beyond that nothing was going to stand in their way.

Bahrain International Airport is a good half hour from the circuit, at fairly high speed. It operates twenty-four hours a day, but over a Grand Prix weekend, movements are restricted because there are normally more than sixty private jets wanting to get out in a hurry. You have to be there when you say you are going to be there. And you cannot just drive up to your plane and leap on. This is a troubled part of the world and one has to go through security checkpoints whether you are a billionaire or a Hollywood starlet.

The traffic was bad that evening, but the driver paid no attention. He went down the outside where there was a queue. There were not many oncoming drivers but those who saw him coming at them understood that they would get out of the way, because that was how it was. The way you drive sends out a message. It tells those around you about who you are. If you drive with assurance and authority, people will assume you are important. If you drive like a sheikh, you are a sheikh. Once on the freeway, it was a drive of pure class: the smoothness, the authority and the choice of route all perfect. Even the security men at the airport looked cowed by the presence of a car driven with such authority.

They got to the plane about five minutes before the slot time, the pilot was already spooling up the engines and as soon as the door was closed he requested take-off. It was all cut very fine, but the little jet hurtled down the runway bang on time and climbed effortlessly into the night sky, curled slightly to starboard and headed up the Gulf. The troubles in the region meant that the flight was going to go through Iranian air space until it reached the Turkish border and from there would turn to the west and fly over the Black Sea to the Romanian coast and then across Hungary, Austria, Germany and Belgium. They had a few drinks and a meal and then they dozed off until the pilot announced that they were beginning their descent into Brize Norton. It was a little later than planned because of the detour to avoid Iraq and Syria.

There were times when Maddie wondered if the whole private jet thing made any sense. A month earlier she had flown off to Australia, leaving her car at Heathrow. Her problem now was that she was returning to Brize Norton, sixty miles from the Heathrow car park. There was a car waiting for her to go home to Netherington, but if she did that she would be stuck there without transport and would need to take a taxi to Oxford and then a train to London. So she asked the driver if he could take her straight to Heathrow. It was nearly two in the morning, but there was no traffic. The driver did not mind. He worked nights anyway and this would make him more money. She slept quietly in the back but the trip was less than an hour. When he dropped her off he asked quietly: "You are aware that today is Easter Monday?" he said. "It's a national holiday."

She had completely forgotten.

She wondered what Izzie and Winslow were up to. For Winslow every day was a holiday so fitting in with his lifestyle was much easier, but getting time with Izzie was more difficult. She considered ringing to see if Izzie was at home, but it was three in the morning and not the time to one call anyone. She was not sure what she wanted to do. If she went home she would spend the day asleep in bed. Perhaps Winslow would come visiting. If she stayed in London, perhaps she would see Izzie.

It struck her that this was a straight choice.

Izzie or Winslow.

Girl or boy.

# Twenty-three

Maddie chose Izzie, or at least the possibility of Izzie. The decision was not an easy one, but she had spent a week with Winslow in Sydney and had not seen Izzie for more than a month. She had missed the female touch. She knew that there were no guarantees. Izzie might have gone away for the weekend. Friday would have been a day off as well, but Maddie decided it was worth the risk. Early in the morning on a bank holiday Monday in England, the roads into London are not busy. She would go and see if Izzie was home. If she was away, Maddie decided she would go back to Netherington and give Winslow a call.

She wondered what time she could call Izzie without it being too early. She did not really know. People don't always want to be woken up on their days off, even by their lover. She had some time to kill. She looked at the fuel gauge, she had plenty and so she set off, deciding what to do when she arrived at each junction. After finally finding a way out of the airport, she found herself in Runnymede. It was still dark as she drove through Old Windsor and round through Windsor itself and then on to Ascot. She saw signs to the racecourse and so turned that way and then continued on the road until she reached a junction with the London Road. She turned right, having failed to see the sign to London and so arrived in Sunningdale, which didn't seem right. She turned left to Chobham. She knew that she was somewhere near McLaren headquarters, and she followed signs to Woking. The A245 seemed like the road to take and she found herself in West Byfleet.

Where on earth was she?

She went over a motorway and concluded that this must be the M25, that loops around the whole of London. Then she was in Byfleet with no signs how to get on to the ring road. After a couple of roundabouts she decided that she would stop and set up the satellite navigation system. There was another roundabout and she turned left, looking for a place to stop, but there was just another roundabout and a big shopping centre. There was no way to get in and so she drove on. It was twilight and she could see a little more now, but decided against the deserted shopping centre. There was a strange building that looked like an old control tower from the 1930s and then another roundabout. She decided to turn left and found herself in a quiet industrial estate. There was a sign for a cul-de-sac, so she took it and arrived at the end of the road, where she could easily stop.

She looked at her watch. It was five forty-five and the sky was getting lighter by the minute. She played with the navigation system and set the destination to Dolphin Square and then decided that she needed some air and so got out of the car, to stretch her legs. It had been a long night. In front of her, behind a series of metal bollards, was a section of what appeared to be banked concrete, overgrown with moss. She looked right and saw that it continued behind the building. She walked a little to the left, where there was a path and she understood. She had somehow arrived at Brooklands, the home of British motor racing and the first permanent race track in the world. She shook her head in disbelief.

That was really spooky.

She went back to the car, feeling rather odd, and followed the instructions she was given. It took her to the A3 and a few minutes later she was heading into London, around the Kingston by-pass, through Putney Vale, over Putney Heath and then downhill into Wandsworth and up through Battersea, until she reached Vauxhall where she crossed the bridge and turned off to park in Dolphin Square. She decided she should arrive with something nice and drove around looking for something to buy. The streets were dead. In the end she finally found a French place and bought four gorgeous-looking croissants and headed back to Dolphin Square. It was six thirty. She rang Izzie's intercom. There was a mumbling voice and then the exclamation "Maddie" and the buzzer sounded and she let herself in. She found her way up to the apartment and as she approached, the door opened and there was Izzie, her hair all in a tangle, but she was smiling. She pulled Maddie through the door and they kissed passionately.

"Shower," said Maddie.

Izzie's eyes sparkled. "Oh yes," she said. "Shower."

They shared a shower that developed into rather more than that and then, wrapped in towels, they had coffee and croissants sitting on the couch. And then with buttery fingers they went back to bed. Maddie was taken aback by Izzie's passion, she seemed that morning to be charged with sexual energy and seemed insatiable. It became a sexual frenzy and Maddie had simply to touch her and she orgasmed.

At first Maddie could not believe what she was seeing, but she was happy to know that she was at least partially responsible. In the end Izzie simply ran out of energy. She could no longer speak. She was catatonic. Maddie held her until she calmed down.

"I cannot explain it," Izzie said. "It is just my brain. I reach a point where I go from one orgasm to the next and then it seems that I pass out. I used to think that it was weird to be so orgasmic, but I looked on the Internet and it seems that there are quite a few women like me. Some have even more than that. There's a mental place where almost anything is possible. I rarely manage to get there, but when I do it is spectacular. One time I was so worked up that I came when my boyfriend told me to react to a click of his fingers. It is all in the mind."

"I'm jealous," said Maddie.

"We can always try," said Izzie, with a smile.

After a while she felt able to walk again and gradually her energy returned. She needed to eat again, desperately. And so they dressed and went out to find brunch. When they returned, they lay curled up together on the couch and watched bad movies until it was dusk outside.

"Do you have to go?" Izzie asked.

"No," said Maddie, "I can stay until the morning, but it will have to be early."

"Like this morning," Izzie said, with a grin.

"I should call Winslow," Maddie said.

He sounded surprised that she was not at home.

"I'll be there later," she said. "I'm with Izzie."

She could not help it. It was payback for the call that had upset her in Bahrain.

"OK, I'll see you tomorrow," he said.

Maddie and Izzie had exhausted all amorous feelings. They had used up all their energy and there were no frustrations left. They were just happy to sleep.

In the morning Maddie left early and drove up the M40 before the traffic jams began. The night had troubled her a little. She kept telling herself that she was not a lesbian and it was all just a question of sensuality. She loved the difference and she was very fond of Izzie, but it was not love, and that worried her.

Back in the office, they had a management meeting to decide what to do about Poppy Denso. They decided that they would keep him a while longer, but if he had not started scoring the same kind of results as Buckett by the Monaco Grand Prix, they would replace him with Kyle Mason. It was agreed that the youngster would start work with the team's simulator immediately, in order to get as much virtual mileage as possible. They had six weeks before the Monaco Grand Prix, which should give him enough experience to be able to get into the car and be competitive.

The team would be home for just a week and so Maddie

decided that she would do as much as possible in that time with Winslow. They would have only the one weekend because Maddie then had to fly off to Shanghai for the Chinese Grand Prix. Maybe they would see Izzie, but she would leave that decision up to Winslow.

When he arrived on Tuesday evening, he seemed a little quieter than usual and Maddie felt that there was something on his mind. She did not ask what was wrong. If he wanted to tell her, he would come out and say it.

She told him about her adventures with Izzie and he explained that it had been the same kind of thing for him when he and Izzie had been together when Maddie was away in Bahrain.

"It is like she was desperate," he said. "It's very flattering to think you are responsible for all that passion, but I cannot help but think that she is a bit extreme. It is not like she needs sex all the time. It's not a nymphomaniac thing, but when it happens, it seems like she goes completely berserk and no longer has control over herself. Her body just takes over."

"I think what she really needs is to calm down and commit to one person," Maddie said. "She needs love and stability."

"Well, I guess you would know," Winslow said. "You must know all her little secrets. You come home and the first thing you do is go to see her. I don't even get a call. I thought I was supposed to be the serious relationship and she was the fun, but I'm beginning to wonder."

He paused. Maddie knew now what was on his mind. She had suspected that it might be this.

"Ever since she came on to the scene, I always seem to not be your first priority," he went on. "And I don't like it. I decided to commit myself to you and the next thing I know, you seem to have gone off the idea. I don't understand it, Maddie, I really don't. I know she's good fun to be with, but what happened to us?"

"You disappeared over Christmas," Maddie replied. "We got really close on the island. We wanted you to be there with us, but you just deserted us. We still don't know what you are were doing - and we don't know when you will take off again. We don't know if you will even come back. If you got yourself killed we wouldn't even know about it. How can one be committed to someone like that? If we are going to be together all the time, we have to be honest with one another and tell the truth."

"You want the truth?" he said. "Maddie, the truth is the last thing you want. It's better for you not to know. It's what I do. Can I stop it? Maybe one day when I have made enough money to never have to work again. But until that happens, I will do what I know - and I'll do it well."

"What is it that you do well?" Maddie said. "I don't know."

"I fix things," he said. "I make things happen. I facilitate. I convince people to do things. Just like I convinced you to do what you did."

"That's not good enough," Maddie said. "Who do you work for? What do you do?"

Winslow sighed.

"Maddie, sometimes in this business you don't really know what you are doing. You don't know who you are working for. "

"And you are pragmatic enough not to care?" she said. "Winslow, that's awful. You could be working for the Islamic State. Or the Russians. You don't know and it seems you don't even care. I'd say that was lacking morals."

Maddie was aware than the conversation had swung out of control. They were getting into things that were way too sensitive and she felt that no good would come of it. But she could not stop herself.

"I mean, do you have any idea who you are working for with our deal?" she went on.

She saw a flicker in his face and she knew she had hit the nail on the head. He was not working alone, as he had said he was. There was someone else.

"You lied to me," she said. "You told me that you were just making money. If that was the case you could retire now. I gave you three million. That is enough to stop working. You could stop forever with that sort of money."

"Yes," said Winslow, "I lied. That is what happens in life! People tell lies. You're doing it yourself right now. Your life is a lie. Chiphurst's success is a lie. Don't be such a hypocrite!"

"And who was it that talked me into doing that?" Maddie said, angry now. "It was the Devil's little helper. Tempting me..."

"...making you rich!" he added. "What a ridiculous argument. You're rotten to the core. Maddie. You cling to these ridiculous ideals of Victorian good and bad. Give it up! You're bad! You are just a crook - and a dyke to boot!"

Maddie had had enough.

"Go fuck yourself, Davenport. Piss off back your narrow little life on your narrow little boat. Go off and kill people, or whatever it is you do. Just don't come back here!"

"I'd rather sleep with a skunk than bed down with you," he shouted.

There was silence. He turned and walked out. The door slammed. She heard the Mercedes roar into life and the gravel crunched. He was gone.

Fuck.

In the space of a couple of minutes, she had become single again. She sat in silence for maybe five minutes. It could have been an hour. She had no idea. She felt herself calming down. And then she did what Maddie Midnight never did.

She cried.

Why was it that all her relationships went wrong? What was wrong with her? She loved Winslow.

She knew that he was a good man, beneath the obvious flaws. She trusted him. She knew that he did not cheat on her, apart from with Izzie. And Izzie was just a sex toy. And then she realized that perhaps that was not true. She loved Izzie as well.

She went to the kitchen to find the rum. This was not a crisis she could handle without alcohol. She would drink a bit and then she would ring Izzie and tell her that she loved her.

Winslow and all men, come to that, could go fuck themselves. But she didn't ring Izzie. You cannot say "I love you" for the first time on a phone. You have to be together, holding one another, looking into one another's eyes.

Maddie had no idea what time it was, but she could not stop thinking. What was it that she and Winslow had been fighting about? Was it that Winslow had lied about their scam, or was it a fight over Izzie? Was that the truth?

She went to sleep on the couch at some point. In the morning she didn't remember much. It had just been a dark world filled with questions, pain and regrets.

She went to work on the Wednesday but she was like a zombie. In the end, she made some excuses and went home. Then she rang Izzie.

"It's all screwed up," she said. "I need you tonight. Can you be there if I come at eight?"

Izzie sounded delighted.

"Of course I'll be there," Izzie said. "What happened?"

"We broke up," Maddie said. "We broke up over you."

She heard Izzie take a sharp intake of breath.

"Over me?" she said in a very quiet voice.

"Yes, over you," Maddie said. "He was upset that I went to see you when I got back rather than going to him. It all got out of hand and we said a lot of bad things. A lot of true things, but true things are not always good."

Maddie drove into London. She had already decided that she would call in sick the next day. She needed time for herself and the team could live without her for a day or two. In six days she would be going off to China and she wondered whether she might be able to talk Charlie into letting her stay out of the office until then. Maybe she would stay at Izzie's for the whole time and play at being a housewife. Izzie was very feminine but she had a lot of masculine ways about her. Her whole "use me" approach was not a feminine thought process. Maddie was quite sure that she could never adopt such an attitude. She needed more on an emotional level. She needed to feel wanted, valued and, if possible, loved.

She decided that she would suggest the idea to Izzie that night, after they had made love, because she knew that the first thing that would happen when she arrived would be sex. Izzie always needed physical stimuli before she could connect on an emotional level.

Maddie parked the car in Izzie's space in the underground car park and went upstairs. Izzie engulfed her, but was calmer than Maddie had expected and it was not long before they were lying together and talking.

"I am jealous of you," Izzie said. "Love is too dangerous for me. I'm not a heroine. I am not an adventurer like you are. I like to be free and wild in the bedroom, but real freedom is way too scary. I'm only a rebel behind closed doors. You go out there and you slay dragons."

Maddie laughed.

"Well, I am envious of your beauty and the freedom of your mind," she replied. "You are not trapped by love. You can switch from one person to another. It seems that when I find someone who wants me, I always end up wanting them to be only with me. I don't want to share you with Winslow. It is stronger than I am. I hated it when I was away and you two were together."

"It's funny," said Izzie, "because although I say I am happy to be your sex toy, it is not really true. I am like you. I like the different experience, but I am attached to you emotionally. It's not the same with Winslow. I like him well enough, but I don't love him. He just makes me feel good."

"And you do love me?" asked Maddie.

There was a very long pause, as Izzie considered.

"You see," she said finally. "You see how frightened I am to make a commitment."

"I'd like it if you could say it," Maddie said. "If you did then we could be a couple."

"I don't know," said Izzie. "I am not sure I am ready for that and I'm sure that you won't be coming out any time soon..."

It was not going to happen. And they both knew it.

"It's best for us to keep it like it is," Izzie said. "It's good. We have all the good things from a relationship and we have none of the bad stuff."

Maddie asked if she could stay and Izzie agreed immediately. She called Charlie and told him that she was chasing a possible sponsorship lead and needed a few days in London, but added that she was saving the team money by staying with a friend. Charlie was happy. He would see her again in Shanghai.

Izzie went off to work early on the Wednesday. She was a hard worker. Maddie needed time to herself and took it easy, sitting on the couch. She decided that the only way to find out what was happening would be to shake the tree and see what fell out.

Winslow had told her, without meaning to, that there was someone else behind the scam and she wanted to find out who it was, but without Winslow to tell her, it was going to be difficult. The only sensible thing was to look closely at the rival teams and see if there were any people who were behaving in a similar fashion to Winslow. It would not be obvious, of course, because if one looked hard at Chiphurst Competition one would not see Winslow Davenport III.

Maddie decided that it might be a good idea to talk to a private investigator to see what he thought.

She did some research on the Internet and decided that the Ingram Detective Agency was the best choice. It was run by a man called Tom Ingram, who did business from a small office on the sixth floor of office building on Regent Street. It was above a Subway restaurant, which at least made it easy to find. She rang and arranged a meeting for the following morning.

The world thinks that private detectives are glamorous, but the image of these people comes straight out of literature. The industry has been forced to change in recent years because the laws of privacy are now very different. Most of the people in the industry are still former policemen or security service employees, but it seems that surveillance is now their primary work. They use the same techniques as previously. Following a suspect, she was told, was done with subtlety, using teams of three interchanging "watchers" to reduce the likelihood of the target spotting a tail. Much of the other information that people want can be found on the Internet.

Tom Ingram was not all what Maddie expected. He was a

slightly shambling figure, with the air of a college professor. He wore a saggy jumper, claret-coloured corduroy trousers and Hush Puppies. His jacket had leather elbow patches.

Maddie shrugged off this bizarre appearance and explained that she thought that Omar Rymer-Jones of the Super Dubai team was up to "some funny financial business" and wanted Ingram to see who else was involved. It was going to cost her two thousand Pounds, but that seemed reasonable in order to get things moving.

If Omar did meet someone interesting she asked that Ingram switch the surveillance team to the new target. Ingram said he would start immediately and within an hour Maddie had received her first e-mail report, informing her that Ingram had called Omar, saying he was from HM Customs and Excise and was enquiring about unusual financial transactions and that he would like to have a chat.

The goal was to rapidly flush out whether Omar was involved in dodgy business and using the tax man was a brilliant way to panic any wrongdoer.

Less than two hours later Rymer-Jones was followed to a pub in Oxford where he met an American. Ingram reported that the pair had "a very serious discussion" and then the American left, making a phone call as soon as he left the pub. The watchers switched to the stranger, while Ingram figured out from the car number plate that he was probably an Orlando Petty, an American entrepreneur who was based in England. It was not clear exactly what he did for a living.

Maddie read all this that evening when Ingram sent her a progress report. Petty, he explained, had driven to London and parked his car in an underground car park in Knightsbridge. He had then gone to a meeting with a man called Max Wysocki.

The name jumped out of the page at Maddie. She knew him. He was the Polish prince they had met at Tarquin's dinner party. Maddie remembered how Winslow had not liked Wysocki, but had insisted they had never met, although Maddie had sensed somehow they knew one another.

She spent half of the next day looking for references to Max

Wysocki on the Internet, and began to build up a picture of his story. She guessed that there had been a Wysocki in the Free Polish Forces in World War II and duly found a suitable reference. It was a typical story. The family had become English after the war because the Russians had invaded Poland and the Poles in the UK did not trust the Russians enough to return. They had all heard about the massacre of Polish officers in the Katyn Forest, even if the news of it had come from the Nazis. The Soviets blamed the Nazis, while they blamed the Russians. No-one was willing to gamble on which it had been and so there was a large Anglo-Polish community.

Within a generation the Wysockis had become more English than the English themselves. Max has attended a public school before spending a few years in the Royal Marines. He had then been recruited as the personal assistant of a Middle Eastern Prince before moving on into the world of banking. It was not really clear for whom he worked.

She rang Tarquin and asked if he could tell her what Max did for a living, making up a suitable story to explain the request. He said that there were a number of "consultant types" who would arrange funding for anonymous parties who required large sums of money in a hurry. It was a high-risk business, but the returns were impressive. The bankers did not let on who or what the money was being used for, but assessed the risks involved and did business based on trust in their abilities to recommend a good deal. Tarquin said that he thought that Wysocki might also be a freelance central banker, employed by governments in developing countries because they did not have anyone of their own with the necessary skills to properly control their economy. Tarquin added that he was not really sure if such people existed, but that was what he had been told by someone or other.

Her researches were not very successful and she concluded that she had two choices: she could approach Max and ask some direct questions, or she could forget the whole thing and go back to minding her own business.

The following day she was outside the address that Ingram

had given her for Wysocki. It was lunchtime. Her plan was simple. She was going to engineer a chance encounter. She intended to follow him and try to eat in the same restaurant.

She carefully positioned herself in a place where she could see the entrance to Wysocki's office building and then she waited. Sure enough, at just before one, Wysocki emerged and strolled across to Harvey Nicholls, where he took the express lift at the back of the store to the fifth floor restaurant. Maddie waited for the lift to return and then she followed.

She emerged in a bright and airy café with a small terrace off to one side. She spotted Wysocki immediately. He was sitting by himself at a table for two. The waitress had already given him a menu. The seating seemed to be free and so she picked an empty table nearby, making sure that he would spot her, and sat down pretending not to have seen him.

It did not take long. She was just reaching into her handbag to fish out a book when a voice said: "It's Maddie, isn't it?"

She feigned surprise.

"It's Max," he said. "Max Wysocki. We met at Tarquin's."

"Yes, of course, " she said. "What a very pleasant surprise."

It was as easy as that.

He was eating alone. She was eating alone. He invited her to join him. She could start asking questions. Job done.

"So what are you doing here?" she asked as she settled down opposite him. "This is lady's country, isn't it?"

"Maybe that's why I am here," he laughed. "I work around the corner and I sometimes come here. It's a nice place and the food is really very good. I recommend the sea bass with seaweed, pak choi and teriyaki sauce, although I had that yesterday and today I think I fancy a chicken burger, although I have no idea what *chermoula* is."

"*Chermoula*?" said Maddie. "Isn't that some kind of green sauce that comes from Morocco and blows the back of your head off."

"Sounds like some kind of terrorist," he laughed.

They chatted inconsequentially for a few minutes and then Maddie went on the offensive.

"I didn't really understand at the dinner party what it is

that you do." she said, sipping from a glass of very good Marlborough Sauvignon Blanc.

"I get paid lots of money to do very little," he said.

"Ah, the perfect deal," said Maddie. "We all love those."

"I cannot really give you details," he said. "It's all rather confidential and I do always try to fly a long way beneath the radar. I think it is better that way."

"So you work in secret finance," Maddie said. "How very mysterious. And I guess that if you have an office round here, you have some international clients. So I would guess that you arrange loans, isn't that what financiers do?"

"That sort of thing," he said. "I make things happen."

"We all make things happen," said Maddie. "The point is what you make happen..."

"I like to be a man in the shadows," he said. "People today don't really understand that. The world is fixated by celebrity. I hate that. One can make a big difference to the world when operating in the shadows. You know some people even take pride in *not* bragging about what they do. They don't need to show off. They are happy to keep their secrets. I'm like that. I don't want to be famous, but if I can make a difference I will."

"Well, that is about as clear as mud," Maddie said.

# Twenty-four

"You don't mess about, do you?' Max said, with a slightly nervous laugh. "You always go straight to the point. It is really rather disconcerting."

"I don't mean to cause offence," Maddie said, "but I just don't get the logic of small talk. Being direct saves time and energy. I'm into efficiency. Why waste time when you don't have to? Life is too short to spend it on worthless chit-chat."

Max thought of saying something else but she could see him pause and switch to a more tactful response, which he delivered with an oily charm. She was searching for the right word to capture him: he was too proud to be unctuous, yet with too much gravitas to be glib or urbane. In the end she settled on "pleased with himself', something which is not unusual in the world of high finance.

"So what's your story?" she asked, wondering if it might throw some light on Winslow's activities.

Max eyed her oddly.

"How did you end up 'doing confidential stuff' for all these important international clients?"

He told her the story that she already knew of his grandfather in the Polish Air Force. At the end of it, she went back to the key question.

"So you raise money for people?" she said.

"Isn't that what bankers do?" he smiled.

"In my experience they write me letters saying that I am spending too much," Maddie laughed, "but I am happy to believe your explanation."

"And you work in F1?" he said.

"You have a good memory," she replied

"And you are with that American chap, Winslow," he said.

"I was," she said. "We broke up."

"I am sorry to hear that" he said. "I always thought he was a rather nice chap."

"That's odd," she said. "He always denied knowing you."

Max laughed.

"A very sound man," he said. "Never give away secrets that don't need to be shared."

"How do you know Winslow?" she asked.

Max paused, thinking. "To be quite honest, I don't really remember," he said. "We were introduced at a party, I think. We did some stuff together in Africa. I think it was something like financing a school. I honestly don't remember the details, but he's a good chap."

"If not a celebrated humanitarian," said Maddie. "I don't get it. You're a banker. He's some kind of a soldier. Where's the connection there?"

"It is probably best that I don't talk about that," Max said. "Sometimes we bankers need to be, how shall I say? A little muscular. And sometimes we need to be protected. I am sure you understand."

Maddie nodded.

"And did you do business with him as well?"

"I don't recall," he said.

"I'll take that as a yes," said Maddie.

Max did not deny it.

"You do sponsoring and marketing?" he said.

"Yes," said Maddie. "I make things happen."

"Funnily enough," he said, "your name came up in conversation not long ago with someone. I don't remember who. And he said that you were quite an operator. I don't think it was Winslow."

"Tarquin?" said Maddie.

He shook his head. "No. Nor Katie. I'm sure it was a man."

"I didn't know we had other mutual acquaintances," Maddie said.

He shrugged.

"I don't remember," he said, "but I guess it will come to me in the middle of the night."

Maddie decided that more questions might seem a little obvious and so she started talking about F1. Max seemed to know all the people she talked about. He was more than just a fan.

"Well, I suppose I must go back to work," he said eventually. "It really has been very enjoyable. We should meet up some time."

He insisted on buying her lunch and then as they were saying goodbye down on the street, a thought came into his head.

"Do you ever see that girl I sat next to at the dinner party," he asked. "Izzie something?"

"Our paths cross occasionally," she said, deciding not to explain to him that they had woken up in bed together that morning and in a few hours would be back in bed together again.

"I thought she was really extraordinary," he said. "She had amazing green eyes. And she was really smart. And sexy too."

"Yes," Maddie said. "I do believe she gets a lot of men chasing around after her."

"I understand that," Max said.

And then he was gone and Maddie strolled up to Hyde Park Corner and then down through an underpass into the middle of the roundabout, by the Wellington Arch. She was thinking as she walked and not paying much attention to where she was going. She needed to know more about Wysocki. She would ask Tarquin. That would give her an excuse to drop in to see Izzie as well. So as not to make it too obvious, she rang Katie and asked for Tarquin's number.

"It's a work thing," she said. "I need his expertise."

Tarquin answered and said that he was having a meeting at the Treasury, but once that was done he'd be very happy to meet her.

"Why don't we have a cup of tea in the park?" he said. "Then you must come and see my office. You remember Izzie, don't you? You two really got on as I recall."

Maddie smiled.

"Yes, we did," she said. "I'd like that very much. I've been meaning to catch up with her, but you know what Formula 1 is like. I'm always rushing about."

"Well, perhaps we three could have dinner?" he said. "That would be fun. I'm staying in town tonight. Katie is coming up in the morning and we're going to the theatre tomorrow night. Anyway, we'll have to check to see if Izzie is free. She's always rather secretive about her love life, but I don't get the impression that she's off anywhere tonight."

"That sounds nice," she said and mentioned that she was staying with a friend on Cheyne Walk, which he accepted without a question.

"Meet me at four at Inn the Park, I think they call it. It's a wooden and glass thing in the trees, opposite Horse Guards. We can have a cream tea, or an Eton Mess. I expect we'll see some MPs in there with their mistresses. You'll just have to pretend that you're my bit on the side. That will boost my credibility. My colleagues all think I am very dull being happily married to Katie."

Maddie laughed.

"I will play the mistress role as best I can," she said. "I've never done it, but how hard can it be?"

It was a lovely afternoon, a sunny Friday in April and London was at its finest. She had time to wander down to the lake and then along the side of it, watching small children feeding a collection of ducks. For a while she sat down on a bench and worked out what she was going to ask Tarquin.

At four she was sitting on the terrace at the Inn. Tarquin was right on time and full of energy.

"Spring fever," he said. "Most animals go a little silly at this time of year. I'm no different. I am not as mad as a March hare, but I do feel rather energised. Will you have tea and scones?"

She tried to say no, but Tarquin was having none of that.

"Two cream teas," he said. "Scones, clotted cream, the lot. And I think we'll have some Darjeeling Flush."

For a while he talked about how the tea was made from the first leaves of spring in the foothills of the Himalayas. She wasn't hungry, but Maddie could never turn down clotted cream.

"Marvellous," he said. "We should all have naughty little secrets, don't you think?"

"Absolutely," said Maddie. "What's yours?"

"Marmite sandwiches," he said. "Childhood. Comfort food. I often have then in the House."

Maddie laughed.

"And you?" he said.

"Clotted cream," she said.

"Splendid," he said. The conversation paused for a moment and Tarquin, seeking to keep it flowing, asked: "How's Winslow?"

Maddie frowned.

"Oh God," said Tarquin. "I've put my foot in it, haven't I?"

"Well, it's not your fault," she said. "Actually, we broke up two days ago."

"What a silly ass he is," Tarquin said. "Doesn't know how lucky he is. I mean. Oh dear."

"Don't worry," said Maddie. "I'm fine."

Tarquin clearly wanted to change the subject and so moved quickly on with some remark about scones and then asked how he could help her.

"I need to know a little more about this Max Wysocki," she said. "He's popped up in some of my dealings and I don't really know what to make of him. I don't know if he can be trusted. Winslow denied knowing him, which is rather strange and no-one seems to know what he does. Winslow told me once that Max was some kind of a crook. Can you help me?"

Tarquin looked serious for a moment. And then, with a

conspiratorial glance left and then right, he leaned forward and said.

"I wouldn't say he's a crook," he said, "but I think he sails rather close to the wind. Some of the people he raises money for are, how shall we say? Hmm... marginal. In the political sense. He's really a bit of a facilitator. He gets people what they want and he's very discreet. You can deal with him and no-one will hear a word about it."

"I'm not going to ask what he's done for you," Maddie said.

"Oh no, nothing like that," Tarquin said. "We've known each other since we were boys. Played Cowboys and Indians together, that sort of thing. We've always stayed in touch. He was a Royal Marine and a bit of a hero in Iraq in 2003 by all accounts and then he was poached by a Saudi, I think it was. The sheikh liked the idea of having a prince as his bodyguard, made him feel important. That got Max into the world of money and old Wysocki has always sharp. He saw a chance and grabbed it. We don't really talk about what he does, but I think he and his people can get a bit rough at times, if you know what I mean. I think also that they do the occasional 'deniable' job, when governments need things done, but don't want anyone to know they are doing them."

"So he knows a lot of secrets?" Maddie said. "He's well-connected?"

"Very," said Tarquin. "Maybe not Prime Ministers and Presidents, but certainly some people with influence."

He nodded.

"And business people too," Tarquin added. "When they need a little of muscle in the wilder places, I think Max helps out. But I also think he does a fair bit of legitimate stuff as well. I think he does things between the Saudis and the Americans. There is a lot money to be made these days with military dealings, but I heard he does real estate as well. And I did hear that he is doing something with data networks. There is this guy called Bilski, who is making a lot of moves in that market and I think Max has something to do with him."

"Bilski?" said Maddie. "I know Bilski. He's one of my sponsors this year. He's providing a big chunk of money to

Chiphurst."

"Really?" said Tarquin. "That's extraordinary. Why would he do that?"

"I don't understand," said Maddie. "Why would he not do that?"

Tarquin looked at her rather oddly.

"Well, I am sure I read somewhere that he owns the whole thing..." he said.

Maddie tried not to look surprised. In the two months that had passed since the change of Formula One ownership, no-one had made any real progress in finding out the identity of the new owner. And yet here was Tarquin coming out with the name.

"Oh dear," he said. "That might be a secret, now I think about it. I think the tax folk wanted to know what was going on with Formula One. It's a big industry for us, you know. When the old lot sold it, I think the Revenue wanted to make sure that it had not gone to some drug cartel or something."

Maddie's brain was racing along. Tarquin was right. Why on earth would Bilski sponsor an F1 team, if he owned the whole business? It made no sense at all.

"I may be wrong on that one," Tarquin said, back-pedalling with all the grace of a swan. It all looked serene, but beneath the surface there was chaos going on.

"Anyway," he added. "I certainly did not tell you. And it may not be true. There is so much stuff that goes over my desk that sometimes I have to admit it is a bit much."

Maddie changed the subject. They talked about ducks for a while and then Tarquin looked at his watch and suggested that they drop over to the office to say hello to Izzie.

"We should have dinner at that nice Italian place," he said. "I'll get her to book it."

He was reaching for his phone.

"Don't call her," Maddie said. "Let's give her a surprise!"

As they walked back past the Foreign & Commonwealth Office, Tarquin mentioned that he was a little worried about Izzie.

"There's something going on with her," he said. "She's

taking time off and seems out of sorts sometimes. That's not like her. She has a habit of getting mixed up with all the wrong men. It is amazing to me how often that happens with beautiful women. You'd think they would find the best and brightest but often they end up with losers. Why is that? Do they do it sub-consciously because they don't think they deserve happiness. I've never really understood women. I mean Katie is perfect for me, but I do find most women to be a complete mystery. Not you, though. I think you're the most sensible woman I know."

"Maybe I am the most masculine," Maddie said.

Tarquin laughed out loud.

"Maddie, have you looked in the mirror recently?"

"Every day," she said.

"And you don't see beauty?"

"No," she said. "I see me. Me is OK, but I'm not an Izzie. She really has film star looks."

Tarquin nodded. "I agree. I think what she really needs is a proper boyfriend; someone solid to give her stability. There must be someone in that F1 world of yours who would bowl her over?"

"Probably," said Maddie.

If Tarquin knew that Izzie was bowled over by her, he would probably have fallen over with shock. Tarquin was old school.

"I fear for the motor racing crowd, Izzie would be rather intimidating," Maddie added. "We mustn't forget that this girl has some serious brains going on. And a lot of men find that rather scary."

"True," said Tarquin.

Getting into the building was something of a challenge without the right paperwork having been done in advance (and in triplicate), because of all the security measures that are a requirement these days, but finally Maddie was signed in and security screened. She and Tarquin walked through a series of corridors to find the tiny little office that served as the centre of his political world.

"It's not much," he said, "but it is quite convenient, if you know which corridor goes where. Even rabbits have been known to get lost in this warren."

They arrived finally in front of a drab door.

There was one of those old brass name plate holders, into which someone had slipped a card that read "Haig & Dalrymple". It gave the impression that this was a world where there was a very rapid turnover of people.

Tarquin opened the door with suitable flourish and a "ta-ta" that served as a drum roll. Izzie was sitting at a desk, facing the door. She looked up with a face that was one of the funnier things Maddie had seen in a while: there was a remarkable mixture of surprise, horror, lust, restraint and feigned coolness - all at the same moment.

"Hal-lo," she said, the second syllable taking on a life of its own, as the various thoughts and emotions collided, like a motorway pile-up.

"Look who I picked up in the park," Tarquin said, in that slightly jangly voice that people from Eton have when making introductions.

Izzie later admitted to Maddie that it was such a surprise that she had forgotten to breathe for a moment. Tarquin was blind to all of this, as only an English public schoolboy can be, and he babbled on about how they were going to go out to dinner together in a bit, and even joked about it being "a threesome". He then apologized to Maddie and said that there was some urgent paperwork that had to be done before dinner, but that Izzie would look after her. Initially it was rather uncomfortable, as they had to make the kind of inane conversation that might be expected if they had not seen one another for several months. The fact that they had woken up in bed together that morning made the whole interlude deliciously comical, but hard to sustain.

While they did this, Tarquin stuck his nose into a draft parliamentary bill, and seemed oblivious to everything. The stilted conversation continued, but Izzie was soon stealing hidden caresses. They were half hidden from where Tarquin was sitting by a filing cabinet and so Izzie stuck her hand up under Maddie's skirt. She continued to talk while her fingers explored. In revenge Maddie squeezed one of Izzie's breasts through her blouse and bra. She could feel the nipple hard beneath her fingers. Izzie wanted more. She pulled her hand out from under the skirt and put her finger to her mouth and gave a satisfied little sigh.

"Would you like a quick tour of the nooks and crannies of this place?" she asked. Maddie nodded. Her cheeks were rather flushed.

Tarquin grunted as the two girls disappeared. The tour was relatively short. They walked down a corridor, turned right and Izzie dragged Maddie into an office that she knew would be empty at that hour. There was a lock on the door, which she snapped shut. She turned to Maddie and the two kissed frantically, messing up their hair and their clothing in the minutes that followed. It ended up being a satisfactory tour for both of them. When they returned Tarquin might have noticed that both were a great deal more relaxed, but he was not paying attention.

"Where did you go?" he asked. Izzie said something about the terrace overlooking the Thames and Tarquin said "lovely" and then went back to the paperwork.

It was almost time for dinner and a few minutes later, with the work out of the way, the three of them walked to the little Italian restaurant in a basement, just around the corner from Parliament. Tarquin was charming as usual, having focused his attention back on them. The dinner was delicious and then, when they reached the street corner, he offered to walk Maddie to the Underground.

"There's really no need," she said. "I'll grab a cab. Cheyne Walk is a terrible place for public transport."

"Don't worry," said Izzie, "I'll look after her."

The girls smiled at one another and Tarquin set off back towards the Houses of Parliament.

The two girls found themselves alone, walking along Millbank. When they reached Lambeth Bridge, they crossed so that they could walk and see the river. They passed Thames House, the headquarters of MI5, the security service, and continued on to the Tate Gallery. Then they reached the Morpeth Arms, a cosy-looking pub where Izzie sometime stopped. They passed Vauxhall Bridge Road, rounded the next corner, crossed St George's Square, and there was Dolphin Square in all of its glory. It is a vast 1930s style red brick building, ten storeys tall, with its countless white windows and three grand arches, two gaslights and a pair of flagpoles at the entrance. There are around three thousand residents in a dozen buildings, all named after celebrated mariners.

Izzie was in a hurry to get home and they went quickly through the gardens to Collingwood House. In the lift they looked at one another, knowing full well what was going to happen, as soon as they close the door of the flat. Maddie bit her lip. The fumbling in the office had been entertaining, but it was not enough for either of them.

# Twenty-five

An hour later, lying in the darkness with Izzie breathing gently beside her, Maddie cleared her head and began to try to piece together what Tarquin had told her during their tea party in the park. There was clearly a much more complicated scam going on than she had imagined. It was safe to assume that Winslow, Orlando Petty and possibly others were at what one might call operational level, reporting to Max Wysocki and perhaps other cut-outs. It was odd that Wysocki would be working with Bilski, but clearly Maddie needed to do more work on that. On the face of it, however, it looked as though there might be a series of parallel scams, with a number of different teams all having been sold the same data. That would explain why the cars looked so similar and why they were performing as they were.

If there were four such schemes going on that would raise about twelve million, but why would a billionaire like Bilski care about such a small amount of money? Maddie chuckled quietly in the darkness. The answer was obvious: twelve million is twelve million and the average crook does not turn his nose up at easy money. But was Bilski really a crook? He did not seem to fit in with that style of criminality and for some reason Maddie felt that the idea of a scam just to generate some extra cash was not at all how he did business.

And if Tarquin was right and Bilski was the new owner of the commercial rights holding company, would he really take money from those who were helping to build his fortune? That was greed of a special kind and somehow even more despicable in Maddie's eyes.

At the same time, the teams paying the money were getting the benefit of the data they were buying, although if four or five teams ended up being more competitive it did not necessarily mean that they would each win a bigger share of the prize money. That only happened if one made progress in relation to the others. If everyone moved up equally, no one really gained. All it did was to make things a little closer and, perhaps, make the results a little less predictable.

And then it struck her. By making the smaller teams more competitive, Bilski might be trying to create a better show, and by doing so he could improve the product that he had acquired and that would mean a higher valuation as and when he wanted to sell it. The better the show, the more money he could make. Could that be it?

"Genius," she said quietly.

Bilski was making money from the scam and making money as a result of it.

It was a double earner.

But why then would he be happy to give money to sponsor Chiphurst? Perhaps, she thought, it was simple. He owned a lot of companies and by sponsoring the team, he could sell more goods, increase his revenues and make more profits.

And yet it was also a way to protect him investment, by strengthening the weaker teams.

She wondered if perhaps she ought to be outraged by all of this, but the truth was that, more than anything, she was impressed. The greatest crimes are always the ones when people don't know they are being robbed. If you don't know it is happening, there is no sense of injustice, no need to investigate, no need for revenge. All those who knew about the crime were being amply rewarded, so no one would rat on the perpetrators, not least because they did not actually know who they were.

Did Winslow know how brilliant a crime this was?

At that moment she suddenly felt a cloud of emotional darkness descend upon her. She loved the sensuality of being with Izzie, but Winslow was more than just sex. Was this what being in love was like? Should she ring him, tell him she was a fool and suggest that they get back together?

Izzie would not mind. She liked sex with both of them, together and separately. Maddie had often wondered if Izzie knew how to love. That sounded cruel, because she was not even sure whether she really understood love. It was all too complicated.

She felt better in the morning. Izzie got up early and Maddie listened to her showering and then tiptoeing around the apartment. When she was finally ready to leave, Izzie leaned over the bed and gave Maddie a gentle kiss on the cheek. It was a sign of genuine affection.

"Where are you going?" Maddie asked, pretending to wake up.

"I'm going for a run," she said.

Maddie groaned.

"I'll give that a miss," she said. "I'll have bacon sandwiches ready when you get back."

"Don't you dare," said Izzie.

They spent a lazy weekend, watching movies, eating unhealthy things and drinking wine, but they went for a walk on Hampstead Heath on the Sunday afternoon and both felt virtuous as a result of the exercise. That night, as they lay together, Izzie once again asleep, Maddie decided that she was going to ring Winslow and ask for forgiveness and plead with him to take her back. She hoped he would. She knew that he had lied to her, but it had not been about another woman or anything like that. It had been about a crime and who was she to judge him on the grounds of morality when she was as corrupt as he was in this respect. They would still have to figure out what to do about Izzie, but she wanted Winslow back.

In the morning Maddie was left alone in the apartment. She did not want to sleep longer and wandered around the apartment naked, looking at herself in the mirror. Then she took a long hot bath, until she was pink and feeling rather floppy. Wearing only a towel, she lay on the couch and felt the coolness of the air beginning to return her body temperature to normal. She then picked up her mobile and rang Winslow.

The answering machine was on. Maybe he did not want to take her call. Suddenly she felt very sad and more than a little lonely. If she had known where to find him, she would have driven there, but a man on a canal boat is hard to find. In an effort to calm herself down, she threw on some clothes and went for a walk along the Thames, down river to Vauxhall Bridge and then across, passing the Secret Intelligence Service building and heading up beside the river to Lambeth Bridge. She tried to call Winslow several times, but the result was always the same. She started to imagine horrible things happening to him. To stop worrying on the way back, she went into the Tate Gallery and tried to find peace among the Blakes and Turners. She liked the vagueness of Turner, but she still felt flustered and troubled. She decided that perhaps some food would help, so she stopped in the gallery café and ate a strange sandwich which involved brisket, caramelized onions, sliced gherkins and crispy bacon. She washed it down with a glass of wine. This made her feel very weary and so she returned to Dolphin Square and slept on the couch.

She woke at three thirty and tried again to reach Winslow. Again there was no answer. She felt wretched and stressed. She tried to take her mind off him by taking a book from Izzie's shelf, sniffing the paper with delight when she first opened the pages, and diving headlong into the story. It was a trashy detective novel, and not really very good. She could not concentrate on it.

She looked in Izzie's fridge and drank what was left of a bottle of white wine. She did not bother with a glass. She rang Winslow several more times. There was still no answer. She tried the book again, but it was no good. Her mind was focussed on one thing and nothing was going to change that.

She was dozing when the phone finally rang.

"You called thirty-two times," said Winslow, with an

amused tone in his voice.

"I did," Maddie said. "I know it is not a cool thing to say, but I miss you. I'm sorry. I don't want us to be like this."

Winslow laughed, but it was a kindly laugh.

"I was going to call tonight and say exactly the same thing," he said. "Maddie, I missed you. I love you. I want to be with you. Let's try again. And let's not screw it up this time."

"Where are you?" she said.

"I've been away from the boat today," he said. "I'm at Marylebone. I'm taking the six fifteen to Banbury.

"Wait for me," she said. "I'll be there as soon as I can. I'll grab a cab."

She threw her belongings into her bag, scrawled a note to Izzie, and was down on the street within five minutes. She hailed a cab almost immediately, but it was rush hour and the going was tough until they had cleared Hyde Park Corner. She told the taxi driver the reason for the urgency and he responded as best he could, but there were jams everywhere, one way systems and little old ladies crossing roads. It was a good half an hour before the taxi finally swung into the forecourt at Marylebone and she jumped out. She didn't have quite enough cash, but the taxi driver was willing to compromise and wished her good luck. She could see Winslow on the platform but knew she could not get there without a ticket because of the automatic barriers and so she queued up. It was six twelve and the person in front of her was taken her time buying a ticket. She considered throwing the silly woman out of the way, but restrained herself and at six fourteen she reached the machine. The credit card machine worked and twenty seconds later she was running up the platform, dragging her bag. A whistle was blowing and when she reached Winslow there was no time for any romance. They bundled one another on to the train. The doors closed behind them.

She knew that she looked a mess, but she didn't care. This was not like in the movies. Real life is sweaty and unromantic. It was rush hour and there were no seats, but they clung to one another and kissed. He put his arms around her and smelled her hair. She nuzzled her face into his chest. The train rattled its way out of the station.

"Oh, what fun we have...." he said.

The journey was fast, with only a couple of stops and less than an hour later they were standing in the forecourt of Banbury Station.

"Daisybelle is right here," he said. "She's moored just round the corner. There's no food. We can dump our stuff and then go and find some dinner."

She nodded. She was happy to be told what to do. She did not want to manage the relationship. He could be the boss.

"I have to fly out from Heathrow on Wednesday afternoon," she said. "So we have a day together."

"A day and two nights," he corrected.

They went to a Chinese and carried their dinner back to Daisybelle in a plastic bag. They ate and drank a couple of glasses of wine, that Winslow had aboard. They did not say much. They were just happy to be in the presence of the other and that was all that they needed.

Finally they settled in the salon with the bottle of rum on the table between them and they began to talk.

"Why did we fall out?" Winslow asked.

"You were upset about Izzie," Maddie said. "At least it felt like you were jealous. You were upset that I went to see her first when I got back from wherever the hell I was. And you said - quite rightly - that we were supposed to be in a proper relationship and she was just for fun. You felt that you were no longer my first priority and you didn't lIke it.

"And then I got defensive and brought up your mysterious life and how I was not happy not knowing where you were and what you were doing. And you lied about acting alone. You said that you were just making money, but that did not match with your argument that you would change your life if you could afford to stop doing what you do. I knew you were lying."

"But you are lying to yourself as well," Winslow said. "You are cheating. You are stealing, so it is not right to condemn me for telling a lie to protect the people I am working for.

And then we both got angry and said bad things. I think I called you a dyke."

"You did," said Maddie. "I didn't really mind that. It's sort of half true."

"It was true that Izzie is a big complication in our plans," he said, "but I was fairly sure that the novelty of our little threesome would wear off in the end. Izzie is just having fun. It is not that serious. And it has been fun."

"Yes, it is fun," she said, "but I'm not certain that it isn't serious."

They paused for a moment. There was not much more they could say on the subject.

"Anyway," said Maddie, "tell me how much you really made from the scam?"

"I cannot talk about it," Winslow said.

Maddie looked at him, took a swig of rum and said: "Winslow, I am not stupid. I know that you are working with Max Wysocki and I know that he is working with Bilski. I think that Bilski did this and I think there are other teams as well."

Winslow sighed. It was a sign of resignation.

"I knew you would one day find out about Wysocki," he said. "I should never had denied knowing him. I'm not sure why I did. After I had said it, I could not come clean because it would be telling you that I could not to be trusted. And I wanted to be trusted. I wanted to build a proper relationship, based on trust and respect. I wanted to settle down a little. And you were the way I was going to do that."

He paused for thought.

"You think Bilski did this with other teams as well?" he asked. "I didn't know that. It never crossed my mind. I thought it was just Chiphurst."

"I believe you," said Maddie.

"I didn't know Bilski until after we had done that sponsorship deal. I asked Wysocki if he could find me some cash to help Chiphurst out. He was the one who put me in touch with Bilski. I didn't know he was running the whole thing.

"So what happened to the money that Chiphurst paid you," she asked. "The three million that we paid you in order to get the Mercedes data."

"You know what happened, Maddie," he said. "It was paid into a company called M&W Enterprises and we bought two houses on Abaco in the Bahamas, each worth one and a half million. Both had five bedrooms and they each have a private dock. But, after we did the sponsorship deal, Wysocki said that the deal was changing and that I was going to get ten percent of the six million commission on the sponsorship. That was six hundred thousand dollars in cash. It was a better deal in the short-term and so I took it. Your one point two million is in your account, but the remaining four point two went straight back to him and was used to buy the houses. So nothing has changed.

"I have six hundred thousand in the bank, but that's not enough to spend the rest of my life living off it. I wasn't lying. I cannot stop working and be a beach bum. I have to work from time to time."

"Unless you become a kept man," she said, "which could happen because I *can* afford to retire."

"But you don't want to," he said.

"No, I don't. I like what I do and I want to go on doing it. It is nice to have financial security, but I am not going to start blowing money everywhere. I am just going to leave it, building up quietly."

He nodded.

"That is wise," he said.

"So how are we going to go on from here?" she asked. "I think we're pretty well suited and we fit together well. The big problem seems to be Izzie. Is that how you see it?"

Winslow nodded.

"She's great," he said. "She's sexy, she's smart, but she is not you and she's in the way. We both know it and while we both like her, we have to find a different path to take. I don't see how she can be a part of that future. It just won't work. Three into two doesn't go. Never has, never will. People pair up and live together. That is how it is."

Maddie nodded.

"The problem is that she doesn't really know what she

wants," she said. "She's still playing at life. She likes all kinds of sex, but I get the feeling that she's just like me. She's not a real lesbian. She just likes the sensations. She'll try anything. She's so attractive she knows that she will always find another man, so she is not frightened of being alone for very long. She doesn't have to make do with what she can get. Women are very picky these days because they are not under any real pressure to settle down. They are happy to cruise along and look for Mr Right. The problem is that the Mr Rights of the world are gone pretty quickly and if you don't get one early on, you end up looking for something that's just not there."

"So what we need to do is to find her a Mr Right?" said Winslow.

"No, I think she has to do that for herself," said Maddie. "In my experience all attempts at match-making end up disastrously. Tarquin and Katie have been trying to find her someone for years and all they could come up with was Max. He can be charming and he is a prince, but he's not my idea of Prince Charming. I can't say he gets me excited."

There was a pause. They both drank more rum.

"So," said Maddie. "We have to explain to her that as much as we don't want to do it, we need to stop seeing her, not because of what it is doing to us, but rather because we want to help her find something real and lasting. We have to tell her that letting her go is really an act of love. She needs to start her own story. What we have now doesn't work and it can't work. She needs commit to one person: male or female."

"How are we going to do that?" said Winslow. "It is going to be tough for both of us to dump her at the same time."

"She wanted us to think of her as a sex toy," Maddie said. "That was what she said. She wanted to have a way out and a complete lack of commitment. I think the best way to explain it to her is to tell her that we are doing it for her. That we want her to have what she needs, but we can't give it to her. She has to find it herself. Maybe I should take her to China and introduce her to some men."

"She meets plenty of men," said Winslow. "She just doesn't like any of them."

Maddie nodded. It was certainly not going to be an easy task. It was going to be painful.

# Twenty-six

Maddie yawned and Winslow followed suit. It had been a stressful day and it was time for bed, to sleep.

"Shouldn't we have sex at least to show that we have made up and are friends again?" Winslow asked, as he followed her down the corridor to the cabin.

"I don't have the energy," she said.

"Nor do I," he replied.

"Let's just sleep," she said. "We have a day and a night together left. Maybe we will feel more enthusiastic in the morning."

"Probably," he said.

They were both asleep within a minute of their heads hitting the pillows.

When they woke in the morning it was raining hard. A thoroughly miserable day. There was no enthusiasm to get up. Lying in bed Winslow explained that they could get to Heyford, where the canal and the railway run together and there is a station. It would take about four hours on the boat.

"There are shops and a pub," he said, "but the train trip to London would be slower although you would arrive at Paddington, which is an easier trip to Heathrow."

Maddie listened to the wind and the rain battering Daisybelle's roof and decided the only thing that made sense was to spend the morning in bed. If there was anyone mad enough to be out walking on the towpath that day, they might perhaps have heard Maddie and Winslow making up. They were rather noisy in their adventures, but they felt that if anyone was walking along the canal on such a miserable day, they probably deserved to hear a little passion to brighten up their lives. Later on they discussed what could be done about Bilski.

"We could tell him we know what he has been doing," Maddie said, "but what will that change? What's done is done. You cannot stop it now. It is already being written into the history of the sport."

"We can argue with him about what should be done, put ideas into his head," said Winslow. "Very often people in his position, with the power that money brings, want others to think that they are good people. They want to feel loved. Maybe we can use that to do some good. He might listen."

"If we explain that we know, he will probably be impressed," Maddie went on, "but he's not frightened of us. Who is going to believe us when everyone involved denies it. Could we even prove it is true? Yes, the cars look the same, but you can bet they are different in many ways.

"The fact that we found out about it is something that he might appreciate," Winslow said. "It is sort of a compliment to him, isn't it? I mean, who else knows? Who else would have guessed? Wysocki knows the plan because he is the cut-out, but apart from him, the whole plan is a secret and will likely always remain a secret. Bilski may be pillaging the sport, but if he sees that there are smart people out there who can spot such things, he might at least moderate his activities."

"Winslow Davenport, you're an idealist," said Maddie. "You're a do-gooder in disguise.

"... and I love you all the more for it."

It was still raining at lunchtime but Maddie was feeling restless. She wanted to set off.

"There are seven locks and ten swing bridges between here and Heyford," Winslow said. "I checked the map. We are going to get wet if we do this."

"I don't care," said Maddie. "A little English rain won't hurt me and we might get a better dinner tonight."

Winslow laughed. So they set off at one. The trip was longer than they had expected and they did not moor at Heyford until seven. Maddie looked magnificently dishevelled as they wandered into the village to the local pub. The food was great and they returned to Daisybelle slightly drunk and rather amorous.

The following morning they walked the short distance to the station and said farewell.

"China is the last place I want to be going right now," she said. He smiled and squeezed her arm.

"Go on, away with you," he said. "I'll see you a few days."

She wondered about the car in Dolphin Square, but that would just have to wait.

She arrived in Dubai in the middle of the night, as often happened with the F1 flights. She found a quiet corner in the vast VIP lounge and had a cup of coffee. She did not see anyone that she wanted to see. There are no time zones in the lounges in Dubai. It is whatever time you want it to be. If you want a gin and tonic for breakfast you can have one. The food available changes at breakfast time, but otherwise you are in a place without time. There are numbers telling you what time your plane will leave, but you never feel attached to reality. The truth is that four thirty in the morning is not very different to nine fifty at night. It really does not matter. You do not really even notice if it is dark outside or not.

Maddie slept for much of the second flight to Shanghai's Pudong International Airport. She wanted to take a ride on the maglev train, the fastest train in the world, but there was a driver waiting for her at the airport and so she put herself in his care and after a lengthy ride in Shanghai's manic traffic, she eventually arrived at the hotel where the team was staying. It was getting dark. As she was checking in, Buckett arrived back from the circuit, pursued into the lobby by a gaggle of Chinese F1 fans, wanting autographs.

"Hey, Cougar," he said. "What are you doing for dinner?"

"I was going to eat with Charlie," she said, "but I just got a text saying that he's not coming. He has some real estate deal in New York. So I guess I am free and available."

"My kind of girl!" said Jimmy with a wink. "How about we meet here at eight?"

Then he was gone, off to a gym or whatever it is racing drivers do when they are hanging out in hotels. The thought made her laugh. With the new generation they are probably up in their rooms, logged on to the Internet, playing online games, or watching porn.

They met downstairs at eight.

"Come on, Hot Dog," Maddie said. "I'm starving."

It was another very agreeable evening and Maddie, once again, had to pinch herself when she found they were talking about literature - with a little bit of F1 chit-chat thrown in.

As always in such places, the F1 teams tend to stay in the same hotels and so there were a stream of people popping by and to say hello.

"They all think I should be hanging out with some sixteen-year-old bimbo," Jimmy laughed. "But I have to tell you that I'm already bored with that. I'm looking for a smart intelligent woman."

"Ah," said Maddie. "Sadly, I'm not available. In any case, I don't do racing drivers. I have too much baggage in that department."

"Re-eally?" said Buckett, with an curious glint in his eye. "Tell me more, you can confess your sins to me..."

She laughed.

"I won't," she said. "Even if you torture me."

He raised an eyebrow.

"No, I'm not into that either," she said. "But I tell you what, I do have a friend I think you would like a lot. She's stunning to look at, has a fantastic intellect and she's a tiger in the sack. And she's only a couple of years older than you."

"My kind of girl," he said. "Tell me more..."

"No," Maddie replied. "I'm going to save her up. I'll bring her along to a race one day, if you are a good boy."

"If I am a good boy I would be going to bed about now,"

he said, and then turned to the waiter. "Do you think we could have another bottle of this wine, please?"

Maddie grinned.

"I am so glad that you are like you are," she said. "It's a real dream to have someone one can sell to sponsors for things other than pure speed. Speed is impressive, but often it is quite dull as well."

Jimmy smiled.

They called it a day at midnight and the following day Jimmy took the Chiphurst around the Shanghai International Circuit and set the fifth fastest time, showing that an extra glass of wine or two really makes no difference at all. The team was buzzing with excitement, but Poppy Denso was not happy. Rosita seemed to have suddenly discovered that Buckett was an attractive young man, and it put Poppy into a state of complete panic.

It was fair to say the team had completely lost interest in Denso. He sensed this was the case and seemed to have given up. He knew he had been found out and he was unlikely to be able to hold on to the drive for another year. It was still early in the season, but he knew he had no answers to Buckett. A better racing driver would have dug deeper, found more inner strength and power but Denso didn't have it. He was a spoilt rich kid from Brazil and one day soon, when his father decided he wanted to retire, he would return home and run the family business. Poppy would still be able to get the girls and would captivate them with stories of F1 and how he had lived in Monaco and how he might have been a World Champion had his luck been a little better. In his mind Poppy was just as good as Sebastian Vettel, Lewis Hamilton and Fernando Alonso.

The only problem was that the results did not support the theory. The mind is a strange and wonderfully delusional organ.

On Sunday, Jimmy was full of energy and fight. Denso arrived, complaining about everything Chinese and muttering something about having been offered some kind of wine with dead mice in it.

"A great delicacy," said Jimmy.

Denso look at him as though he was completely mad.

At the start of the Grand Prix Jimmy shot off the line and was in third place by the time they went into the first corner. It was clear that he had a chance to get second, but he pushed too hard, his tyres faded and in the final laps he dropped back to fourth. The Chiphurst team was already getting used to success and was dissatisfied with the result.

"Hey Cougar," he said. " I did my best. Couldn't do any more."

"You want a ride to the airport, Hot Dog?" She asked. "I'm gone in fifteen minutes."

"I'm with you," he said.

They were back in London by lunchtime on Monday, having spent much of the journey laughing and joking rather than sleeping, as they ought to have been. They parted at passport control. Maddie went through quickly enough but Jimmy, being a US citizen, had to wait in a long queue. She did not see him after that. Her bags were quick to arrive and she was on the way London to pick up her car from Dolphin Square before he appeared.

She got home before lunchtime and spent the afternoon doing some washing. That evening Winslow came to see her and she explained that it would be a great idea to try and get Izzie and Jimmy together.

"And what happened to match-making being a bad idea?" Winslow asked.

"Truthfully?" she said.

"Truthfully..." Winslow replied.

"I don't want us to dump Izzie," she said. "I want Izzie to dump us. It would be better for everyone that way. I don't want to hurt her and I think it might."

"Really?" said Winslow. "She always says she just wants to be a sex toy."

"Yes, but I don't believe her," said Maddie. "I think that's just bravado. I think we mean a lot to her. I think she's been dumped too many times in the past and she only says what she says to be ready if it happens again. If she calls herself worthless and gets dumped, it doesn't hurt as much, does it? What she needs is someone to build up her sense of self-worth, someone who will love her and stick with her, through thick and thin. At the moment she's in a cycle of self-defeat."

"I thought we said that we'd dump her and tell her that it is an act of love?" Winslow said. "Isn't that half the truth?"

"Sort of," said Maddie. "But that won't help her, will it? If she finds someone else and dumps us, then it is much better for her..."

Winslow sighed. He did not understand women. How such beautiful creatures would sometimes be unable to see their own beauty.

What Maddie was saying made some sense, but there were one or two practical problems with this strategy. What were they going to do with Izzie before they got her together with Jimmy? And what chance was there that the two of them would hit if off?

"There's only one way to find out," Maddie said. "We have to put them together as quickly as possible so we can see what happens..."

"...at the weekend," said Winslow. "Dinner at your house."

Maddie nodded.

It was the obvious answer.

The next morning Maddie sent e-mails to both, inviting them to dinner. She had checked Jimmy's schedule and there were no functions she knew about. A message came back straight away: he was free and would love to come. Izzie responded in a similar fashion a couple of hours after that.

"Nothing more we can do," Maddie told Winslow that evening, while they were doing the washing up. "It's now down to chemistry. We have lit the blue touch paper and now we must retire and wait for the fireworks. If you see what I mean..."

That week seemed to go very quickly for Maddie. Once an F1 season begins, the pace of life does seem to accelerate. Those who go racing are here and there and suddenly March has become August. They get a short break and then August turns into December.

Charlie was in the office all week, but he was not in a good mood as he was trying to work out what to do about the Denso problem. He had been a team boss for many years and suffered many different problems, but he had never been keen on conflict and always looked for ways to avoid unpleasantness. It was an admirable feature, but perhaps not the most useful thing for an F1 team principal.

The Chiphurst factory was humming with activity. Success is such a great motivator as it gives everyone confidence and ambition to get better and better. It was great to be part of the excitement. Everyone was smiling, and work was being done. Charlie had talked to HR about weeding out any discordant voices and there had been a couple of "promotions" to solve the problem. Chiphurst Competition was a happy ship.

On the Saturday morning, Maddie and Winslow were up early and visited a number of farm shops, in order to try to get the best quality produce available. They spent the afternoon quibbling happily in the kitchen, like witches around a steaming cauldron. The result of these combined efforts were some bite-sized fish cakes, with a rather lurid green sauce, created from cucumbers and fresh dill.

"Maybe I should use this on my face," said Maddie, "to improve my complexion. They say cucumber is a magical fruit. Or is it a vegetable? I don't know."

"Slop some on your face and see what happens," said Winslow.

The fish cakes would be followed by Winslow's version of a navarin of lamb. He explained that this is a dish that celebrates the coming of spring, being a mix of fresh lamb and young vegetables. It would be served with crunchy spring greens and some crusty baguette to help mop up the sauce. Following French traditions, cheese would be next, an interesting concoction called Oxford Blue, a creamy soft blue cheese, a little like Cambozola, but made in England.

To finish, Maddie had prepared a plum crumble, although this had to be done with fruit that had been preserved over the winter months.

They had chosen lovely wines to go with everything and Maddie had laid out a beautiful table. It was all ready with plenty of time to spare and the two of them sat around, waiting for the appointed hour. Izzie texted that she was on the train and Winslow was sent off to Oxford Station to pick her up. She arrived, looking fit and happy. The three had a drink in the kitchen and Izzie spotted that there was a fourth place at the table.

"Who's coming?" she asked.

"My driver," said Maddie. "Jimmy Buckett. He's an American, but he's a very unusual racing driver. He decided to race rather than going to Princeton."

Izzie nodded.

"I cannot say that I know the name," she said. "Should I?"

"He's new," Maddie replied, "but I think he is going to be a big star one day. He finished second in a race recently."

"OK," Izzie said. "That's pretty good, is it?"

Winslow laughed.

They heard Jimmy's car crunching over the gravel outside. He was bang on time. Maddie and Izzie watched his arrival from the kitchen window. He looked cool and relaxed and was carrying a big bunch of flowers and a little green box that Maddie guessed would be chocolates.

"Yummy," Izzie said, quietly. "He's a hunk, isn't he?

Maddie turned and smiled and then headed to the back door to let him in.

"Cougar," Jimmy smiled. "I brought you a present. Well, two actually. Flowers and macaroons, proper French ones not those awful dry things the English eat."

"Come on in," she said, stepping aside.

Jimmy walked past her and into the kitchen. Izzie was standing there. Buckett stopped dead in his tracks. If they had been cartoon characters his eyes would have come out on stalks and his tongue would rolled out from his mouth and hit the floor with a loud thud. Little hearts would have floated in the air around him.

Maddie followed him into the kitchen and was aware that Izzie too was just standing there, gawping and unable to say anything at all.

"This is Izzie," Maddie said. "Izzie, this is Jimmy Buckett."

Jimmy held out his hand and Izzie shook it. Maddie would later tell Winslow that she was sure that just before the two hands met a blue spark jumped between them and she heard a tiny crack of electricity flying through the air.

As this was happening, Winslow walked into the kitchen.

"And this is Winslow, my other half." Maddie said. "He's a fellow colonial, but more of a rebel than you New Jersey boys."

The two men shook hands.

Jimmy said nothing. He did not know that Maddie had "another half" and it was quite a surprise. Izzie too was silent.

"So, you're the famous Hot Dog," said Winslow. "Maddie told me all about you."

"Let's go through to the sitting room and have a drink," said Maddie, shooing Izzie and Winslow out of the room. "You two, go and make us some drinks."

As soon as they were gone, Jimmy said: "Is that her? Is this the girl you were talking about."

Maddie nodded.

"Wow!" Jimmy said. "I mean wow!"

"Cool your jets, Hot Dog," she said. "Just remember she's is my lesbian lover and we share Winslow."

Jimmy looked at her oddly.

"You're kidding me, right?"he said.

Maddie giggled.

"Get in there," she said. "I think Izzie's looking for a bit of adventure. You could be just the man."

"What do you mean could be?" he said. "I am. No question about it."

It was her turn to give him an odd look.

They went through to the sitting room, where Izzie had settled in an armchair and Winslow was pouring four glasses of red wine.

"Is your name really Buckett?" Izzie said, with what felt like rather shocking directness.

Jimmy nodded as he settled into the other armchair.

Maddie sat down on the couch and was joined by Winslow, once he had handed out the wine.

"Well, you know we can't ever get married," Izzie said. "There's no way. I'm not changing my name to Izzie Buckett!"

"I don't blame you," Buckett replied. "It's OK. I'll just shag your brains out and then dump you. That is what men are supposed to do, isn't it? When we revert to primal behavioural patterns?"

"And you'll grow old all alone," Izzie said. "A sad little apeman in forest of loneliness, without a campfire to welcome you. And all the ape ladies will have to resort to lesbianism to get their kicks."

"Cool, said Buckett. "My kind of tribe!"

Maddie shook her head in utter consternation.

This was indeed a very curious romance.

Izzie and Jimmy were staring at one another, each with what appeared to be a quizzical look on their face

"Did I mention that Izzie went to Harvard?" Maddie said, trying to fill the silence.

"Am I supposed to be intimidated by that?" Buckett said. "I like stunning, intelligent women with slightly bisexual tendencies."

"Looks like we're the perfect couple then," said Izzie.

And with that she took a big slug of wine, stood up and crossed the room. She sat down at Jimmy's feet, turned towards him and said: "Do you like buying diamonds?"

Maddie laughed out loud.

Jimmy looked puzzled.

"I love diamonds," said Izzie.

She then leaned her head on Jimmy's knee and he stroked her hair. They had known each other for less than five minutes.

# Twenty-seven

Life can be strange sometimes. For no reason at all, two people will meet and they will know instantly that they have found their soulmate. Everything will be right and the rest of the world around them will cease to exist or to have any real value.

It had happened to Maddie once in her lifetime, at a party in her teenage years, when although entirely sober, she had found herself kissing a guy five minutes after they had met - despite having arrived at the party with her then boyfriend. She had never really been able to explain why it had happened. It had been entirely instinctive and she had accepted that it had definitely gone beyond the bounds of polite behaviour. She had known it at the time, but she had no control over it. Convention became utterly irrelevant. She just wanted to kiss him. It seemed that he had felt the same way. It was some strange kind of chemical thing between them. The relationship had been lively, from a sexual point of view, but it did not last long because they had little in common, apart from chemicals. It had taught her a basic truth about life: beneath the veneer of human society, there is still the power of the animal that lurks in us all. We may kid ourselves that we are civilised, but in the end it is all down to chemicals. She tuned back into the conversation. A wide-eyed Winslow was asking where Jimmy was from, and the latter was talking about rural New Jersey.

Maddie took a sip of the wine, felt its goodness slip down her throat, and watched with delight as Jimmy's fingers played with Izzie's hair. It was probably the strangest thing she had ever seen, but sometimes life was like that. One forgot conventions, readjusted and went on as normal, as though nothing untoward has happened; as if Izzie and Buckett had been together for months. She looked at Izzie and saw a glow of complete happiness, the like of which she had never before seen, despite their many intense moments together. Izzie smiled back at her. And in that moment of connection between the two, there was a pang of sadness as well. They had shared so much, yet both knew, in that very instant, that it was over, although both recognized that perhaps they should mourn for a millisecond or two.

Maddie shrugged. She was entirely happy with Winslow. The chapter with her and Izzie was over. In the end it had been absurdly easy. Life can do that. It throws up endless problems but, now and again, it solves them brilliantly.

After about half an hour of chit-chat, Winslow got up, headed for the kitchen and said: "I must do the dinner". He left the other three sitting in silence for a few moments.

"This is so cool," said Jimmy. "It's fantastic, in the real sense of the word. It is just like a fantasy."

Izzie smiled.

"For me too," she said. Jimmy stroked her neck affectionately. He was getting over the shock now, and feeling more relaxed.

"Hey Cougar, tell us how you hooked up with Winslow? Was it a *coup de foudre*?"

Maddie laughed at the thought that a non-French racing driver in the modern era might use such a phrase, but then began to tell them the story of how she and Winslow had met in a hotel to discuss a deal and how they had not got on.

"Actually," she said, "we didn't start to like each other until we went to California to do the sponsorship deal that allowed Chiphurst Competition to put *you* into the car."

They chattered a little longer and then Winslow called out from the kitchen that it was time to go through to the kitchen for dinner. The food was excellent and the conversation lively. Izzie and Jimmy continued to behave like a couple who had been together for months and when the coffee was done and the evening was winding down, Jimmy finally said: "I guess we'd better be going".

Izzie got up and said "I'll get my stuff", as though it had always been the plan, and disappeared upstairs to pick up her bag, which had been put into the spare room.

"You treat her right, Hot Dog, or I'll be round to break your legs," said Maddie, with the sweetest smile one could possibly imagine.

"And I'll nail your hands to the table," Winslow added.

"OK, I get the message," said Jimmy. "But you really don't need to worry. Did you not see what happened? Did you not understand what it means? We're not just playing. I can't tell you why or how, but we just know. It will work out. Maybe we'll have some ups and downs, but she's the one I've been looking for. And she knows it too."

"It is all very strange," said Winslow. "Damnedest thing I ever saw."

"I can't help you," Buckett said. "It's weird, but we just know. Straight away. No need for fireworks. We didn't even have to discuss it. It was like magic. It's stunning, really, to feel such a connection with someone that one has never met before. I guess it is all about chemicals in the brain or something. I was reading somewhere that It's not quite as basic as we think. It can be more than just physical attraction. Sure, that is part of it, but we create these maps in our minds of what we want and we can analyse a lot of this stuff in just a few seconds. If we meet someone who fits the map then we can be instantly enamoured with them. It's about intellect, humour, sex appeal, warmth and I don't know what else. I don't really understand it, but I know it's right. All we have to do is to accept our feelings and not be scared of them, so when she got up and came and sat on the floor by me, that was it. I knew straight away."

Izzie reappeared, with her bag, and there were farewells and thank yous.

"Sorry to desert you like this," she Izzie to Maddie, "but there really is no choice. I have to go. This is my man. I've found him. I can't even describe how I am feeling right now. I know it's right. I just know it..."

"It usually takes more than a handshake and two sentences," said Maddie with a smile, "but I guess I understand. It sort of happened to me once, but as you can see, it didn't work out..."

Izzie shrugged.

"This one will," she said.

They hugged.

And then suddenly Izzie and Jimmy were gone and Maddie and Winslow were left standing in the kitchen, looking at each other. They shrugged.

"It's a fucking strange world," he said, as he turned to the sink and reached for his favourite yellow rubber gloves. Maddie helped him with the washing up. They worked in silence. It felt good just to stand next to one another.

"You know what it feels like?" she asked, after a few minutes of silence. "It feels like I'm standing on the rim of the Grand Canyon for the first time, or in the middle of the desert, looking up at the stars. It is only at times like this that you really understand the power of nature and how unimportant we all are, in the overall scheme of things."

Winslow nodded.

"Still," he said, "by a happy miracle we seem to have solved our problem of how to end the fun and games with Izzie. They were fun while they lasted..."

Maddie smiled.

"Yes, they were. I explored all kinds of things I'd always wanted to explore."

"Me too," said Winslow. "And it taught us what? That we like boring old normality? That mankind has tried all manner of different relationship models and this one is still the one that works? That it is entirely natural that boy meets girl and they settle down and have kids?"

"Steady on," said Maddie. "That's not in my thinking at the moment."

"You know what I mean," Winslow went on. "People might sometimes feel trapped in relationships and nowadays society let's them walk away, but what do they do? They go and look for the same thing again, hoping that this time it will work out."

"And sometimes it does," Maddie said, kissing him on the cheek. "Come to bed. I feel inspired by all this magic. Let's see if we can make some more."

Winslow in his yellow rubber gloves was not perhaps the leading man that Maddie had imagined for herself in earlier years, but now somehow he fitted the bill perfectly.

"Show me some magic," Winslow said.

They had a lazy Sunday, relaxing and then walking across to the pub in the early afternoon. Maddie wondered whether to call Izzie or Jimmy, to find out what had happened, but Winslow advised her to wait.

She was late for work on Monday, only half an hour or so, but she immediately saw that something was seriously wrong at Chiphurst.

"It's Denso," Cheryl said. "He flew his helicopter into a cliff or something. It's not good."

"When did it happen?" Maddie asked.

"This morning, very early," she said. "Rosita said he left at about seven."

"She wasn't with him?" Maddie said.

"It seems there was someone else," Cheryl said, rather sadly.

"Good grief," said Maddie. "And there was I thinking racing drivers could be sensible..."

Charlie appeared in the doorway. His face was ashen.

More news emerged from France in the course of the morning, but it was not good news. Poppy had been at Paul Ricard on the Sunday, playing with motocross bikes. He had stayed overnight in the Hôtel du Castellet, next to the circuit. There had been a woman with him, but no-one knew her name. He had called Rosita early in the morning to say that he was flying home to Monaco and then he went across to the aerodrome, where he had parked his helicopter and had flown off, heading down to Cassis, presumably to show his passenger the views of the Calanques, the steep-sided inlets of the sea. He had then climbed up to fly alongside the impressive Cap Canaille. He had probably been showing off and flying close to the twelve hundred foot cliff that they call the Falaises de Soubeyranes. The police said that they thought that there was an updraft, or a downdraft and maybe a rotor had hit the cliff but, whatever the case, the helicopter had gone straight down into the sea.

"Get Kyle Mason on the phone," said Charlie, when he heard the assessment. "We may need him."

"Forget it, Charlie," Maddie said. "We do need him. Full stop. They are not going to find Poppy sitting on a life raft, are they?"

Charlie stopped, thought about it, and sighed.

"No, you're right," he said. "Do you think we should fly down there? I never know what to do in these situations."

"Let's wait and see," said Maddie. "We don't want to get in the way."

"And to think I was just about to fire him," said Charlie, rather wistfully.

"He had one race left," said Maddie. "It's such a waste."

"I don't know," said Charlie. "There are some people who are not meant to grow old like the rest of us. We used to have a lot of them in Formula 1. These days the drivers are not the same mavericks that they used to be. Nowadays, they plan their careers and have investment portfolios. They are just different. I think I preferred the old days when there were more cowboys."

Later in the day Jimmy rang Maddie. He had heard the rumours and wanted to know more.

"I'm afraid he's gone," she said. "It's not confirmed yet, but it is true."

"He was a decent guy," said Buckett. "Crazy, but not a bad person. Apart from stealing Lorenzo's girlfriend."

"I think it takes two to tango," said Maddie.

"True," Jimmy said, "but if she jumped on him, he didn't have to say yes, did he?"

"And you would refuse Rosita?" Maddie asked.

"Cougar," he said. "I would have done. She's absolutely not my type. I'm not one of these guys who will fuck just anyone, just because they are there. I always want proper relationships."

Maddie was not sure whether to believe that one.

"Anyway," he added, "I am now very happily in a relationship. Saturday night was a great success."

"That's too much information," Maddie said.

"I just wanted to say thank you for putting the two of us together," he said. "It's brilliant."

"Just don't let her affect your performance," said Maddie. "We need you more than ever now."

There was a pause in the conversation.

"I guess you're going to put Kyle in the car," he said.

"Yes," said Maddie.

"It's so sad," Jimmy said. "So very sad. It's kind of worse that it didn't happen in a racing car. Let me know if there's any more news about Poppy."

"It won't be good," said Maddie.

"I know," he said.

It was not good news. The French police divers soon found the wreck of the helicopter and reported there were two bodies that would need to be recovered.

They tried to call the Denso family in Brazil, but it was clear that they were in a terrible state. They did not know what to do. The police told Charlie that there was not going to be a funeral any time soon. There would need to be a post-mortem. They heard nothing at all from Rosita since the first call that morning. They tried ringing the apartment several times and then sent someone round to knock on the door. The concierge said Rosita was gone. She had upped and left for Brazil, wearing sunglasses and taking only five suitcases of clothing.

There was nothing they could do except go on as normal.

"It's what he would have wanted," Charlie explained when

he announced the bad news to the factory.

Mason was in the simulator the next day and was soon beginning to find his feet. He was doing two or three simulated Grands Prix every day, using different circuit programmes. His lap times were good, but Buckett would still have an advantage when they got to Barcelona.

While they waited for news from the Denso family, Maddie tried to keep the team moving forwards. She sent an e-mail to Bilski, in the name of "Maddie and Winslow", inviting him to have lunch with them on the Friday in Monte Carlo, at the *Chèvre d'Or* in Èze. A reply came back, saying that the concept was perfect, but that Bilski did not find Èze much to his taste and proposed that Maddie and Winslow present themselves on a certain dock at a certain hour and they would be picked up by a tender belonging to a yacht named Shangdu.

They would have lunch, a private one, as requested, but on the Shangdu. That way, Bilski wrote, they did not need to worry about people with big ears. Maddie smiled at the thought and, while slightly irritated that her invitation had been turned around, but she was sure that the Shangdu would be decorated with exquisite taste and that they would get a decent lunch aboard.

She informed Charlie that if he had other functions planned that day, she would not be able to attend.

"I'm planning to have an absolutely horrible hangover that morning," he said. "I'll be on my yacht and only nurses in uniform will be allowed aboard. And they'll be made to walk the gangplank if they're found not to be wearing black suspenders."

Maddie remarked that she would get the word out to her friends in the nursing trade.

"I love nurses," said Chiphurst. "You know there are only three certainties in this life, don't you? Death, taxes and nurses".

The week dragged on. On the Thursday, Maddie and Winslow decided that they would drop out of circulation completely for the weekend. They would shut down their mobile phones and disappear off to find the Daisybelle, which was moored in the Grand Union.

Maddie left work at five on Friday and by seven they were there. She brought only minimal clothing and pondered the idea of putting together a kit that would stay aboard the old barge, so that in future she did not need to worry about even that. When she suggested it to Winslow, he said it was a great idea and that he would clear out a compartment for her stuff.

"It's not like you're going to need any ball gowns," he said. "Working clothes only!"

They were getting ready to go to the local pub, when Maddie's phone rang. She had forgotten to turn it off.

It was Buckett.

"I just wanted you guys to know that we're moving in together," he said. "We're looking at High Wycombe. So that Izzie can get to work and I can be close enough to get to the team."

"And you've known each other for what... a week?" Maddie said. "Impressive. So the love affair is still a raging inferno?"

"She's amazing," he said.

"I know," said Maddie. "If I were you, I would get her to ask Tarquin if he has any cottages available on his estate. That would be a good way to do it."

"I don't know who Tarquin is, or where that is," he said.

"Tarquin's a friend of mine and he's Izzie's boss," Maddie explained. "He lives on a vast estate which is hidden away, not far from Henley. That would be a great solution because she could then work at home some of the time, because that is where Tarquin lives. That office of hers at Westminster is a real rabbit hutch. I expect that Tarquin has something on the estate."

"Cool," said Buckett. "I'll ask her."

Maddie shut down the phone. They walked down the road to a pub called The Queen's Orb. It a quaint little place and the food was agreeable enough. They drank a bottle of Merlot and then returned for an early night.

The plan, Winslow told her, was to get up early and be on the canal several hours before "the grockles" started to arrive." Maddie groaned.

"Don't worry," he said. "I'll do the hard work. You just have to make the breakfast. The only down side of the plan is that we really need to have sex right now, so that we can get plenty of sleep."

Maddie turned, walked over to the doors and shut them, pulled down the blind and turned to Winslow, as she started to unbutton her shirt. He scrambled to draw the curtains in the salon.

"You want to convert this dinette thing into a bed, or do you want to just fuck me on the table top," she asked, as she removed her jeans. "Come on, Winslow. I need you right here... right now."

The dinette was not converted into a bed.

The following morning, as she was laying the table for breakfast, she giggled as she remembered what the table had been used for the previous evening. Tables were not always comfortable, but they were useful when the mood was right. It had been fun.

She managed a pretty decent bacon and eggs, with fried bread (Winslow's favourite English delicacy) while he was steering Daisybelle. He did not want to stop and so they took it in turns to eat, so as not to waste time. She enjoyed being the captain, although wearing only a jersey over the tee shirt she had slept in was rather unusual attire. The air was cold and crisp, with occasional gusts of wind that blew through her unkempt hair, but for Maddie all seemed well in the world.

When Winslow re-emerged from the cabin, she was despatched to wash up and to take a shower in order to be ready for "lock duty", which Winslow said would be required in about twenty minutes. They spent the morning going from one lock to the next, Maddie doing menial tasks between each one. Being the crew on Winslow's ship was a busy life. Finally she made them both coffee and sat down next to him as they chugged towards lunchtime.

By midday the canal was busy and things took a lot longer, particularly the locks, so they decided to moor up. They had thought about perhaps going to a pub for lunch, but the only one they passed, seemed to be full of people. Maddie made a couple of sandwiches and they opened bottles of beer. After that, they battened down the hatches, closed the doors and curtains and spent the next couple of hours in bed.

As the afternoon turned to evening, the canal traffic thinned out again and they set off, stopping only when darkness had engulfed everything. They were within easy reach of another lock, with a pub beside it and so for dinner they had a steak and kidney pie and chips.

Sunday morning was a lazy one. They could hear church bells echoing across the fields, but they were feeling ungodly and stayed in bed until late. They decided to have lunch in the same pub, which was offering a very agreeable roast, with proper Yorkshire pudding and some delicious, if rather heavy, treacle pudding and custard.

"I'll tell you what," said Maddie, "this canal boat business is not good for the figure!"

"You just need more exercise," said Winslow with a wink.

By the time they got back to the Daisybelle, neither had much energy to go on and they spent the afternoon lying on Daisybelle's roof, enjoying some surprisingly warm spring sunlight and waving at passing boats.

Winslow pondered pushing on further, but there was no real goal, and in the end they moored near a road and Winslow unloaded the di Blasi and rode away to get the Mercedes. He returned, picked up Maddie and they headed back to Netherington, leaving Daisybelle locked. Maddie made a soup from whatever she could find in the fridge, the freezer and the store cupboard. They spent the evening in front of the fire, listening to music.

It had been a perfect weekend.

Back in the office on the Monday, Maddie had to make plans for the race in Spain. There was still no word from the Denso Family nor from Rosita. They could do nothing.

On the Wednesday night Maddie arranged to go to London, where she had dinner with Buckett and Izzie, in a rather flashy establishment in Knightsbridge. They were still completely enamoured by life and by one another, without either of them ever questioning the logic of their relationship.

They were already talking about getting married.

Maddie had given up worrying about them and let them talk about their plans. They had been in contact with Tarquin about a cottage on the estate and he had thought it was the perfect idea, because it meant that he could spend more time at home and if they needed to go to London, they could travel together. There was an empty office in the estate and one of the cottages had just come up for rent and the happy couple were going to visit the following week. The Thursday would be the first night they would spend apart and neither was looking forward to it. They had discussed the idea of Izzie going with Buckett to Spain, but had decided against the idea. However, Buckett made it very clear that she was going to be coming to be in Monaco with him, at least on race day.

Maddie met Jimmy and various other team members, including Kyle, on the Thursday morning at Heathrow and before too long they were at the Circuit de Catalunya, in the less than glamorous northern industrial suburbs of Barcelona.

"I hate this place," Buckett confided. "The track is no great challenge and you cannot eat dinner before nine. It's bad for my metabolism!"

In qualifying Kyle Mason did a solid job, much better than Poppy would have done. Jimmy was ninth and Kyle eleventh, underlining Jimmy's belief that the Spanish track gave you a good idea of the performance of the car, but did not really allow the drivers to make much of a difference.

They had a minute of silence on the grid for Poppy, as this was deemed by some of those in ties and blazers to be the thing that they ought to be seen to be doing. The drivers stood around looking awkward and feeling self-conscious. They were not by nature very good mourners.

Finally it was time to race and Buckett made a tremendous start to run sixth at the end of the first lap. Kyle was thirteenth having been a little too cautious. It was a tough fight after that but the car was not quite strong enough for Jimmy to retain the place and he fell back during the second pit stops. Sixth was nonetheless a good effort and Mason made up a place to finish 12th, which was deemed to be a good solid F1 debut.

As usual, there was a race to get out after the Grand Prix, with Charlie having rented a jet for the occasion. This was waiting for them at Girona, sixty-five miles up the motorway from the circuit, towards the French border. From there it was a short seven hundred mile hop to Brize Norton. This meant they could be back in the UK before it got dark.

Charlie and Maddie left immediately after the race, while Jimmy and Kyle piled into a hire car half an hour later, having done the necessary work with the media and engineers. It was, by all accounts, a rather exciting drive for the two youngsters, although Jimmy said that they did manage to stay on the road at "almost" all the time and were "generally" on the right side of the road. They arrived in Girona just minutes after Charlie and Maddie, as their bags were being loaded into the plane.

They were back at Brize Norton in just under two hours and a taxi took Maddie and the two drivers to Heathrow, where they picked up their cars. She was still home before nine and Winslow appeared half an hour later.

# Twenty-eight

There was a little over a week to go before Maddie's busiest race weekend of the year: the Monaco Grand Prix. It is a time when everyone remembers they are your friend, and they all want to know if you, by any chance, you have any tickets or passes available. The problem is everyone wants to be seen in Monaco. Oddly, it is one of the worst places to go as a VIP guest, as there is nothing to see from the paddock. It is cramped and the facilities available for hospitality are over-priced and usually rather run down.

The people at Penkoz had grand plans for their first Monaco Grand Prix and Maddie had done the best she could for them. The locals in Monaco are descended from pirates and renting venues, hotel rooms and catering is wildly expensive. Greed has no bounds in this part of the world.

In this respect F1 does not help itself. There is always some daft sponsor with too much budget, who is willing to pay too much for everything, thus giving the impression everyone will do the same. As a result, the teams do very little themselves, beyond entertaining in the paddock or on the yachts they have rented (elsewhere) for the occasion.

Despite all this, in the eyes of the world, Monaco remains the very essence of F1 glamour. They call it "the storybook principality" and it is hard to argue against it. The Côte d'Azur is a spectacular area, with its own delightful microclimate, protected from the northern weather by the vast cliffs that rise above the Mediterranean. It is so warm that they can grow bananas along this coastline, which was once dotted with villas of the rich and famous. With time, it gradually became over-developed and the process was worst of all in Monaco, where the fiscal advantages offered by the Principality meant ever-increasing demand.

The Grand Prix is a spectacle for the crowds to watch and a thrill for the drivers. Winning Monaco is special.

There are still a few elegant hotels along the coast between Monaco and Nice, but there is a tendency these days for everything to be overdone. The new rich of today and showy folk.

And yet, when you walk around the harbour on one of the nights during the Grand Prix weekend, you cannot help but be sucked into the romance of the place. It's still Cary Grant and Grace Kelly in *To Catch a Thief*. Walking on the quayside, listening to the chattering of the rich on their yachts, the chink of expensive glass, the fizz of opened champagne and the gentle lapping of waves on expensive hulls, it is hard not to be seduced by the magic of Monaco.

The old town barely exists these days, but if you follow the coast road through Cap d'Ail to Èze and Beaulieu you can imagine just a little what it must have been like in the old days. There is money by the trainload, peace and quiet, and even a veneer of class.

The odd thing is the Monaco Grand Prix begins a day earlier than all the other F1 events and there is then a day off halfway through. It means the first day of running the cars is largely meaningless, unless one smashes the car into a wall, which happens rather a lot. Fortunately for Chiphurst, this was not the case this particular year and Buckett drove exceptionally well and set the third fastest time, getting everyone (not least the international media) very excited. By Friday morning the volatile Italian press had already started rumours suggesting Buckett would be at Ferrari the following year. Mason was ninth, which added to the impression that he too was something a little special.

Traditionally, Thursday night in Monaco is a big party, as no-one in F1 has much to do on the Friday. Maddie had done the partying when she was younger and didn't really have any great desire to do anything more than having a quiet dinner up in the old town at a little Italian place called Pinocchio. It is always much quieter up there. She and Winslow drank a bottle of rosé and after a slow and enjoyable dinner they wandered around the old town for a while, following the Avenue Saint-Martin to the cathedral and then going up a tiny street and under an arch to emerge back in the Place du Palais. From there they wandered slowly back to where they were staying in Fontvieille and closed the door on the world.

The next day they arrived at the quayside at the appointed hour and a tender with the name Shangdu written discreetly on the side was waiting for them, with a cheerful young sailor, blond and well-muscled, at the wheel. They were helped aboard and then the tender navigated its way through the mess of the harbour and out into the open sea.

There were yachts moored at intervals, but eventually they spotted the Shangdu itself. She was a big yacht, not as grand as some on the Côte d'Azur these days - usually flying Russian flags - but she was discreetly impressive.

There was a boarding staircase they could see that would vanish cleverly into the hull when the yacht was ready to depart. Further forward was a tender bay, with overhead cranes ready to lift the tender straight out of the water and carry it aboard. Hydraulic doors on the side of the yacht would then clamp shut and the vessel would be ready to sail.

They climbed the staircase and emerged in what was obviously the main salon. A very pretty dark-haired girl with a New Zealand accent was there to greet them. She wore a white tee shirt with Shangdu embroidered on it and a navy blue that finished halfway up shapely thighs.

"Do come this way," she said, and led them to a table on the terrace at the back of the salon. "Can I get you a drink? A chilled rosé perhaps?"

It seemed a most sensible suggestion.

"Mr Bilski is on the telephone at the moment," she said. "He will be with you shortly."

Before she could leave, Bilski appeared.

"Maddie, Winslow, how lovely to see you again," he said. "I see you've already met Gorgeous. She is the best hostess in the Mediterranean."

"I prefer 'on' the Mediterranean, rather than in it," she said with a gorgeous smile.

She disappeared in search of drinks and what Bilski referred to as "nibbly things". He sat down with them. They were aware that the yacht was preparing to set sail.

"I thought we'd go for a little trip," Bilski said. "We'll stop somewhere away from the crowds for a pleasant lunch. Something a little more civilised than Monaco harbour. There are so many barbarians about there these days. The captain suggested that we moor off Cap Ferrat. I am very fond of it. One day I really must buy a house there, but I am not sure I want to have Russians for neighbours. You never know if they won't be gunned down on the lawn or murdered in their beds."

The engines rumbled into life beneath them and the Shangdu edged gracefully forwards, gradually building up speed.

"This is quite a yacht," Winslow said.

"It's not bad," Bilski said. "There are much bigger and better ones these days. There is so much money about, but one does not really need it all, and I certainly don't need all the ex-spetsnaz heavies who seem to go everywhere with these Russian rich. I presume that they are worried that someone will kill them, although I suppose that is what you have to expect when you steal as much money as most of them have done. Anyway, for me, the Shangdu is perfect. There are five or six staterooms, I actually don't know. I don't really prowl about downstairs that much. There are some crew quarters.

"If there are visitors who want to come by helicopter I have this terribly clever device. I don't even know what it's called.

It folds up into a big box-shaped thing. It's all hydraulic and lives in the tender bay. You lift it out and unfold it and it creates a big floating platform. You can attach it to the stern of the yacht and use it for helicopters or as a place to have big dinners and dancing parties. Or you can tow it off into a shallow bay, anchor it and it can be an artificial island. All you then need is Gorgeous with a picnic basket and all is well.

"We also have a couple of cars in the tender bay, so we are not stuck in a port when we go visiting places."

Winslow was impressed.

"Would you like a tour?" Bilski said. "I am really rather proud of it. This is my deck. My cabin and my office are over there. Upstairs, there is a another stateroom and a thing we call the sky lounge, which sounds like something at an airport, but is really only a bigger outdoor eating area. We use that when the sun is low, otherwise it gets too hot.

"Up there, we also have the bridge and the captain's cabin. Above that, there is a sun deck and a nice little plunge pool thing, so that one can keep cool. At the rear of this deck, just over there, you can see stairs going down. We have a swimming platform at the back. There is also a place where we store all the toys: jets skis, windsurfers, diving equipment, bicycles and so on. I think we might even have a motorcycle or two. In front of that is the engine room and then the tender bay. On top of that I think we have the galley and the staff quarters, but I honestly never go on that part of the ship."

The yacht was already passing the imposing Musée Océanographique de Monaco and they could see the entrance to Fontvieille harbour. They would soon be at Cap d'Ail.

"So tell me, Maddie," Bilski said. "What is this all about? You said that you had something important to talk about."

Maddie took a deep breath.

"I have figured out who you are and what you are doing," she said. "And I don't like it. Now, I'm trying to decide what to do about it and I'd like to hear your views on the subject."

She watched Bilski intently, as she was talking, but he did not seem to react at all. She had expected something.

"You say you have figured out exactly what I have been doing," Bilski said. "Perhaps it would be good to start out by telling me exactly what you know and what you suspect, then I depending on that, I will explain, and give you a full and unexpurgated version of the truth."

Maddie was surprised by the reaction, but she explained that she knew that Bilski was the new commercial rights holder of Formula 1 and described the scheme that he had created for Chiphurst. She said that she was certain that as many as four other teams had agreed to the same scam, each without knowing about the others. This meant that Bilski had made around twelve million, depending on the commissions he had paid in each case.

The goal of all this, she said, was probably not the money but rather to try to balance the performance of the teams and to give the smaller teams a better chance of competing. By doing this, Bilski was going to create a much more competitive championship and thus have a better product to sell to the world. The runaway triumph of Mercedes the previous year had not been that good for the TV viewing figures and this was a way in which interest in the sport could be revived.

Bilski smiled.

"Well, I'm afraid that you have me pretty much banged to rights," he said. "And I am really very impressed that you have been able to figure it all out..."

"... without any help from me," said Winslow. "She had the whole thing worked out before she even told me."

"Very impressive," Bilski said. "Really, very impressive. You have the whole story. OK, so let me try to justify myself. I think when I have explained it, you will think less harshly of me."

He smiled at her and Maddie could not help but think of her grandfather.

"The first thing that you have to understand is my attitude to money. I am not at all like the last owners of this business. What is money? Maddie. If you stop and think about it. It is only really important if you don't have enough of it. Once you have enough, there is no real value in it. There is an argument, of course, about how much is enough, but when you have a couple of hundred million and you have bought all the toys that you want, then money is a pretty worthless commodity. It becomes a means of keeping score.

"My view is that if you have it and you do not use it in some positive kind of way, you are reprehensible. The great industrialist Andrew Carnegie once said that to die rich is to 'die disgraced' and I agree with that. Carnegie put his money where his mouth was. He started with nothing, built his empire in steel and sold it for four hundred and eighty million dollars in 1901. I am not sure how they work these things out, but I believe that was something like seven point five billion in modern terms. He then spent the rest of his life, nearly twenty years, giving it all away. His charitable institutions are still operating to this day, still making grants to improve education and doing things that improve the world that we live in.

"That is how I look at it. I don't see any point in keeping your money. Your children and their children will only be messed up by it. Those who are born wealthy, don't respect money, they don't understand it because they have always had it. They rarely have the motivation that made their parents wealthy. It is too easy for them, from the moment they are born. People like me get rich because we want to be rich. We need to be rich. We need to drag ourselves free from the apathy of the masses. We get money because we want it so much and we will do anything to get it.

"So I don't value money," he went on. "And I don't need monuments to myself. What's the point? One day all human life will disappear. We are just specks of dust in a vast explosive universe and nothing is permanent. Everything will disappear. What we have that is valuable are the people around us, not just our loved ones but all people. We have sunlight, we have beauty. We must not forget these things. We must enjoy them for what they are. All that matters is making other people happy, making them smile and making sure that the world remains beautiful and unspoilt.

"The reason I bought the Formula One group is that F1 is something that makes people happy. It inspires them, it is their passion. It is their way to escape the drudgery of life.

"Motor racing is a passionate sport, generally involving very passionate and colourful people. It is also a fantastic money-making machine. But it is a machine that needs to be oiled, maintained and improved. The problem is that in recent years the sport has been drained rather than nurtured. The people who have been running it have grabbed as much as they could grab and while they were doing this, the sport - this wonderful thing of value - has been drifting without direction, because the people in charge had all the money they wanted and could ever need and so it became a battle over ego. The mess they created is not fixable in any rational way. Everyone argues with their own self-interest at heart and no one can agree on anything. The only way to change that is to find a way to appeal to the self-interest of each party. If you can do that then anything is possible.

"That's the secret of making money. You give people what they want. That is all that I ever did. And that is what I am doing now.

"So I looked at the sport in great detail and identified the things that I felt were wrong with it. And then, when I had done that, I set out to fix those problems."

He paused for a moment and a gust of wind ruffled his hair.

"The major problem as I saw it, was that people were not working together to make the sport stronger," he went on. "It may be a battle between different companies on the race track, but they have shared interests as well. The value of their success is best increased by working together, but they could not do it because they were too busy fighting and seeing things only from their point of view. What we needed was less back-stabbing politics and a better show.

"Bernie gave some of them power because he had no choice but to do it, to keep them in line, but he did it knowing they would never agree on anything. So he remained the powerful one, because he held the purse strings. This worked fine, but now it is failing because the system favours the big, rich teams. And they will not change anything, so what we needed was a way to share the technology, without them knowing about it.

"With technology today, nothing is safe. You can steal anything and create exact copies and no one will ever know. It really is that simple. We don't want the teams racing with the same cars - that will always fail in the end - what we want is them racing cars that are less expensive, but more closely matched. When the sport was growing up, this was achieved because people were finding new technologies, but after a while the cars had to be slowed down and this meant it was no longer the same. The difference between the cars for a long time was simply the aerodynamics and the people who spent the most, achieved the most. It became a question of money.

"It was a great idea to change the engines, to make the sport relevant to the industry. Brilliant, but the downside of that was that the formula needs to mature so that they will all be racing engines that are basically the same. The difference is that the technology is useful, whereas aerodynamics is a complete waste of time, energy and money.

"So we needed to negate the power of aerodynamics, by making sure that everyone had basically the same thing, which would put the emphasis back on to the engines and the drivers; where the spotlight should be.

"The sport needs to be about heroes," he added. "People relate best to people."

Bilski paused. Maddie was nodding. The logic was right.

"Do you know what STD stands for?" Bilski asked her. "The company that now owns the business. It is an acronym for Stacking The Deck."

"Stacking the Deck?" said Winslow.

"Sure," said Bilski. "Arranging the cards so that they are dealt out so you get the result that you want. Not leaving anything to chance. When I bought this business it made money. It was doing OK. It was turning over one point eight billion dollars a year, but it was hopelessly dysfunctional and not performing as well as it could have been doing. Half the money was going to the teams. Fair enough. They are the stars of the show, but Ferrari was getting more than its fair share. Far more. Why? Because they were a bigger name. You know a Hollywood A-List star compared to the C-Listers at the back of the grid. But that wasn't right because Ferrari has not made a good movie in ten years. They were getting paid extra but not delivering star performances any longer. And the rest of the money was going to these private equity guys. They borrowed against future profits to get cash. They loaded the business with debt. Their investors were happy, but they were screwing the sport. They didn't care - and that made me angry. Personally, I think they were a pretty pedestrian and unimaginative bunch. What these suited idiots did not understand was that a real entrepreneur builds a business. Rather than dividing and conquering the cast, you get the whole cast working together. You build a team and you use imagination and energy to create more potential for earning.

"Those guys were greedy, but they put nothing back. Where was the promotion? Where was the investment? Where was the marketing? They did nothing but take."

He paused again. He was hungry.

"I've built several fortunes," he went on. "The thing I know better than anything is you do it with the help of your workers, not by exploiting them. There is enough money in this game for everyone to be happy. Taking it all was just despicable - and bad business.

"My goal was to fix the whole thing and make it work as it should work, but by the time I got my hands on it, there were problems. The smaller teams were dying on their feet with no-one helping them. The federation had failed in its duty to keep the sport healthy. They had taken some money to shut up, waiting for the sport to fall apart. The federation should not be in that position, but these kind of organisations are always run by the wrong kind of people. It is all about ego or money. So what I needed was a quick fix that would not come back and bite me. I needed to protect myself while I was fixing the problems, so it was all done on a need-to-know basis. Only Wysocki and I know the whole story. He is there simply to protect me. I don't know how you made the connection, but well done for finding it.

"I think my plan was pretty good. I have one cut-out per team, one marketing person to fiddle the books and one engineer to take the data without any questions. Everyone got what they wanted. We delivered the same car to all five of the smaller teams and they didn't even realize it. Of course, you must remember that an engineer who is copying someone else's car is always going to make cosmetic changes to ensure there is no way of being caught, but in the critical areas the aerodynamics are identical, although they have all been developed along different lines, so they have become less alike as the weeks have gone by.

"The overall effect is that these teams are now much closer to the big teams and so we have great races and unexpected results. The business is more attractive than it used to be. It is worth more money and it can make more money. My next step is going to be to use what we have achieved to show everyone that working together is best and get them to do it, so we can all make more and more people will see and want to come in and take part. What the sport needs now, more than anything else, is a cost cap. That's easy enough to achieve. You just ignore the federation and get the teams to sign a document saying they will accept a certain level of budget..."

"... how do you do that?" said Maddie.

"By offering them more money," said Bilski. "If you tell them they can have an equal share of eighty-five percent of the revenues, rather than the current percentage, split unevenly between them, they are all going to sign up for it, aren't they? OK, I accept that Ferrari might make a fuss, but that is fine. They can go and race somewhere else. They have played hardball with F1 too many times in order to get themselves in a position where they getting more than one hundred million before any prize money is divided amongst the teams: that is just wrong. If they don't like it my way, that is fine, they can go and race at Le Mans. I am afraid it has to be my way or the highway...

"We all know this is not a real option for them, because no-one gives a toss about Le Mans. It is a race with one day of coverage. After that, they have to pay to tell the world what they have achieved. In F1 they need only to invest in the racing because the sport delivers the message for them.

"Ferrari knows that. They'd quickly crumble if you called their bluff, particularly when you explain to them how we can all make more money by working together and embracing new ideas.

"I have proved if you can control the technology, you can reduce the spending, haven't I? I gave half the teams the same chassis and left them to do the aerodynamic work. They all saved money, they all had better cars and no-one knew I had done it. I gave each team about thirty million worth of research and development in exchange for three million. And I gave you the profit. As a result we have stronger teams and a better championship. And no-one knows. What does that tell you?

"I have shown you don't need to spend money you don't have. I have proved it is possible to cut costs by making sure money is not wasted. No-one needs to know you all have the same chassis or the same suspensions. What is important is the aerodynamics and the engines. We need to cut down the cost of the engines and put some restrictions on wind tunnels. They do that already but it could be more. But you know the important thing, above all else, is to have a public budget cap. That way the sport looks like it is efficient. We need to attract new funding. Too many people think F1 is just about ridiculous uncontrolled spending - and it is! We need more manufacturers to come into the sport. They all want to develop the technology F1 is using, but they don't want to be associated with the wild excesses of spending everyone thinks about when you mention F1. They can spend as much as they like developing their engines, I don't care. But they must agree to supply engines at a certain price to a number of teams. They can have their own teams if that is what they want, but they have to give the same material to everyone."

360 - Maddie Midnight

"That's sensible," said Maddie.

Bilski sat back and smiled.

"The brilliant part of the plan is it is almost impossible to uncover. No designer is ever going to admit to cheating. And if they did they still don't know where the data came from, so why would they admit it? They understand the data is good and they use it. They know it will make them look good so they keep the secret to themselves. They save money on the R&D and get more success. It is a win-win.

"We buy the marketing people's loyalty and, of course, once they have taken our money they are effectively silenced. They are not going to admit they are corrupt. Are they?

"Anyway," he added, "now the cut-outs will fade away, the cars will be developed. No-one will be any the wiser."

"And," Maddie with a smile, "you have the teams paying for the scam."

"So who was the loser in this?" said Bilski. "The rich teams with the unfair advantage? Yes, but then again who has the most to gain from the sport growing?

"You want a level playing field? This gives you it - and it does it in such a way it is not obvious and the public never knows about it. It's an elegant solution, so elegant in fact that it is invisible."

"Except to me," said Maddie.

# Twenty-nine

"Yes," said Bilski, "except to you. But Maddie you have to understand this is the best thing to happen in F1 for years. In any case, why is it so unfair? The old system was worse because small teams had no chance at all of winning anything. So I've given them a leg-up to off-set the big team advantage. Is it fair that teams like Ferrari and Red Bull get paid vast premiums because they were politically important at a certain moment? Those benefits are not really about their histories, are they?

"That was a retrofit explanation to justify the money. It was not good for the sport. It divided the teams, so they could not work together to put on the best show possible. My idea helps to level the playing field and no-one knows it is happening. The whole thing is laced with deniability. You can argue two wrongs do not make a right, but sometimes they do. You have to fight fire with fire. Giving everyone the same basic starting point is not a bad idea, but you cannot make it happen. To my mind, there are no rights and wrongs in the F1 business. There is only action and inaction.

"And the money I made has been ploughed back into the business. How do you think you ended up with the sponsorship money? You said the team was struggling and so I used the money to help you and to protect the future of

Chiphurst Competition. Is that a bad thing? I used the money from your rivals to make you stronger. Actually it should be like that. That is a good business model. I've made a step in that direction without them even knowing it is happening."

Bilski paused.

Maddie was looking out across the water. It did all make sense, she had to admit. Yes, he was manipulating everything, but it was in the best interest of the sport.

"If F1 was stronger and fairer it would create a better show, based on what was supposed to be important: ingenuity, innovation and skill."

"I am still struggling with it," Maddie admitted. "Sport is sport and you cannot script it."

"But I am not scripting it," said Bilski. "I am leaving it up to you guys. The sport is more unpredictable than it used to be. It pushes the drivers to the fore. They are humans - unpredictable beasts. We want characters. We want real men who take risks and make mistakes and are not afraid to say what they think. What we do not want is the hideaway heroes of today. The guys who say 'No comment' in press conferences when there is a hard question.

"And we need to ship in bus-loads of great-looking women and let nature take its course!"

Bilski stopped and laughed. It was a gentle laugh, almost kindly.

"We don't want people who are glove puppets for the sponsors," he went on. "We want heroes. We need people who want to promote the sport. We want people who realise F1 will work for them. If you have a new movie you are promoting, movie companies should know that if they bring the stars to an F1 race, we will give them plenty of promotion. You want the media to help? Easy, make them feel wanted. Give them hotel rooms, fly them to the races on charters. Save them a few dollars and they will make the money back for you. Give them access to great stories. Feed them celebrities. That would stop the negativity, make the coverage more positive. OK I accept that you will never fix the Daily Mail, but it will always be out of step with the others and might change because of that. Nothing is impossible if you look for solutions rather than reasons why things won't work.

"Ecclestone created the current situation because he had to do it. He was scrambling to stay in control. I was able to buy the business because I convinced Bernie he was going to lose in the end. He did not know how I was going to fix it, but he recognised he was going to lose. I gave him an elegant way to leave. He didn't want to stop, but the thing that really motivates him is winning and as much as he didn't want to stop, he didn't want to lose. That was why he went. I showed him life would be better without that. He is going to build an empire in something else now...

"All I want is to make this a great sport and make a decent profit. I am not here to screw the sport like the goons who came before me. They were just milking it and killing it. They were fools. Successful fools. The financial world is full of them and none of them understand why the world hates financiers. They do not understand they are extremists and there is a happy medium where progress can be made and everyone can work together to build an even more profitable business. I gave them the money they wanted and told them to get lost.

"Above all else, we need to do proper marketing," he went on. "We need to engage with the fans, build a bigger fan base, figure out ways to get the younger generations involved. We need new style races, more like the festivals that you see each year in Melbourne and Montreal. Do you know that in Montreal more people came to the Grand Prix to party than come to the Grand Prix? That's brilliant. That's driving business for a city.

"We need to cut out the greedy people and we need to be transparent in our dealings - once we have the whole thing sorted - but we don't want to do anything stupid like having an IPO. Above all else, this business needs a benevolent dictator."

"And that's you?" said Maddie.

Bilski nodded. "Yes, that's me, but I will never tell. I like to stay out of the limelight."

The yacht had arrived off Cap Ferrat. They could see back across the bay to Èze, with its viaduct high up above the water. They could see the delightful little port at Beaulieu and the rock up near La Turbie which they call the Tête de Chien.

"Goodness me, I've talked a lot," Bilski said. "Let's eat. I'm starving."

He led them upstairs to where Gorgeous was waiting. As soon as they settled down she explained they were going to have a very *provençal* lunch, with some nicely-chilled rosé from Château Vignelaure to accompany the baguette "tradition" and a large pot of *tapenade noire*.

Bilski rolled up his sleeves. Eating, he said, was serious business. Gorgeous hovered discreetly, appearing where and when she was needed, but otherwise being invisible.

The wine was perfectly chilled and delicious.

"When I took over this business," Bilski said, "the TV revenues were about eight hundred million dollars a year. That sounds a lot, but it really isn't much when compared to what some of the other sports have been getting in recent years. The NFL did a deal a couple of years ago to run from 2013 until 2022. That was worth three billion a year to the teams. The Premier League in the UK did a  four point eight billion for three years just for the domestic rights.  And not long ago the NBA did a nine-year deal worth twenty-four billion just for the US market. So I think that F1 is underperforming in this respect. However, I don't think switching to pay TV is a good idea. F1 is good content, but not at any crazy price. If you have pay TV then you drive the fans away. It makes your finances better in the short term, but over time your audience dies away because new fans do not stumble upon the sport and get sucked in by it. It's absolute short-termism; the philosophy of men who are greedy for the sake of being greedy. Motor racing is still a niche business. NASCAR, which is basically a one-market sport, was able to do a deal worth eight point two billion over ten years, so being a global sport we really ought to be able to do better than that.

"I still believe the best model is to broadcast the races on free-to-air television, so that everyone can watch them for nothing and the local TV stations can pay for the rights by selling time to advertisers. They also do their own promotion, which makes it easier for the sport. The problem with this is they cannot pay as high a fee as a pay TV channel."

"Perhaps there will come a time when it is generally accepted one has to pay for sport on TV," said Maddie. "I don't think the moment has yet arrived, but the world is changing. Live sport is one of the few activities that gets people really excited, but even real fans baulk at paying prices for premium viewing. I still believe F1 has to be seen by as many people as possible and going to pay TV is disastrous in terms of numbers."

Bilski nodded.

"Perhaps we need to wait and go with cable operators who bundle F1 content with Internet access, cheap phone calls, TV and online radio," he said. "That would help them attract new customers and you would get maybe five bucks from each customer. With our kind of viewing numbers that would mean two point five billion a year. The cable operator is also going to be doing the advertising for you, so the overheads are low.

"Maybe in the end we can go to direct-to-consumer at, perhaps, a dollar a race, or something like that, and that has potential to raise more than ten billion a year. It's absolutely massive. The trouble is we need attitudes to change a little more before that becomes acceptable, but in the meantime I really don't think it is wise to drive your fans away. We need to encourage them to watch our activities by providing them with the best content at sensible prices.

"Rather than taking all the money, I think the commercial rights holder should make some serious investment because that will create more revenues in the longer term. We have to look to the future. It is no good trying to survive on an audience of 50-60 year-old men. We need to open an office in Hollywood and deal with the movie and TV people. They are always looking for ideas and motorsport is exciting and colourful. We need to start out trying to make cartoons or animated features for kids, we need to use the Internet and create good computer games. You should not be jumping on anything published on Youtube, we should be broadcasting the exciting moments in order to draw in viewers.

"The numbers we have seen in the cinema and gaming industry are stunning. The animated feature films Cars and Cars II between them produced something like a billion at the box office. But they also made twelve billion in merchandising. That is all about car racing. That is our territory! The game Grand Theft Auto V made eight hundred million on its first day on sale. Why do F1 games not make that much? Because they are boring. They need spicing up. There are tons of ways I can see to make more money.

"So you ramp up your revenues by being smart rather than mean and if we do that we can cut the race fees and get races where we want them to be and not in places where people can afford it. That way the ticket prices will come down. I will insist on that, and then the grandstands will be full and we will be making new fans.

"The cost cap I propose will be self-policing. If it is in the rules, the big companies involved in F1 will make sure it is respected, because they do not want to be found to have cheated. A cost cap is no different to measuring the width of a rear wing. It is just a measurement. They can try to hide money if they want to, but forensic accountants will find it. In any case, having a cost cap is a bit like mandating profits and if they have profits they have buyers and the value of the teams goes up.

"And if the tracks are given more money then they can use some of it to build better facilities to make themselves more attractive to the ticket-buying fans. They have to compete with fans staying at home so you need to have big screens for replays, good quality food, plenty of retail outlets and a real experience. That's what you don't get on TV. Lower fees would mean that we could race on the streets overlooking New York City and in places like Long Beach. You have to make the events into carnivals and you have to make the stars into good role models."

The *tapenade* had given way to a delicious *pissaladière*, a tart made from caramelized onions. The glasses of rosé were refilled, they slipped quickly down again.

"The really key thing F1 has entirely missed is its target market should not be old men, as the previous owners thought. The person we are selling to should be a mother in her thirties or early forties. Women with kids between the ages of five and sixteen. Mothers are the people who decide how the family's leisure money is spent. The men may want to do things their way, but the women usually win the argument.

"So we have to sell the sport to them. We have to have heroes who are people to look up, the sport has to be wholesome and healthy, with nice fair-minded kids, not evil little shits who will win at any cost. They don't all have to have lobotomies, they can still be characters, but we need them to be good sportsmen.

"We also need to drive forward with media technology so we can offer better experiences for the TV viewers and gamers. There is a whole lot can be done with virtual technology. You can get into the paddock if there were some cameras dotted about. Why not? It can still be the inner sanctum, but the public can see it is as well. With Google Earth you can go anywhere.

"And there is huge savings to be made in the industry if people don't try and cheat one another over transportation and freight. Why not charge what is actually costs, rather than needing to jack up the prices? And why take all the TV production equipment around the world? It can only be a matter of time before we are able to do all the TV production work from a permanent studio in England. The pictures from the cameras can come down the cables, different feeds can be edited for different markets and the finished result can go out as it does from the circuits. Why do we need to transport all these people around the world and make life difficult for ourselves? All you need is the cameras. I am not even sure that you need operators in all cases. Obviously cameramen are good in some ways, but not all cameras need them. With all the GPS data that we have available the cameras can be programmed to react if there is an incident near them. And all the data should be available as well, free of charge. They have amazing stuff in Race Control. We should use that as well.

"And then, of course, we have all the old content sitting around being wasted. We should be making our own documentaries, we should be using all this stuff. We should be encouraging film makers to make movies. I don't really see why we need to have photographers, to be quite honest. If we buy their archives they can retire as rich men. We can hire the young guys to work for us and create a central picture library with shots available to anyone who wants them, at a sensible price, so even Internet sites can afford them.

"I think also there should be some kind of budget-balancing structure that makes sure the small teams can survive and maybe even allow us to have promotion and relegation. You have to have new blood. I don't know how that would work, but it would be a good thing to have.

"I think we should help journalists as well, but make sure there are standards upheld. You have to have writing with bite. Trying to tone it all down for the sponsors makes no sense to me. I think we should probably set up an F1 university, where you can go to study how to do all these different jobs. We should not be leaving the running of the sport to chance, we should be teaching the best and the brightest how to do it."

Gorgeous appeared with a *salade niçoise*, with seared tuna and salty anchovies.

Bilski was full of ideas, which for a man of his age was impressive.

"I think the key point we need to remember is that while we are a sport for two hours every fortnight, we are also a major industry. We should be getting the same kind of government grants other sports get. We should be democratising the sport so a fast kid in a kart can have the money to move up the ladder if they keep on winning. It is all possible. We should have our own F1-branded shops, selling stuff to people at reasonable prices not the crazy fifty dollars for a tee-shirt attitude that exists today. I know some teams don't want to do it, but I don't think they should have the choice. They should have to be part of the merchandising operation and they should have to provide stuff at sensible prices. If they want premium brand lines as well then they can, but we just want to shift produce. And we can do that in many different ways. We can create some really big loyalty programme promotions, allowing people access to premium merchandise if they buy a certain product. You get a collector's item if you pay for an F1 magazine. That sort of thing."

It all made perfect sense to Maddie.

"I think the one thing we have to remember is while the technical exercise is valuable when it comes to engines," she said, "the technology can be used to improve road cars and help to increase efficiency. There really is very little value for the real world in the chassis, aerodynamics and suspension design. We need to keep it because F1 is unique only because every car is different, but at the same time we need to control the spending on the parts that don't matter. And we have to remember we are in show business and we have to compete with other sports and other leisure activities. We have to embrace the fans, not drive them away. We need to have a massive marketing department that helps everyone in the sport and we have to be willing to embrace anything people would like to promote. There are all kinds of barter deals that can add to the value of the sport."

"It sounds like we agree on a lot of things," said Bilski.

"It does," said Maddie. "But I still struggle with the scam. I understand why you have done it, but I see it as manipulation of the sport."

"It clearly is," said Bilski, "but it was required. I really felt we had to do something and no one would agree to anything, so I found another way. We still have good racing. I had to choose between right and wrong, but the truth is doing wrong was the right thing to do. Everyone is happy, if only because they don't know any different.

"What's wrong with that?

"In any case," he went on. "Only you and Winslow know the whole story and if you tell the world, where is the evidence? You implicate yourself in a scandal you cannot prove."

Winslow chuckled. It was brilliant.

"Look, Maddie," Bilski said. "Look at it this way: if you knew you could fix your financial situation for life by having sex just once for, let's say, five million. Would you do it? Would you lower yourself just once for the good of the cause? Or would you refuse and have to go on struggling, but feeling righteous?

"I play fair in business and I always have and I'm not greedy, but this was a necessary evil. We live in an imperfect world and we must make if it what we can."

Gorgeous delivered a lovely piece of *banon* cheese, served with some early cherries.

"So Maddie, you have proved yourself to be very clever and I like that," he said. "I like good brains and you obviously have one. If I offered you the job of marketing director of the Formula One group, with a suitably disgraceful salary I suppose that would sound a bit like a bribe, to stop you talking. Would you see it that way?"

"I don't know," said Maddie. "I'd like to do that, but the ethics are a bit worrying."

Chewing on a cherry and a piece of delicious *banon*, Maddie stared out across the waters off Cap Ferrat and remembered what Professor Quirk had said to her. "I am this day fourscore years old," she said aloud. "And can I discern between good and evil?"

She was the one who had to choose.

She knew it and sighed.

"Mr Bilski," she said. "I think I may have misjudged you."

# Thirty

On the trip back to Monaco, they discussed how things could change in the F1 business and Bilski said it was vital to do things gradually and quietly.

"Success is about the little things," he said. "The nuances of behaviour. It's about drivers saying more, behaving in a slightly different fashion. If you try to do things suddenly and dramatically it always looks fake - and it will be. The change needs to be - and I hate the expression - organic. It needs to feel natural. The drivers need to become more comfortable with being themselves. I have huge respect for these guys, and I want them to do what they want to do, not what some trainer, team boss or sponsor has told them they have to do. I don't want fake heroes. I want the real thing. So please, Maddie, do me a favour. Go and get Jimmy Buckett to win this fabulous motor race. That would be such a good story. It would really boost interest in F1 in America, and everybody loves a David and Goliath battle. The underdogs are always much more popular than the big combines.

"The other thing is to try and get the team to do something new and interesting in terms of promotion every race weekend. It doesn't have to be elaborate, but every little thing helps to change the sport."

When they got back to the mooring outside the harbour,

they bid Bilski farewell, thanked him and Gorgeous for a great lunch, and waited for the tender to be prepared.

"Out here one can keep a low profile," said Bilski. "No-one knows I'm here. I like it that way."

"No-one knows who you are," said Maddie.

"Let's keep it that way," said Bilski.

They went back to the apartment they were renting in Fontvieille, but there was not much time before there were functions to attend. Winslow was not invited and so he stayed in the apartment.

"I think I might go home on Saturday night," he said. "I don't see the point in being here. I'm just in the way..."

"Can you stay until Sunday morning?" she said. "I have an idea and I need my man beside me."

"Really?" said Winslow. "Can't you get Hot Dog to go with you?"

Maddie pouted. "No, I want you!"

Before heading out for the evening, Maddie rang Izzie in London and asked her if she could get herself to Farnborough Airport on Saturday morning. They wanted to give Jimmy a surprise on Saturday night.

"I was coming down on Sunday morning," she said. "If I come earlier I don't think he'll be very rested for the race," Izzie replied, without a hint of humour.

Maddie smiled.

"Well, you'll just have to wear him out quickly and get him asleep before midnight," she said. "You're a talented girl, you'll figure it out."

They discussed whether she needed a hotel room or whether she could stay at Jimmy's new place.

"I'm not sure if it's furnished or has any creature comforts," said Maddie. "He's a boy, so don't expect anything out of Ideal Home. But I expect he has a bed."

"That is the primary requirement," Izzie said.

"And bring an elegant dress," said Maddie. "I need you looking super special."

"I'd better have a hotel room," said Izzie. "I'll need clothes for Sunday as well."

"We'll get you home on Sunday night," said Maddie, "unless of course if he wins, in which case you're just going to have to be late for work on Monday."

"Tarquin will understand," said Izzie. "He knows about Jimmy and is very excited. He said I needed more of a social life."

"You did..." said Maddie.

Once the call was done, she headed out for the sponsor dinner and on the way had time to enjoy the atmosphere. Monaco is more than just a motor race. It's part of the social calendar. And, of course, it is still unbelievably spectacular. What F1 drivers do with their cars in such small spaces always amazed Maddie. It is a place where a driver can still make a big difference - at least in qualifying. The race is often frustrating because overtaking, while not impossible, is very difficult and tends to result in contact between the cars. This is not really surprising when one considers that the circuit has not much changed since the first event in 1929. They have put in some more tarmac in places, but it is still a track where qualifying well is vital if one wants the chance to win the race. If a driver gets pole position at Monaco, he should be able to win, even if he is slower than the cars behind him. But, he has to stay away from the walls...

The teams focus on the Q sessions, because once those are done, the order is often set. Despite this drawback, Monaco remains the most famous Formula 1 race of the year and the one that every race fan wants to see at least once in their life. It is still an extraordinary event where one can see drivers doing unimaginable things with their cars.

Buckett made his Chiphurst dance between the barriers on Saturday. It was a joy to watch and he made no mistakes. But the best he could do was third fastest. Third on the grid.

"Sorry guys," he said over the radio on his slowing down lap. "That is as fast as this car will go. If you can find another driver who can do better, you ought to hire him and dump me."

The comment was picked up on the international TV feed.

"Message received," Blenkinsop replied. "We will discuss

firing you later. Brilliant job, lad. Quite brilliant."

The two cars ahead of Jimmy on the grid were the pair of factory Mercedes, which was logical when one considers that the Chiphurst was a Mercedes copy. The field was pretty close in terms of speed, but life was tough for Ferrari, which seemed to have been outgunned. The fastest of the red cars was back in twelfth place on the grid, a result that sent the Italian media into a tailspin and by Sunday morning there were calls for firings and resignations. It was always the same and irritating to team members, who understood that progress requires stability, the absolute opposite of the demands of the media.

"I'd hate to be a Ferrari driver," mused Jimmy during the debrief. "Sure, you get to wear the red overalls and all the girls like you, but they have to deal with so much crap. I mean, we all have to deal with some crap, but those guys really earn their money."

After qualifying, the paddock cleared out quickly. It was quiet in the garages. People had parties to go to and only a few specialist journalists were left tapping away on their computers in the Media Centre. The port area was humming with life, thumping music coming from the bars down at the Rascasse corner, where one can dance on the race track. Across the harbour there were dinner parties on every boat. No-one was going to bed early that night.

On the other side of the old town, in Fontvieille, where most of the F1 drivers have apartments, life was much quieter. Buckett did his duty with a couple of VIP functions with sponsors and then went home to his recently-rented apartment. It was almost empty. There was a bed, a table, some chairs and a television. He had ordered a couch, but there had been trouble agreeing a date for delivery. The refrigerator was almost empty. Jimmy had barely been there since becoming a F1 driver. The Internet, at least, worked and so he was happy enough. He wondered whether to invite Izzie to help him decorate, or whether it was better to decorate and then invite her and see what she thought.

His mobile rang and the word "Cougar" came up on the

screen.

"Allo-allo-allo,"he said.

"Hey, Hot Dog," she said. "I need a favour..."

"Cougar," he said. "You know I cannot do sex now I am with Izzie. Unless..."

"In your dreams," Maddie laughed. "I need you to put on a tuxedo and be ready downstairs in about half an hour. I promise you'll love it. We are going to go and play James Bond at the Casino. I promise you'll be home in bed by eleven."

"Only if it's with you," he said.

"You never know," said Maddie, "maybe one day your dreams will come true..."

Jimmy laughed.

She had been busy since qualifying ended and had rung around and managed to borrow an Aston Martin for the evening. Winslow was bullied into a dinner suit - but he looked delicious. She told him to go, get a taxi and pick up Izzie at her hotel and to meet them at the Casino at nine thirty. She called a photographer and asked him if he wanted some exclusive pictures.

"I want this in all the magazines," she told him, "from Paris Match to National Geographic."

"I'll remember to get some foliage in the picture," he said sarcastically.

She knew there would be other people around Casino Square with mobile phones and pictures would quickly start appearing on social media sites.

And if they didn't, she could make sure that they did...

Once that was done, she looked at her watch and knew she had to get a move on. It was all a bit of a rush, but she arrived at the front door of Jimmy's apartment block bang on time. He was ready and waiting.

"Get in," she shouted. "I'm not getting out of this bloody car more than once. God knows what would end up in the newspapers if I tried that in this dress."

Jimmy laughed.

"I suspect that God already knows what you have to offer,"

he said. "He will have seen it all before."

"I am sure you're right," she said. "Shut up and get in the car, you idiot."

Jimmy skipped around the car, opened the door and said: "Wow, Cougar, you scrub up well."

"I look better standing up," she said.

Jimmy was going to say something, but decided against it.

"You look pretty good yourself," she said.

"I look better lying down," he said.

They smiled at one another. Silly smiles.

"So what's the story?"he asked as Maddie pulled away, driving sedately through the tunnel under the palace leading down to the port area.

"We're going up to the Casino for an impromptu photo shoot," she said. "We're just playing up the racing driver image. F1 drivers these days never do this sort of stuff and so it's a great opportunity to get a load of coverage. I should have thought of it before. We are telling a story that makes you the hero, so make sure you behave like one. The photographers are not allowed inside, but I guess we can lose some money on the roulette tables, just for a while."

Jimmy nodded.

"Sounds fun," he said. "I love losing money."

"So, you're my date," he said. "Izzie will be jealous..."

The traffic was bad, but despite the crawl up the hill they reached the Casino in ten minutes. No-one recognised him.

Maddie remarked that it was funny how people always look at the driver of a car and never at the passenger.

She brought the Aston Martin to stop at the bottom of the Casino steps and a *voiturier*, dressed in a peaked cap and smart uniform, appeared and opened Jimmy's door. He jumped out, skipped around the car and opened Maddie's door.

"I want to see you get out!" he said, with a big smile.

"Pervert," she said, keeping her legs together as she manoeuvred herself out of the car. He took her arm and, she handed the keys to the valet.

"Wow," said Jimmy. This is quite a place. I never really

stopped to look. I always pass by rather fact..."

"Keep it that way," Maddie said. "Inside this building they have individual gambling chips worth more than a quarter of a million dollars, so it is way more dangerous than a racing circuit."

At that moment Winslow and Izzie appeared at the top of the stairs. She looked sensational.

Jimmy laughed with surprise.

"You minxes," he said. "I've been set up."

He unhooked his arm from Maddie's and with a polite "excuse me" he bounded up the stairs and took Izzie in his arms and kissed her.

Maddie heard a photographer's flash-gun going off.

She followed him up the stairs, quite slowly, and took Winslow's arm. There were some more camera flashes and then the two couples, turned and went into the Casino and asked where to go to find some roulette tables.

The girl at the reception desk smiled a very sweet smile and said, in perfectly-accented English:"I am terribly sorry, but I don't believe that Mr Buckett is yet twenty-one. I am afraid I'm not allowed to let him gamble.

"You're kidding me?" said Maddie.

"Rules of the house, I'm afraid. If we break them for Mr Buckett, we will have to do the same for all manner of ghastly spoilt children."

Maddie saw the problem.

"Do you have a place where minors can get milk and cookies?" she said. The sarcasm went clean over the receptionist's head.

"No roulette?" said Jimmy.

"You have Izzie," said Maddie. "You've already won the jackpot."

Buckett smiled at that one and nodded. Cougar was right.

"Well, it doesn't really matter about the gambling," Maddie said. "We've got the photos. Jimmy, an Aston Martin. Stunning girl. Job done. We'll stick around for half and hour and then head off."

At that point a manager or under-manager arrived. He

apologised for the inconvenience and then proceeded to amuse them with tales about the building

"You know," he said. "We have a room here known as The Morgue where we used to put the bodies of the gamblers who had lost all their money and decided to shoot themselves right there at the gaming tables. I believe it happened quite a lot."

They ordered some cocktails.

"Give that man a mojito," said Izzie, pointing at Jimmy.

"Mojitos all around," said Winslow.

It was, in the end, an agreeable experience. The setting was sumptuous.

"I feel like The Great Gatsby," said Jimmy.

Buckett loved the fact that Izzie had come early.

"But you know," he said, "it's a really very bad idea. I am horny teenager and I am supposed to race tomorrow?"

"Don't worry," said Maddie. "Izzie has very specific instructions about to how to deal with you.."

"Really?" he said with a smile. "Can we leave now?"

Maddie looked at her watch. They had done enough.

She texted the photographer: "Leaving in five minutes".

She waited and an SMS came back. "Ready and waiting".

"OK, chaps," Maddie said. "Go put on a show. You take Izzie in the Aston. Leave it outside your place. Stick the keys in the exhaust pipe."

Winslow and Maddie watched them leave and saw the flash guns going. She turned to him and said "Let's walk". Jimmy and Izzie were still waiting for the Aston, but Winslow and Maddie slipped quietly down the stairs and, arm-in-arm, they strolled down the hill. They were halfway to Sainte-Dévote before the Aston passed them.

The harbour was spread out beneath them, a panorama of expensive boats and glittering lights, all in the shadow of the palace.

"This place is magic, isn't it?" Maddie said.

Winslow disappeared off to the airport very early in the morning and Maddie then got ready for the day ahead and then set out to walk to the paddock. She exchanged text messages with Jimmy, in part to organise breakfast and in part to make sure that he was up and ready for the day ahead. The plan was to meet in the Chiphurst hospitality unit for breakfast. Jimmy and Izzie arrived together on a scooter, attracting more photographs.

It was going to be a busy day. Maddie had a group of guests to look after and decided to let Izzie tag along. They had a tour of the garage, met the drivers and then it was time to have lunch. For that they were going to have to go up to the apartment that the team rented each year for an obscene amount of money, although it was worth every penny.

Getting to the VIP apartment was not easy, but they had a minibus to ferry the guests to the back of the Caravelles building on the Boulevard Albert 1er. This block is sixteen storeys high and overlooks the entire port area. Charlie had rented the same fourteenth floor apartment every year since the 1970s. This belonged to an elegant old lady, now ninety-four. She was a great beauty and had married a wealthy, but much older man. He had died when she was still in her forties and she had inherited an unseemly amount of money, which she had been happily spending for the last fifty years. The apartment was probably now worth about four million dollars. The old lady never stayed for the race, going off to stay with  friend Sheila, at Saint-Jean-Cap-Ferrat. She made enough money each year from the Grand Prix not to need to use up any of her remaining capital.

The apartment was rather old-fashioned in terms of its decoration, but it was the best possible viewing point. They moved the furniture around, provided food and wine all day and no-one ever went home unhappy. In truth, rather a lot of them went home *too* happy...

The apartment boasted a view of the start-finish line, the first corner at Sainte-Dévote, the climb up the hill towards the Casino, where the cars disappeared from view. One could also see the exit of the tunnel down at harbour level, the chicane and the straight down to Tabac, the entire swimming pool complex and the entry of the Rascasse corner. In addition, there was a giant TV screen located halfway up the hill. The most important thing about the apartment, however, was that it had a wide terrace, sufficient for a normal sized table with chairs. Maddie had found that it was best to have fewer guests than some other organizations, so the terrace was not so much of a squeeze. Every terrace, every window and every balcony had people, all gazing down at the action below. There was excitement in the air, brilliant sunshine and Monaco harbour in front of them.

She and Izzie has lunch in the team motorhome. Jimmy stopped by for a few minutes but then Maddie had to break them up

"Go win the race!" Izzie said. "For me."

Jimmy smiled, blew her a kiss and disappeared to have a discussion with Blenkinsop. By the time Maddie and Izzie got up to the apartment, the cars were lining up to leave the pit lane.

"Great view," said Izzie.

Maddie smiled: "It doesn't get better than this."

Izzie squeezed her arm.

"Oh, I don't know," Izzie said "Christmas on the island was pretty good."

Maddie felt herself blushing, an odd reaction and it caused Izzie to laugh out loud.

"I don't remember you doing much blushing on the island..." she whispered.

Maddie did the rounds of the VIPs before returning to stand next to Izzie. Below them, the crowd on the grid was thinning out and everyone, apart from the TV crews, had stopped moving while the *Hymne Monégasque* was played. The beautiful people were traipsing away down the pit lane. Maddie wondered if they would even stay for the race, now that their faces had been seen on the TV broadcast.

And then the engines began to roar into life.

Maddie waited until the cars set off on the final parade lap before explaining to the VIPs what was going to happen when the cars came back.

It was not long before the field was back in the port area, coming out of the tunnel and braking for the chicane, the colourful bodywork glinting in the sunlight. The cars went down the short straight to Tabac, snaking backwards and forwards, trying to get heat into the tyres and the brakes. They were snarling like caged cats.

Izzie was quiet, her eyes following Jimmy's car. The field disappeared from view around the Rascasse Corner and then, they watched them coming out of the final corner and lining up on the grid, directly below them.

"This is it," said Maddie. "Here we go."

The start of the Monaco Grand Prix is always spectacular. The distance to the first corner is short and the pressure is on for the drivers to make up positions. The problem is that the Sainte-Dévote corner is tight and slow and the cars have to go through in what amounts to single file. The first corner is quite often a big mess. Usually there is a Safety Car at some point during the Monaco race and, more often than not, it is at the start. If not, the leading cars, running free on their own, can build up a big advantage straight away, as those behind fall over one another.

The Safety Car can be very useful because it means the tyres will last longer, and so helps teams which have cars that have heavier tyre wear.

Maddie was hoping for an incident to help Jimmy against the Mercedes.

As the five lights on the start line gantry came on, one by one, the engines revved up into a crescendo of noise. When all the lights were lit, there was the moment that Maddie loved most of all. And then all hell broke loose.

The lights went out and the cars shot off the line at incredible, but slightly different, speeds. Jimmy was a little faster away than Lewis Hamilton, who had been on pole position, but Nico Rosberg was better than both of them. Jimmy tucked in on the inside line behind the two Mercs, as they headed down to the corner, side by side, with Lewis on the inside. It was going to be very tight, as neither man wanted to concede the corner.

Maddie saw it first.

"They're going to go wide," she shouted. At that instant

Rosberg's car suddenly slowed and Hamilton's went ahead. Lewis had held on a fraction longer than he ought to have done, in order to secure the advantage. Now he had to keep it all on the road. This meant that a gap was opening on the inside. Rosberg could not get to it, but it was there for Jimmy and he pointed the Chiphurst straight into it.

In F1, you don't look a gift horse in the mouth.

He was careful to leave Hamilton just enough room to avoid a collision, but Jimmy knew that the Chiphurst would have more momentum as they accelerated up the hill. Inch by inch he pulled ahead.

High above them Izzie and Maddie were yelping with glee. This was the perfect start. Jimmy Buckett was leading the Monaco Grand Prix, with the two Mercs snapping at his rear end, both drivers annoyed at themselves. By the time they reached the top of the hill and turned into Casino Square, Hamilton was close enough to be considering a move on Buckett for the lead, going down the hill towards Mirabeau, but then yellow flags and Safety Car boards came out. Further back someone had crashed and the race was neutralised. Hamilton's chance was gone. Jimmy didn't know what was happening behind him. He didn't care. It didn't matter. He knew that his only focus was simply to keep it all together, to stay calm.

"Good job there," said Blenkinsop over the radio. "You know what to do. Keep everything as warm as possible. It could be a while. Maldonado has smashed up his Lotus."

When you are running behind the Safety Car, you need to try to make sure that your tyres stay hot, although that is often impossible. If no-one has much heat in their tyres at the restart, everyone is scrambling and there is a chance people will make mistakes. It is frustrating and it is all too easy to lose concentration and make an unforced error. It is a tense period.

"Waiting is far worse than racing," Maddie said.

For three laps the cars snarled around and then finally the lights on the roof of the Safety Car stopped flashing. The race would start again when the cars reached a white line painted across the track halfway up the hill from Rascasse towards the final corner. Jimmy felt his tyres were not hot enough and so he slowed everyone else down, to make sure they were all in the same boat. He dictated the pace and was trying to catch the others out.

Normally he would have accelerated flat to the floor coming out of Rascasse, but he wanted Hamilton to do that and have to lift off. It was a gamble. He waited and then shoved the accelerator hard. The car shot forward, the tyres grabbing at the road and he threw the machine into Noghès, the tight right-hander on to the start-finish straight. He prayed that the rear end would stay off the wall, but he knew it would be close. Hamilton was not caught out, but was a fraction more cautious in the corner, although there was not much he could have done. Buckett hugged the inside line down past the pits. If Hamilton was going to overtake, he was going to have do it on the outside. Going into Sainte-Dévote, Jimmy moved out to the middle of the road, blocking any move from the Mercedes. Defensive driving is an important skill in F1, particularly if you don't have the fastest car. He had to place the Chiphurst in exactly the right place in every corner, making sure that there was nothing that Hamilton could do. And he had to watch for moves in unexpected places. The one bit of good news was that Hamilton was having to watch his mirrors for Rosberg. It was going to be a cat-and-mouse game. The pressure was on.

It was clear that Lewis had the better car, but he did not have quite enough to get ahead. Jimmy knew he was quite capable of using force, if the opportunity arose, but Lewis was a clean driver in general, so Jimmy concentrated on leaving no chinks in his armour.

The key now for Jimmy was to preserve his tyres. The longer he could go with the set he had started the race on, the better his chances of victory.

"Focus, focus," he said to himself. "Stay calm. Place the car. Make him do the work. Back him up as much as possible."

He knew the most dangerous place on each lap was on the run between the exit of the tunnel and the chicane beside the harbour, but that was dictated by the momentum one carried through the corner, before the tunnel, the downhill right-hander, known as Portier. Hamilton thought about making a move a couple of times in those early laps, but he was worried about getting the car off the racing line, because dust and bits of discarded rubber would hurt the tyres.

Jimmy had been planning to stop on lap forty-five of seventy-eight, switching on to harder rubber for the final laps. Hamilton's plan was almost certainly the same. But now it was a question of who could go furthest on that first set of tyres.

If Lewis could go longer and stay as fast, Jimmy would be beaten. The alternative was to pit when there was clear track behind them. If Hamilton did that, Jimmy would need to follow him, to cover the move.

The length of time needed in the pits and the fact that overtaking is difficult, means teams usually make fewer stops in Monaco than at other tracks. It helps that the circuit is smooth and there are no really high-speed corners to increase the tyre wear.

There are people who say that Monaco is dull and processional, but that is only because they do not understand what they are watching. This is like dancing Giselle, or playing Mily Balakirev's Islamey on the piano. It's like threading needle after needle after needle, never making a mistake.

Several times Hamilton tried to pull alongside Buckett going into Sainte-Dévote, but Jimmy had him covered. He watched for a surprise attack at the Fairmount Hairpin and made sure that Portier was perfect every time. He did the same thing lap after lap and it became a kind of rhythm. The Mercedes was the faster car, but Hamilton was given no opportunities, yet he continued to stalk the Chiphurst.

"Go longer," said Blenkinsop on the radio. Jimmy wondered if perhaps he could go to lap fifty.

On lap forty-six he went down the hill to Portier as usual, but Jimmy turned in just a fraction earlier than normal. The Chiphurst touched the kerb on the inside corner and was knocked slightly off balance. The car lost a little momentum and went into the tunnel slightly slower than usual.

"Dammit, dammit, dammit," Jimmy shouted into his helmet."

He sensed Hamilton was there and was going to try this time. Jimmy feared he was going to lose the race. The only option was to crash into the Mercedes, but Jimmy was not that kind of a driver. They were side-by-side coming out of the tunnel, Jimmy hugging the inside to block a move. Hamilton braked a fraction later, sliced across ahead of the Chiphurst and took the lead.

"Don't let him get away," Jimmy said out loud. "Stay with him."

Hamilton had lost momentum with the move and was slow at the exit of the chicane, but there was nothing that Jimmy could do to get the place back. Now the roles had changed. He was happy to see that Rosberg was nowhere to be seen. It was just the two of them in the fight.

For the whole of the next lap he was staring at the rear end of the Mercedes - but it was not getting any smaller. Hamilton could not get away from him.

The battle was not lost.

Lewis was now doing to Jimmy what he had done to him earlier, but Buckett's tyres felt good, and he could see that Hamilton was beginning to struggle, just a little. All those laps behind the Chiphurst had meant that Lewis's tyres had been a fraction hotter and had degraded a little more. It was impressive that he had still managed to get ahead, but Jimmy knew it was because he had made a mistake. There was no escaping that.

He wondered how long it would be before Hamilton went into the pits. Perhaps he could get the Mercedes strategists to panic. Into Portier on lap 50 Hamilton slid a few inches wider than the perfect line. Jimmy had the momentum, he pulled out to go for a pass. Lewis held on, held on, held on and then they both braked for the chicane. The message had been delivered. Were they worried?

As they went through Rascasse, Blenkinsop suddenly said: "They are bringing him in. Stand on it! As fast as you can go.

Kill the tyres. Now. This is your chance!"

Hamilton peeled into the pit lane and Jimmy went through Noghès with the abandon as at the restart after the Safety Car. In Sainte-Dévote he drifted the car right out to the barrier, every inch was important. When he got back to Rascasse the radio came to life.

"I want another lap like that," Blenkinsop said. "Come on boy. Only perfection is good enough."

Jimmy was not listening. He was in a zone of his own, seeing only what he needed to see, being inch-perfect.

"You have twenty-seven seconds lead, he heard Blenkinsop say as he was going through Casino Square. I want twenty-eight. Can you go another lap?"

"Yes," Jimmy said. "One more. I'll give you thirty seconds. Just don't mess me up when I come in."

The driver is the man who gets all the glory in motor racing, but he is always the front man for a team of people, each individual playing a key role. If a mechanic fails in his task, the car will fail. If the strategist calls the wrong strategy, the team is defeated. If the engineers cannot find the right set-up for the car, the driver cannot perform at his best. And so it goes on. The most visible illustration of this teamwork is the pit stop. A driver can race his heart out all afternoon and be screwed by his own team with a bad pit stop.

Buckett said a little prayer as he headed the Chiphurst into the pit lane at the end of lap fifty-two. He was careful to position the car perfectly for his crew. In the blink of an eye, the tyre guns were firing, the wheels were off, new wheels were put on and the guns fired again. And then the signal in front of him blinked green and Jimmy nailed it.

"Speed limit," said Blenkinsop.

Driving in the pit lane in an F1 race is the most frustrating possible feeling for a racing driver. He's chugging along at sixty kilometres per hour, knowing that his rivals are closing in.

"White line," said Blenkinsop.

Jimmy jammed his foot to the floor. He sensed a silver object away to his left. He knew what it was, but he knew too that Hamilton was still on his way into Sainte-Dévote corner. Jimmy had done enough. He felt a surge of energy. This was a race he ought to win. Now, he had tyres that were six laps newer than Hamilton's. He needed to get them fully up to speed, but each corner helped. He could feel the grip coming as he curled through Massenet and Casino Square. By the time he got down to Mirabeau they felt right. It was all coming together. A perfect entry into Portier and he was launched into the tunnel. He looked back. He was pulling away.

"Nice and easy," said Blenkinsop. "Keep it nice and easy."

Hamilton is not a guy who ever gives up, but he knew that his chance of victory was gone. Perhaps he could  risk it all and close in, but passing the Chiphurst was impossible. It was not worth skittering alongside and bumping bodywork.

Lewis had to think about the World Championship. Buckett had nothing to lose. Winning titles is all about knowing when to hold, knowing when to fold and always getting the job done. He would settle for second. He would push Jimmy in the closing laps, as much as he could, hoping for a mistake, but if Buckett could stay ahead, he deserved the win.

And now came the real pain. The waiting. Lap after lap ticked by, but in seemed that each lap was taking longer. Jimmy tried to get back into the rhythm he had earlier enjoyed, but it was harder now.

The suspense spread through the team. No-one dared to smile. They were waiting, The tensions were building up inside each one of them. Up on the balcony in the Caravelles, Izzie was looking tense. The VIPs had all gone quiet, they were glued to the TV screens inside the apartment. The TV cameras cut to Charlie. He was trying to look cool and unworried, but Maddie could see the strain in his face.

"Come on Jimmy," said Izzie, quietly.

The magic number was seventy-eight. When Jimmy crossed the line  for the seventy-eighth time, barring incompetence, the chequered flag would be waved and he would have won the world's most famous motor race. Yes, Le Mans is big, Indianapolis and Daytona too, but Monaco is the first word that people say when you ask them to name a motor race.

Blenkinsop kept quiet. Each lap he would simply say the number of laps remaining.

At the end of lap seventy-seven the radio crackled.

"One to go," said Blenkinsop.

"Just hold it together," Jimmy told himself and he talked himself in. "We go up the hill... through the square... down the hill... through the hairpin... down to the sea.. through the tunnel.. around the chicane... around the swimming pool... through the Rascasse... And, last corner."

There was one last burst of acceleration. He looked in his mirror. There was Hamilton, jinking the Mercedes through the corner behind him.

Up on the terrace Izzie and Maddie were jumping up and down with joy.

"We have to go..." Maddie said. "We have to get down there."

Even Hamilton smiled. The kid had beaten him. He didn't like it, but you had to respect the newcomer.

The scenes that followed are the same every year, with joyous celebrations, national anthems, spraying of champagne and then interviews, then more interviews, and more interviews. Eventually, the drivers return to the team for manly bear hugs and other hoop-la.

As they ran through the streets, trying to get back to the paddock, Izzie was as happy as Maddie had ever seen her. That made her happy. It was hard not to get caught up in it all. She wanted to, but deep down she knew how the success had been achieved. Yes, they had all done their bit, but beneath the victory was the secret that only she and Elfin knew. It pained her. She felt robbed of the joy. She pretended she was happy, but she could not be genuinely delighted. Elfin could do it. It was a mark of the man, she thought.

It all made sense when Bilski explained it and she tried to convince herself that two wrongs do make a right, but she was not convinced. The happiness of those around her made her smile, but she did not feel like a winner. All she really wanted to do was to go home to Winslow. He had been wise enough not to be there. She rang him. He knew.

"Look at how Jimmy drove," he said. "Look at the team work. You know how hard it is to do this. Let them have their joy. Half of human history is not what it appears to be. There are thousands of things we don't know and will never know. You are judged by the results and not how they were achieved. If no-one knows, no-one suspects, then you can enjoy it. Only you know the difference. And if you feel that you have failed, you know, it's really a good thing. It shows that you are a good person. We learn from failure and from pain. You always learn more lessons when you lose than when you win. Losing makes you stronger. If you feel pain in this hour of victory then you must use that and resolve to win properly in the future."

Maddie sighed. As always, it was good advice.

"I love you, " said Maddie. "You are the best thing that ever happened to me. I don't know how I lived before I met you, but I feel bad about myself today. I have not been true to myself."

"Blame me," he said. "I got you to do it, but if I hadn't done that, would Chiphurst even have got here?"

"We'll never know," Maddie said, "but what I do know is that I want to do it properly next time. I don't want to work for Bilski, as much as it is a great offer. I have unfinished business. I need to win for me. I am not going to fake it."

"Just like in bed," he said. "It's all or nothing. If it isn't right, you don't pretend. You never take the easy way out. I love you, Maddie Midnight."

Maddie knew that the evening was going to be painful, but it had to be endured. There is nothing worse than being an unhappy person surrounded by a crowd of people enjoying themselves. But she felt she deserved some pain.

It was decided at some point that she, Jimmy, Izzie and Blenkinsop would go out and have a pizza. No-one would expect them to do that. Then there would be a big party which Charlie was planning at Jimmy'z, the famous (and wildly over-priced) nightclub over by the Sporting Club.

"Where else could we do it? he said.

They were all heading off in different directions to reconvene later, when Charlie took Maddie by the arm and said: "Walk with me".

There were people cheering them but the noise faded.

"You know," he said. "Today is down to you, more than anyone. You suggested Elfin, you found the money. This is your day, Maddie - and I want it to be a special day for you. A day you will always remember.

"I've been thinking for a while about this. I am getting too old for this game. And, let's be honest, my kids are not going to do much good running a racing team. They are too spoilt. My fault, I know, but I want Chiphurst to go on, after I am gone. I want it to be a F1 legend. And I want you to do that for me. So I decided the other day that I am going to give you half the team. I'm keeping fifty percent and I am staying on as chairman, so it is still my team, but when the time comes, then you will become the chairman and the team will be your team. It must still be called Chiphurst, but it will be yours. The kids can sell their shares and waste their money."

Maddie stopped in her tracks.

"But..." she said.

"There are no buts," Charlie said. "I fully accept that Midnight Racing is a much sexier name than Chiphurst Competition, but there are limits to my magnanimity..."

"I don't know what to say," Maddie said.

"When you have nothing to say," he said, "Say nothing."

Maddie Midnight laughed. It was good advice. Things would have been very different if she had followed that advice that night at the Berkeley, when she had got herself into a pickle about the colour of her pubic hair.